Lauren St John

The White Giraffe
and
Dolphin Song

Two African Adventures

Illustrated by David Dean

Orion
Children's Books

This omnibus edition first published in Great Britain in 2011
by Orion Children's Books
Originally published as two separate volumes:
The White Giraffe
First published in Great Britain in 2006
by Orion Children's Books
Dolphin Song
First published in Great Britain in 2007
by Orion Children's Books
a division of the Orion Publishing Group Ltd
Orion House
5 Upper St Martin's Lane
London WC2H 9EA
An Hachette UK Company

9 10 8

Text copyright © Lauren St John 2006, 2007
Illustrations copyright © David Dean 2006, 2007

The Orion Publishing Group's policy is to use papers that are natural,
renewable and recyclable products and made from wood grown in sustain-
able forests. The logging and manufacturing processes are expected to
conform to the environmental regulations of the country of origin.

A catalogue record for this book is available from the British Library

Printed in Great Britain by Clays Ltd, St Ives plc

ISBN 978 1 4440 0471 7

www.orionbooks.co.uk

· Contents ·

the White giraffe

LAUREN St JOHN

For Sophie, aged 10,
who, like me,
loves horses and shy giraffes

1

People like to say that things come in threes, but the way Martine looked at it that all depends on when you start counting and when you stop. For instance, she could say that one bad thing happened along with three good things, but the truth was that the one bad thing was the very worst thing in the whole world, another was so small she didn't really notice it at the time, and something else that she first thought was bad luck later turned out to be the best kind of fortune anyone could wish for. Whichever way you added it up, though, one thing was certain. The night Martine Allen turned eleven years old was the night her life changed absolutely, totally and completely and was never the same again.

It was New Year's Eve. At the time, Martine was asleep in bed and she was dreaming about a place she'd never been to before, and the reason she was so positive was because it was too beautiful ever to forget. As far as the eye could see there were lawns lined with exotic flowers and trees. Behind them, rising into a clear sky, was a mountain made majestic by granite cliffs and lush green forests. Children were laughing and chasing moths through beds of dusky-pink flowers and, in the distance, Martine could hear drums and soaring voices. But for some reason she felt apprehensive. Dread prickled her skin.

All at once, the sky began to boil with a turbulent violet light and a thick tablecloth of steel-grey cloud raced down the mountain. The day turned from sunny to sinister in seconds. Then one of the children shouted, 'Hey, look what I found!'

It was a wild goose with a broken wing. But instead of helping it, some of the children began tormenting it. Martine, who could never bear to see any creature hurt, tried to stop them, but in the dream they turned on her instead. Next thing she knew she was on the ground crying and the injured bird was in her arms.

Then something very peculiar happened. Her hands, holding the wild goose, heated up to the point where they were practically glowing and electricity crackled through her. She saw, in a swirl of smoke, black men in horned antelope masks and rhinoceroses breathing fire, and heard voices as old as Time. She knew they wanted to speak to her, but she couldn't hear what they were saying. Suddenly, the bird stirred. Martine opened her palms and it shook out its wings and flew into the violet sky.

In the dream, she looked up smiling, but the other children didn't smile back. They stared at her with a mixture of horror and disbelief. 'Witch!' they chanted, 'witch, witch, witch,' and they began to chase her. Martine fled sobbing up the mountain, into a dark forest. But her legs were unimaginably heavy, hooked thorns tore at her ankles and she was losing her way in the cloud. And all the while it was getting hotter and hotter. Then a hand grabbed her and she began to scream and scream and scream.

It was the sound of her own screams that finally woke Martine. She shot up in bed. It was pitch dark and it took a few seconds for her to realize she'd been asleep. None of it had happened. There was no mountain and no bird. She was safely in her bed in Hampshire, England, with her parents sleeping soundly across the corridor. Heart pounding, she sank back into the pillows. She was a bit dizzy and she still felt very, very hot.

Hot? How could it possibly be *hot?* It was midwinter. Martine's eyes flew open. Something was wrong. Frantically she fumbled for the bedside lamp, but for some reason it wasn't working. She sat up again. An orange light was flickering beneath the bedroom door and grey ribbons of smoke were drifting up from it.

'Fire!' yelled Martine. 'Fire!'

She leapt out of bed, caught her foot in the blankets and crashed to the ground. Tears of panic sprang into her eyes. She wiped them away roughly. If I don't think clearly, she told herself, I'll never get out alive. The corner of the door turned molten red and broke away and a plume of smoke poured in after it. Martine began coughing violently. She clawed at the floor for yesterday's sweatshirt, discarded there when she put on her pyjamas. Almost cheering with thankfulness when she found it immediately, she tied it round her face. Then she scrambled to her feet, heaved up the window and leaned out into the starless night. What was she supposed to do? Jump?

Martine stood paralysed with terror. Far below her, the snow glinted mockingly in the darkness. Behind her, the room was filling with smoke and fumes and the fire was roaring like a factory furnace. It was blisteringly, murderously hot – so hot that she felt as if her pyjamas were melting off her back. The window was the only way out. Swinging her legs over the sill, she reached out and grabbed a clump of ivy. It was as wet as lettuce and came away in her hand. Martine almost toppled after it. She tried again, this time knocking away the packed snow and groping behind the vine for a pipe or a crevice or anything at all that would give her a handhold. Nothing!

Martine's eyes streamed. Moments remained between her and disaster, but she jumped back into the room, snatched the sheets off the bed and knotted them together, tying one end to the bed leg nearest the window. There was no time to test it. She just had to hope that it would hold. As fast as she dared, she climbed out of the window, clinging to the sheet-rope with both hands. She knew very well that it wouldn't reach the ground but it might get her a little closer.

She was still high in the air when her hands, stiff as fish fingers in the gusting Arctic wind, lost their grip and she crashed into the snow. Martine dragged herself upright, shivering, and hobbled along the side of the house to the front. She was soaked to the skin and one wrist was aching, but as soon as she rounded the corner, she no longer thought about that. She was too busy taking in the appalling scene before her. Her home was a raging inferno. Flames leapt in every window and coils of smoke billowed into the night sky. A crowd had gathered on the lawn and all along the street doors were opening and more people were rushing to join them. Sirens announced the rapid approach of the fire brigade.

'Mum! Dad!' yelled Martine, and she ran round the side for the front of the house.

Shocked faces turned in her direction. There was a collective gasp. The Allens' elderly next-door neighbour opened her mouth when she saw Martine rushing across the lawn but no sound came out. Mr and Mrs Morrison, who lived further up the street, were also rooted to the spot, but Mr Morrison, a burly former rugby player, shook himself into action at the last moment and managed to catch Martine as she flew by.

'Let me go,' sobbed Martine, but even as she spoke she knew it was too late. The walls of the house were collapsing in a molten heap. Within minutes, there was nothing left. The fire brigade had arrived, but the most they could do was put the flames out.

Mrs Morrison put her arms around Martine and held her tightly. 'I'm so sorry, my dear,' she said. 'I'm so sorry.' Others came over to console her, and Mr Morrison gave her his coat to put on over her pyjamas.

Through the screen of Martine's tears, the still-glowing embers and bubbles of the firemen's foam shone like rubies and diamonds in the fading night. Only a few hours ago, she'd been enjoying a birthday dinner with her parents. They'd made pancakes and filled them with almonds, bananas and melted chocolate and shaped them into cones they could eat with their hands. Martine and her mum had laughed at her dad, David, who was talking so much that he hadn't noticed that his pancake was leaking chocolate down his shirt. Only one thing had happened that Martine now thought strange.

They'd been on their way up to bed. Martine's mum had kissed her and gone on ahead and Martine was walking up the stairs with her dad. When they reached her bedroom door, he hugged her goodnight, ruffled her hair and told her he loved her, just as he always did. But then he said something odd.

'You have to trust, Martine. Everything happens for a reason.'

And Martine had smiled at him and thought how lovely her parents were even if they were sometimes a little weird and she'd gone into her room, not knowing that they were the last words he would ever say to her.

Not knowing she would never see either of her parents again.

2

It was Mr Grice from Social Services who told Martine that she would be moving to Africa. Cape Town, South Africa, to be precise.

'*South Africa!*' cried Martine. 'Why South Africa?'

'Well,' said Mr Grice, 'it seems that your only surviving relative is, in fact, living on a game reserve in South Africa. A Mrs Gwyn Thomas who, I'm told, is your grandmother.'

Martine was stunned. 'I don't have a grandmother,' she said slowly.

Mr Grice frowned. He reached into his pocket for his glasses and consulted his file again. 'No, I assure you there's no mistake. I have her letter here.'

He handed Martine a sheet of cream writing paper.

Dear Mr Grice,

Thank you for your condolences on the sad loss of my daughter, Veronica Allen, and her husband, David, two of the finest people I have ever known. I was unaware that my daughter had stipulated that I should have guardianship of their child, Martine, if anything ever happened to her. However, I will accept the responsibility. It is the least I can do. I enclose an air ticket to Cape Town and £150 for the girl's expenses. I rarely go into the city and would be grateful if you could ensure that she is adequately clothed for the South African weather.

Yours truly, Gwyn Thomas.

There was something about the tone of the letter that bothered Martine. Her grandmother didn't seem at all enthusiastic about the prospect of taking her on. Quite the reverse. From the sound of things, she expected Martine to be a burden. She couldn't even face the prospect of buying her a few summer clothes. She had clearly adored Martine's parents, but that didn't mean she wanted to be stuck with Martine. And what about her grandfather? There was no mention of him.

Martine handed the letter back to Mr Grice. 'I'm not going,' she said. 'She doesn't want me and there's no way I'm going to live with somebody who doesn't want me. I'd rather stick pins in my eyes.'

Mr Grice looked at her in consternation. It had been a trying morning and he had a feeling that it was about to get worse. What was the matter with his supervisor that she was always giving him the difficult jobs?

'But Mrs Thomas is your legal guardian,' he tried.

'I'm not going,' Martine repeated stubbornly, 'and you can't make me.'

Mr Grice gathered his papers together in a messy bundle, knocking over a glass of water in the process. 'I'll be back,' he told Martine, ignoring the puddle and the ink turning to watercolour on his documents. 'I have to make a phone call.'

Martine sat staring at the smoke-stained wallpaper in Mr Grice's office feeling much more afraid than she'd let on. The past few weeks had passed in a blur. For the first nightmarish five days after the fire she'd stayed with the Morrisons, until their sons returned from a college rugby tour. Then she'd moved in with a friend of her mother's who was unable to cope with a grieving child. Finally, she was driven off to the house of Miss Rose, her English teacher, who was going to take care of her until her future was decided. Everywhere she went, people wore over-bright smiles and were full of helpful suggestions. But as soon as she left the room, she could hear hushed conversations in which the words 'orphan' and 'all alone in the world' were frequently used.

Martine was too dazed and heartbroken to care. Most of the time she walked around with a crashing sensation in her head, as if she was falling into a well with no bottom. She couldn't eat; she couldn't sleep; she couldn't cry. The question she kept asking herself over and over was *why*? Why had she been saved and her parents hadn't? It seemed so unfair. The firemen had praised her bravery and told her she'd done the right thing. They said if she'd opened her door even a crack to try to get to her parents, she would have been swallowed by the blaze. But it was hard not to feel guilty. And what happened to her now? Was she really going to be sent away to a stranger in South Africa?

It was then that she spotted a cream envelope on Mr Grice's desk. There was something familiar about it. She picked it up and studied the address on the back. It was written in neat blue pen and it read: Gwyn Thomas, Sawubona Game Reserve, Eastern Cape, South Africa. Martine searched her memory. Where had she seen that handwriting before? Then it came back to her. She'd watched her mum opening these envelopes every month for as long as she could remember. Nothing had ever been said about them, but Martine had always detected a change in her mum after she'd read the letters. She seemed to smile more, to laugh more easily. To Martine, sitting abandoned and confused among Mr Grice's dusty files, it was all the more upsetting that her mum had never told her that the letters came from her grandmother, or even that she had a grandmother at all. Why was it such a secret?

Martine thought about the signature on the letter: Gwyn Thomas. It sounded so stern. She found it difficult to grasp that such a person might be her grandmother, let alone that she might have to call her Grandmother or, worse still, Granny. She couldn't even think of her as Gwyn. For some reason the whole name – Gwyn Thomas – stuck in her head.

Mr Grice returned to the office shaking his head. 'I'm afraid your options are extremely limited,' he said. 'I've managed to find you a bed in the children's home in Upper Blickley—'

'It's okay,' Martine interrupted, 'I've decided I'll go to South Africa after all.'

Mr Grice heaved a huge sigh of relief. 'Well,' he said, 'that settles it.'

Right from the start, it was obvious that everyone around Martine was much more excited about her new future than she were. 'A *game reserve in Africa*,' said Miss Rose in awe. 'Just think, Martine, it'll be like spending your life on safari.'

Mrs Morrison seemed to be convinced she'd be eaten by a tiger. 'You'll have to be vigilant,' she told Martine. 'But oh, what an adventure it'll all be!'

Martine rolled her eyes inwardly. Mrs Morrison was the kindest woman in the world, but she was absolutely clueless when it came to the animal kingdom. 'There are no tigers in Africa,' Martine had to keep telling her. 'Not unless they're in zoos.'

Apart from that one detail, she herself knew very little about Africa. When she tried to picture it, all she could come up with was big yellow plains, umbrella trees, mangoes, dark faces and baking hot sun. She wondered if wild animals literally roamed the streets. Would she be able to have one as a pet? Martine's mum had been allergic to animals so Martine had always been kept away from them, but ever since she was tiny she'd yearned to have one of her own. Perhaps she could get a monkey.

Then she remembered the tone of her grandmother's letter and the crashing feeling came surging back. Gwyn Thomas didn't sound like the kind of person who would say yes to a primate in her living room. If she even *had* a living room. For all Martine knew, her grandmother could live in a grass hut.

At school, most of her classmates seemed to have forgotten that barely three weeks had gone by since her home had burnt to the ground and that she was hardly going to South Africa out of choice. 'You're sooo lucky,' they kept telling her. 'You'll be able to learn to surf and everything. It'll be so cool.'

Listening to them, Martine thought that the one good thing about moving to Africa was that she'd never again have to enter the grim gates of Bodley Brook Junior. She didn't fit in here. Come to think of it, she'd never fitted in anywhere with children her own age, but somehow it hadn't mattered when her mum and dad were around because *they* were her best friends. Her dad had been a doctor who worked very long hours, but in the summer he took time off and they'd go camping in Cornwall, where her mum would paint and she and her dad would swim or fish or he'd teach her a little first aid. And every

23

weekend, come rain or shine, they always had fun, even if it was only making pancakes. Now it was over and there was a hole in Martine's heart.

On Saturday morning, the day before she was due to fly to Cape Town, Miss Rose took her shopping for summer clothes on Oxford Street in London. An icy grey rain was falling and the entire road was a sea of frenzied consumers and tourists poking umbrellas in each other's eyes, but nothing could dampen Miss Rose's enthusiasm.

'Look at these cute shorts!' she said to Martine as they fought their way around Gap. 'What a great baseball cap! Oh, I can just see you in this stripy red T-shirt.'

Martine just let her go on. If the truth be known, she felt ill. Her stomach was a bubbling cauldron of nerves and her mouth was dry with fear at the prospect of what tomorrow would bring. 'Whatever you think,' she kept saying as Miss Rose presented her with clothing options. 'Yes, it's nice. Yes, I'm sure it'll be fine.'

She ended up with two pairs of khaki shorts, a pair of jeans, four T-shirts, a baseball cap and a pair of tough, camel-coloured hiking boots. The only time she was forced to put up a fight was when Miss Rose tried to insist on a floral-print dress. Martine, who had cropped brown hair and bright green eyes, had refused to wear a dress since the age of five, and she had no intention of starting now.

'I'll get bitten by a snake if I don't have proper protection,' she told Miss Rose.

'But surely you run the same risk if you wear shorts?' protested her teacher.

'Yes,' said Martine, 'but that's *different*. Have you ever seen an explorer who didn't wear shorts?'

Back in Hampshire that evening, Miss Rose cooked a farewell dinner for Martine – a roast chicken with crispy potatoes, garden peas, homemade Yorkshire pudding and onion gravy. Mr and Mrs Morrison came over and Mrs Morrison presented Martine with a pair of binoculars that had belonged to an old uncle.

'To help you spot the big cats,' she told Martine.

Martine was very moved, particularly when Mrs Morrison also gave her a large slice of homemade chocolate cake carefully packed in a lunchbox for her journey.

'I wish you much happiness, dear,' Mrs Morrison said emotionally. 'Remember that you'll always have a home with Mr Morrison and me.'

Mr Morrison just grunted in agreement. He was a man of few words. But when his wife turned away to thank the teacher for the meal, he put his hand in his coat pocket and brought out a carved wooden box. 'To keep you safe,' he said in a low voice, giving it to Martine. Then he opened his car door and started the engine.

'Ready, love,' he called to Mrs Morrison. 'See you, then, Martine.'

Martine waited until she was alone in Miss Rose's spare room that night to open the box. Inside she found a pink Maglite torch, a Swiss Army knife and a first-aid kit. She could hardly believe her eyes. She laid everything out on the bed and spent several rapturous minutes reading the survival leaflet that accompanied it all. The generosity of everyone was very touching. After a while, she repacked her presents carefully, turned off the light and lay on the bed. A full moon beamed in through the window, laying a silver path across the room.

Despite herself, Martine began to feel excited. By tomorrow night she'd be on a plane bound for Africa and a life she could not even begin to imagine. For better or worse, Fate was closing a door on the past.

3

The first thing Martine noticed was the heat. It rose from the airport runway in a soupy, silvery haze so thick that the horizon appeared to bow under the weight of the blue sky and all the planes had wavy edges as if in a dream. Back in England, it had been a freezing winter's night with the weather report forecasting gales and heavy snow, but here Martine felt as if she was burning up. She stood without moving, a small, deathly pale eleven-year-old, and watched the other passengers board the yellow bus to the terminal.

'Wake up, love, you don't want to be left behind.' A bald man in a Billabong surf shirt was leaning over her.

'Where's Mum and Dad? Are they waiting for you?'

Martine wanted to burst into tears and scream so loudly that everyone in the airport could hear her: 'Yes, actually, I do want to be left behind. And no, my mum and dad are not waiting. They'll never be waiting.'

Instead she mumbled: 'I-I'm just . . . I'm not . . . I . . . Somebody's meeting me.'

'You don't sound very sure.'

'Harry, what are you *doing*? I'm fed up to the back teeth with you. The bus is leaving and if you're not here in five seconds, so am I,' a woman called shrilly.

'I'll be fine,' Martine told the man. 'Thanks for asking.'

'Really?' He reached out a damp pink paw and patted her hard on the shoulder. 'Cheer up, love. You're in Africa now.'

The woman at the information desk at Cape Town airport tapped a little drum roll on the counter with her purple nails and squinted over Martine's head at the queue that was beginning to form. Her name tag described her as 'Noeleen Henshaw, Assistant Supervisor'.

'My girl, it's not that I don't want to help you,' she told Martine in a nasal voice, 'but I'm going to need a few more details. Now, what does your grandmother look like?'

Martine tried to conjure up a picture of the

grandmother she had never seen. 'She's got grey hair,' she said hesitantly. 'And glasses. I think she's got glasses.'

Noeleen Henshaw sighed. 'When did you last see your grandmother?'

'Well, I . . .'

'Do you have a phone number for your grandmother?'

'Just an address,' admitted Martine. For much of her journey, she'd been taken care of by a cheery flight attendant named Hayley whose job it was to 'look after unaccompanied minors', but as soon as they landed in South Africa Hayley had pointed her in the direction of the airport bus and just as cheerily waved goodbye.

Noeleen gave an exasperated shake of her henna-red hair and looked again at the queue. 'Sweetie, I think the best thing for you to do is to sit over there, where I can keep an eye on you. If your grandmother doesn't pitch up, I'll try to find someone to help you.'

'Okay,' Martine said uncertainly. 'Thank you.'

She picked up her suitcase and her new olive-green rucksack – a present from Miss Rose – and walked back into the arrivals hall, taking a seat under the 'Welcome to South Africa' sign. Never in her life had she felt less welcome. More than an hour had gone by since her plane had landed in Cape Town and still no one had arrived to collect her. Martine was close to tears. Her worst fears had been realized. Her grandmother hadn't wanted her and so she hadn't bothered to come and fetch her. What Martine was going to do now with no money and nowhere to stay, she had absolutely no idea.

Added to which, she was weak with hunger. It was ten o'clock in the morning and all she'd had to eat since the previous evening was Mrs Morrison's chocolate cake. The food on the plane had been inedible. The scrambled eggs were watery, the rolls had the consistency of tennis balls and the main meal smelt like pet food. Martine made up her mind that she would never fly again without extensive supplies of cake and maybe some ham sandwiches for good measure. Opposite her, a smiling customer left the Juicy Lucy stand with a mango smoothie and a large muffin. Martine's stomach rumbled enviously.

'Miss Martine, you will be thinking we have forgotten you,' boomed a voice so deep that it rumbled in her chest like a bass drum. Martine looked up to see a mahogany giant bearing down on her, arms outstretched and the broadest smile in Africa on his face. He had a scar in the shape of a question mark on one shining cheek and a tooth on a leather thong around his neck. He was wearing a bush hat with a zebra-skin band, and khaki hunter-type clothing that had seen better days.

'Miss Martine?' he queried, and burst into gales of laughter. Without waiting for her to reply, he gripped her hand and pumped it up and down furiously. 'I'm Tendai,' he said. 'I'm very, very happy to meet you. Your grandmother has told me all about you. She was very sorry that she couldn't be here to collect you, but, oh, what a morning we have had! Late last night we received a call to say that, due to a mix up with some paperwork, a shipment of elephants we were expecting at the weekend was being delivered early this morning. There was nobody to supervise their arrival except your grandmother and myself, and she had to stay until the vet had checked each one. I offered to fetch you instead. I forgot that a man of the bush knows nothing about the highway! I have been driving all over Cape Town! I hope you can forgive me. I will get you home to Sawubona just as fast as I can.'

Martine hardly knew how to respond to this torrent of words, but she immediately warmed to the big, gentle man who delivered them. He carried nature with him, almost like an aura.

'Pleased to meet you, Tendai,' she said, adding shyly, 'Of course I forgive you.'

These words provoked a further bout of laughter. Picking up her suitcase and tucking it under one arm as if it weighed no more than a hen, he led the way out into the sunshine.

4

Afterwards Martine would always remember her first journey to Sawubona, which Tendai explained was a Zulu greeting. He was from the Zulu tribe himself. They took the coastal road out of Cape Town, riding in his battered jeep past a series of magical bays and inlets. The sea was navy-blue against the clear sky. Some beaches were wild, with flying spray and forests growing almost to the shore. Some had rainbow beach huts and surfers riding the breakers on bright boards. Some had colonies of penguins or seals. And all of them were overlooked by the mauve-grey cliffs of a flat-topped mountain, which was called, for obvious reasons, Table Mountain.

After about an hour they turned inland and Martine was amazed at how quickly the scenery changed from a heathery type of vegetation and became like the Africa she'd always seen in photographs. Pale spiky thorn trees and ragged shrubs dotted the long yellow grass, which glowed beneath the blazing summer sun as if it was lit from underneath. The empty road stretched on for ever. Martine wound down her window and the dusty, animal smell of the bush poured into the jeep.

Tendai talked about Sawubona along the way, describing his job as a tracker at the game reserve. Sawubona, it turned out, was not just a game reserve, it was a wildlife sanctuary, and it was Tendai's role to check on the progress of every animal in the park. About a quarter of the animals at Sawubona had been born there, but all the rest had been rescued. Some came from drought-stricken areas or game reserves or zoos that had gone out of business. Others had been brought to Sawubona with injuries or because they'd been orphaned in hunts or culls.

'In twenty years,' Tendai said, 'I never saw Henry Thomas, your grandfather, turn a single animal away. Not even one.'

This was the first mention there had been of her grandfather and Martine pricked up her ears. But Tendai's next sentence caught her totally off guard.

'I'm so sorry, Miss Martine, that I wasn't here at his side, watching over him, the night that he died.'

Martine's head was already spinning from jetlag and lack of food and this news made it spin a little more. It

33

was clear that it hadn't occurred to Tendai that she might not know she even had a grandfather, let alone that he had died.

She said carefully: 'Would it be okay if you told me what happened?'

Tendai's hands tightened on the steering wheel. 'Yebo,' he said. 'I can try.'

It turned out that nearly two years had passed since her grandfather's death and yet the events surrounding it were still shrouded in mystery. The police theory was that Henry had stumbled upon a gang of poachers trying to steal a couple of giraffes or maybe kill them for trophies. It had happened on a weekend when Tendai was away in the north of the country visiting his relatives – a weekend when Sawubona was at its most vulnerable. There had been a struggle. When it was over, Henry had been fatally wounded and the giraffe left for dead.

'There was no telephone in the village where I was staying,' said Tendai, 'so I never knew that this terrible thing had happened until I returned on Monday. By then it was much too late. In the summer, many Zulus ask the Rain Queen to bless their fields with rain, but that week it seems she had been listening far too well. For two days, the storms had been washing away the tracks and the police and their vehicles had been driving all over the ground. By the third day, when I came, there was no sign to be found.'

None of the hunters had ever been caught. To this day, nobody knew whether Henry had been murdered or just shot by accident in the struggle. Most puzzling of all was why the poachers had fled without the giraffe they had so obviously come for.

'Did the police manage to find any clues?' Martine asked worriedly. It was sad to hear about her grandfather, but it was even more disturbing to know there were killers on the loose in the very place she was expected to make her new home.

'Tch, those baboons! Don't worry, little one, even the spider leaves a trail. It might take some years, but eventually we will find those who did this. Maybe, if we are patient enough, they will even find us.'

The Zulu's face had darkened during the conversation and now he gave himself a little shake, as though remembering that he and Martine had only just met and perhaps he was saying more than he should. He smiled his amazing smile. 'Your grandfather had a warrior's heart,' he told her. 'He was the *best* game warden. Number One.'

Martine felt a pang for the grandfather she had never known. He sounded like a good man. The new game warden was a young man by the name of Alex du Preez. There was something in the way that Tendai said his name that gave Martine the impression that Mr du Preez was not on Tendai's list of top-ten favourite people.

35

They were passing a village of thatched huts and scattered houses with sunflowers and maize stalks in the yards. A group of African children were playing soccer in a field. The jeep slowed and turned into a driveway overhung by banana palms. At the end of it was a pale-green house with a corrugated iron roof. A peeling Coca Cola sign was propped against one wall. Three chickens wandered out through the front door.

Martine climbed out of the jeep. 'Is this my grandmother's house?' she asked, unable to hide her surprise. She wasn't sure what she was expecting, but it wasn't this.

'No, chile, Tendai is jus' bringin' you to see me.'

Martine turned around to see one of the fattest women she had ever encountered waddling towards her across the threadbare lawn. She was wearing a traditional African dress in the most brilliant colours, with a matching headscarf of banana-yellow, Kalahari-red and lime-green. 'I tole him you would be hungry,' the woman continued in a voice as warm as buttermilk, 'and I see I'm right. Look at you, chile, you just skin'n'bone.'

'Miss Martine, meet my aunt, Miss Grace,' said Tendai with evident pride. 'The best cook in the world.'

They followed Grace into the little green house. It occurred to Martine that her grandmother might not know about this unscheduled stop, but she was too hungry to care. The smells coming from Grace's kitchen were divine.

She and Tendai made themselves comfortable on hand-made wooden chairs in Grace's simple but spotless lounge. There was a woven grass mat on the floor and an out-of-date calendar on the wall, depicting a tropical island.

In a matter of minutes Grace emerged from the kitchen with two huge plates containing omelettes made from fresh farm eggs and wild mushrooms, a heap of crispy bacon and tomatoes fried with brown sugar. Martine felt as if she hadn't eaten in years and she savoured every mouthful in silence. By the time she had finished, she agreed with Tendai wholeheartedly: Grace *was* the best cook in the world.

She turned to Grace to thank her and found her watching her intently.

'Chile looks just like Veronica,' Grace commented to Tendai.

Martine jumped as if she had been scalded. 'You knew my mum?' she cried.

'Aunt!' shouted Tendai, leaping to his feet. 'I told you not to say anything.'

'Quiet, boy,' ordered Grace. 'There be too many secrets at Sawubona. The chile has a right to know the truth.'

'What truth?' demanded Martine.

'Miss Martine,' said Tendai, 'I'm sorry, we must go now.'

'But . . .'

'Please!'

Martine looked from one to the other, her head buzzing with questions that it was clear she was not going to be allowed to ask. Grudgingly, she turned to follow Tendai out to the jeep. Grace grabbed her arm.

'Wait,' she hissed. She put her hand on Martine's forehead and Martine felt an electric current pass through her. Grace's eyes widened.

'You have the gift, chile,' she whispered. 'Jus' like the forefathers said.'

'What gift?' Martine whispered back.

But Grace just shook her head. 'Be very careful. The gift can be a blessin' or a curse. Make your decisions wisely.'

5

In the yard, Tendai had the engine running. As soon as
Martine climbed into the jeep, he put his foot on the
accelerator and they bounded over the potholed drive
and onto the main road. Heat wavered like a watery
mirage above the tarmac.

Tendai seemed agitated. 'I'm sorry, Miss Martine. I
shouldn't have taken you there. Perhaps you would be
kind enough not to mention it to your grandmother.'

Martine barely heard him. Her forehead was still
tingling from the pressure of Grace's hand and her mind
was rushing like an express train through her past. She
was trying to remember something, *anything*, that would

39

explain what had just happened.

'But what did Grace mean about my mum? Did *she* ever live at Sawubona?'

'Please,' begged Tendai. 'Those things you must ask your grandmother.'

He drove on in silence for a few minutes, before turning right onto a sandy road lined with a high wire fence. Arching over the entrance and supported by two white pillars was a black wooden sign etched with the words 'Sawubona Game Reserve.'

The jeep stopped and Tendai pointed out of the window. 'Can you see the buffalo?'

Martine dragged herself reluctantly back to the present. She squinted into the sun, but could see nothing except an endless expanse of trees, dusty shrubs and grass, sprawling under an electric-blue sky. On the horizon was a range of mauve mountains. A black eagle circled lazily overhead.

'No,' she sighed. 'I can't.'

'Don't look *through* the bush,' instructed Tendai, 'look *into* the bush.'

Martine did and gradually the shrubs resolved themselves into the muscular black hides of around thirty buffalo. She could make out their curved horns and intense faces between the trees.

Then she spotted the bull elephant. He was standing under an umbrella tree, his curved tusks and grey bulk almost completely camouflaged. Like the buffalo, he seemed as ancient as the land itself. But even from three hundred yards away, his deadly power was apparent.

Martine stared at him in awe. She was beginning to feel overwhelmed by all she had seen and heard since leaving the airport. 'Wow!' she said at last. 'He's huge and so . . . so still. I've only ever seen wild animals on television. What else do you have here?'

'Twelve other elephants,' Tendai recited proudly, 'eight ostriches, one hundred and fifty springboks, ten wildebeest, eighteen kudus, twenty zebras, six lions, four leopards, seven warthogs, a couple of troops of baboons, a few waterbucks and a . . .' He stopped. 'That's all.'

'And what? You were going to say something else.'

'It's nothing,' Tendai said. 'The local tribes believe that a white giraffe has come to Sawubona. The Africans have a legend, which says that the child who can ride a white giraffe will have power over all the animals, but it is only a myth. We have had no giraffes, not even ordinary giraffes, at Sawubona for nearly two years now, but people keep coming to me to report that they've seen this white one. The tribesmen say that it's an albino giraffe, as white as a snow leopard. If it's true, that would make it one of the rarest animals in the world. There is no proof. I have never seen it and I am in the game reserve every day.'

Martine had an odd feeling of déjà-vu, almost as if she'd had this conversation in another life. 'But do *you* believe it exists?' she asked eagerly.

Tendai shrugged. 'From time to time, I have seen tracks, but they always disappear. I follow them for a few hundred yards and then they just vanish into thin air.'

'So maybe it *is* true!'

The Zulu laughed. 'It is not always the one you follow who makes the tracks, little one. In the old times, some tribes would tie the hooves of animals to their feet to lead other hunters away from the herds, and your grandmother says that in the mountains of Asia people have tried to fake the footprints of the Abominable Snowman. Maybe this is what is happening here!' He grinned at Martine. 'If the white giraffe does exist,' he said, 'it must be very shy.'

The gears clanked and they moved off down the road. When they reached a high iron gate, Tendai jumped out to open it. On the other side was a driveway lined with huge red and orange flowers, an immaculate lawn and a white-painted thatched house. Nerves bit into Martine's stomach. In a few minutes, she would meet her grandmother for the first time. Would Gwyn Thomas be glad to see her? Would she be kind? Would she, even though she hadn't really wanted her, learn to like Martine? And what if she didn't? What then?

6

The door of the thatched house opened and out stepped a tall, slender woman in her early sixties, wearing jeans and a short-sleeved khaki shirt with a symbol of a lion on the pocket. Her hair was tied back in a ponytail. Martine was still taking in the fact that her grandmother was dressed in denim when Gwyn Thomas marched up to her and, without any introduction, took her face in both hands. Up close, Martine could see that her fair hair was streaked with white and that her chestnut-brown skin was etched with a million creases. She looked at Martine with an expression that was impossible to read.

'You're all grown up,' was all she said. She turned to Tendai. 'You're very late, my friend. You haven't been visiting that crazy old magic woman, have you?'

Martine realized with a shock that she was referring to Grace. 'We got lost, Grandmother,' she said quickly. 'We were driving all over Cape Town. I've seen the whole city!'

In a flash, her grandmother turned on her. 'In this house, we speak only when we are spoken to.' She wheeled round abruptly and stalked back inside.

Tendai followed her with Martine's suitcase. He didn't look at Martine as he passed.

Martine walked after them, her heart thumping. A ginger cat sat washing itself on the front step. It regarded her curiously as she approached.

'Oh, boy, this is going to be fun,' Martine muttered under her breath. But the ginger cat simply yawned, closed its eyes and lay down in the sun to sleep.

Tendai appeared at the door. 'Your grandmother is waiting for you,' he said.

With Tendai gone, Martine felt more alone than ever. She stepped into the house and looked around. It was cool and peaceful inside, with polished stone floors and big, comfy, worn leather chairs. Another cat, this one black and white, was curled up on the lid of an old piano and there were oil paintings of cheetahs and elephants on the walls. The bare beams and thatch gave the room a sense of space and calmness.

Her grandmother emerged from the kitchen with a glass of milk and a plate of egg sandwiches. She motioned for Martine to take a seat at the dining table. Martine hated egg sandwiches and she was still full of Grace's delicious food, but she wasn't about to say so. She began picking at the bread.

'I don't have fizzy drinks here,' her grandmother said. 'Don't believe in them.' She stood at the head of the table like a lioness, her blue eyes locked on Martine as if in challenge.

'Okay,' Martine said warily.

'The first thing you need to know are the rules of my house. Please don't touch anything that doesn't belong to you, and that includes the piano. No running, no shouting, no cursing, no sweets. I don't have a television. I go into Cape Town twice a year, so there'll be no shopping for you. No fast food. We grow our own vegetables. You'll be expected to make your own bed and help out around here. I can't abide laziness. Any questions?'

'Can I breathe?' Martine asked cheekily.

'No answering back!' her grandmother roared.

Martine shrank into her chair. The egg sandwiches lay untouched.

'Give them to me,' her grandmother said, snatching them up. 'I should have known that crazy old woman would be cooking for you. Well, you can eat them for dinner. I won't tolerate waste.'

The rest of the day went downhill from there. Martine was dizzy and a bit tearful after the long flight and the adventures of the morning, but after she'd showered her grandmother insisted on driving her to the tiny town nearby – a single street of shops known as Storm Crossing – to buy a school uniform and some brown lace-up shoes. At the clothes shop, where she was fitted with two white shirts, two navy-blue skirts, a windbreaker, a blazer that had a lynx cat with fur-tipped ears on the badge, and a grey tie, Martine discovered to her horror that she was expected to start school the very next day, without even the shortest break to adjust to her new surroundings.

'There'll be plenty of time for that,' her grandmother told her. 'You've missed too much school already.'

As if that wasn't bad enough, at dinner (thankfully, not the egg sandwiches) Martine slipped on the polished floor as she carried her grandmother's favourite teapot back to the kitchen. It smashed to pieces.

'Oh, what *was* Veronica thinking?' her grandmother ranted. 'I knew this would happen. How can I be expected to look after a child?'

She refused to allow Martine to help clean up the mess. Martine just crept quietly upstairs to bed with tears running down her face. She felt utterly bereft. She was in deepest, darkest Africa with no parents and no friends, living with a grandmother who plainly couldn't stand the sight of her. Really, it couldn't get any worse.

As far as Martine could tell, there was only one positive in her new life and that was Sawubona itself. She was already falling in love with it. The sun had been setting over the game reserve when they returned from the shops and a herd of springboks was moving in a dusty column down to the waterhole in front of the house. Martine had managed to escape from her grandmother's clutches long enough to go down to the bottom of the garden and watch the springboks through the high game fence.

She'd had to pinch herself several times. Yesterday she'd woken up shivering in grey, gloomy England and now, just a day later, she was sitting under a copper sky streaked with purple, with the evening sun warm on her skin. The young springboks were bouncing around the shallows as if they had mini-trampolines attached to their hooves, and the guinea-fowl, which she'd earlier seen waddling along the roadside like plump, blue-speckled kings, were crying in the trees as they settled down to roost. Martine stretched out on the grass and let her nose fill with the heady smells of an African evening – cooking fires, wild animals, herby grass and nature in abundance. She'd never experienced anything quite like it.

Her bedroom, too, was something a bit special. It was up in the attic, with a window cut into the thatch. Although very tiny, it had plenty of character and charm. There was a bookcase crammed with books about animals and Africa against one wall and a bed made with crisp white sheets, a patchwork quilt and large soft pillows. But the best part was that it overlooked the waterhole, a brown dam surrounded by thorny bush.

Tendai had told her that most of the reserve's wildlife gathered there at dawn or at sunset.

Now, however, it was night-time. The mattress sank beneath Martine's weight. She dried her eyes on her sleeve and wondered if it was really true that her mum had lived at Sawubona. It cheered her to imagine that this might once have been Veronica's room; Veronica might have read these books or snuggled into this very quilt. But why on earth had she never told Martine about this place?

So tired that she could barely put on her pyjamas, Martine slid between the sheets, her head whirling with snapshots from the long day. The last thing she thought about before she went to sleep was the white giraffe.

7

Next morning Martine woke feeling as if she was going to the dentist. For a long time she lay there with her eyes screwed tightly shut, because that way she could pretend that none of it had happened. Her home had not burned down, and her mum and dad were not gone for ever, and she had not been sent to the wilds of Africa to live with a total stranger. Finally, when she could avoid it no longer, she opened her eyes. A vast sky of the most incredible blue filled her vision. The clock on the bedside table said 6.05 a.m. Right on cue, an orange-breasted bird fluttered onto a thatch beam outside her window and began singing a song of pure happiness.

Tirrootiree, tirrootiree.

Propping herself up on one elbow, Martine gazed out over the game reserve. The waterhole was draped with early morning mist and streaked with gold from the sun. A dozen or so elephants were splashing around in it, wallowing in the mud and spraying each other with their trunks. Zebras were grazing nearby. She shook her head in wonder. The scene didn't take away the anguish in her heart, but it definitely helped.

Even so, she walked downstairs on leaden feet. Her grandmother was sitting at the kitchen table, her hands wrapped around a coffee mug. When Martine entered, she stood up quickly and said: 'Good morning, Martine, I hope you slept well.' Her voice shook slightly, as though she was nervous. Before Martine could speak, she went on hurriedly: 'There is a boiled egg in the pan and some bread in the toaster and anything else you might need on the kitchen table. On the counter over there, you'll find a lunchbox containing sunscreen, yellow cling peaches from the garden and some cheese and chutney sandwiches. I have to go out now to feed the young elephant, but I'll be back at 7.30 to take you to school.'

Martine was still stammering a thank you when the stable door banged behind her grandmother and a gust of cool air blew in. It wasn't an apology, but Martine already knew that it was all she was going to get.

The dentist feeling returned on the fifteen-minute drive to school, most of which Martine spent squirming in her new uniform, hating the skirt and not knowing what to say to her grandmother. And it didn't diminish when Gwyn Thomas drove her through the gates of Caracal Junior and she saw the hordes of healthy, confident children who were to be her new schoolmates. They were every shade of honey, cappuccino and chocolate. None were the colour of Martine – that is to say, a sort of unhealthy grey-white. After her grandmother had left her at the door of the headmistress's office with a gruff but kindly 'Have a good day. Tendai or I will collect you at four,' she stood pressed against the wall, trying to be as inconspicuous as possible.

'Be with you in a mo,' called a voice when she knocked. Martine could hear someone speaking on the phone. While she waited, she took in her surroundings. Her old school, Bodley Brook, had resembled a concrete prison, with a tarmac playground and peeling beige corridors, reeking of disinfectant. The toilets had been covered in graffiti. This school didn't even look like a school. It was more like a lovely campsite. Log buildings made from glowing chestnut timber were scattered about grounds laid with emerald lawns and huge trees. Behind a wooden fence, a swimming pool sparkled.

'You can close your mouth now. We still have the same boring old lessons you had back home. You know, long division, dead kings, punctuation!'

The expression on Martine's face must have said it all, because the Cleopatra-haired vision standing in the doorway wearing wooden parrot earrings and a long purple dress laughed merrily and, pulling her into the room, added: 'Only joking. Our lessons are, of course, extremely interesting. I'm Elaine Rathmore, the headmistress, and you must be Martine. Welcome to Caracal Junior.'

Martine wondered if every woman in Africa had a big personality and eye-popping clothing or if it was just coincidence that she'd met several in a row.

Mrs Rathmore ushered her into a chair, saying, as if she knew what Martine was thinking: 'And now you really can close your mouth.'

Once she'd got used to Mrs Rathmore's sense of humour, Martine couldn't help liking the headmistress, who was very down to earth. Mrs Rathmore explained that despite appearances Caracal Junior was a school like any other, but it did have a strong focus on the environment. All the buildings were heated with solar energy, many school projects concerned conservation and the canteen served only organic meals. They went through a copy of the rules together and Mrs Rathmore explained the schedule. Then they went for a tour of the grounds. Apparently sport was a 'big deal' at Caracal Junior, which had produced many champions. There was a gymnasium with a climbing wall and the sports fields stretched for several acres.

'If you have a gift for sport – or anything else for that matter – we'll find it,' Mrs Rathmore promised.

Martine, who knew perfectly well that she didn't have a gift for sport – had in fact been hopeless at every sport she ever tried – thought back to Grace's words: *You have the gift, just like the forefathers said.* What was the gift? Was it to do with science, maths, art or even music? Or something she couldn't even guess at? *Be careful,* Grace had cautioned her. *The gift can be a blessin' or a curse. Make your decisions wisely.*

What kind of gift came with a warning?

'Lucy van Heerden . . . one of our talented prefects,' Mrs Rathmore was saying. 'Lucy is in Miss Volkner's class with you, Martine. Martine? We haven't sent you to sleep already, have we?'

Martine blinked.

An elegant blonde girl was standing in front of her holding out her hand. Martine shook it and was surprised to find that it was ice cold. Judging by Lucy's caramel tan, she spent every spare hour surfing or sunning herself on the beach.

After asking Lucy to take Martine under her wing, show her the ropes and give her a 'very special Caracal Junior welcome' Mrs Rathmore went on her way in a billowing cloud of purple, leaving Martine with her glamorous new classmate.

'Jeesh, but you're white,' Lucy commented as soon as the headteacher was out of earshot. 'Where are you from? Iceland?'

'England,' mumbled Martine. If she was awkward and self-conscious to begin with, she now felt a million times worse.

Lucy giggled. 'I'm kidding,' she said, giving Martine a friendly punch that almost knocked her over. 'Come on, we're late for Miss Volkner's class, but at break I'll introduce you to the rest of the gang.'

At lunchtime Martine discovered that the gang to which Lucy had referred was the 'Five Star Gang', a group of the most popular kids in the school. Along with Lucy, there was her twin brother Luke, also blond and good-looking with caramel skin; Scott Henderson, who was driven to school each morning in a red Lamborghini; the school rugby captain Pieter Booker; and a black boy named Xhosa (which, if you were English and couldn't make the clicking noise that the Africans made, was pronounced 'Corza') Washington, who was the son of the local mayor. They all had the latest haircuts and a way of wearing their uniforms that made them seem like designer clothes. Most kids idolized them and Martine noticed that whatever they wanted, they got. Even the teachers seemed to give them special treatment.

During break, Lucy introduced Martine to the Five Star boys and several other children. On the whole, they seemed a friendly bunch and a couple of them went out of their way to make her feel included. Martine sat in the sunshine eating her cheese and chutney sandwiches, smiling and nodding, and wondering how it was possible to be in such a pretty place, surrounded by laughing children, and still feel like the loneliest, most miserable girl on earth. All the old feelings that she'd had at Bodley Brook came flooding back. It was not just that she felt shy and clumsy. She didn't fit in, full stop. None of the things they talked about – surfing, hair gel, pop music – interested her. But what did interest her? Martine didn't know. Reading, she supposed. And the white giraffe. She was very, very interested in the white giraffe.

It was while she was thinking about this that she noticed a small figure sitting alone under a tree in the distance.

'Oh, *him*,' Lucy said with distaste when Martine asked what the child was doing there. Her nose wrinkled. 'He's either deaf, dumb or a nutcase. We can't work out which.'

Over the next few days, Martine learned that the boy's name was Ben and that he was of mixed race, with a Zulu father and an Asian mother – a dancer from India, so the story went. Martine was small for her age, but he was as thin as she was and not much taller.

If you looked at Ben closely, you could see that he was far from weak. His brown arms and legs were strong and wiry. But most children didn't take enough interest in Ben to find that out. He was an outcast. Hardly anyone ever spoke to him. This was partly because in the three years he'd been at the school Ben had never uttered a syllable. The teachers had long since accepted that he was mute, mainly because he answered their questions on bits of paper and was consistently top of the class, but to the Five Star Gang, who claimed they'd once seen him holding a completely normal conversation with his dad in the car park, he was a source of both irritation and amusement. Every lunchtime, he would take his backpack and disappear to the furthest corner of the school playing fields. There, he would sit under a tree and read a book. His nickname was 'Buddha Ben', because he had a habit of burning incense and never retaliated if you stole his book, or forced him to do your homework.

Martine found it upsetting that everyone was so mean to him. She made up her mind to try to befriend him, but the first afternoon an opportunity presented itself Lucy waved her over and asked her what she was up to and she couldn't bring herself to admit that she'd been on her way to talk to 'Bonkers Ben', as Lucy called him. Next day she put it off for some other reason and after a while she stopped thinking about Ben altogether.

8

Those early days at Sawubona were among the hardest of Martine's life. At times, she felt as if she was undergoing some sort of test, almost as if she was being prepared for something. Everything added to her sense of isolation. It was like being a castaway on a desert island. There was no one she could turn to for comfort or advice. No one who would hold her if she cried. Certainly not her grandmother. Still, she couldn't help noticing that whenever she was feeling particularly upset or down, Gwyn Thomas would suddenly and unexpectedly make an apricot pie for dinner and serve it up with thick Jersey cream, or leave a vase of wildflowers on her bedside table, or say something like, 'Martine, I could do with your help when I go to feed the baby elephant tonight.'

The little elephant lived in an enclosure in the sanctuary close to Tendai's house. He had been rescued from a Zambian zoo that had gone out of business. Tendai had named him Shaka, after the legendary Zulu warrior king.

'So he'll grow up to be a great leader for the herd, despite his early trials, just like Shaka,' was his remark to Martine.

Shaka was one of several animals in the sanctuary, which was a sort of hospital and holding area for new arrivals before they were relocated to the main game reserve. At present, Tendai and Samson, a wizened, white-haired man who looked at least one hundred and four years old, were tending to a jackal that had been hit by a car and had a leg in plaster, an owl with an infected eye, a springbok with a nasty abscess and an orphaned bushbaby. The bushbaby was one of the dearest creatures Martine had ever seen, with huge brown eyes in a tiny grey ape-like face, a long curling tail and paws like a koala, made for climbing.

One of Martine's chores was to make sure the sanctuary animals had water morning and evening, and she'd also been allowed to feed Shaka three times. Once, when she was giggling at his wobbly gait and funny pink mouth gulping at his milk pail, she'd caught her grandmother watching her with an enigmatic, almost pleased expression. But even on those occasions when she seemed to be making an effort to be nice, Martine still couldn't shake off the feeling that her grandmother didn't want her there.

Much to her frustration, she hadn't yet been allowed into the game reserve itself. Martine consoled herself with the thought that at least she could see the wildlife through the fence, and devoted all her spare time to reading up on the animals in the books she found in her room. She'd been fascinated by the facts she'd learned about giraffes. For instance, the spots on each giraffe are as unique as fingerprints; no two are alike. And although their necks are very long, they have the same number of vertebrae as other mammals – seven. Nowhere did she find any mention of white giraffes.

It was the animals at Sawubona that made Martine's life bearable. She'd never imagined she would live in a place with lions at the bottom of the garden. At night, when they were hunting, she could hear their spine-tingling roars, and just knowing she was so close to them was unbelievably thrilling. Curiously, creatures of all shapes and sizes seemed instinctively to know when she needed a friend. Take her grandmother's cats, Warrior and Shelby. They showed no interest in Martine at all except when she was feeling miserable, and then she could hardly move without them rubbing themselves against her legs and clamouring to sleep on her bed. And on two occasions the baboons had appeared in the garden when she'd had an awful day at school and performed so many funny antics that she got a stitch from laughing.

The second time it happened, Tendai came to the house on an errand while Martine was watching them. He crept up beside her and said teasingly: 'So, little one, this is what you get up to when you are supposed to be doing your homework?'

Martine was spluttering an excuse when he cut her off with a chuckle. He told her that according to Zulu folklore the baboons had once been lazy field hands. Instead of removing weeds from the crops, they spent their days sitting on their hoes, gossiping or sleeping in the sunshine. They sat there for so long that eventually their hoes became tails and the weeds attached themselves to their bodies and became hair.

'You'd better watch out,' Tendai said. 'If you sit here too long without doing your homework, you might grow a tail and we'll have to put *you* in the game reserve.' He grinned over her shoulder. 'Isn't that right, Mrs Thomas?'

Martine swung round guiltily to find her grandmother shaking with mirth, her blue eyes dancing.

'Tendai,' Gwyn Thomas managed at last, 'you're pure gold.'

But none of this stopped Martine from lying awake at night aching for her mum and dad. Or from wondering about the secrets at Sawubona. After nearly three weeks on the game reserve, she was convinced that Grace was right – there *was* a wall of silence at Sawubona. Everything she asked about met with the same blank response.

'A white giraffe!' exclaimed her grandmother when Martine mentioned the tale Tendai had told her. 'As if a white giraffe could go missing at Sawubona!'

'But Tendai said he saw some tracks.'

'Martine, if there was a giraffe in the game reserve, don't you think that Tendai, who can track the path of a python across bare rock, would have found it by now?'

Martine had to admit her grandmother had a point.

But there were other secrets at Sawubona. For starters, there was the mystery of why her grandmother was on a mission to keep her out of the game reserve. And there was no question that that was what was going on. Sawubona was a private reserve, owned by her grandmother, but on weekdays it was open to tourists and visitors who pre-booked appointments. They were guided round by the game warden Alex du Preez or Gwyn Thomas herself. That still left weekends. Yet every Saturday her grandmother had a thousand excuses for not allowing Martine to go into the reserve, from a shortage of staff to the late delivery of fuel to Sawubona. 'You wouldn't want Tendai to run out of petrol when a charging elephant was around, would you, Martine?'

She'd also overheard Gwyn Thomas warning Tendai not to take Martine anywhere near Grace, to whom her grandmother again referred as that 'crazy old magic woman'.

'I won't have it,' she told him. 'I don't want her filling

Martine's head with silly ideas. Grace is out of bounds as far as Martine is concerned.'

All of this added to an air of secrecy that Martine could almost touch. She snooped about as much as she could and eavesdropped on one or two conversations, but she found nothing that could answer her biggest question: why had Mum never told her about Sawubona? She'd found several books belonging to Veronica on her bookshelf and now knew her mum had probably spent much of her life here, but there was nothing to explain why she'd never told Martine about it.

Nor did Martine understand why her grandmother continued to maintain a stony silence on the subject. She found it odd that Gwyn Thomas never once said a word about her own daughter. Even if she was still grieving, one would have thought she might occasionally say something like: 'This was your mum's favourite meal,' or, 'Your mum loved to play the piano.' But no, there was nothing. There were plenty of photographs of her grandfather, a silver-haired version of Harrison Ford, with her mum's sparkling green eyes, but none of her mum and dad, even though her grandmother had described them in her letter to the social services as 'the finest people I have ever known'. And Tendai, who evidently did know something about her mum, refused point blank to give her any information.

'Please, Miss Martine,' he kept saying, 'you must ask your grandmother.'

One evening, when Gwyn Thomas seemed to be in an

unusually good mood, Martine plucked up the courage to do just that. A huge storm was raging outside and they had just eaten dinner.

'Grandmother,' Martine began, 'before Mr Grice wrote to you, did you know about me?'

'Of course I did, Martine,' said her grandmother impatiently. 'What kind of question is that?'

'Then why didn't I know about you?'

'That's your mother's business and none of yours,' her grandmother said, her voice rising. 'Your mother made decisions in order to protect you. If you knew why she had done the things she did, you would be more grateful.'

'How can I be grateful when no one will tell me the truth?' Martine burst out.

'Martine!' thundered her grandmother. 'I won't tolerate this rudeness. Go to bed at once.'

Martine jumped to her feet. 'Fine,' she said. 'I will go to bed. But I am going to find out the truth about my mum and everything else that's going on around here and nobody is going to stop me.'

Upstairs, Martine sat on her bed watching rain lash the window. It was pitch black outside. Tears ran down her face. She'd lost count of the number of times she had cried since she had moved to Africa. She wished she could be back in England with Miss Rose or Mr and Mrs

Morrison, but somehow she knew in her heart that she was exactly where she was meant to be – in this wild, amazing place with its strange, hostile people.

'Everything,' her father had told her, 'happens for a reason.'

Martine couldn't for the life of her imagine what that reason could possibly be and right now she didn't care. She just knew that she needed a friend.

Outside, the wind slapped and banged around the house and the thunder cracked as if a thousand boulders were breaking across the heavens. Lightning split the sky. Martine gasped. A white giraffe was standing beside the waterhole and it was looking straight at her! For a split second, their eyes locked, the small, sad girl and the slender young giraffe, and then the sky went dark. Martine pressed her face to the glass, desperate to try to see the white giraffe again, but it was impossible. There was no moon and the rain was coming down in sheets.

Martine felt so crushed she could hardly breathe. It was like getting the best present you could dream of – a pony, say – and then having it snatched away again before you even had a minute to enjoy it. It was almost too much for her to bear.

She tried to pull herself together. Had she seen the white giraffe or hadn't she? Could it have been a trick of the light? From this distance, there'd been something almost ghostly about it. In the lightning's blue flicker, it had had a phosphorescent glow. But when she relived the instant their eyes had met, she was certain. The white giraffe was out there. It had looked at her as though it was looking *for* her.

Martine had a sudden urge to rush out into the game park and find the shy creature. She knew there could be terrible consequences. She had been forbidden from ever going into the game reserve by herself, and not even Tendai would risk going in on foot after dark. Snakes, scorpions, lions, buffaloes and even leopards were all on the prowl at night and many of them would be out hunting. Martine was well aware that if she disobeyed the order she could be attacked or gored or worse.

For a long time she sat at the window trying to decide what to do. She couldn't stop thinking about the white giraffe.

At last, she made up her mind. She took off the shorts she'd changed into after school and put on her jeans, boots and navy-blue school windbreaker. Behind the bookcase, she'd concealed the carved wooden box Mr Morrison had given to her. She removed her torch and knife and put them in her back pocket. At the door of her bedroom, she listened. The only sound was the slowing rain, muffled on the thickly thatched roof.

As silently as she could, she tiptoed down the stairs. The timber boards were old and with every creak Martine fully expected to hear her grandmother's enraged shriek or feel her hand on her shoulder. But nothing stirred.

When she reached the kitchen she stood for several minutes, breathing deeply and taking comfort in the reassuring hum of the fridge. Then she unlocked the kitchen door. There was something very final about the click it made as it swung shut behind her. She checked her watch.

It was one minute past midnight.

9

Out in the garden, the storm had slowed to a drizzle. Confronted with the sights and smells of the African night, Martine's courage almost deserted her. Had her grandmother's bedroom light not come on right at that very moment, she would have rushed back inside. But it did. Martine decided that if she had a choice between her grandmother and a hungry lion she'd rather take her chances with the lion.

The air was perfume-sweet with the scent of fallen mangoes and gardenia blossoms. Martine set off blindly through the dripping trees in the general direction of the game park gate. The one useful thing she'd overheard during her investigations the previous week had been Tendai telling her grandmother the new code for the padlock. She'd made a point of committing the numbers to memory. When her hands touched the cold metal gate, she felt for the heavy chain that bound it and the lock that secured it. Only then did she switch on her torch and enter the numbers on the wet dial. The padlock clicked open! Martine stared down at it, unable to believe that it had been so easy. She realized then that she'd been secretly hoping all along that something would happen to prevent her from going into the game reserve. She glanced over her shoulder. Once more, the house stood in darkness. Whatever happened now, there was no turning back.

Martine stepped through the gate and stifled a cry of terror. Two red eyes glared at her. The bushes shook violently and a waterbuck sprang up so close to Martine that its fur actually brushed her. With a shake of its horns, it bounded away into the blackness.

Martine's heart smacked wildly against her ribcage. She tried to imagine what Tendai would do in a similar situation. Not that he was likely to be in a similar situation, but if he were she was sure that everything would be about staying calm and thinking clearly. 'Focus,' she thought. 'I have to focus. I *can* do this.'

More than anything in the world, she wanted to find the white giraffe. Why, she wasn't sure; she just knew she had to do it. And as frightened as she was, just doing something for herself and rebelling, even in a small way, against the stifling atmosphere of her grandmother's house, made her feel good.

The beam from her torch picked out the path that led down to the waterhole, where the frogs were competing in a noisy chorus. Blue lightning shuddered over the mountains on the far horizon. Martine set off as quickly as she dared, trying to avoid the puddles. Even so, her jeans were soon soaked through. In places the grass was taller than she was and cold droplets drenched her hair and ran down her neck.

As she walked, unseen creatures slithered and scurried and hopped away through the undergrowth. Martine tried not to imagine the worst. She wasn't sure which she was most scared of, snakes and creepy-crawlies or man-eating carnivores, but she fervently hoped that she didn't meet any of them. After what seemed an age, the temperature dropped and she saw she'd reached the water's edge. She tried to pinpoint the exact spot where she had seen the giraffe. She was pretty sure it had been beside the old gum tree that stood, like a startled skeleton, on the left bank of the waterhole.

As if sensing danger, the frogs fell silent. Tendrils of mist hovered over the water and the night air was laden with threat. Martine quelled the butterflies in her stomach. She'd come too far to go back now. She lifted her torch and shone it into the surrounding bush. Nothing moved. Not a mouse, not a lion, not even a bird. Disappointment hit her like a blow. What had she been thinking? A mythical giraffe! She'd risked her life in pursuit of a fairytale and now she had to try to get home in one piece.

Sheer instinct warned Martine something was behind her. The same sixth sense told her to turn around very, very slowly. A Cape cobra was coiled in the mud barely six feet away from her, hood spread wide, swaying in the yellow torch light. Martine recognized it immediately as one of the most poisonous snakes in Africa, more deadly even than the mamba. Its golden colouring was unmistakable. So was the band around its throat.

The cobra's lips parted and its black tongue flickered out evilly. Martine dropped her torch in panic. It rolled behind a boulder and dimmed to a faint glow.

Then it went out.

In the split second before she was plunged into darkness, Martine saw the cobra draw back its head to strike. Helplessly, she waited for its lethal bite.

It never came. Instead, a pale blur exploded from the trees. There was a hideous hissing sound and the flash of flying hooves. The last thing Martine saw before she crumpled to the ground was the white giraffe.

Something was tickling Martine's face. Something that blew warm, sweet air reminiscent of a freshly mown lawn on a summer's day in England. Or strawberries at Wimbledon. Or the rose garden in Greenwich Park in London, which she had visited one spring on a school excursion.

There was something else in the scent, too, something

wild and exotic and . . . African.

Africa!

Martine suddenly came to and realized that she was not dozing in the hammock in her garden in safe, suburban England. She had illicitly entered a South African game reserve in the middle of the night, and something was sniffing at her and possibly preparing to eat her. Cautiously, she opened one eye. A pair of liquid-black eyes framed by impossibly long lashes stared down at her.

'You saved my life,' she said.

The white giraffe drew back with a nervous snort. It gave a half rear, like a horse, and retreated to a safe distance. Martine climbed carefully to her feet. The white giraffe towered over her. The sky had cleared a little and in the dim light of the watery moon, Martine could see it was an immensely beautiful creature. Its coat shimmered like sunlit snow and it was patterned all over with patches of silver tinged with cinnamon.

She reached out her hand to it and it wheeled around and made as if to flee before sliding to a halt, breathing hard and shaking. The wildlife book in her room had explained that although giraffes are basically very gentle creatures they are quite capable of using their long front legs to kick with force if they feel threatened. But something told Martine that this particular giraffe would never hurt her.

She reached out her hand again and took a couple of steps towards it. 'It's all right,' she said soothingly. 'It's all right. I only want to stroke you, not to harm you.'

This time the giraffe stood still. When her fingers made contact with its skin, it quivered with fear, but didn't move away. Martine felt a tingle of electricity run up her arm – the same tingle she'd felt when Grace had put a hand on her forehead. In that instant, she had a strange sense she knew exactly what the animal was thinking. She knew, for example, without having any idea why, that its name was Jeremiah – Jemmy for short. And she knew that Jemmy was lonely. Every bit as lonely as she was.

'I'm alone, too,' Martine confided to the giraffe. 'Five weeks ago, I lost everything I loved in a fire in England. Now I live with my grandmother who doesn't want me, and go to a school where I don't fit in.'

The white giraffe watched her warily. He didn't respond. Instead he sidled restlessly out of range so she could no longer touch him. Perhaps, thought Martine, he was waiting for a sign that he could trust her. And who could blame him? If she wanted to get close to him the first thing she was going to have to do was to prove to him that she was a friend. But how?

Then it came to her. In England, her mum and dad had had a poster in their bedroom of a dove being released into a sunset. On it was written: *If you love something set it free. If it comes back to you it's yours. If it doesn't it never was.* Martine could remember as if it were yesterday her mum's voice reading it aloud to her, and then saying with a smile: 'Isn't that wonderful, Martine? And it's true. The more you love something, the more you have to give it space to find its own way in the world.

That way you'll know that if it comes back to you, it's because it truly cares for you.'

As miraculous as it was that she'd found the white giraffe, Martine knew she had to walk away from him. She took a last lingering look at him. Her heart ached, as if she was losing a friend she'd only just made, but somehow she knew they'd meet again. For reasons she didn't fully understand, she felt like their souls were already entwined.

'Thank you for saving my life, Jeremiah,' she said, adding hopefully: 'See you soon.'

With that, she began picking her way through the mud to the grassy track. She was a bit hazy on the fate of the cobra but she hoped it was either extremely dead or cowering in its burrow. She wasn't sure she would survive another encounter with it.

She was almost there when a twig snapped like a firecracker in the darkness. Martine had never been much of an athlete, but she was on the verge of sprinting like an Olympian for the house when she spotted a reflection in the water. The white giraffe was following her! She pretended to walk on. The mirrored giraffe stepped gracefully after her, its white-gold coat and silvery patches flowing across the steely water like an elegant ghost. Martine paused. The white giraffe paused. She continued. The white giraffe continued. She swung around abruptly.

The giraffe slid to an awkward stop in the mud. He contemplated Martine from his great height. He seemed inquisitive now, rather than afraid. Martine craned her neck and tried to read his expression. She decided that it was like gazing into the eyes of the wisest creature on earth and the most innocent at the same time. Her overwhelming impression was one of gentleness.

She waited to see what the giraffe would do. At first nothing happened, but then he lowered his head, millimetre by millimetre, until his slender nose was close enough to touch. Again Martine smelled his clean, newly cut grass scent. She longed to put her palm against his satiny white jaw but she forced herself to stay still.

Then something extraordinary happened. The giraffe rested his head on Martine's shoulder and made a low, musical fluttering sound.

For one perfect moment they stood there – the small girl and the white giraffe – mirrored in the moonlit water. It was only a minute, but it was long enough for the emotions and confusion of the past few weeks to leave Martine in a rush and suffuse her with a feeling of contentment. She knew then that she'd come home.

A lion roared. In the eerily quiet aftermath of the storm, the sound blasted through the night as though the beast was about to pounce on them. Martine and the giraffe were in full flight – in opposite directions – before either of them had given the matter any conscious thought. There were no goodbyes. By the time she'd reached the safety of the garden, the white giraffe had vanished as if he had never been.

10

Back in her room, Martine fell into an exhausted sleep. When her alarm woke her at six, she forced herself to spring out of bed, pull on her wet, muddy jeans and rush out into the early-morning sunlight, pausing only to splash icy water on her face. She knew she had to find an excuse for the state of her clothes. By the time her grandmother emerged to feed Shaka at six-thirty, Martine was on her knees in the vegetable garden, weeding furiously.

Gwyn Thomas could hardly believe her eyes. 'Whatever are you doing, child?' she asked. 'You're absolutely filthy.'

'I'm just trying to clear the weeds away from these carrots,' Martine said brightly. 'I've been doing some thinking and I've realized that I need to start helping you a bit more around the house.'

'Well . . .' said her grandmother. 'Well, I . . . well, thank you, Martine.'

Neither of them mentioned the row of the night before. However, Gwyn Thomas, who generally served up an unchanging breakfast of boiled eggs and marmite soldiers, made Martine a special treat of fresh paw paw and mango, a South African porridge called Jungle Oats, and homemade bread with Cape gooseberry jam. Martine was just savouring the last incredible bite when Alex du Preez's grey Landrover came roaring up the drive.

Martine scowled. She'd only met the game warden once but she'd disliked him on sight. He was what her mum would have described as a 'snakeoil salesman', over-familiar and full of insincere patter. He gave her the creeps. She couldn't believe he had any empathy with animals.

His freckled face, topped by a shock of strawberry-blond hair, appeared at the front door. 'Good morning, Mrs Thomas, Martine,' he said breezily. 'How are you ladies on this beautiful day?'

'Very well, thank you, Alex,' said her grandmother, smiling. 'What brings you here so early?'

'Ma'am, I'm just heading into Storm Crossing to buy some zebra feed. I know you've got a lot to do so I thought it might be helpful if I gave Martine a lift to school today.'

'Why Alex, it most certainly would. I've got the vet arriving first thing to check on Shaka and the two buffaloes who had that awful fight yesterday, and a party of twenty-four Swedish businessmen coming at ten. I really do appreciate your thoughtfulness. Wait a moment while I get her packed lunch.'

Martine's heart sank. She trailed out of the door after Alex's stocky frame.

Once on the road, Alex started up a stream of boring chatter in his thick South African accent. Martine, who wanted nothing more than to lose herself in a dreamy reverie about her encounter with the white giraffe the previous night – he'd followed her, and rested his satiny head on her shoulder! – gave him a series of one-word answers, but it didn't seem to discourage him.

'You're a smart little thing, aren't you?' he said as they stopped at the single traffic light in Storm Crossing. 'I bet you're much better than I was at school work.'

'I'm eleven,' Martine said rudely. 'Don't talk to me like I'm a five-year-old.'

A sly look came across Alex's face. 'Okay,' he said. 'If that's the way you want to play it. You haven't by any chance come across a white giraffe at Sawubona, have you, Martine?'

Martine did her best to keep the shock from showing on her face. 'The white giraffe doesn't exist,' she answered. 'Everybody knows that.'

Alex put his hand in his pocket and took out Martine's precious torch. He threw it on the cracked leather seat beside her. She itched to pick it up but didn't dare.

Alex gave a cruel laugh. 'Be like that then.' He put the torch back in his pocket. 'The thing is, Martine, the white giraffe, if it did exist, would be very, very valuable. Your grandmother, for instance, would really benefit from the sale of such an animal. I mean, we're talking about tens of thousands of dollars here, not chicken feed. Now I would hate to think that you would jeopardize the future of everyone on Sawubona by poking around in things that are none of your business. How do you think your grandmother would feel about that?'

Martine was livid. How dare he talk about Jemmy as if he was just another animal to be hunted down and turned into money? She was pretty sure her grandmother didn't know about his ideas either.

'And how do you think my grandmother would feel if she knew about *your* little secret?' she retaliated, just to test him.

Alex's blue eyes blazed. He pulled into the school, slammed on the brakes and reached across her to open the door. 'My girl,' he said, 'you are playing with fire now.' He smiled grimly. 'And you know what happens to people who play with fire . . .'

Martine tried to be strong until she was out of the jeep, but as soon as she turned away from him the tears began to pour down her face.

His laughter followed her all the way across the schoolyard.

11

It is possible that Martine would have continued to settle into Caracal Junior and, in spite of her shyness, would eventually have made friends, but on her third Sunday in Africa something happened to change everything. It all started with a school outing to the Kirstenbosch National Botanical Gardens in Cape Town, a place, Miss Volkner told them, of 'incomparable marvels when it comes to the plant kingdom'.

Throughout the week Miss Volkner had drummed them into a state of excitement about it, promising them a weekend treat they would never forget, during which they would explore things like the Fragrance and

Medicine Gardens, and enjoy a special picnic at the foot of Table Mountain while watching a world-renowned African band.

Martine had looked forward to the trip with some trepidation and was very relieved when, a very short time after boarding the bus at Caracal Junior at noon on Sunday, she found she was enjoying herself. There was a good atmosphere on the way into Cape Town and some of the children were telling jokes and singing. 'Why was six cross?' Sherilyn Meyer asked Martine. 'Because seven ate nine! Eight, ate, do you get it?'

Martine was laughing harder than she actually meant to when she caught sight of Ben – alone, as usual, at the back of the bus. She looked away guiltily. Maybe today she would try to find a way to speak to him. To distract herself, she reflected on the conversation with Alex two days previously. The way he had talked, anyone would think there was a conspiracy at Sawubona to preserve the secret of the white giraffe until it could be captured and sold for a king's ransom. And yet both Tendai and Gwyn Thomas had insisted to her that it was a myth. Either Alex knew more than they did, or they were lying.

Martine thought again about her encounter with the white giraffe; about the moment when she had first seen him towering above her, shimmering white like sun on snow, with patches of silver tinged with cinnamon. A shiver of excitement went through her. Nothing on earth would stop her from seeing Jemmy again – no storm, no lock, no game warden, no threat. Nothing was more important than the white giraffe.

The squeal of the bus brakes interrupted Martine's thoughts. They were entering Gate Two at Kirstenbosch Botanical Gardens. As she waited to get off, she stole a glance at Ben. He didn't seem to have noticed that the bus had stopped. He was staring out at the paradise of trees and flowers and Table Mountain rising into the blue sky behind it, and his face was alive with anticipation.

At the Kirstenbosch Nature Study School, smiling staff greeted them with a fruit juice and a lecture on the Botanical Gardens, which had been established in 1913 and were spread over a massive 528 hectares. After that, they were split into three groups of eight. Two of the groups were to explore Kirstenbosch with an education officer, but Martine's group, which consisted of four members of the Five Star Gang (everyone except Pieter), plus Sherilyn, a big sporty boy called Jake, and Ben, was to be led by Miss Volkner, who had done a special course at the centre to enable her to guide them.

Their first stop was to be the Fragrance Garden. They set off over the manicured lawns, where tourists picnicked and guinea fowl hovered hopefully for titbits, crossing a bubbling brook along the way. It looked innocent enough, but it had a brutal and bloody history as an escape route of slaves in the days when the British ruled the Cape colony. 'Legend has it that one slave who escaped here was eaten by a leopard and all that was found of him was his skeleton,' Miss Volkner told them. 'Ever since then, this has been known as Skeleton Stream and the area above it as Skeleton Gorge.

'The older forest beside it is called *Donker Gat*, Afrikaans for Dark Corner.' She added for effect: 'Many a child has been lost up there.'

An echo passed through Martine – a sort of chill. Her eyes followed Miss Volkner's pointing finger up the forbidding slopes of Table Mountain, where forests of yellowwood and ironwood sprawled in a dense green carpet. The scene looked familiar, as if she'd seen it before in a photograph. Goosebumps rose on her arms. Less than an hour ago the sky had been clear with only a few wisps of cloud over the mountain, but already the day was turning ugly. They had been warned about the unpredictability of the weather. For no particular reason, Martine suddenly felt apprehensive.

The Fragrance and Medicinal Gardens were wonderlands of aromatic plants and healing herbs, but Martine found it difficult to concentrate. At the Dell, they drank from an ice-cold spring in a bird-shaped bath and then it was on to the Cycad Ampitheatre, where Miss Volkner explained that the palm-like cycads were actually living fossils that were around in the time of the dinosaurs. 'Some of them are two hundred million years old,' she said. 'Can you believe that? Two hundred *million* years old.'

The final stage of their journey was the Fynbos Walk on the lower slopes of the mountain. Fynbos was one of the world's six plant kingdoms and was unique to the Cape Region. It consisted of heathery type bushes like the bright red Fire Heath, Silver Trees, reeds, lilies and pink, velvety proteas, which were South-Africa's national flower. Sprawling alongside the winding paths in a blaze of colour, it made for a spectacular display. When they reached the Protea Garden Miss Volkner showed them the orange-headed nodding pincushion flower, a favourite nectar of the sugar birds. Just then, her beeper went off. She checked it with a grimace, the wind whipping her curly hair.

'Okay, everyone, pay attention,' she called. 'One of the other children has suffered an allergic reaction to a bee sting and I'm urgently needed back at the Nature Study School. It would be a shame for you to miss out on seeing the sugar birds feed, so I'm going to trust you to stay here quietly and wait for them. Under no circumstances is anyone to go wandering off. Luke and Lucy, as prefects, I'm putting you in charge. If I'm not back in the next twenty minutes, follow the signs to the concert area and I'll meet you there.'

As soon as Miss Volkner was out of sight, mayhem erupted. No one apart from Martine seemed to have the slightest interest in seeing the sugar birds feed. There were a few other visitors in the Protea Garden, but the noise of the children soon drove them away. Martine decided that now would be a good time to try to talk to Ben. She walked through the flower beds in search of him, but he was nowhere to be seen.

'Where's Ben?' she asked Lucy.

'Who knows,' the blonde girl said disinterestedly. 'Probably hugging a tree or something.'

Sherilyn interrupted: 'What's happening to the sky?'

Eight heads tipped upwards. The wispy cloud had become a vaporous grey blanket. It had consumed the top half of the mountain and was sliding furiously down the cliffs towards Kirstenbosch, driven by the wind. But the really creepy part was the sky, which boiled with a queer violet light. It looked less like a storm was approaching than some weather phenomenon, like a tornado or a tempest.

'Please can we go back now, guys? It's freezing,' whined Sherilyn, but the prospect of extreme weather had added to the atmosphere of silliness and the other children started chasing moths through the Protea Garden.

The sound of marimbas, conga drums and African voices rising in exquisite harmony came to them on the gusting wind. The band had started playing.

A flash of memory seared Martine's brain. It was the music from her dream, she was sure of it! That explained it. That's why Kirstenbosch was so familiar. Her dream was becoming reality. And this was the exact scene! The looming grey mountain, the plum-coloured light, the swallowing cloud and the children chasing moths through the proteas. Any minute now, someone would go: 'Hey, look what I found . . .'

'Hey!' Luke was standing by a stack of wooden stakes of the sort used to create fences. His voice was excited. 'Look what I found.'

The others rushed to his side, Martine included,

although warning bells were clashing like a sixty-piece orchestra in her head.

An Egyptian goose lay on the ground. It was a large bird with reddish-brown and white wings, but one of those wings hung broken and its webbed feet curled limply at its breast. It stared up at the peering faces with one red eye. Though it flapped feebly, it was unable to move. Luke scooped the bird up and it honked hoarsely in protest.

'I bet it's been attacked by a fox. Miss Volkner said there were foxes around.'

'Put it down, Luke,' Lucy snapped at her brother. 'It's probably diseased.'

'Yah, Luke, it's dirty,' agreed Jake.

Martine tried to speak, but no sound came out.

'Maybe we should put it out of its misery,' Luke suggested. 'You know, hit it over the head or something.'

Jake laughed. 'How 'bout a *braai,* a nice little barbecue. We can put it on a spit. Should be enough to go around.'

Martine found her voice. She said tearfully: 'Please leave it alone. Please don't hurt it.'

'Ah, poor little English girl,' jeered Luke. 'Cwying like a baby. You want it? Here, have it. Catch.'

He launched the goose at Martine, who flailed blindly for the brown blur and, unprepared for the weight of it, tripped and toppled over backwards. Somehow she managed to hold onto it through her fall. She struggled into a kneeling position with the goose still cradled in her arms, her face flushed scarlet with anger and embarrassment. The other kids burst out laughing.

'Did you see that?' Jake crowed delightedly. 'That was priceless.' He mimicked Martine's windmill arms and plaintive voice. 'Pleaaase don't hurt it.'

Caught up in the madness of the moment, none of the children noticed that Martine had closed her eyes and was trembling violently. She was remembering the goose in her dream. That goose too had had a tiny pulse beating in its throat and brown silken feathers that were warm to the touch. This bird's eyes slid shut as she watched it.

Martine's first thought was that she had to try to save it. Her second was, *How*? Then a voice in her head, a voice she recognized as Grace's, said: 'You know what to do, chile.' And right at that instant Martine realized that she *did* know what to do; that she had always known, all her life. Her hands ceased trembling and heated up to the point where they were practically glowing. After a few seconds the Egyptian goose jerked and its eyelids flickered. She loosened her palms. It shook out its wings and flew into the darkening sky.

The world swam into focus again.

Her classmates were staring at her with a mixture of fear, horror and disbelief. The colour had drained from Luke's face and he was backing away from her as if she was possessed. 'Hey, how did you do that? What are you, some kind of witch?'

Martine was just as bewildered as he was. In the instant when her palms were at their hottest, she'd felt a power as ancient as the earth go through her like an ocean wave, and had seen, in a puff of smoke, a procession of what she could only imagine were spirits – Africans in antelope masks and rhinoceroses breathing fire. Dazed and shaky, all she could think was: So this is it. *This* is the gift.

'What is it?' Luke was yelling at her. 'Is it black magic? Voodoo?'

'Maybe she's an *umthakathi*,' accused Xhosa, 'a witch. Be careful, she might change into a bat or a bird.'

Martine stuttered: 'I'm not an um . . . I'm not a w-witch.'

'You know, in South Africa, some people say that there is only one thing to do with an *umthakathi*,' Xhosa said. 'They must be eliminated. Otherwise they will do evil things.'

Martine cast a desperate glance down the mountainside, hoping to see the sturdy figure of Miss Volkner coming to call them for the picnic. But no one was there.

'You wouldn't?' she said in a small voice.

Nobody answered, but Jake took a threatening step towards her. Martine made a move towards the path that led to the main centre but the other children cut her off.

She looked beseechingly at Lucy, but the blonde girl was wearing the supercilious expression she adopted whenever anyone spoke about Ben.

That's when she knew that they were serious.

Martine spun on her heel and fled into the twilight, screaming for help as she went, but the band drowned out her cries. She ran down a short hill, over Nursery Stream and into an evergreen forest. Only then did she realize her mistake. Ahead of her was a daunting wall of 330 steps. She halted, panting, unsure what to do, but the clattering of feet and cries of her pursuers on the wooden bridge jolted her into action. She flew up the steps as if the hounds of hell were on her trail. With every one, the agony in her legs increased and her breath burnt like acid in her chest. At the top was a road but no signs. Martine knew that she wouldn't be able to keep going for much longer, so she plunged into the wilderness of yellowwood trees. Better to be lost than to be caught.

Once in the greeny dark of the forest, she could no longer hear the noise of the city, just the tinkle of streams and the faint whisper and twitter of birds, bats and snakes high up in the canopy. Cloud oozed through the branches and hung above the narrow path. Higher and higher Martine climbed. When she paused to suck air into her fiery lungs, she caught a panoramic glimpse of the hazy city miles below and of the Botanical Gardens, now in miniature like a village made of Lego, with toys for cars. Behind her, she heard the shouts of the children as they entered the forest. She dragged herself forward, wild asparagus thorns hooking her ankles, but even as she did so she knew she couldn't run any more. Her legs were too rubbery to support her.

All at once, an arm shot out from behind a tree and she was yanked sideways into a hollow. Martine opened her mouth to scream, just as she had in that long ago dream, but she was so startled and breathless that all she could manage was a small whimper before crumpling into a bed of leaves. She steeled herself for a blow, but none came. Squinting up through the misty darkness, she made out the face of her captor. Ben! He wrapped his arms protectively around her and, despite being small, he was warm and solid and she could feel the thud, thud, thud of his heart.

'Martine,' called Jake in a sing-song voice, 'where *are* you?' Leaves crunched under the feet of the gang as they hurried by.

Ben put a finger to his lips. He reached down and picked up a handful of small stones and threw them as far as he could. They made a series of popping noises as they landed, like tiny bullets.

Luke shouted: 'Over there! Come on everyone.'

There were whooping noises and the cracking of fallen branches as they pounded away down the track, cloud swirling after them.

Martine became aware that Ben was shaking with silent laughter. He laughed so hard that he doubled over and had to hold his stomach.

'What is it?' Martine whispered. 'What's so funny?'

Ben straightened up long enough to point at a sign propped against the tree. The base of it was still damp with fresh soil. On it was written:

WARNING: RAW COMPOST TANK.
DO NOT ENTER.

12

Martine said nothing to her grandmother about the Botanical Gardens drama, which had ended with six of her pursuers falling into a stinking stew of fermenting horse manure, rotting fruit, decaying leaves and squashed bugs. Sherilyn had escaped because she hadn't been able to keep up with the others, but the search party who found them had discovered her babbling incomprehensibly after an encounter with a lynx cat with glowing yellow eyes. Miss Volkner was apoplectic with fury. She was particularly enraged that no one would own up to what had happened. Even Mrs Rathmore lost her sense of humour and said that if it wasn't that she thought the six had been punished enough by missing out on the band and picnic, and being mercilessly teased on the bus to Storm Crossing (where they were made to sit at the back, hungry and glowering, like the broken survivors of a pongy mud-wrestling competition), they would have spent the rest of the term cutting the school fields with nail scissors.

What nobody could figure out was how Martine and Ben came to be sitting quietly on a picnic rug near the band, enjoying hot-buttered corn and big slabs of milk tart. Miss Volkner had her suspicions and told them she'd be keeping a very close eye on them, but it was the wrath of the Five Star kids Martine feared most.

'We'll get you for this,' Scott Henderson had hissed as he boarded the bus, dripping, and somehow she didn't doubt that they would.

Fortunately for Martine, ever since her grandmother had found her helping out in the garden the morning after the row, a truce had been declared at home. So much so that Gwyn Thomas finally relented and allowed Martine to go with Tendai when he did his rounds of the reserve the following weekend. He picked her up in the jeep at four thirty on Saturday morning, when dawn was nothing but a smudge in a star-speckled sky, and drove her to Sawubona's highest point, an escarpment densely covered in aloes, proteas and a shrub that smelled like curry. Cacti clung to the lichen-plastered rocks.

The track that led to the top of the escarpment was badly eroded and treacherous so Tendai and Martine walked the last part of the way, and the sky was etched with fiery hues when they reached their destination. While Tendai unpacked their breakfast, Martine made herself comfortable on a boulder still warm from the heat of the previous day. Far below her was the biggest dam on Sawubona. As the sun rose and her eyes became accustomed to the honeyed light, Martine could make out herds of buffalo, springbok and elephant drifting down to the water. White egrets watched from the trees like the stiff paper birds of Japanese origami.

Martine thought that she had never breathed in purer air, seen a more lovely view, or heard any choir more amazing than the singing of the birds that morning. She wished her mum and dad could have been there to share it, but it made her feel good to think that her mum had probably visited this spot and watched the same sunrise. Tendai made a small fire and brewed up a pot of condensed milk-sweetened tea. He handed Martine some hot African bread made with maize meal, cooked in the coals in tightly wrapped banana leaves, and they munched contentedly and watched the animals in the valley below.

After a while, Martine said: 'Tendai, can I ask you a question?'

'Yebo.'

'Sure?'

'Yebo.'

'How did you get the scar on your face?'

Tendai laughed, but it was a bitter laugh devoid of his usual bubbling good humour. 'It was a long time ago, little one. Too long ago to be important. I was an angry young man, that's all.'

Martine could tell that he didn't want to talk about it, but curiosity got the better of her. 'Did an animal attack you, or did you get into a fight?'

Tendai unbuttoned his khaki shirt and Martine clapped a hand to her mouth. His back and broad chest were crisscrossed with fifty or sixty thick, raised scars. It was as if someone or something had tried to cut him into a million pieces.

'What animal would do this?' he said harshly. 'No, little one, animals might scratch you, or bite you, or even rip you apart in hunger or in fear, but only a man can crush you inside, in your heart, for no reason other than the colour of your skin.'

Martine swallowed.

Tendai had a faraway expression on his face. When he began to talk, it was as if he was seeing something that had happened in another land, in another lifetime. He had been twelve years old when his parents had moved from a peaceful village in the Drakensberg Mountains to the notorious township of Soweto, near Johannesburg, in search of work.

'For many years,' Tendai recalled, 'it was as if the devil himself had moved to Soweto and turned it into hell. But it was a hell just for black people. Whole families lived in corrugated iron shacks without toilets or running water.

When darkness fell, we burned fires to keep away the cockroaches and rats, and armed gangs roamed the streets.' He stopped. 'Perhaps I should not be telling you this. Your grandmother might not like it.'

Martine got up off her boulder and moved nearer to him. 'Please, Tendai,' she said, 'I want to know.'

In spite of the hardship of life in Soweto, Tendai considered himself luckier than most. His mother was a trained teacher and she'd helped him study in their shack. He worked hard and dreamed of one day being able to return to the mountains and buy a farm of his own. When he was seventeen, he managed to get a job as a clerk at a railway station. He was prouder than he had ever been in his life. There was only one problem. Every day he walked five miles to work and almost every day he was stopped by police wanting to check his papers. At that time it was illegal for a non-white – a man of colour – to go anywhere without identification.

'One policeman in particular, it was as if he hated me without even knowing me. Sometimes I felt that he was just waiting to catch me out.'

Martine realized she was trembling. 'And did he?'

Tendai nodded. 'He caught me without my papers. My mother had washed my shirt and had forgotten to return the papers to the pocket after it was dry. This policeman began to strike me with his baton and shout at me for having no identification. When I reminded him that he had checked it many times before, he called me names. Then he tore my shirt. I had kept my temper all this time, but when he tore my shirt – without it, I couldn't go to my job – I'm sorry to say I punched him as hard as I could.'

After that, Tendai remembered very little. When he regained consciousness, he was in a prison hospital, covered in the weals of a sjambok, a whip made of rhinoceros hide. When he was released from jail nine months later, he found that his parents had been taken away by the authorities. He never saw them again. At eighteen he was a broken man, living rough on the streets of Johannesburg, when Grace sent for him.

'It was Grace who taught me that the best revenge is forgiveness,' Tendai said. 'Sometimes the thing that hurts your enemies most is to see that you are not like them. Grace introduced me to your grandfather, who changed my life. He believed in a South Africa where men of all colours are equal. Not everybody does.'

'Why not?' asked Martine. For some reason the face of Alex du Preez, as he threatened her, swam into her mind.

'I don't know, little one,' Tendai said tiredly. 'I just don't know.'

They packed up the breakfast things, threw sand over the coals and headed back down the escarpment. The grass was still wet with dew but the early-morning sun was already hot on their skin. As they walked, Tendai gave Martine her first lesson in bushcraft. He picked an aloe leaf and showed her how to squeeze a gel from it that could soothe burns or rashes, heal wounds or calm itching.

That was impressive, but the aloe couldn't even begin to compete with the marula tree, which was practically a one-stop pharmacy. Not only did its golden yellow fruit soothe stomach aches, Tendai told her, but it had four times as much vitamin C as an orange. Its leaves were great for dressing wounds or treating insect bites and its bark reduced inflammation. And that wasn't all. The stone of the marula fruit contained an oil that the Africans prized as nose or ear drops, or lit in its shell as a natural candle. The Zulus even believed that if a person suffering from measles rose before dawn, went down to the tree without speaking to anyone and bit the bark, they'd be cured.

Martine gazed around her in wonderment. With every passing day, she felt more and more that she belonged here. It was as if the landscape itself was creeping into her soul. She thought of it as a language. Every new bird call, every breath of wind, every new plant and each fresh encounter she had with the local people or animals was like learning a new word. Put together, it made up the language of the bush. She hoped that if she studied hard enough, she'd be as fluent one day as the tracker was.

'Show me more,' she urged Tendai, and he did. He taught her how to identify a multi-layered orange mushroom that was delicious if it was roasted, and how to make a cone of leaves to trap dew or rainwater. He even showed her the 'toilet paper' tree, which had soft fronds that came in handy if you were far from home and caught short!

Best of all, he taught her how to make a natural compass. First, he selected a straight stick of about a metre long. He pushed it into the ground in an area away from any grass or vegetation, so that it cast a clear shadow.

'When you're sure that the stick is standing up nicely, you mark the tip of the shadow with your finger, or a twig,' he told Martine. 'Wait fifteen minutes. When the shadow moves, mark the tip again. Draw a straight line through the two marks, like so. This will be your East-West line. If you now put your left foot on the first shadow mark and your right foot on the second one, you will be facing roughly north. There are more accurate ways of doing it, but for you, I think, this is the easiest.'

Martine could have gone on listening to bush lessons all day long, but she knew Tendai had work to do, so she thanked him and they continued down the escarpment. The path was overgrown and their way was frequently blocked by cacti and massive boulders. Once, when Martine was about to jump from a rock onto a soft pile of leaves, Tendai's arm shot out and he pushed her back so hard that she slipped and grazed her bare knee. She was opening her mouth to ask, a little crossly, what he was doing, when she saw Tendai's sombre face. Lying in the leaves, completely camouflaged by the browns, greys and yellows, were a dozen baby Berg adders. Tendai assured her they were every bit as poisonous as their mother.

Martine was shaken. It was the second time in less than two weeks that her life had been saved. 'What would have happened to me if I'd been bitten?'

Tendai smiled. 'But you weren't.'

'But what would have happened if I had been?'

The Zulu refused to answer. 'With any snake bite, you must stay as calm and quiet as possible. Try to identify the snake and walk slowly to get help.'

Urine, it turned out, was an excellent antiseptic and the perfect thing to use if there was no water nearby when a cobra spat in your eye. Martine tried to imagine herself calmly peeing into a cup or even her hand and then using it to wash out her eyes. 'Ugh,' she thought, and shuddered as she remembered her close shave with the cobra the other evening. She resolved to give snakes a wide berth in the future.

Tendai saw her expression and erupted into laughter. 'Don't worry, Little One. Snakes usually do their best to avoid people and seldom bite unless they are cornered or threatened.'

'Mmm,' murmured Martine doubtfully.

13

When they reached the jeep, Tendai put the breakfast things in the cab and took out his rifle. They set off on foot across the valley. The sun was so searing that even the earth smelled baked and the sky was as blue as a kingfisher's wing. At this hour of day there was no shade to speak of, but the lacy-leafed thorn trees were alive with bees, cooing doves and crested grey louries, which her grandmother and Tendai referred to as 'Go-away' birds. These were the sounds Martine had come to associate with Africa.

She stuck close to Tendai, who walked with his hand on the trigger of his rifle, alert for elephants, buffaloes and lions, the most unpredictable animals in the reserve. He noticed everything. He showed Martine a nest of hoopoe bird babies, a comical chameleon and the spoor of a female leopard and two cubs. He could even tell how big the cubs were and how fast the little family had been travelling.

The more Tendai talked, the more obvious it was that he knew Sawubona like he knew his own heart. Martine felt safe with him. With his gravelly voice and patient way of explaining things, he reminded her of her father.

All at once, Tendai broke off. He made a clicking noise of irritation and took some pliers out of his pocket. They were in the valley to search for snares, wire nooses or iron-jawed traps left by poachers, which strangled animals or broke their limbs and left them to die slowly. Martine watched him as he sprang a trap, almost invisible in the long grass, and cut the rusty wire binding it to a tree.

'I don't know what to do any more,' he said as they walked into the welcome cool of a grove of trees. 'No matter how many snares I remove, they are always there the next day. And recently we've started to lose our big game as well. A lion and a buffalo have disappeared in the last month. I wish we could employ a guard, but money is very tight.'

Listening to him, Martine began to feel frightened for Jeremiah. What if her giraffe (she'd already begun to think of Jemmy as *hers*) had his legs broken in a steel trap?

'Tendai . . . ?'

The Zulu put his finger to his lips. He indicated that she should creep forward quietly and crouch with him behind a tree. They sat motionless. After a few minutes, a magnificent kudu bull stepped gracefully into the clearing in front of them and stood in the dappled sunlight. He seemed to be listening for something. Martine thought that next to Jemmy he was the most gorgeous animal she had ever seen. He had spiral horns and almond-shaped eyes in a broad, fawn-coloured face. Long silky white fur traced the line of his throat and delicate white stripes adorned his back, which was humped at the shoulder.

'He's amazing,' she whispered to Tendai, who grinned down at her.

BANG!

A bullet ripped into the tree trunk above Tendai's head, simultaneously spraying him with splinters and terrifying Martine. Before they could move, a second bullet hit the kudu in the throat. Blood spurted from its neck in a fountain and it dropped to the ground and lay still. Martine screamed.

Alex came strolling through the trees, smoke rising from the tip of his rifle. His blond hair was standing up in sweaty spikes.

'Sorry about that, guys,' he said. 'The sight on my gun's been playing up. Lucky I missed you, hey! I was trying to hit that kudu over there. From where I was, it looked like it was caught in a snare.'

Tendai was incandescent. 'There was nothing wrong with that kudu, nothing,' he shouted. 'Where is the snare? What did you have to go and shoot it for?'

'What can I say?' Alex mused chirpily. 'These things happen. At least it'll make good eating.'

This incensed Tendai even more and the two men started to argue. Neither of them noticed Martine steal away and run as fast as she could to the fallen kudu. His eyes were glazed over and his lovely fawn coat was scarlet with pulsing blood. The rifle blast had left a big jagged hole in his white-bearded throat.

Martine bent down beside him. She was in a trance, just as she had been when she held the wild goose. Ordinarily, she would have been inconsolable at the mere idea of anyone shooting an animal, but today she didn't feel any sadness at all. Instead she felt charged with energy, as if the purest, most perfect electricity in the world was coursing through her veins. Her hands became boiling hot. She put them over the kudu's heart. There was a faint beat, already fading.

Martine thought fast. Shock and loss of blood had caused the kudu to lose consciousness and she knew from the first aid her dad had taught her that without emergency treatment he would be dead in minutes. But that didn't mean he couldn't be saved. The bullet had pierced the kudu's throat, passed straight through its windpipe and made a clean exit. If Martine could stem the blood and heal its failing heart, then maybe, just maybe, the kudu would breathe again.

In the distance, she heard Alex snap sarcastically: 'The trouble with you, Tendai, is you always put sentiment before business. A dead animal is not always a disaster, my friend. Sometimes it's just a furry bit of money.'

Martine shut him out and put her hand over the hole in the kudu's throat. Blood bubbled through the gaps in her fingers. Every second counted. She scanned the area around her, desperately searching for something that could help to seal the wound. There was nothing but pale dirt, tufts of dry grass and a big anthill. An anthill! Martine had a sudden flashback of Miss Volkner telling the class how the Shangaan tribe had once used soldier termites, which had very large mandibles or pincers, to 'stitch up' wounds. What made it so effective, Miss Volkner had told them, was that the saliva of the ants worked as a natural antiseptic.

'The down side,' she'd added, with what Martine had thought was unnecessary relish, 'is that, after the soldiers have locked their jaws, you have to rip their bodies off. That way, they won't be tempted to let go.'

Martine had been squeamish about the decapitation of the poor termites at the time and, as she watched them making their way innocently home past her left knee, she didn't feel any better about it now. But she also knew she had to save the kudu.

The soldier termites were easy to spot. They had bulbous red heads on tiny cream bodies and their black mandibles waved in the air like weapons. As quick as a flash, she brought the edges of the wound together in a neat line, grabbed a passing soldier by the end that didn't bite and held its pincers to the pink flesh. It clamped down hard. Before she could think about it, Martine whipped off its rear. It worked! The soldier's black mandibles curved into the kudu's skin exactly like a stitch. She picked up another termite and did the same thing again, telling herself that at least it had died for a good cause. It hadn't just been stepped on by mistake or something. In under a minute, twenty termite heads sealed the wound as tightly as any surgeon could have done. Not a trickle of blood escaped.

Martine placed her hot hands over the kudu's dying heart and began pressing down every few seconds. Under her touch, the beat grew stronger and the kudu's skin became warm. When he opened his eyes and saw Martine he appeared confused, but not frightened. He climbed to his feet shakily and, with a flick of his tail, bounded weakly away.

She watched him go, flooded with an indescribable feeling of joy. All she could think was: Dad would have been proud of me.

That's when she realized that somehow, without realizing it, she was finding her feet in her new world, and because of that, happiness was creeping up on her again. Three times in the last few weeks – saving the Egyptian goose, finding Jemmy and now healing the kudu – she'd had to do things on her own, with nobody else's help, even when she was very, very scared, and each time something amazing had happened. And that made her trust herself more.

Even so, she was scared to look at the two men in case they'd witnessed what had just taken place. Fortunately, it seemed they hadn't. Alex had his back to her and Tendai's view was blocked by the game warden's body.

They were still arguing. She used a tuft of grass and some spit to wipe the blood off her hands and walked over to them.

'Kudu's gone,' she announced casually.

The men stopped ranting and stared at the spot where the kudu had been.

Tendai rubbed his eyes. He went a funny grey colour. His gaze went from Martine to the clearing then back again.

'Where's the kudu?' roared Alex. '*Where's the kudu*? It was dead. How the hell could it have moved?'

'He felt better,' said Martine. 'He decided that it wasn't a great idea to hang around while the sight on your gun isn't working.'

Alex made a move towards her as if he were going to throttle her with his bare hands.

'*You* again,' he snarled. 'Remember what I told you. Be very, *very* careful. Next time you might not be so lucky.' He turned to Tendai. 'And as for you, just for the record, you should know that it's not the new South Africa on this game reserve.'

He picked up his gun and stormed off into the trees.

Martine waited until she heard his truck speeding away.

'He could have killed you,' she said.

The Zulu was sitting on the ground with his head in his hands. There were two ugly gashes on his face caused by ricocheting splinters. He lifted his head. 'Please don't say anything to your grandmother.'

'Tendai!'

'*Please.*'

'Okay,' Martine agreed unhappily.

They were silent for a minute. Then Tendai said: 'My aunt was right, wasn't she, Little One? You have the gift.'

Martine didn't answer.

'The kudu,' persisted Tendai. 'It was dying. What did you do to it?'

'It was resting,' said Martine. 'The kudu was just resting.'

And with that Tendai had to be satisfied.

14

The combination of Alex's bizarre behaviour and the bone-crushing snares Tendai had destroyed in the valley had unnerved Martine so much that rather than waiting for the white giraffe to find her, as she'd promised herself she would, she became determined to find him again. For once, luck was on her side. Eight days after her outing with Tendai, a Sunday, her grandmother received a call to say that a close friend of hers had been rushed to hospital. The hospital was in Somerset West, a couple of hours' drive away, and Gwyn Thomas would have to spend the night. She wanted to take Martine with her, but Martine convinced her that it would be much better if she stayed at Sawubona.

'I don't want to be tired for school in the morning.'

'That's true, although I'm surprised to hear you say so,' retorted her grandmother. 'But in any case I'll be worried about you here on your own.'

'I won't be on my own,' Martine assured her. 'Warrior and Shelby will keep me company and if I'm scared I can call Tendai. Besides, I've got some homework I need to finish.'

At two o'clock she waved goodbye to her grandmother, smiling what she hoped was her most trustworthy smile. That in itself made Gwyn Thomas suspicious and before half an hour had gone by Tendai was at the door, checking up on her. Luckily Martine, who really did have a school project to finish, was already sitting at the dining room table surrounded by books, so she had no difficulty convincing Tendai that she was absolutely fine. 'I'll phone you in a second if I'm not,' she promised.

Homework done, she went up to her room, shut the curtains on the afternoon sunshine, set the alarm and hopped into bed. She had a long night ahead of her and she needed all the sleep she could get.

It was one a.m. when Martine entered the game reserve, nerves tingling, and she knew within seconds that there was going to be trouble. She crouched down in the thick grass and scanned the bush carefully. Lights were flickering in the trees. At this hour, that meant one of two things. At best, it was Tendai or Alex patrolling the reserve, in which case if she was discovered and her grandmother got to hear about her escapade, her life would no longer be worth living. At worst, it was a gang of poachers – possibly even her grandfather's killers. Either way, it was a monumental disaster. Unable to get back without being seen, she used the grass as cover to make it as far as the trees and then flung herself under a clump of bushes.

Presently, she heard voices. The men were speaking softly, but it was a fine night and the sound travelled clearly over the water.

'I'm telling you, man, this better not be another one of your wild goose chases,' said one. 'If we don't deliver this thing very soon, M . . .' – the name was lost on the wind – '. . . is going to get ugly. He's not used to being kept waiting.'

'When have I ever let you down?' a second voice demanded. 'I'll find that blasted animal if it's the last thing I do.'

The voices came nearer and one of the men stepped out of the trees. He walked to the water's edge and squatted to examine the mud with his torch.

'Bullseye!' he crowed.

Another man emerged from the shadows. Martine tried to get a good look at him, but despite the full moon he was too far away to be anything other than an indistinct silhouette.

'What's up?'

'Giraffe tracks,' the first man replied. He stood up. 'Now all we have to do is find the giraffe.'

There was a whisper of leaves and Martine whipped round in fright. It was Jemmy. Unheard, the giraffe had crept up almost beside her and now he loomed over her, outlined like a shimmering white giant against the blue-black sky. His eyes were locked on the two men.

'Jemmy!' Martine whispered. 'You've got to go. Run! Get lost!'

He didn't move.

'Jemmy!' hissed Martine as loudly as she dared. 'RUN!'

The white giraffe seemed to notice her for the first time. His liquid black eyes swept from her to the men and back again. He was shaking. Every inch of his body was poised for flight, but something was stopping him.

Abandoning all thought for her own safety, Martine jumped from her hiding place. 'Go, Jemmy,' she pleaded, drumming her fists against his leg, 'you've got to go.'

The white giraffe shoved her purposefully with his nose. That's when it hit Martine: he wanted her to come with him.

'There it is!' cried one of the men, and Martine went cold with terror. Behind her, she could hear shouts and the high-pitched whine of an engine firing into life. There was no escape. In a matter of minutes, she and Jemmy would be caught. Unless . . .

'Jemmy,' yelled Martine, and she ran to the nearest

climbable tree. For several petrifying moments it seemed as if Jemmy was not going to follow her, but all of a sudden he did. Martine pulled herself up onto the highest branch she could reach. There was no time to think. In particular, there was no time to think about how she'd never ridden any animal, not even a Shetland pony, and that she wasn't all that good at riding a bicycle. She simply swung onto Jemmy's back and grabbed a handful of mane.

The first panicked surge of the white giraffe nearly sent Martine flying. Self-preservation stopped her from falling off. Before she could adjust to the fact that she was ten feet off the ground – on the same level as a startled owl – they were bolting into the night. Martine leaned forward the way she'd seen horse riders do in England, gripped with her legs and tried to avoid looking down.

They swept through the dark trees at an incredible speed, the giraffe galloping with a rhythmic, rocking-horse stride. How he avoided colliding with the overhead branches or getting a hoof caught in a root was a mystery to Martine. Nevertheless, once she got used to his sloping back, she found it surprisingly easy to ride him. He was broad and comfortable and his fur was like satin. Soon it seemed like the most natural thing in the world to be racing through the moonlight on the back of a young giraffe.

The sound of the men died behind them. After a while, Martine could hear nothing but the wind in her ears and the sharp cries of the night birds as they flashed by. Gradually, the trees gave way to open grassland and she could make out the shadows of the game reserve animals and smell the sweet smell of the bush at night. Zebras looked up blinking as they passed, a bushbaby swung torch-like eyes on them and a couple of lionesses bounded after them hungrily before stopping to lie in wait for easier prey.

After about a quarter of an hour they reached the lower slopes of the mountain that marked Sawubona's northern boundary and Jemmy slowed to a walk. His neck was wet with sweat and he was breathing hard, like a racehorse on the gallops. He seemed to be searching for something.

Martine was so exhilarated by the experience of riding an actual giraffe that at first she barely took in her surroundings. It was *awesome,* if a little vertigo-inducing, to see the world from this height. When she did look around, she found that they were in a barren clearing, littered with rocks and shale, at the base of a granite cliff. An air of desolation hung over the place. Usually the African night was alive with the sound of cicadas, frogs and nocturnal creatures, but this area seemed devoid of any life. Even the temperature seemed lower. Nothing grew here apart from a single, twisted tree, which had taken root in the cliff itself and was shrouded in a tangled mass of moss and parasitic creepers. Due no doubt to the gales that ripped around the mountain, it had grown stunted and misshapen over the years and now, Martine thought with a shudder, it stood among the boulders like a sinister sentinel. She couldn't think why the white giraffe had brought her to this awful place, but he seemed very agitated. She began to feel concerned.

Through the night came the rumble of an engine. It was heading straight towards them. A searchlight swept the slopes above their heads.

'Jemmy!' Martine cried. 'What are you *doing*? We've got to get away!'

Beneath her, she felt the white giraffe's hindquarters bunch as if he were preparing for a mighty leap. Martine put her arms around his neck and hung on for all she was worth. Until that moment, she'd been too full of the miracle of the ride to wonder where Jemmy was taking her or what would happen when they got there. Now reality was setting in. She dreaded to think how many bones she would break if she did crash to the ground, or indeed how she'd manage to crawl home and explain her injuries to her grandmother. Assuming, of course, that she wasn't eaten, bitten, stung, trampled, gored or shot by poachers along the way. But there was no time to think about that now.

From standing, Jemmy took six breathtakingly fast strides and an enormous leap. In the instant before the jeep burst into the clearing and the world went black, Martine understood why Tendai had never been able to follow his tracks. The white giraffe had simply evaporated into thin air.

15

How they managed to survive this leap into the unknown, Martine later had no idea. One minute they were in the creepy clearing and the next Jemmy had launched himself directly at the cliff-face, and Martine was being sucked at by gravity and strangled, mauled and scratched by hairy vines and vicious thorny branches.

At last they came to a foaming, trembling halt. They were in complete darkness. It was some time before Martine's eyes adjusted to the light and she was able to take in the fact that she was still on the giraffe's back and still in one piece. It was even longer before she was able to figure out a way to slide safely to the ground.

Back on solid earth, she felt small and inconsequential again, but also elated. For the time being, at least, she and Jemmy had outwitted the poachers. She took her grandmother's kitchen torch from the pocket of her school windbreaker and prepared to expect the unexpected. She had willingly climbed onto the back of a wild giraffe (even though there were probably very good reasons why no one else in history had ever attempted to ride one) and had been whisked away to a deeply unpleasant place with an even more unpleasant tree. Then, just when she thought things couldn't possibly get any more surreal, the white giraffe had hurled himself at a mountain.

They could be anywhere.

She switched on her torch. Relief flooded through her. Nothing fantastical had occurred – at least nothing involving any magic, black or otherwise. And Jemmy hadn't actually jumped through bare rock. He'd simply leapt through the veil of creepers covering the tree into the crevice that lay behind it. Because the crevice ran at an angle almost parallel to the cliff itself and was disguised by foliage and the great twisted bulk of the tree, it was invisible from the outside. Martine marvelled that even the animals had ever found it. Not that many of them had, if the silence was anything to go by.

Drawing a wide arc with her torch beam, she discovered that she was in an exquisite little valley of perhaps an acre, surrounded on three sides by high sloping walls of sheer granite and on the fourth by massive chestnut boulders stacked five deep. The effect was of being on the inside of an uneven pyramid. The mountainside wall leaned at such an angle that it overhung the boulders like a ledge, creating a roof over the valley. Seen from below, it was obvious that even if someone were to climb the mountain and glance down, they still wouldn't notice the valley. It was completely hidden.

That wasn't the amazing part, though. Judging by the rectangle of blue-black sky she could see, a fluke of nature had ensured that there was enough space between the ledge and the boulders to allow sunlight into the valley for at least part of every day. That explained the presence of several acacia trees, a favourite food of the giraffe, the lush carpet of grass and the fragrant white orchids springing from the valley's floor. There was also a pool of water in a hollowed rock, fed by a clear stream.

Martine knew she was standing in the white giraffe's secret sanctuary. Jemmy had everything he needed to survive here. Everything, that is, except love and company. No wonder he was so lonely. She ran a soothing hand over Jemmy and marvelled once again that he stood still under her touch. If he would let her, she planned to give him all the love and company he could possibly want. He need never be lonely again.

In the meantime, a million questions ran through her mind. Who had first discovered the Secret Valley? Had any other human being ever been here? Did anyone apart from the animals know it existed?

She set out to explore the valley perimeter, combing the walls with her torch. That's when she saw it – a black triangle between two rocks. It looked like some sort of tunnel. Immediately she felt an overwhelming urge to investigate. She was well aware that there were probably smarter things she could do in her present situation than go poking around in black holes, but try as she might she couldn't think of any. She checked on the white giraffe. He was over by the stream drinking deeply, his front legs spread wide, his silvery nose wrinkled against the bubbles.

Martine debated what to do. What if she'd used up all her luck for one evening? But there was something almost magnetic about the space. She felt as if it was pulling her towards it – *calling* her, even. She had the oddest sense that going into the tunnel was what she was meant to do. That that's what she'd end up doing whether she decided to or not.

Retying her bootlaces purposefully, Martine walked on uncertain legs towards the black hole. Her heart was in her mouth.

It was a tunnel, one that smelled strongly of wet rock and animals that dwell in dank, dark places – spiders, baboons and the like. Leopards enjoy those places as well, but Martine consoled herself with the thought that Jemmy would hardly have lived as long as he had if a carnivore resided close by. After one last attempt to talk herself into staying in the lovely valley, she stepped inside.

The tunnel was not much taller than she was and even a small adult would have had to crouch, but gradually it widened and became less claustrophobic. After a while, it turned back on itself. She was beneath the mountain now. From there, the ground rose sharply in a series of steep steps, slick with froggy algae. Martine put the torch between her teeth and scrambled up in an undignified fashion. She made a mental note to smuggle her giraffe-fur, grass and slime-covered jeans into the washing machine before her grandmother noticed them. The vegetable garden excuse was not going to work a second time.

She was halfway up the last step when a hideous screech echoed from the chamber above her. Martine nearly flew over backwards. Her torch flashed around madly as she grabbed a ledge to save herself. Within seconds, the air was filled with a blizzard of flapping wings and high-pitched squeaks. She had unleashed a colony of bats!

In England, Martine had known girls who went around saying that they had a phobia about bats, even though they lived in suburbia and had never encountered them outside Dracula films. She herself had never much cared for the idea of them. But since her arrival in Africa she'd come to realize that they were actually quite cute. Far from being blood-sucking vampires, they were just flying mice that enjoyed fruit. Until, that is, they got caught in your hair.

'Eeek,' spluttered Martine as she tried to disentangle their scratchy feet and clammy wings without being bitten. 'Eeek!'

When the black whirlwind subsided, she picked up her torch, dusted herself off and saw that she was in a cave – one the height and size of a small church. But what struck her as strange was that the feeling in the cave was different from that of the tunnel, which was simply damp and cold. The cave had a distinct atmosphere. Martine took a lungful of its dense, heavy air and was immediately swamped with the same light-headed, time-travel sensation that she'd felt in some of the cathedrals and historic buildings her parents had taken her to in England – Leeds Castle or the Tower of London. There, too, she'd had a real sense of the generations who'd occupied them before. It was almost as if certain people in certain eras made their mark on a place so thoroughly that the spirit of them never left. But why should she feel that here?

Moving cautiously so as not to alarm the bats, Martine shone her torch around the cave. What she saw next made her cry out in wonder. Every wall and every rock was covered in paintings! Some of them were nothing more than crude charcoal line drawings, faded with the years. Some were stick figures. And some were so rich in texture and hue that they seemed to leap from the walls like naked flames. But every one of them lived and breathed. They spoke to her from across the ages as clearly as if their creators were standing in front of her, telling her of battles lost and won, feasts and famines, times of pestilence and times of plenty.

Martine sank down onto a rock. Half of her felt like a child at Christmas; the other half felt dizzy. What was happening? What was this all about? Jemmy, the kudu and now the cave pictures . . . ? What did it all mean? Oh, if only she'd been able to have a proper conversation with Grace on that first day in Africa. Martine was sure that Grace held the key to at least some part of the mystery. She had, after all, known about the gift.

So much was happening so fast. Martine tried to remember her life with her mum and dad. Already bits of it were fading. One thing she did recall was being petrified of the dark and spending sleepless nights convinced that something monstrous lurked under her bed. Several times she'd even crept into her parents' room. Yet here she was, alone in a cave in the dead of night, and she felt completely unafraid. Confused, yes, but not afraid. Nor did she feel alone. It was as though her mum and dad were watching her, as though they knew about her and Jemmy. She smiled to herself in the dark.

She knew that she owed much of her newfound confidence to the white giraffe. Loving Jemmy had given her a reason to smile when she was sure that she'd never smile again, and being brave for Jemmy, as she'd had to tonight, had made her reach deep inside for some strong, steady part of herself that she hadn't even known existed until then. In return, the white giraffe had overcome his fear of humans to save her twice and allow her to ride him. If he hadn't trusted her, he wouldn't have brought her here. She vowed that as long as she lived she would never tell anyone about the Secret Valley. If the paintings were ever found, Jemmy's sanctuary would be flooded with reporters, scientists and tourists. The ancient spirits would be chased away. The world would come trampling in.

Martine stared at the paintings. One of her mum's books had contained pictures just like these. They'd been painted by the San people, as the Bushmen were known, centuries before the white man ever came, using iron ore, china clay and oxgall. She wondered if these pictures, too, had been painted by the Bushmen, or if some other tribe had done them – perhaps Tendai's tribe, the Zulus. She got up off the rock and went over for a closer look. Her head was still spinning and she still had millions of questions, but mostly she just felt lucky to be able to witness this.

Holding the torch above her head, she walked around the cave. The red, gold and black images unfolded before her, like scenes from an old sepia-toned movie. Martine was entranced. Despite their simplicity, they conveyed lives of great beauty and sorrow. There were fantastic scenes of animal migration, tribal dances, and men confronting rhinos and elephants armed only with bows and arrows. She was halfway round when she noticed a painting of a giraffe. It was one of a series, most of which featured herds of giraffes surrounded by men with spears. In each new picture, the herds became smaller and smaller and more and more bloody giraffes lay on the ground. Soon there were just two left. Then they, too, were on the ground and a man lay on the ground with them. But it was when she saw the next painting that Martine's head really started whirling. It showed a white giraffe suckling from an elephant. At first, she was sure that the colouring of the giraffe was merely a trick of the light, but when she compared it to the previous images it was definitely paler. She traced the giraffe with her fingertips. The rock was cold to the touch but somehow it, too, had a kind of energy.

She had to force herself to look at the final picture and when she did the emotion was overwhelming. The hue of the image was different, almost as if it had been created with a metallic paint. In it, a child was riding a white giraffe. To the left of them was a fire and to the right was a line of animals of different species.

'The child who can ride a white giraffe will have power over all the animals,' Tendai had told her when she arrived. And although some dreamy part of her had entertained fantasies about riding Jemmy, she'd never really thought about what it meant because she had never believed for a second it might come true. Why would she imagine she'd be able to ride a giraffe? Nobody else in the world ever had.

The child who can ride a white giraffe will have power over all the animals.

For the second time that evening, Martine's knees gave way and she had to sit down on another rock.

Grace had been right. The forefathers had known she was coming.

· 16 ·

In the excitement of the night, Martine had forgotten about the poachers or the fact that she was miles from home with dawn rapidly approaching. Even supposing she was able to steer Jemmy – who was not, after all, a schooled horse – in the general direction of the house, there was no way she could allow him to leave the Secret Valley if there was any possibility that the hunters were still out looking for him.

After a last bemused glance at the giraffe paintings, Martine ran to the cave exit and slipped and slithered back down the rocky steps, adding a fresh layer of moss to her jeans. The tunnel seemed longer than she remembered and she was very grateful to reach the tranquil valley and hear the welcoming call of the white giraffe. She rushed over to Jemmy, put her face against his velvet fur and cuddled him for several minutes. Only then did she switch off her torch and grope her way to the valley entrance. Standing on a rock, she peered over the edge of the crevice. The dense foliage of the tree blanketed out most but not all of the view. A stamp-sized gap showed a patch of sky, which was that brilliant blue that precedes first light. Martine could also make out the front half of the poachers' rusting Ford pickup. It was empty.

Seeing the truck gave her an idea. Like a lot of her ideas recently it was a bit crazy, but if it worked it would be the perfect solution. She was going to get the poachers to give her a ride home!

Martine ran through the dark valley to Jemmy's side. She stood on tiptoes and he put his head down and nuzzled her affectionately. 'Stay safe, my beautiful friend,' she said. A little self-consciously, she added: 'I love you.'

She returned to the valley entrance, climbed cautiously over the sharp rocks that guarded it and began to wriggle through the tangle of sticky creepers. Lying on her belly beneath the sinister tree, she waited and listened. Twin points of light were bobbing through the trees. The poachers were returning to their vehicle!

For a second Martine's limbs were filled with the same helpless weakness she'd felt on the night of the fire, but she propelled herself forward. If she hesitated now, it was over. Tearing herself free of the vines, she sprinted for the truck and flung herself on the back. A tarpaulin lay in a heap near the cab. Martine dived under it, gagging at its rotten-meat odour. Then she lay still. She hardly dared breathe.

Footsteps crunched across the stony ground. The truck rocked as the men got in and the doors slammed with unnecessary force. They weren't speaking. Despite her predicament, Martine managed a smile. She pictured them seething, each blaming the other for a wasted, torturous night among the creepies and crawlies. With any luck, it had put them off hunting for life.

The old truck gave a harsh metal wheeze and jolted into action. Martine's plan was to wait until the poachers slowed down to open a gate or cut the fence and then jump out. Assuming that she didn't injure herself in the fall, she should then be within easy walking distance of the house.

In the meantime, she was determined to try to get a good look at the men. Using the tarpaulin as a cover, she raised herself up inch by inch until her eyes were level with the bottom of the dusty cab window. The first pink stirrings of dawn were in the sky and Martine saw immediately why she'd found it so difficult to make out the features of the men at the waterhole. They were dressed in grey long-sleeved shirts with black balaclavas masking their faces. All she could see was their hands – the driver's powerful paws gripping the wheel, and his accomplice's hairy ones holding his rifle.

She lay back down again. One of the men was black,

with a tattoo of a tiger on his wrist, and one was white. It didn't really tell her anything. It didn't even tell her if they were the same men who had shot Henry Thomas and the two giraffes. All it told her was that men of different colours broke into game reserves and hunted for animals.

A light bulb went on in her head. What if the clue lay not with the men but with the giraffe?

From what Tendai said, the police and everyone at Sawubona had always assumed that the poachers had been after ordinary giraffes, mainly because it was ordinary giraffes that had been found dead, and most people believed that the white giraffe was only a legend. But what if they had been trying to catch the white giraffe instead? That would change everything.

Martine wriggled deeper into the folds of the stinking tarpaulin. It made total sense. For the poachers to have known of the white giraffe's existence within hours of its birth, they must have had very close links with Sawubona. That meant they were either friends or relatives of someone who worked on the game reserve, or they worked at Sawubona themselves. Martine shivered at the thought of these possibilities. She knew that Alex had befriended her grandfather in the year before he died and had been promised the job of game warden if anything ever happened to him. Alex had also threatened Martine herself, had shot the kudu and found it amusing, and had made it clear that he knew the value of the white giraffe and was very sure it existed.

But maybe he was too obvious a suspect. In Martine's

mum's favourite detective show, the villain had never turned out to be the weird postal worker with the limp or the gun enthusiast or the eccentric, wart-ridden spinster. It was always the least obvious person – the clean-cut doctor, the wholesome housewife or the new vicar.

The least obvious person at Sawubona was – and Martine felt guilty for even thinking such a thing – Tendai. He claimed he'd been away in the north of the country at the time of the shooting, visiting his relatives. But what if he hadn't been away at all? What if he'd been right here? What if the reason he didn't find the poachers' tracks was because he didn't want to?

But no, that didn't work either, because Martine *refused* to believe it was true. She would trust Tendai with her life.

The vehicle slowed. Martine readied herself for the jump. She dreaded to think what would happen if the driver or his gun-toting companion noticed her reflection in the mirror.

In the end it was easier than she expected, largely because the poachers swerved to avoid a startled springbok and Martine flew over the side. She landed in a clump of dewy, elephant dung-padded grass, which had the double effect of cushioning her fall and quickly obscuring her from view. It did not, however, improve the fragrance of her jeans. By the time she had established that her left leg was bruised rather than broken, all that remained of the poachers was the fading drone of their engine. She checked around her for animals in search of breakfast. She was not, as she'd hoped, close to the house but she could see the faint outline of the Sawubona sign and knew that she was close to the road.

With dawn unfurling like a scarlet silk banner above her head and the birds competing to announce the arrival of another perfect summer's day, Martine managed a limping jog through the bush to the game gate and was home in under ten minutes. Usually her heart would have been full of the magnificence of the morning and the fizzing freshness of the air, but today all she could think about was the danger Jemmy was in and how close they'd both come to falling victim to the hunters.

A couple of hours later Martine had showered and put on her uniform, and she was in the process of shoving her jeans to the very back of the washing machine and thinking how nice it was to have the house to herself, when she heard what sounded like a rally car race in the yard. She rushed outside expecting to see her grandmother returning from Somerset West and was confronted instead with an extraordinary sight. Police were spilling out of two squad cars. But that wasn't what stopped her in her tracks. In the centre of the lawn, roped together like the baddies in a cowboy film, were the poachers. Their balaclavas had gone and their faces were as sour as milk, but there was no mistaking them.

Tendai, Alex and her grandmother were in a huddle in the driveway, talking intensely, but they broke apart when Martine walked up.

'Martine, thank goodness you're okay,' said Gwyn Thomas, rushing forward. Her overnight bag and car keys were still on the lawn where she'd dropped them. 'I've just arrived home to find police swarming all over Sawubona. Alex here has managed, almost single-handedly, to catch the poachers who have been plaguing us for nearly two years.'

'*Alex?*' Martine burst out before she could stop herself.

Her grandmother gave her a reproachful look. 'Yes, Alex,' she said. 'In an act of extraordinary bravery, he shot out the poachers' front tyres as they left the game reserve. Then he radioed for help and managed to pin one of the men to the ground until Tendai could get there and assist him to catch the other.'

'It was nothing, ma'am,' said the game warden. 'That's what you hired me for. I just wish I could have done it sooner.' He put his arm around the Zulu's shoulders and said warmly, 'But I couldn't have done it at all without Tendai's help.'

Martine caught Tendai's eye, but he looked away quickly.

Her grandmother glanced at her watch. 'We'd better get you to school, Martine,' she said. 'If you collect your things, I'll take you in myself.'

Martine, who in the space of ten hours had ridden a white giraffe, escaped from men with guns, and seen her destiny written on a cave wall, was struggling to cope with this unexpected turn of events, but she went crossly back to the house to collect her lunchbox and rucksack. Alex, the hero! How sickening. How *maddening*. Was it really possible that she'd been mistaken about the strawberry-blond troll?

She was on the kitchen step when footsteps pounded up behind her. 'Martine,' called Alex. 'Wait up.'

Martine turned with a black scowl, but the arrogance that usually marred Alex's face had been replaced by a puppyish eagerness.

'Martine,' he said, 'I owe you a huge apology. Over the past year I've become so obsessed with catching the people who were stealing your grandmother's animals that at times it's clouded my judgement. I don't know what came over me the day I drove you to school. Threatening you like that – it was unforgivable. But I was worried that a stranger to Sawubona, someone not familiar with the wildlife, might get in the way of my investigation. All I can say is I'm sorry. If there's anything I can do to make it up to you, let me know.' He reached into his pocket and brought out an exquisite kingfisher feather. 'Peace offering?' he asked.

Martine accepted it grudgingly but didn't answer. She was remembering the bullet splitting the tree above Tendai's head and the haunting eyes of the fallen kudu.

Alex's mouth gave a twist. 'Ja, I know what you're thinking. The kudu: why did I shoot it? Believe me, it hurt me to do it. But I'd become suspicious of everyone by then and it was a test. I wanted to see how Tendai would react. And he reacted like a man who cares about animals should react. So he was in the clear. But you never know in this game. When there's a lot of money at stake, even the best can be tempted.'

Martine wasn't convinced, but then she didn't *not* believe him either. She decided that the best way forward was to trust nobody and say nothing. After the night's adventures, one thing was perfectly clear: she and Jemmy were on their own.

It was late summer in South Africa. More than a month had gone by since Martine had first met Jemmy and in that time her life had changed beyond imagining. Not that it had all been easy. After her flight from the Secret Valley, nine agonizing days had passed before she caught so much of a glimpse of the white giraffe, and then it had been so dark and the vision of him so fleeting that she sensed he was there rather than saw him. Naturally, her grandmother had chosen that very evening to embark on an all-night session with the game reserve accounts and there was absolutely no chance of Martine sneaking out undetected. She just had to sit in her room and fume.

By the tenth day she was ready to tear her hair out. It didn't help that ever since the incident at the Botanical Gardens, the Five Star Gang had tormented her. They put chocolate on her chair so that when she stood up she had a brown sticky mess all over her uniform. It happened at nine a.m., which meant Martine had to spend the rest of the day being sniggered at by the whole school. She found 'umthakathi' and 'witch' scrawled all over her books, and on another occasion she opened her pencil case to find a hairy baboon spider – an African tarantula, lurking inside. Martine screamed so loudly that Miss Volkner immediately banned her from speaking for the rest of the day.

Not that that was very difficult. After what had happened at Kirstenbosch few children talked to Martine anyway. The Five Star Gang had turned them against her. And Ben, to whom she would have liked to speak, remained a mystery. When he passed her on the way to class, his mouth curled up at the edges as if he was happy to see her, but he never spoke. Even after he rescued her, he hadn't said a word. And at break he no longer sat under the far tree in the playing fields but took himself away to some unknown location.

All these things conspired to make Martine feel tearful and lonely again, even though she was getting along much better with her grandmother. With the white giraffe gone, the emptiness she'd felt after losing her mum and dad returned. What if Jemmy was caught in a snare? What if he, too, was gone for ever? Oh, why hadn't she spent any time trying to teach him some sort of signal so that she could call him?

She scoured the books in her bedroom and in the school library for more information on giraffes, hoping to learn something that might help her, but the only new fact she came across was that the Romans had called the giraffe 'camelopardalis', meaning camel marked like a leopard, which was interesting but of no use at all.

Then, out of the blue, she had a brainwave. It happened when she came across a book on dogs on her bookshelf. In his youth, her grandfather had apparently been a very fine dog trainer and there was a jade box on top of the cabinet in the living room containing three of his old dog whistles. In a rare moment of sharing, her grandmother had told her that one of the whistles was completely silent to the human ear because it was pitched at a frequency that only dogs could hear.

But what if giraffes could hear it too?

That night, Martine crept out to the garden and experimented with the silent whistle. For nearly an hour she blew and blew, but nothing happened. Martine stood shivering and frustrated under the mango trees, convinced that she'd never see Jemmy again. Then, a miracle. The white giraffe came striding out of the darkness and stood beside the skeleton tree. Martine did a double take. She'd imagined seeing him again so many times that she wondered for a second if she'd conjured him up. But he was real. Not only that, he was looking right at her, just as he had done on the night of the storm.

Martine didn't even pause to check for lions or leopards. She just went tearing through the game park gate and running and stumbling along the waterhole track, sending all manner of night creatures fleeing for their lives. When she reached the giraffe he lowered his head and she flung her arms around his neck with such enthusiasm that he snorted with alarm and backed off a little, even though he was obviously just as pleased to see her. 'Jemmy,' said Martine, 'thank you for coming back to me.'

In her fantasies, she'd always followed this moment by hopping on the white giraffe's back and being whisked away to the Secret Valley, but in real life Jemmy was an untamed animal as tall as your average tree, and Martine knew as much about training wildlife as she did about riding a monocycle on a high wire at a circus, so there were one or two practicalities to overcome.

She found, for instance, that there really was such a thing as beginner's luck. The first time she rode Jemmy he stood quietly beside a tree and allowed her to climb onto his back, but this concept seemed to have vanished from his mind entirely. Now when she attempted it, Jemmy waited until she was suspended between the tree and his back before spying some juicy acacia leaves and moving away. Martine had to improvise a sort of flying dive and latch on to his neck. There she dangled until her arms nearly came out of their sockets. At that point, she tumbled the very long way to the ground.

Jemmy didn't understand what he'd done, but he made his low, musical fluttering sound and nuzzled her with his silver nose until Martine forgot about the agony in her coccyx and remembered how much she adored him. I have to be patient, she told herself. She also tried to put herself in his position. If she was a giraffe and someone rubbed the back of her forelegs and tugged gently on her knees, she figured that eventually she'd understand that they wanted her to lie down. So she experimented with Jemmy and, after some trial and error, he did. And before the night was over, Martine was flying through the moonlight again on the back of a young giraffe.

That was only the start of it, though, because she then had to learn to steer Jemmy and stop him. It didn't happen overnight and there were several close calls over the next few weeks while they got to know each other – once the giraffe shied away from a bristling porcupine and Martine was nearly impaled on its black and white spines – but through it all Jemmy was gentle and loving and when he did grasp what she was trying to teach him, he grasped it completely, and it was as if he'd always known it.

For Martine, it was then that the door opened on the *real* Africa, the hidden Africa; the Africa that few human beings apart from the bushmen ever witnessed. Those nights with Jemmy were the most magical of Martine's life. It was rare for the other animals to notice her and those that did seemed to accept her as an extension of the white giraffe. Safe on Jemmy's high back, she was able to watch baby warthogs play and move close enough to elephants to touch their parched, grooved skin. Once, when Jemmy was drinking from a lake as black as ink, she found herself just yards from a party of bubble-blowing hippos. With their tubby bodies, piggy eyes and tiny ears, hippos were among the cutest creatures in the wild, but they were also among the most lethal. Their huge pink jaws could bite boats as well as people in half – and frequently did – so Martine took special care to stay still and respectful whenever she was anywhere near them.

But her favourite thing was to ride the white giraffe up the escarpment where she and Tendai had had breakfast, swivel round so she could use his withers as a pillow and his hindquarters as a footrest, lie back and gaze at the canopy of stars. So clear and cold were the nights, with summer sliding into autumn, that she was able to see the Southern Cross and Orion's Belt and even Mars, glowing red in the navy-blue sky.

Sometimes she talked to Jemmy about what had happened to her. About the night of the fire and how scared and heartbroken she'd been. About her mum and dad and how much she missed them. About school and her struggles to fit in. About the Egyptian goose and the kudu, and the strangeness of her gift. Jemmy's ears flickered back and forth and he made his musical fluttering sound, and somehow she felt that in his giraffe way he understood everything and she felt comforted.

The whistle, it turned out, worked perfectly. Jemmy always responded to it if he could hear it, although how long it took depended on where he was in the reserve. Martine took to wearing the whistle around her neck, even at school, because it made her feel close to Jemmy. It also meant that she didn't have to hunt for it when she went sneaking out to see him late at night. But as much as she missed him, she was very careful to vary the hours when she called him and never to do it more than twice a week. She was well aware that each time she went into the reserve she was taking a risk.

Still she continued to get away with it and she managed to persuade herself – mainly because she wanted more than anything for it to be true – that she and Jemmy could go on like this for ever.

· 18 ·

Apart from her mum and dad, the person Martine thought more about than any other on those star-flung nights was Grace. It was Grace, she was convinced, who held the key to the questions she had about her gift. She'd never forgotten the African woman's wonderful food, nor how warm Grace was to her on that traumatic first day and how determined she'd been that Martine should know the truth about the secrets at Sawubona. Yet Martine hadn't seen her since. Once or twice she'd considered bunking off school to try to find her, but she wasn't sure where Grace lived and Tendai refused to be part of it.

'Your grandmother might not like it,' was his last word on the subject.

Later that same evening – at half past midnight to be precise – Martine thought how much less Gwyn Thomas would like it if she could see her granddaughter crouched low over the neck of a white giraffe as he galloped at full pelt for the black mountain that marked Sawubona's boundary. She was going in search of answers. If Tendai and her grandmother weren't going to tell her anything about the past, and if she was banned from seeing Grace who possibly could, then she would find the information for herself in the only place she could think of to look: the Secret Valley.

It was a balmy night. The wind in her face was pungent with the smell of the bush, and the moon was a bold yellow sliver. As she rode, she remembered a wonderful bushman legend she heard from Samson, the old man who cared for the animals in Sawubona's orphanage. In the story, the moon was a man who had angered the sun. Every month, when the moon was full, the jealous sun would take his knife and cut away a piece of him until only a thin slice remained. The moon would plead for that piece to be left for his children. His wish granted, he would build himself up again until he was once more prosperous and whole.

Martine snapped into the present to find they'd reached the barren clearing. The twisted tree glared at them, guarding its secret like a living beast. Martine tried not to look at it. Knotting her fingers through Jemmy's mane, she urged him forward. Vines and branches tore at her skin as he jumped. It was like being ripped from his back by an octopus. Then, just as suddenly as before, it was still and dark. She was in the Secret Valley. All she could hear was the tinkling of the stream and the giraffe's rapid breathing. The scent of orchids wafted up to her. Above her head, the gap in the valley roof showed a rectangle of blue-black sky sprinkled with stars.

She slid down Jemmy's neck and switched on her torch. The tunnel entrance was in front of her, as spookily inviting as before. A prickle of fear brushed her skin. What if something went wrong? Nobody knew where she was. Nobody even knew about the Secret Valley. In the unlikely event anyone ever found her, all they'd stumble across would be her bones, just like the slave at Skeleton Stream. But she banished these thoughts from her head. She had an hour at most to look for the truth. She needed to start down the tunnel.

Martine stood in the centre of the cave, bathed in the radiant glow of the paintings. She filled her lungs with its dense, cathedral air. The time-travel sensation she'd felt before, the vivid sense of generations past, was stronger than ever. There was something humbling about it. It made her feel as tiny as an ant or a fleck of dust in a gale – at the mercy of some immense, unseen power. She went over to the painting of the white giraffe and its child rider and traced its shining outline with her fingertips.

'I see you found the message from the forefathers, Chile.'

Martine tried to yelp but her throat sealed up with shock and she just gulped like a haddock out of water.

Grace stepped out of the shadows. She was draped from head to foot in Zulu tribal dress. Beaded jewellery in all the colours of the rainbow adorned her arms and throat.

'Grace!' croaked Martine. 'What are you doing here? How did you get here? Who else knows about this place? Does Tendai?'

'So many questions,' said Grace. She smiled, but even in the wavering torchlight Martine could see that the smile didn't reach her eyes. She seemed burdened somehow, weighted down with worry. 'Come,' she said. 'Come sit with old Grace.'

Martine followed her to the corner of the cave, where the water-hewn rocks made a natural bench. They sat side by side, gazing at the gallery of copper and ochre paintings. Martine was still reeling from the bombshell of finding the woman she'd wanted so much to see, here, in this sacred place.

'What you got to understand, chile, is that this arl started a long time ago, before my grandmamma was born and her grandmamma before her, when Bushmen lived on the land you now call Sawubona. Everything that will come is already written. You see for yourself your story, and that of the white giraffe, on this here wall.'

She raised her arm and Martine saw for the first time that there was an order to the pictures; their tales of beauty and tragedy unfolded like the plot of a novel.

'Grace,' Martine asked in a hushed tone, 'what happened to the people who stayed in this cave?'

'They perished, chile, arl but one – a girl. The elders of our tribe say that it was a disease brought by the white man – chicken pox or some'at, but nobody know for sure. As the end drew near for each of 'em, they painted their stories and the legends of the forefathers on these walls. Then there was just one. She was found by one of my grannies from long, long ago – a *sangoma,* a traditional healer, like me – in tha place outside the valley. My mama say that on that day the *sangoma* call down so many favours from the gods that fire rained from the heavens and scorched the earth so bad that nothin' could ever grow there no more.'

Martine thought about the barren clearing and the glowering tree, misshapen and parasitic, and had no trouble believing the tale.

'After the Bushman girl was well,' Grace went on, 'she brought the *sangoma* here, to the Memory Room. She made har promise that only har first-born daughter and har first-born daughter after har – all *sangomas* – should know the secrets of the caves. And you, Chile, the chile who rides the white giraffe.'

Martine stared around the cave with new eyes. 'But why me? What does it have to do with me?'

'The answers are right here on the walls,' Grace said again, 'but only time and experience will give you eyes to see them.'

Martine looked harder than ever at the paintings, hoping that, in spite of Grace's words she'd find the answers now, when she felt she most needed them. But their fiery colours just blurred before her vision and only one image stayed clear: the child on the white giraffe.

'Grace,' she said, 'does Tendai know about the white giraffe?'

'He ain't sure,' replied Grace. 'Tendai, he still a young man and young people are always suspicious of the old ways. They call it mumbo jumbo. *Supastishun.*' She studied Martine with strange glittering eyes. 'But not you, huh?'

'No,' said Martine, 'not me.'

It was on the tip of Martine's tongue to ask Grace how she'd known she would find her in the cave on this particular night and at this particular time, but she decided against it. Some things were better left unsaid.

Instead she asked: 'Grace, why did you come here tonight?'

Again Martine thought she saw a shadow pass over the African woman's face. 'I come with a warnin',' Grace said heavily. 'Your time is almost here. Dark forces be comin' and they will stop at nothin' to get to the white giraffe. Be very careful. Trust in your gift and it will keep you safe.'

Martine had a sudden premonition of danger. She'd convinced herself that, with the poachers caught, no one would bother Jemmy ever again. But even as Grace spoke, she knew her words were true. The hunters would be back.

'I don't care what happens to me, but how can I save the white giraffe?' she pleaded.

In answer, Grace opened the beaded pouch that hung from her neck. She took out a handful of small corked bottles that sparkled in the torchlight. Their contents were orange, brown, mustard yellow and a peculiarly vile green. She smiled, and this time her eyes did light up and crinkle at the corners.

'Grace is gonna teach you a little magic,' she said.

For the next hour, Martine – who knew that she should be getting back but was too entranced to care – had a crash course in Zulu traditional medicine. She learned about plants like Mother-in-law's Tongue, which is a remedy for pain and earaches, Rooibos tea, which can cure stomach cramps and allergies, and many other healing herbs besides. Afterwards, Grace handed the pouch full of bottles to Martine.

'Thank you, Grace,' she said, 'I'll keep them in a special place.'

Grace looked pleased. 'You're mos' welcome. You have your healing gift, but sometimes you will need a little extra help.'

There were so many questions and no more time to ask them, but there was one thing Martine had to know before they parted.

'Grace,' she said, 'why doesn't my grandmother want me here?'

'She do want you here, chile. She do. Your granny loves you soooo much. But she has her story just like you have yours.'

Martine was about to tell Grace that her grandmother had no feelings for her whatsoever when Grace cut in: 'Now *I* want to ax you somethin'. I got a cousin of mine who works down at your school and he tells me that you're arl the time arl by yourself. Why you don't find yourself some friends to play with? It ain't good to be alone.'

Martine dropped her eyes, embarrassed. 'But I have got a friend. The white giraffe is my friend.'

'That's right, the giraffe is your friend. But every chile needs someone their own age, a human bein', to talk with. To *share* with.'

'Well, maybe there's no one I want to be friends with,' Martine said defensively. 'Who would understand about Jemmy? Who would understand about this?'

For a long time Grace made no comment. Finally she laid a hand on Martine's shoulder. 'You will find the friend you seek in the last place you look.'

· 19 ·

Three days later Martine was walking across the playing fields after a netball game, her head still full of her encounter with Grace, when she heard raised voices coming from Black Horse Ravine. Her first thought was that someone was in trouble. Black Horse Ravine was a deep gorge with a fast-flowing river, which lay beyond the boundary fence of the school. It was so treacherous that the punishment for even entering the dark pines that fronted it was ten detentions. But Martine didn't hesitate. She climbed over the fence and ran into the trees. When she was out of sight of any passing teacher, she squatted down and listened.

Straight away, she recognized the voices of the Five Star Gang. They seemed to be taunting somebody. 'You think you're pretty clever, don't you? Did you really think you could make fools of us and get away with it?'

'Tell us the truth or you're going for a swim. It was your twisted little brain that came up with the plan to humiliate us at the Botanical Gardens, wasn't it? Answer us. And don't pretend you can't speak. The teachers might be taken in by your deaf and dumb act but we are not.'

There was no response from their captive.

'He's such a waste of space, isn't he?' Scott said. 'I mean, look at him. You're a runt, do you know that. I've seen chickens with more meat on their bones.'

'You're a loony, has anyone ever told you that? You're a freak.'

'You're like one of those sad-looking dogs you find down at the shelter,' jeered Luke. 'Say: "I'm a mongrel, Luke." What are you? Say: "I'm a mongrel . . ."'

Martine had until then been crouching behind a boulder, too scared to intervene. But at those words, the memory of Tendai's story came burning through her like liquid fire. With a yell of fury, she burst out of the trees. Luke and Scott had hold of Ben and were forcing him to stand on the edge of the ravine. Lucy was laughing her high-pitched laugh and Pieter was sitting on the ground nearby looking slightly green.

'What are you . . . ?' Luke was saying to Ben.

He didn't see Martine until she was right in front of him and then he just stammered: 'M-Martine! What the . . . ?'

'I'll tell you who Ben is,' Martine heard herself saying. 'He's my friend, that's who he is. He's also the boy who beat you by about fifty metres in the hundred metres at the school championships, Luke. And he's the boy whose homework you keep borrowing, Lucy, because you're too thick to do your own. As for his parents, well, at least he's got a father, Scott. When was the last time you saw yours?'

A shocked silence followed her outburst. The Black Horse River roared far below them.

'My f-father . . .' stammered Scott. 'Oh, forget it. This is no fun. Come on, Luke, Lucy, Pieter. Let's leave these losers to their pathetic little friendship.'

He dropped Ben's arm so abruptly that the boy teetered for a moment on the edge of the ravine before finding his balance and stepping away.

'I haven't finished with you,' Scott growled.

'Let it go, Scott,' snapped Pieter. 'Enough is enough.'

They left noisily, kicking at pine cones, cursing as they went. Martine and Ben were alone.

Martine suddenly felt shy. 'Are you okay?' she asked hesitantly.

It struck her for the first time that Ben was very handsome. He had topaz eyes like a lion, shiny black hair and white, even teeth. When he spoke, his voice was soft and he pronounced each word clearly and separately, like a newsreader.

'I appreciate your help,' he said, 'but I prefer to fight my own battles.'

For several days after the incident at Black Horse Ravine, Martine went back to feeling nervous again at school. She was convinced that the Five Star Gang would want to get back at her somehow. Instead, something completely different happened. They wouldn't leave her alone. By standing up to them, she seemed to have earned their respect. Lucy van Heerden presented her with a box of homemade condensed milk rusks to say sorry and all five of them went out of their way to be nice to her.

Martine was cool with them at first – she was still angry about the way they'd treated Ben at the ravine and the wild goose at the Botanical Gardens. But they kept telling her that both were just games that had gone too far and that they felt really bad about them, and gradually she came to believe they'd changed. That didn't mean that Martine wanted to be bosom buddies with them, but it did mean that when their close friend Sherilyn offered her a slice of carrot cake and wanted to sit with her she accepted, and when Xhosa asked her about life on Sawubona, she was happy to go along with that too. She kept remembering Grace's words: *You will find the friend you seek in the last place you look.* Maybe Grace had been right about that too.

Of course, Ben was still Ben and he still spent all his free time by himself. Ever since Martine had intervened at Black Horse Ravine he seemed to have gone out of his way to avoid her. Lucy had given him a box of apology rusks too, but he'd later been seen handing them out to some homeless children. At break, he once again sat cross-legged under the distant trees with his palms resting on his knees and turned upwards. Some days Martine was convinced that he was meditating.

Now that she knew he wasn't mute – that he actually had a beautiful speaking voice and was, as she'd thought all along, very smart – she spent a lot of time puzzling over why he never talked to anyone at school. Finally she'd come to the conclusion that he just couldn't be bothered. Maybe school and the people in it didn't interest him. Maybe he was only here because he had to be. Maybe he was happiest when he was in nature, like Tendai. But just when Martine had made up her mind to get to the bottom of the riddle that was Ben once and for all, two things came along to preoccupy her. She began to get the distinct impression someone was going through her locker. Nothing was ever taken and the changes, if there were any, were subtle ones – exercise books curled up at the corners as if they'd been flicked through, items shifted or replaced in a different order – but it was still creepy. Then a tiny watercolour she'd done of Jemmy went missing. She spent so long searching for it that she was late for her next lesson.

'Ah, Martine,' said Miss Volkner when Martine burst in. 'Good of you to join us.'

Martine was mumbling an apology when the teacher interrupted: 'We were just discussing African folklore. Lucy asked a question about giraffes.'

'Giraffes!' cried Martine.

'Yes, those creatures with the funny long necks,' said Miss Volkner. 'Do you have a problem with that? I'd have thought you'd be the class expert, living on a game reserve.'

Martine was about to deny that she knew anything at all about giraffes when something stopped her. It wasn't often that she got a chance to talk about her favourite subject. Besides, she thought mischievously, she could have a bit of fun with it.

'No,' she said. 'I mean, no I don't have a problem with it.'

'Good, then perhaps you can tell us what you know.'

So Martine, flushing a little with shyness, told the class how the ancients had regarded giraffes as the most innocent, delicate and timid of all the wild animals, but also brave enough to fight dragons. How the Venda people called them *thutlwa*, 'rising above the trees', and how other tribes saw a giraffe in the stars as the Southern Cross. She also told them some facts. That giraffes can reach speeds of thirty-five miles per hour and that it takes them ten years to reach their full height of seventeen feet for females and nineteen feet for males.

Miss Volkner was clearly taken aback. 'If you applied yourself to your school subjects with even half the diligence with which you appear to study wildlife, your grades would improve dramatically,' she said somewhat sarcastically.

'Miss Volkner,' asked Sherilyn, 'has anyone ever ridden a giraffe?'

'No, they haven't, Sherilyn. I don't know why that is. Maybe they're not as intelligent as horses. Certainly they wouldn't be as comfortable.'

Martine stayed quiet, thinking to herself: If only they knew! If only they could see me and Jemmy racing across Sawubona's plains in the moonlight!

'Maybe it's because they're too stupid,' said Lucy, with a sly glance at Martine. 'I mean, it's not as if they do anything. They don't hunt or build nests or webs or have any purpose that I can see. All they do is stroll around and look pretty.'

Instantly Martine's temper flared. 'They *do* have a purpose,' she snapped, turning on Lucy. 'They act as lookouts for the other animals. They're very intelligent and have incredible eyesight and hearing, and they warn other animals if a predator is approaching. Their ears are so amazing they can even hear whistles that only dogs can usually hear.'

As soon as it was out of her mouth, she regretted saying it, but it was too late to take it back.

'How do you know?' challenged Luke. 'About the whistle, I mean?'

'I just know, okay?' answered Martine, anxious to change the subject. 'I read it in a book or something.'

In the last row of the class, Xhosa stopped playing computer games and sat up straight.

'Miss Volkner,' he said, 'if Martine knows so much about giraffes, how come she hasn't told us about the white one that's supposed to live at Sawubona?'

'The one in the legend?' asked Miss Volkner. 'Is this

true, Martine? I didn't know there was anything in it. You mean there actually is a white giraffe?'

Martine went red.

'The white giraffe doesn't exist. Everyone knows that.'

'Well, let's say it did exist,' said Miss Volkner. 'I want you to draw it on the board for us. Use your imagination.'

Heading off for a swimming lesson afterwards, Martine felt shaken and guilty. The bad feeling that had come over her when she let slip the remark about the whistle returned with a vengeance. She tried to console herself with the thought that the only people who'd heard her say it were a bunch of hair gel and pop music-obsessed kids – and Miss Volkner, who was a vegetarian – and they were hardly likely to go out hunting for the white giraffe. And yet the butterflies continued to boil away in her stomach.

It was a Friday afternoon and the school was almost empty when Martine returned to her locker. After swimming, she'd tried again to find the little watercolour, but with no success. She opened the door and stood staring in, frowning slightly. Again she had the feeling that someone had been tampering with her things. Out of the corner of her eye, she saw Gwyn Thomas's car pull into the car park. Martine removed her rucksack and empty lunchbox from the top shelf.

She knew that she was keeping her grandmother waiting, but she continued to stare into her locker. The longer she stood there, the more feverish and worried she felt. Something else was missing; she was sure of it.

It wasn't until she was halfway back to Sawubona that it hit her.

The silent whistle was gone.

20

Martine tossed and turned all night and woke bleary-eyed at dawn. She felt sick. Not only had the whistle been stolen, but someone had changed the combination on the game park gate so she couldn't get in to find Jemmy. And that was not all. At some point in that awful night, she'd opened her window and leaned out into the wild wind, hoping to catch a glimpse of the white giraffe, and had seen instead a swoop of white light. Seconds later, darkness blanketed the game reserve again, but by then she was sure that the poachers were back and that they wouldn't be leaving without the white giraffe.

As scared as she was, Martine had forced herself to dress quickly and tiptoe down the stairs and out of the front door. Outside, the wind buffeted her and stung her skin, and the trees tossed like ocean waves. Martine ran barefoot down the sandy track that led to Tendai's house. Apart from Grace, there was nobody else she trusted to help her. The animals in the orphanage skittered in their cages as she passed and she wished she could stop and soothe them. But every minute wasted would give the poachers more time to get away, so she ran on, thankful when the lights of Tendai's front porch shone through the swaying trees. Panting, she rang the bell. Nobody answered. That's when she noticed that the door was partially ajar. She pushed it with a finger and it opened.

'Tendai,' Martine called, 'Tendai, are you awake?'

But the house was silent. The bed hadn't been slept in and the remnants of a half-eaten meal lay on the table, as though the tracker had left in a hurry. When she checked round the back, his jeep was gone.

Martine sank onto a garden bench, defeated. So perhaps Tendai was involved after all. She walked on wooden legs back to the house, undressed, and climbed weakly under the covers. She wished she was brave enough to wake her grandmother and admit everything, but she couldn't face it. She'd been through too much. She just hid under the covers, feeling like a coward, and hoped that it would all go away. When sleep finally came, she was haunted by nightmares in which Tendai and the Five Star Gang were in league and they were chasing her through a forest. The branches were catching fire as she ran, and she knew that they'd only rescue her if she told them where to find the white giraffe. So she confessed, and they just laughed and left her to face the fire anyway.

In the harsh light of morning, the nightmare seemed more real than ever. Martine imagined Jemmy hearing the silent whistle and trustingly following the sound to his doom, and felt like the worst, most evil person on earth. She wanted to die. The most horrific images kept going through her mind. She saw Jemmy being skinned and used as a rug in some rich man's home, or being whipped and made to perform tricks in a circus, or even freezing to death in some Siberian zoo.

Worst of all, it was her fault. The secret of the white giraffe had been hers to keep, and it was her carelessness that had given it away. There was no reason for her to take the whistle to school, let alone the little watercolour of Jemmy. How could she have been so stupid? It was almost as if she'd wanted to be found out; wanted everyone to know that *she* was the girl in the legend, the one who could ride the white giraffe. After years of being an outsider, it was her chance to be special.

Now 'special' was the very last thing she felt.

Martine decided that she had to leave Sawubona immediately. She didn't deserve to be there. She would go back to England on the first flight available – she would stow away like a boy she'd once read about, if she had to – and Mr Grice could find her a bed in a children's home.

There was a knock at the door. 'Martine?'

'Go away!' shouted Martine, burying her face in her pillow. 'I'm not going to school.'

The door opened and her grandmother came in. She sat down on the edge of the bed. 'I know,' she said quietly.

Martine took the pillow off her face. 'You *know*?'

'Yes, I do. I know about the white giraffe. And if I'd told you that sooner, none of this would have happened.'

Martine's heart skipped a beat. 'Has something happened?'

Gwyn Thomas gave a heavy sigh and handed Martine a strand of silver tail hair. 'Tendai found this tangled in the game park gate. Last night he received a hoax call from a man claiming to be a passer-by, who said he had seen some buffaloes breaking through a hole in the game fence and that they were loose on the road. When Tendai got there, there was no hole and no buffalo. It was a trick to get him out of the way. He spent an hour searching for them before racing back to the reserve, but by then it was already too late. I'm sorry to have to tell you, Martine; the white giraffe is gone.'

She stood up and walked around the bed to the window. 'You see, Martine, you were right to be angry with me that night you wanted to know about your mother. There *are* too many secrets at Sawubona. But I thought I was protecting you. I thought I was protecting the white giraffe, too. But now it seems I've done everything wrong.' She turned to Martine. 'I'm so sorry I've hurt you,' she said.

Martine didn't know what was going on, but she was

so relieved someone was still speaking to her that she jumped out of bed and took her grandmother's hand.

'It's okay,' she said. 'It's okay. But I don't understand what you mean about the giraffe. This is all my fault.'

Her grandmother was silent for a long time. When she finally looked up, her face was etched with sorrow. 'Sit down,' she said. 'There's something I need to tell you.'

After Martine had made herself comfortable, her grandmother went out of the room and returned with tea and hot buttered English muffins and a large package, which she tucked between the bed and the table. Only when she was sure Martine had eaten her fill would Gwyn Thomas go on. She started by taking a present from the plastic bag and handing it to Martine.

'I've been meaning to give this to you since the day you came to Sawubona,' she said, 'but somehow there never was the right moment.'

Martine took it from her with a puzzled frown and unwrapped it carefully. Inside was a heavy rectangular scrapbook crafted from hand-made paper and pressed with wildflowers of the Cape. 'It's beautiful,' she told her grandmother.

She opened it. On the first page was a series of photos of a little girl with wavy brown hair and sparkling green eyes, playing with a lion cub.

'My mum,' breathed Martine. On the next page was a

poem Veronica had written, followed by pictures of her riding horses through the reserve at Sawubona, taking a curtain call in the school play and splashing in the waves. There were wedding photos and holiday photos of Veronica and David, arms around each other, laughing, in the early days of their marriage. And on the final page, there was a picture of her mum and dad standing in front of the house at Sawubona, cradling a tiny baby.

'That's you,' Gwyn Thomas said.

Martine's whole world shifted on its axis. 'I was born in *Africa*?'

'You were born at Sawubona.'

'Then why . . . ?'

'That's where your story begins,' her grandmother said. 'You see, Martine, the night after you came into the world Grace came to tell us that she'd had a vision that you were the child in the African legend, the one who has power over all the animals. She said that in years to come a white giraffe would be born on Sawubona and that fate would ensure you were brought together. That you were twin souls.'

A faint smile tugged at her grandmother's lips. 'Well, you can probably imagine our reaction. Grace has always had the gift of second-sight but we'd never actually heard her predict the future before, and somehow this just sounded so far-fetched. So initially, we were sceptical and then we were just amused. Veronica giggled and said she couldn't wait to see the faces of the other mothers at the Pony Club when her daughter turned up on a white giraffe.

'But Grace became angry and told her that it was not a joke. She led us to the window and there we saw a spectacle I will never forget as long as I live. Lions and zebras, leopards and springboks and other animals that usually prey on each other or fight with each other were lined up against the fence in perfect harmony, and they were looking towards the house. It was as if they knew something. After that, we took Grace very seriously. She said that along with the power – what she called the 'gift' – would come enormous responsibility, and that although it would bring much beauty and happiness into your life you would also experience great hardship and danger.

'Well, your mother was furious. She was scared to believe what Grace was saying but she was more scared to ignore it. What made it even harder for her was that Grace insisted that sooner or later you would have to follow your destiny, whether you wanted to or not. Well, Veronica refused to accept that.'

Martine was spellbound. 'So what happened next?'

'Well, after talking it over with your father, your mother decided that she could stop the course of destiny by taking you away from Africa, keeping you away from animals and severing all ties with Sawubona.

'Your grandfather and I were devastated, but we understood her reasons – she was convinced it was the only way to keep you from harm – and we also felt that there was a chance the plan might work. So that's what we did. Within two or three days of your birth, as soon as you were able to travel, you went to England.'

'It must have been very hard for you,' Martine pressed. 'Saying goodbye to my mum and dad and knowing you might never see them again.'

'It was the hardest thing I've ever done,' her grandmother said with feeling. 'But for a long time it was worth it because Veronica was so happy. She believed – we all believed – that it had worked. Then four months ago, shortly before Christmas, I went to Grace's house for dinner. When I got there she was reading the bones – African *sangomas* throw bones the way Western fortune tellers use crystal balls and tarot cards – and she answered the door in such a state, perspiring and talking gibberish, that I thought she had a fever. She said the bones had told her that a tragedy would bring you back to Sawubona. She wanted me to phone Veronica right then and say anything, even lie and say I was ill if I had to, just to bring you all back to Sawubona. She said that if you came of your own accord, the gods might be appeased and the tragedy would be averted.

'Of course, I was very alarmed. It was hard not to be. But I tried to reason with her. I said that perhaps the bones were mistaken and that, apart from the fact that I had no intention of lying to my own daughter, she could hardly expect a whole family to move continents for a second time on the basis of her visions. After all, we'd seen no evidence at all that the first one might come true. We ended up having a terrible row about it. She was my friend but we haven't spoken since. She was always adamant that you shouldn't be taken away from here. She kept saying that the forefathers had predicted your coming. I just told her she was mad. To be truthful, I really hoped she *was* mad.'

Gwyn Thomas took a ragged breath and for the first time since coming to Sawubona Martine understood the extent of her grandmother's loss. She squeezed her hand and was rewarded with a grateful smile.

'So I told your mother what she'd said,' Gwyn Thomas went on. 'For Veronica, it was the final straw. She said that for years she'd had to suffer the heartache of being away from me, her dad and her beloved Africa. Finally, she'd found happiness. David had a good job, you were growing up wonderfully, and you all had lots of plans for the future. She was not about to uproot you a second time for what would probably, in the end, turn out to be nothing more than superstitious gabblings.

'It was the last time we spoke. Days later, I received a call to say that your mum and dad had lost their lives in a house fire. I blamed myself. I felt that if only I'd worked harder to convince them to leave, it would never have happened. Then the will was read and I was told I was your sole relative. We had always agreed that I wouldn't be your guardian if your parents died, because that would mean you would have to return to Africa. But the will had recently been changed. Why Veronica changed her mind, we'll never know. It seemed the cruelest of ironies. After everything we'd done to keep you away from Sawubona, you were destined to return after all.'

Martine suddenly realized she had been holding her breath. 'Phew! Now I understand why you didn't want me to come here.'

'Yes,' said her grandmother. 'And I feel very ashamed about the way I've treated you. At first, I must admit I resented you. Every time I looked at you, it reminded me that it was because of you that your mother had gone away and I hadn't seen her for eleven years. Later, I was afraid to get close to you. I thought that if I loved you and you were taken away from me, it would be like losing Veronica all over again.'

'You're not the only one who lost my mum,' Martine said pointedly.

'I realize that now. But by the time I came to my senses, I had already driven you away.'

'I haven't been driven away,' Martine assured her. 'Maybe we could start again.'

Her grandmother touched her hand. 'You're very wise. No wonder the forefathers chose you.'

At those words, Martine suddenly recalled the ghastly events of the night.

'But what about Jemmy?' she fretted. 'What did you mean about protecting Jemmy?'

Her grandmother looked confused.

'Jeremiah. *The giraffe!*'

'Of course! Well, a few days after the poachers attacked your grandfather, the local Zulu chief came to see me. He told me that in the hours before the hunters arrived at Sawubona our female giraffe had given birth to a snow-white calf. She and her mate later died trying to protect him, but somehow – it might even have been because Henry arrived to distract the men – the baby giraffe managed to get away in the struggle. According to the chief, it was rescued by an elephant whose own calf had been still-born and she had taken it to a secret place. The chief said that the giraffe had special powers and that it was the rarest animal on earth. On no account should anyone ever find out about it. He said that if anyone ever asked me about it, I had to deny it existed. I couldn't even tell Tendai or your mother. And when you came I tried everything in my power to keep the two of you apart so that the prophecy would not be fulfilled.'

'Grandmother, Jemmy is my best friend,' Martine confessed.

'I won't ask how the two of you became so close,' her grandmother remarked drily. 'I suppose that explains why your clothes are always covered in mud and strange grasses these days, and why you're always yawning on the way in to school.'

'I'm sorry,' Martine said. 'I didn't think you'd understand. And now it's because of me that Jemmy has been stolen. Somehow I have to try to find him. Grandmother, do you think you might be able to help me?'

'No,' said Gwyn Thomas. 'But I know someone who can.'

21

The pale green house looked exactly the way Martine remembered it. The rusting Coca Cola sign was propped against one wall, the lawn was even more threadbare and the chickens were still scratching hopefully on the porch in the sunshine. It was mid April and Martine found it hard to believe that barely three months had passed since she had climbed off the plane at Cape Town airport. It felt like for ever. She remembered Grace's words on the first day: 'The gift can be a blessing or a curse. Make your decisions wisely.' The sick feeling returned to Martine's stomach. Her decisions might have cost Jemmy his life.

A small boy materialized at the front door. 'I'd like a word with that crazy old woman,' said Gwyn Thomas. 'Is she home?'

'Who you be callin' crazy?' purred Grace, looming up behind the boy. Martine found it incredible that she appeared to have got even fatter. 'There's only one crazy old woman round these parts and that'd be Gwyn Thomas.' She reached out a massive paw and stroked Martine's hair, giving no indication that she'd seen her only recently. 'Chile looks like she could use summa Grace's good food. What you been feeding her?'

'We haven't come here to be insulted,' Martine's grandmother said primly. 'We need your help.'

'Uh huh,' said Grace, putting her hands on her hips. 'I be listenin'.'

'Listen, Grace, I know we've had our differences,' Gwyn Thomas said. 'I don't blame you if you never want to speak to me again. But if you ever cared for me at all, you'll help Martine. She's lost something she loves and you may be the only person in the world who can help her to get it back.'

Grace smiled, revealing a lot of pink gum and very few teeth. 'Old woman,' she said, 'why didn't you just say so?'

Without ceremony, she turned and walked back into the house. Martine and her grandmother followed the swish of Grace's dress, a riotous blend of indigo, sunshine-yellow and burnt honey, patterned with African prints. She led them to the living room, which smelled familiarly of chopped wood, mealie-meal and a million cooking fires. The out-of-date island calendar

168

was still on the wall and the same grass mat was on the floor. A vase full of peacock feathers had been added to a teak table.

Grace went into the kitchen and reappeared with two steaming plates of mealie-meal porridge drenched with buttermilk, cinnamon and cane sugar. Martine was queasy and not at all keen on eating, but Grace stifled her protests with a flat: 'You're arl bones.'

Afterwards, Martine was glad that she had. The porridge was fantastic. It poured into her veins like molten lava, warming her bones and clearing her head. When she was finished, Martine told Grace what had happened to Jemmy, giving her as much detail as she could about the poachers' chase.

'One question, chile,' Grace said when she had finished. 'Did you ever see the face of any of them hunters?'

Martine glanced uneasily at her grandmother.

'Go on,' urged Gwyn Thomas.

'Well, I didn't see either of their faces, but I think that somebody at Sawubona might be involved. I think it could be . . .' Martine faltered. She didn't want to make her grandmother angry again.

'It could be Alex,' she said at last.

'No!' cried her grandmother. 'Your grandfather trusted Alex with his life. I won't have you saying—'

'ENOUGH!' commanded Grace. 'The chile has spoken. Now we must listen for the answers.'

She heaved herself off the chair and drew the curtains. The room was plunged into blackness. A match flared and Grace placed a candle on the table. She sat down on the grass mat with a grunt, her broad face and deep-set eyes glittering eerily. Out of her blouse she produced a small leather pouch, which she proceeded to empty on the ground in front of her. As far as Martine could tell, it contained a collection of small bones, a portion of porcupine quill, a guinea fowl feather and a couple of elephant hairs. Grace closed her eyes and began to chant.

Nothing happened for several minutes and then a low, rhythmic pounding began to emanate from Grace's chest, like the sound of a distant drum. Before Martine's startled eyes, a thin spiral of blue smoke rose from the objects on the floor. It flattened out and blurred images began to flash across it, too fast for her to take in. There were mountains and men in loincloths and headdresses, great herds of animals and bloody battles, and once she thought she saw a giraffe, but it was gone before she could be sure.

Grace's eyes rolled back in her head. 'Water,' she moaned. 'I see blue, blue water and boats that go up to the sky. The men are going far. They be hungry for tha power. The white giraffe is there, but not for much longer. I see much pain, much pain, much pain . . .'

'Stop!' shouted Gwyn Thomas.

The smoke disappeared. Grace's eyes swam back into her head. She was shaking. She looked up at Martine.

'Go now, chile. Soon it will be too late.'

'But where?' cried Martine. 'Where have they taken him?'

'Boats that go up to the sky' can only mean one thing – the dockyards in Cape Town,' interrupted her grandmother. 'Hurry, Martine. I think they're taking him abroad.'

22

Maybe Gwyn Thomas had driven as fast as she did on the way into Cape Town before that day, but Martine seriously doubted it. As it was, the needle on the ancient red Datsun quivered as if it was about to burst through the glass. Martine could tell that her grandmother was very anxious. But she was also very determined. She had agreed to drive Martine to the docks but no further. 'If Jeremiah isn't there, we'll have to call the police,' she'd said firmly. All Martine's protests had been in vain.

The two hours that it took to reach the ocean seemed the longest of Martine's life. Every possible obstacle conspired to delay them. A police roadblock. A traffic jam. A busload of disembarking senior citizens. Three loose cows ambling across the road.

And all the while Grace's prophecy kept running through Martine's head. *The white giraffe is there, but not for much longer. I see much pain, much pain, much pain . . .*

They were on an inland road and soon the wine estates, with their pristine white Cape Dutch buildings and lavender-lined drives, were followed by shanty towns reminiscent of the Soweto Tendai had described to Martine. Mile upon mile of rusting iron and water-stained plywood shacks, worm-ridden dogs and shifty, hungry-eyed youths. Children played in the dirt with wire toys. The thought of Tendai brought back the memory of the day they'd spent together at Sawubona.

Gwyn Thomas pulled off the highway and took the coastal road down to the waterfront. The forbidding crags of Table Mountain were draped in thick cloud. When tall grey cargo ships and cranes lifting containers came into view, she slowed the car to a crawl. Martine was ready to explode with impatience but she knew that they had to find a place to hide the car. An overgrown track provided a solution. They bounced over the weeds and stones and parked under a flat-topped pine tree. Gwyn Thomas opened her door and started to get out of the car. Martine put her hand on her grandmother's sleeve.

'Grandmother. This is something I have to do on my own.'

'I don't think so,' Gwyn Thomas said wryly. 'You're eleven years old and you're an hour and a half from home.'

But Martine stood her ground. 'It's my fault that

Jemmy's been captured, and if he's hurt, that'll be my fault too. I've got to be the one to try to find him.'

Gwyn Thomas sat back down and closed the car door. A battle was going on behind her eyes. 'Where is this all going to end?' she said, and Martine had a feeling that she was talking about much more than the disappearance of the giraffe.

She put a hand on Martine's shoulder. 'All right, go and look for your precious Jemmy. But if you're not back in forty-five minutes, I'm calling the police. I'm not taking any chances. The pain of losing one child was terrible. I couldn't bear it if I lost another.'

Martine leaned forward and gave her a kiss on the cheek, and was surprised to see her grandmother's blue eyes fill with tears.

'Thanks for everything,' she said.

She hopped out of the car and ran back along the track to the main road. The ocean wind cut through her thin T-shirt like a knife and the salty air tingled in her nostrils. At the bottom of the hill, behind a high fence fortified with coils of razor wire, lay the shipyard. Beyond it, the sea was a churning, white-capped green. The shipyard was buzzing with activity and she could hear dogs barking – guard dogs, perhaps. Martine waited shivering behind a tree for a couple of cars to pass. She was beginning to regret that she hadn't brought a jacket. She put a hand on the medicine pouch that Grace had given her at the Secret Valley. In the car, her grandmother had commented on it, but Martine would say nothing about it except that it had been a gift from a friend to bring her luck. Now she drew courage from it.

She had also brought along Mr Morrison's Swiss Army knife for good measure. If she could get to Jemmy, she was sure that she could help him.

When the road was clear, she sprinted to the gate and slipped behind the wooden guardhouse. She'd intended to try to talk her way in, but when she peered through the salt-smeared window there didn't seem any real need. There were two security men in the hut. One was watching rugby on TV and stirring a cup of tea, his chair balancing precariously on its rear legs. The other was on his radio, his back towards the window. He was having an argument. 'Who're you calling an idiot? Over.'

Furious crackling followed.

Martine didn't wait to hear any more. She ducked under the barrier and ran for the mountainous lines of blue, red and grey containers. With every stride she expected to hear voices yelling for her to stop, but no one seemed to notice her. Except . . .

A snarl that almost turned her blood to yoghurt brought her to a terrified halt. A rottweiler was blocking her path, his lips pulled back over teeth as savage and numerous as a crocodile's. In spite of the icy breeze, Martine began to sweat. Instinctively she fixed her green eyes on the rottweiler's big yellow ones and focused all her energy on dominating him, telling him that if he dared to prevent her from saving Jemmy, she'd personally feed him to the sharks. Then she commanded him to lie down and let her pass.

To her astonishment, the rottweiler sank to the ground with a piteous whine. He put his paws over his eyes. If Martine hadn't been so scared, she would have laughed.

She stepped over him and sneaked forward until she came to a gap between two metal containers. Through it, she could see the docks. There were three grey ships and a blue and white tugboat in the harbour. The shipyard itself was bustling with workers. Martine estimated that there were about twenty-five crates and several expensive cars in the process of being loaded. There was no sign of a giraffe. Time was running out for Jemmy and she didn't know where to start. How could she even begin to search three ships the size of skyscrapers? What had she been thinking? Why hadn't she just called the police as her grandmother suggested? Why did she always have to do everything the hard way? Why was she always so stubborn?

Suddenly she was grabbed from behind. 'Let go of me,' she screeched, and began to fight and squeal like a wounded warthog. She and her assailant hit the ground with a thud. Martine lay on her front, groaning, too winded to move.

'I'm arresting you for trespassing on private property,' said a clear young voice. 'You have the right to remain silent . . .'

Martine rolled over, still breathing heavily.

'You!' she cried.

A pair of lion's eyes gazed calmly back at her. 'Hello, Martine,' grinned Ben.

23

Martine scrambled to her feet, ignoring the hand Ben held out to her.

'You could have been a bit more gentle with me,' she said crossly.

'I apologize,' said Ben, who seemed to be struggling not to laugh. 'I didn't recognize you until we were in mid-air. But you are trespassing, you know.'

'What about you?' Martine accused. 'Isn't that what you're doing?'

'My father is a sailor.' Ben pointed to one of the tall grey ships. 'That's his boat over there – the *Aurora*. *I* have permission to be here.'

Martine sighed. She could see that she had no choice but to tell Ben about Jemmy and just pray that he didn't try to stop her. As briefly and quickly as she could, she explained about her betrayal of the white giraffe, about the hunters, and about Grace's prediction. She also told him about her grandmother, parked behind the pines, waiting. Lastly, she told him how much Jemmy meant to her and how desperate she was to save him.

'Please, Ben,' she said, 'please say you won't stand in my way.'

Ben's face was serious. 'For ages now my father has worried that his ship is being used to smuggle rare animals out of the country, but he didn't want to notify the authorities until he was sure. If the giraffe is on board, I think we can get to him, but we must go at once. The *Aurora* sails for the Middle East in thirty minutes.'

Before Martine could get used to this new Ben – a Ben who spoke and smiled and was a million miles away from the introverted geek he appeared to be at school – he was striding confidently across the shipyard, beckoning for her to follow. He wore ragged jeans, heavy boots and a sleeveless black t-shirt and his arms, though thin, were sinewy and strong. Martine ran to catch up with him.

'What do you think you're doing?' she enquired breathlessly. 'Do you really imagine that we are just going to walk onto the ship and walk off with a giraffe?'

'*We* aren't,' said Ben. '*You* are.' He smiled. 'Trust me. Sometimes the most obvious way is the best way.'

As if to prove him right, a commotion erupted on the

jetty. A crate had broken while it was being hoisted onto the deck and what looked like an antique table and several highly polished chairs were bobbing around in the greasy green harbour. Men were cursing and shaking their fists and two guard dogs were going berserk at the end of their chains. Ben took no notice of them. He strode coolly across the gangplank of the ship, onto the deck and through a low doorway. Martine scuttled in after him.

Below decks, the ship was a warren of corridors, galleys and scrubbed, anonymous cabins. They walked as quickly as they could along miles of battleship-grey passages and down two spiral staircases, their footsteps ringing like church bells on the steel. Finally they came to a storage room. A swarthy man was hunched over a computer. He jumped up when Ben tapped at the door and shouted something in a foreign language.

Ben gave him a radiant smile. 'Captain Holloway is asking for you up on deck,' he said politely. 'I'm not sure what it's about but it seems to be urgent.'

The man glared at him suspiciously. He reached for his radio.

'I'm pretty sure it's an emergency,' Ben said again.

Muttering, the man snatched up some papers and scurried away along the corridor. Ben waited until he was out of sight and then darted into the room.

'Martine! In here!'

He locked the door behind them and opened a filing cabinet. In it, hanging from brass hooks, were hundreds of keys. He began to sort through them methodically, laying them on the floor. Martine checked her watch. It was just after midday. The boat sailed in twenty minutes. She dreaded to imagine the consequences if they hadn't found Jemmy by then.

There was a knock at the door. Ben put his finger to his lips. The knock turned into hammering. Martine was a nervous wreck. Ben remained perfectly serene. He examined each key meticulously as if he had several spare hours up his sleeve, seemingly unconcerned that he was participating in an illegal animal rescue, or that a raging Russian was now attacking the door with what sounded like a fire extinguisher. The pounding ceased and there was the steel echo of footsteps running away.

'*Please*!!' Martine panicked.

'Got it,' said Ben, holding up a bunch of keys. 'But we don't have much time.'

He unlocked the door and the two of them shot across the passageway and down two spiral staircases, darting into a cleaning cupboard when a couple of grease-stained engineers popped out of a side door. Martine judged that they were now on the bottom of the ship. The air reeked with fumes. The floor shuddered and there was the low grinding roar of great engines coming to life.

'Do you think we're going to make it?' whispered Martine.

Ben didn't answer. They had reached an intersection of corridors and he was trying to decide which way to go.

'Oy, oy,' thundered a voice. 'What have we here?'

Out of the gloom came a sun-reddened man with

immaculately cut grey hair. He was marching towards them with a ferocious expression on his face.

'Good afternoon, sir,' Ben called out cheerfully.

The man's demeanour changed. 'Good heavens, Ben,' he said, 'I didn't realize it was you.' He looked at Martine and frowned. 'The two of you shouldn't really be down here, you know. This section is supposed to be off limits, and we're sailing in fifteen minutes.'

'I'm so sorry, sir. I was showing my friend Martine around the ship and I lost track of time. I must admit I'm also a little bit lost.'

'That's not like you, Ben,' chuckled the man. 'You know this boat almost as well as your father does. If you take that passage to the cargo section, you'll find a lift going up to the deck. Hurry now. You don't want to end up in Dubai. Ha Ha!'

Ben thanked him profusely and they ran off down the corridor. Soon they came to a large steel door. A red-lettered sign warned staff that they entered at their own risk and disclaimed any responsibility for injuries, psychological trauma or death caused by the biting, kicking or venomous inhabitants within.

Ben pressed the keys into Martine's hand.

'This is as far as I go. It's more than my father's job is worth for me to be caught down here. When you come out, take the lift up to level three and cross the gangplank. As soon as you're on the jetty, look left. You'll see a path leading up the hill to a pair of tall gates. I'll make sure they're open.'

Martine hesitated. There was one more thing. 'Do you

181

think you could try to get a message to my grandmother?'

Ben nodded. 'It's a promise. Good luck. You're on your own now.'

It took Martine five tries to find the right key. And all the while the ship creaked, seethed and groaned like a wounded beast. Once or twice, Martine was convinced she felt it shift in its moorings. Finally, the lock clicked. She wrestled open the heavy steel door, feeling hopeful for the first time that day. As she entered, a nail caught her T-shirt sleeve and ripped a small hole in it. She pulled herself free, barely noticing it.

As soon as the door hissed shut behind her, the stench of oil, animals, manure and sea water came at her in a sickly wave. She was in a cramped container area lit with flickering neon tubes. Scores of crates and boxes, many draped with tarpaulins, were stacked in untidy rows in the shadows. Martine rushed over to those nearest to her and peered inside. There were glass cases full of writhing snakes, cages crammed with crestfallen parrots, and boxes full of whimpering monkeys. There were trunks packed with animal skins, antelope horns, grain and alcohol, and a huddle of depressed sheep cowering in a crate that was plainly too small for them. The last container on the row housed an enormous blue-bottomed male baboon. When she lifted up the cover, it lunged at the bars of its cage, yellow teeth bared. Martine almost jumped out of her skin.

There was no sign of the giraffe.

Martine had never felt more helpless in her life. Her heart ached for all these creatures. The majority had been treated with less regard than a shipment of coal or rice. As if they had no feelings or needs. As if they were immune to thirst or hunger and impervious to pain. But she knew that there was no way on earth for her to save them all now. It was looking increasingly unlikely that she'd even find Jemmy.

She tried to think logically. There were no obvious labels on the containers, but that didn't mean they weren't marked in some way. There had to be a system of identifying them. She studied the boxes nearest to her. Each had a number scribbled on the lower right-hand side of the door. A twinge on her upper arm reminded her of the nail that had torn her sleeve. Something had been swinging from it. Some sort of notebook? Seconds later she had it: No.144, giraffe, Aisle C.

She saw No.144 right away. And if she'd been thinking more clearly, she'd probably have spotted it sooner. It was a black-painted container, higher and wider than the rest. She dashed over to it and whipped the tarpaulin aside. Jemmy was lying on the floor, his legs at odd angles. His white and silver coat was covered in cuts and matted blood. He seemed to be dead.

'Jemmy!' sobbed Martine. 'Oh, Jemmy. What have I done to you?'

Jemmy raised his head at the sound of her voice. His

eyes were dull and empty.

Martine fell on her knees beside the container. 'Jemmy, please don't die. I love you so much.'

The white giraffe flopped down again and his eyelids drooped. His breathing was shallow. Martine undid the bolts on the cage door and knelt down beside him. She began to stroke his face and neck, feeling again the now familiar tingle.

'Please wake up, Jemmy. Please.'

There was no response.

Martine closed her eyes and put her hands on the white giraffe's heart. Unbidden, technicolour memories of their time together came flooding into her mind. Of the evening she first saw him, standing in the storm, shimmering against the night sky. Of the unforgettable moment when he rested his head on her shoulder. Of lying on his back high up on the escarpment, staring at the Milky Way. Of their exhilarating rides among the elephants and lions of Sawubona.

Through it all, Martine was aware of her hands becoming hotter and hotter and a pure feeling, like love, flowing through her.

A huge shudder went through Jemmy's body. He gave a great gasping breath, as if trying to reclaim the life that had nearly been taken from him. His eyes opened at the same time as Martine's. The light came back into them and Martine knew in that moment that he still loved her and still had faith in her.

Martine pressed her face against his velvety shoulder and gave him a kiss. She sat up. Fingers trembling, she fumbled in the pouch for one of the bottles that Grace had given her on the night they'd met in the cave. 'For bleedin' or to numb any pain,' she'd instructed. Privately, Martine had resolved never to use it. It was the most alarming colour and the smell of it – somewhere between minced-up frogs and Brussels sprouts – made her want to vomit. But right now she had very few options. She knew she had the power to heal but she wasn't yet sure how much her gift could do. She'd got the impression from what had happened with the kudu that she still needed the help of traditional medicine in certain situations. Martine didn't know how badly injured Jemmy was or even if he was capable of walking, but she did know that they had no chance of getting out of the shipyard unless he could gallop. She removed the cork from the bottle and, holding her nose with one hand, daubed the mixture onto his cuts with the other. It sizzled on application.

The ship gave a lurch that almost sent her flying. She held her watch up to the light. Only six minutes till they sailed.

Martine was frantic. The mixture would have to work its magic along the way. She stroked the white giraffe urgently. 'Jemmy,' she said, 'we have to go.' After what seemed an eternity, he lumbered to his feet and stood there swaying. Martine started for the door and breathed a sigh of thanks when he followed her, stumbling a little.

They were almost at the exit when a glint of gold and black caught Martine's eye. Leopard cubs! Martine was pretty sure that they, too, had been stolen from

185

Sawubona. They could even be the cubs whose spoor Tendai had shown her at the escarpment. But even if they were there was no way she could help them now. They were lying in a heap in the corner of their cage, clearly doped.

With a last anguished look at the cubs, Martine guided Jemmy through the steel door and into the cargo lift. It was at least three times the width and depth of a normal lift, but the giraffe still had to bend his neck. He snorted with alarm. Martine pressed the button for level three and the lift began to rise. She realized then that she hadn't thought past the point of rescuing him. With her on foot and the white giraffe running crazed with fear around the dockyard, pursued no doubt by men with guns, disaster would quickly follow. She would have to ride him.

Jemmy was quaking in the clattering, claustrophobic lift, but he stood quietly when she indicated that she was going to try to mount him. Using the support rail as a foothold and doing everything she could to avoid touching any of the cuts on his neck or shoulders, Martine scrambled onto his back just as the lift juddered to a halt. One minute to go. The doors opened. Alex du Preez was standing in front of them, talking on his mobile phone.

'In the end, it was much easier than we thought,' he was saying. 'Like taking candy from a baby.'

He saw Martine and Jemmy at the same moment they saw him. His face went the colour of a frozen Christmas turkey. He dropped his phone and whirled around.

'Raise the gangplank!' he roared. 'STOP THEM!!!'

'Run, Jemmy,' screamed Martine, but the white giraffe was already in full flight. He swept across the deck, striking Alex a glancing blow with his hoof as he went. Alex dropped like a clubbed seal. There was a loud grinding noise and the gangplank began to rise. On the jetty, men were shouting and pointing and tearing across the dockyard from all directions. The ship began to move. Martine's heart was ready to burst out of her chest, but Jemmy never hesitated. He galloped up the gangplank as it rose and took a flying leap. Martine looked down. There was nothing below them but ocean.

· 24 ·

The first thing Martine noticed when she and Jemmy crashed down onto the jetty was the police cars. They were streaming through the shipyard gates in a blizzard of flashing lights and sirens. The second thing she saw was the path leading up the hill.

'That way,' she cried.

Jemmy had stumbled when he landed and then swerved to avoid the guard dogs, and Martine had nearly fallen off. Now she clung hard to his mane and gripped with her legs as he steadied himself and raced up the slope towards the iron gates. They were open, just as Ben had promised. As they galloped through, Martine caught a glimpse of Ben behind the wall. He had an excited grin on his face and he was waving.

Martine lifted her hand and smiled back. 'Thanks, Ben,' she shouted, 'I won't ever forget this.'

As they left the shipyard it occurred to Martine that she didn't know the way to Sawubona. Nor had she given any thought to the complicated question of how to ride a wild animal through the traffic in Cape Town. But she needn't have worried. Jemmy was guided by the instincts of his ancestors to follow the sun on an unerring course for home. He never faltered. He turned away from the city, with its hooting cars and crowded beaches, jumped over a stream and began to run as if his life depended on it. Which, in a way, it did.

For the first mile, Martine fully expected the police cars to come screaming over the horizon, but they didn't. Nothing interrupted the steady thud-thud of the giraffe's hooves. Apart from a brief pause for a drink when they crossed a rushing river, Jemmy ran without tiring, leaping fences whenever he came to them. Whatever Grace had put in the foul-smelling potion, it had worked a miracle.

They travelled inland, away from the suburbs and the stormy coast. Sometimes the landscape was nothing more than parched grey desert, with ostriches strutting jauntily through the scrub. At other times, low-slung hills gave way to valleys carpeted in wildflowers, purple mountains of protea and heathery fynbos, or golden acres of wheat. They travelled so swiftly and so silently that few people saw them go by. And those who did either toppled over in a dead faint, checked their mugs of tea for alcohol content or carried on about their business with little more than a shake of their head, convinced that their eyes were deceiving them.

Only when they reached the outskirts of Storm Crossing did Jemmy slow to a walk. The sun was still shining but a fine misty rain had begun to fall. Martine had learned from Tendai that the Africans called these beautiful showery afternoons 'monkey's weddings'. Ahead of them, Martine could see a crowd of people gathered. As they drew closer, people started coming out of their houses and shops and pointing and clapping, and once or twice Martine thought she heard cheering. She tried to persuade Jemmy to take a different route, but he turned down the main street. From the bakery onward, men, women and children lined the street three deep. From her lofty perch, Martine could see for hundreds of yards in any direction, but there was no sign of any festival or passing parade. It was only when a group of little kids began chanting her name that she realized that all the fuss was for her and Jemmy.

Martine could hardly take it in. They passed a police car parked outside the post office. Alex was glowering in the back in handcuffs. He shot Martine a poisonous glance as she went by. A smartly dressed black man, whom Martine recognized from the newspapers as Xhosa Washington's father, was being led out of the mayor's office by two constables, protesting his innocence as he went. Behind the police car was Tendai's jeep. An outraged mewing was coming from inside. The leopard cubs, thought Martine, and she could have wept with gladness.

The jeep doors opened and Tendai emerged beaming and covered in scratches. When he saw the white giraffe and Martine riding high, he took off his hat and stared in amazement. 'The white giraffe,' he said. 'So many times, I wished . . . I hoped . . . he's truly a creature of the gods, little one, like a horse made of stars.'

Martine smiled down at him, tears of happiness in her eyes. The only thing missing now was her grandmother.

As if reading her mind, Tendai said: 'Your grandmother is waiting at Sawubona for you, little one. She knew your friend would carry you home safely.'

Martine thanked him and Tendai opened the jeep doors again to deal with the leopard cubs. Later, he would tell her that he'd suspected for a year that Alex was stealing animals from Sawubona, but he'd never come close to proving it.

'I just didn't want to believe it,' he confided to Martine.

After Alex's arrest, detectives found that he was the mastermind of a massive poaching operation that had lasted nearly three years. During that time, he and his accomplices – one was Xhosa Washington's father, the mayor, who had processed the export licences – had sent hundreds of animals, many of them rare, to collectors around the world, the main culprit being an oil-rich sheikh in the Middle East. He wanted them for his private safari park. There, they were hunted and eaten at exotic feasts, or stuffed and their heads and skins used to decorate the sheikh's mansion walls. The poachers Alex had heroically caught at Sawubona were a rival gang that he was only too pleased to get rid of. He certainly hadn't done it to protect the animals.

When questioned, Alex was adamant that Martine's grandfather's death at Sawubona had been an accident, claiming that a gun had discharged when Henry was wrestling with another member of the gang. He insisted he'd patched Henry up as best he could before fleeing with the other men. He also said that he had taken the job at Sawubona in an 'attempt to put things right'. How Martine laughed when she heard that.

It would be some time, however, before any of this was known, and for now all Martine was aware of was that Jemmy and the leopard cubs were safe. She smiled so much her cheeks hurt. When she caught sight of the Van Heerden twins ducking red-faced into an alleyway, embarrassed, no doubt, by the part she suspected they'd played in helping to steal the silent whistle, she began to laugh out loud.

'What a difference a day makes,' she thought to herself.

It was almost sundown by the time Jemmy turned into the sandy road that led to Sawubona. Doves were cooing in the thorn trees and the air smelled the way it had on Martine's very first evening at the game reserve – of cooking fires, wild animals and herby earth and trees.

The fading sky was threaded with gold. Ahead of them was a perfect rainbow. It arched over Gwyn Thomas's thatched house and ended in the game park, close to the waterhole. Martine had a lump in her throat. She and Jemmy had been through so much together. He was her best friend and her loyal protector and she loved him more than anything else on the planet. But he needed his freedom. Once again, she was going to have to let him go.

When she reached the game park gate nearest to the house, Martine put her arms around Jemmy's neck and he lowered her to the ground. 'Goodbye, my beautiful friend,' she said. 'I'll miss you.'

But Jemmy refused to leave. He made his musical fluttering sound and pushed his nose against Martine's chest. She ran her hand over his silken mane and cinnamon-tinted patches. 'I'll always be here if you need me, I promise,' she said tenderly. 'But right now you need some rest and for that you need to go home to the Secret Valley.'

Martine watched the white giraffe gallop away through the reserve until she could no longer see him. He'd be back, she was sure of it. She resumed her walk to the thatched house, where her grandmother was waiting.

As she approached the gate, she saw Grace. The sangoma was seated on a tree stump in her indigo, yellow and burnt honey dress, wearing a matching headdress. She gave a pink-gummed smile, stretched out her arms and swept Martine to her mammoth breast for an ecstatic squeeze. 'You done well, chile. The forefathers, they be very proud of you,' she said.

The last remaining dark cloud lifted from Martine's heart. 'Thank you, Grace,' she panted when she managed to extricate herself. 'But I still feel very ashamed. I let everyone down. Jemmy trusted me and I behaved so stupidly.'

'We arl make mistakes, chile. That's human. But not everybody has the courage to admit what they done and go out into the world to try to mend things. You be very brave. Like I told you, the gift can be a curse, not just a blessin'. When arl was said and done, you made your decisions wisely.'

'But Grace, surely this wasn't the reason I was chosen?' asked Martine. 'I mean, I know I managed to save Jemmy, but it was my fault he was stolen in the first place.'

'You're right, chile,' replied Grace. 'This ain't the task that you been chosen for. This be a test, nothin' more. There be many, many challenges to come. You will travel to the ends of the earth and have a whole lotta adventures before you're done.

'This is not the end, you see. This is only the beginning.'

AUTHOR'S NOTE

The idea for *The White Giraffe* came to me out of nowhere one blustery winter's day in London. I was walking along the street when all of a sudden an image popped into my head of a girl on a giraffe. When I was a child I actually had a pet giraffe and I thought: Wouldn't it be the coolest thing on earth to be able to ride a giraffe? And right then, the entire story, even the names of the characters, came into my head.

I went home and wrote it down. I thought: one day when I've retired, I'll have a tinker with it. Soon afterwards I went to Africa, and the whole time I was there, the book was on my mind. When I returned to London, I was busy with other projects but I decided to spend a few hours every Saturday writing it. Well, the first Saturday came and I wrote the first chapter. It just came to me as if I was watching a movie. After that, I couldn't stop!

And it was so much fun. I was writing during a grey, rainy winter in London, but every morning I'd sit at my computer and think: Where shall I go today? Within seconds I could be sitting with Martine and Tendai, enjoying a campfire breakfast on an escarpment, looking down at a herd of buffalo and watching the sun come up over the African bush.

For me, the best part was being able to revisit the landscape of my childhood. When I was Martine's age, I lived on a farm which was part game reserve, in Zimbabwe, which borders South Africa. Apart from our giraffe, Jenny, we had two ostriches, a wildebeest, a herd of impala antelope, and a troop of monkeys. As a family, we were animal crazy and so apart from hordes of cats, dogs and horses, we were forever adopting stray goats, or taking in wild orphans, like our two warthogs, Miss Piggy and Bacon.

For a long time I wanted to be a vet. I had a "vet kit," full of syringes and bandages I used to patch up injured birds, or antelope, or other animals that were carried to our door. My father did a lot of non-emergency animal treatment on the farm, so I learned from him. My first job, at seventeen, was veterinary nursing. Those experiences helped a great deal when I wrote about Martine's gift of healing.

I was fascinated with bushcraft. I spent a lot of time alone in the game reserve, so I was constantly at risk of being bitten by snakes, chased by ostriches, or even devoured by one of the crocodiles on the river beside our house. As a result, I was always on the look out for survival tips. There's a scene in the book where Martine uses soldier termites to stitch up a wound, and that's something I've actually tried, although using a leaf rather than a living creature. It works!

The reason I set the story in Cape Town, South Africa, rather than Zimbabwe, is because I wanted the best of both worlds – the awesome scenery of the Cape, with its ocean, mountains and vineyards, and Zimbabwe's savannah. In South Africa, real savannah occurs much further north than I've located it. Storm Crossing, where Martine lives, is a fictional town about two hours from Cape Town, and Sawubona has a mix of savannah and *fynbos*, a plant kingdom unique to the Cape.

Grace and Tendai are composites of Africans I've known. I sometimes feel that if the only experience a person ever had of Africa was what they saw or heard on the news, they could be forgiven for thinking that the whole continent was mired in disease, famine and conflict. It is true that large sections of it suffer from those things, but in between are areas of breathtaking beauty, rare and amazing wildlife and beautiful, talented, giving people, like Tendai and Grace.

In African culture, the wisdom of grandmothers is greatly valued and many traditional healers – *sangomas* – are women. The training of a sangoma can take as long as seven years. A good sangoma – and Grace is among the best! – is expected to master the techniques of divination, the treatment of mental and physical disorders, plant and animal medicine use, ritual, chant and song, and soul ascension. Although Grace's mother was Zulu, her father's ancestry is Caribbean, so Grace's accent is Afro-Caribbean in a sense and not strictly South African.

People often ask if Martine and I are alike and I'm quick to say that we're not. However, she and I do have one thing in common and that's a passion for saving animals. A lot of us feel that our pet is our friend, and that's definitely true of me. When I was Martine's age, I often felt isolated, or not as cool as everyone else, and although I did have lots of friends, my relationship with my horse Morning Star was the most special of my childhood. I suppose I wrote *The White Giraffe* for anyone who understands what it's like to fall completely in love with an animal and have them love you back.

My hope for *The White Giraffe* is that it is as enjoyable to read as it was to write. If it encourages even one person to want to help wildlife, or to visit, or want to know more about Africa, that would make me incredibly happy.

Lauren St John
London, 2006

Dolphin Song

LAUREN St JOHN

For my godson, Francis,
who is not quite old enough to read this book
but who loves dolphins and sharks with "big teef".

1

When her teacher first told the class that they were going on an ocean voyage to see the 'Sardine Run', Martine Allen had a funny vision of the silver, tomato sauce-covered sardines that come in cans, only whole and wearing matching silver trainers in which they'd sprint along the South African coast.

But that wasn't it at all. The Sardine Run was, Miss Volkner told them, one of the greatest wildlife spectacles on earth. It was a migration by sea. Every June and July, millions of sardines left their home off the Aghulas banks on the west coast of South Africa in pursuit of their main food, the nutrient-rich plankton flowing eastwards on the cold current. The sardines swam after the plankton with their mouths open, gobbling it up as they went. They in turn were pursued by tens of thousands of predators, including dolphins, dusky, ragged tooth, and bronze whaler sharks, and great flocks of Cape gannets with fledgling chicks.

Joining this caravan would be Martine and her classmates. Miss Volkner explained that they would follow the Sardine Run up the KwaZulu-Natal coast, before continuing north to Mozambique, where they would help count the population of dugongs.

'What are dugongs?' Martine whispered to Sherilyn Meyer, and was told that they were those 'cute, lumpy, grey things . . . You know, sort of like a cross between a hippo and a seal. The old sailors used to think they were mermaids.'

The whole class was in a fever of excitement at the thought of ten whole days off school in mid-term, and on a cruise ship no less. So was Martine, until her teacher handed round some notes on the trip. Top of the list of what to pack was:

1 Swimming Costume

Martine put up her hand. 'Excuse me, Miss Volkner, but why do we need a swimming costume?'

There was a lot of giggling, and Miss Volkner couldn't resist a smile. 'It's called a *sea* voyage because we're going to sea, Martine,' she said. 'There'll be endless opportunities to snorkel, dive and splash around in the waves, and I don't think we want you swimming without a costume!'

More laughter.

'But what if . . . ' Martine tried to get the wording right, ' . . . what if some of us preferred not to swim?'

'Why ever would you not want to get into the water?' asked a surprised Miss Volkner. 'The reefs are glorious. Trust me, Martine, once you've swum in the open ocean, where the seabed might be as much as half a mile beneath you, we won't be able to keep you out of the water.'

Somebody else asked a question then, so nobody noticed that the colour had drained from Martine's face and that, beneath her desk, her knees had started to tremble.

That night, the sharks came for Martine for the first time. They circled her in technicolour nightmares, their deep-set dead eyes on her flapping white limbs as she struck out across tempestuous seas. Over the weeks, the dreams increased in frequency and intensity to such an extent that Martine became afraid to go to sleep. Two nights before she was due to leave on the school trip, she took the extreme measure of sitting up in bed with a stack of books on her head so that they'd crash to the floor and wake her if she nodded off. Unfortunately, by then she was so exhausted that the third time they toppled she barely heard them. She simply scooted down in the sheets and gave herself up to the sharks.

She was battling to stay afloat and uneaten in an ocean so icy that her limbs felt paralyzed, when a disembodied voice cut into her dream. 'Wakey wakey, Martine! We'll need to go soon if we want to get to the beach while it's still early.'

Martine forced herself into consciousness. It was morning and a blurry figure was sitting on the edge of her bed. She blinked and it swam into focus. Her grandmother, dressed, as usual, in denim jeans but wearing a pale blue shirt instead of her khaki work one with the lion on the pocket, was watching her with sharp indigo eyes.

'How many times have I told you not to sleep with the window open?' Gwyn Thomas reproached her gently. 'No wonder you have nightmares. You're freezing. June is winter in Africa, Martine. Try to remember that.'

Martine struggled to free herself from the cold tentacles of her dream. 'I was drowning,' she said blearily. 'There were sharks and I couldn't breathe.'

'*Of course* you were drowning,' said Gwyn Thomas, leaning forward and briskly shutting out the biting, antelope-tinged air. 'You were all caught up in the blankets. And what are these books doing on the floor?'

Martine disentangled herself and sat up. She didn't want to worry her grandmother by telling her how bad the nightmares had become. 'I was trying to find something good to read.'

'And you thought you'd start with *The Enthusiast's*

Guide to Model Railways and the *Jeep Engine Repair Handbook*?'

Martine didn't answer. She was too absorbed by the view from her bedroom window. Beneath the thatched eaves, a herd of elephants straggled around the distant waterhole, grey ghosts in the wintry dawn mist. She'd been at Sawubona for six months now, and she still couldn't believe she lived on a game reserve in South Africa; still got a thrill every single morning when she opened her eyes, propped herself up on one elbow and looked out over the savannah wilderness she now called home. Those things didn't take away the knot of sadness that had dwelled inside her ever since her mum and dad had died in a New Year's Eve blaze in their Hampshire home in England, but they definitely helped.

It helped, too, that she had a new family. It wasn't a replacement family, because no one could ever replace the parents she'd worshipped. But at least she didn't feel so isolated anymore. Along with her grandmother, there was Tendai, the big Zulu who had recently been promoted from tracker to game warden. Tendai taught her bushcraft skills to help her survive the beautiful but deadly African landscape, and took her for campfire breakfasts up on the game reserve escarpment. Martine adored Tendai, but she had a very special relationship with his aunt, Grace, an African medicine woman and traditional healer – a *sangoma* – who also happened to be the best cook in the world. Grace's ancestors were both African and Caribbean and she alone knew the secret of Martine's gift with animals, and many other secrets besides.

Last, and to Martine's mind, most important, was her white giraffe, Jeremiah (Jemmy for short). Martine thought of Jemmy, who she'd tamed and could ride, and Ben, the boy who'd helped her rescue the white giraffe when he was stolen, as her best friends, although since Jemmy couldn't talk and Ben was mostly silent, they hadn't actually confirmed that.

'Some time today would be nice,' Gwyn Thomas said pointedly, and Martine remembered that she was supposed to be getting up. She glanced at the bedside clock and stifled a groan. Six a.m.! Sometimes she wished her grandmother was more of a fan of Sunday morning lie-ins.

Gwyn Thomas saw Martine's expression and her eyes sparkled with amusement. Once, those eyes had only ever studied Martine with coolness or hostility but these days her tanned face was more usually creased in a smile.

'You must be so excited about leaving on the school trip tomorrow,' she said. 'Ten whole days at sea. Ten whole days of history and nature and, I suppose, a little adventure. I envy you, I really do. I almost wish I was going with you.'

'Want to swap places?'

Gwyn Thomas laughed. 'For a minute there, you sounded almost serious, Martine. You are looking forward to it, aren't you?'

'Absolutely,' said Martine with as much conviction as she could muster. She swallowed a yawn. 'Can't wait.'

'I'm glad to hear it, because you've been looking quite pale recently. You could do with some sea air. Well, I'll see you downstairs in a few minutes. I'm just packing a picnic for our beach walk.'

'See you downstairs,' Martine said brightly, but as soon as the door swung shut behind her grandmother, she put her head in her hands and closed her eyes. She knew very well why she was having the shark dreams and it had nothing to do with sleeping with her window open in winter, getting tangled up in blankets, eating cheese before bedtime, or any of the other things people said caused nightmares. She was getting them because of something that had happened almost exactly a year ago.

She and her parents had been on holiday in Cornwall, England. On their last afternoon there Martine's dad, a doctor, had received an emergency call to help some boys who'd fallen down a cliff. Martine's mum, Veronica, was recovering from a bout of flu and was having an afternoon nap, and her dad had asked Martine if she would mind reading or drawing for a while because he wanted her mum to get plenty of rest.

But it was a roasting hot day and after a while Martine was bored and decided that if she nipped down to the beach and put her toes in the sea, she could be back before her mum woke up. When she got down there, though, the water was so inviting that soon she was up to her knees and then her waist. Then, out of nowhere, a wave had knocked her flat. It had dragged her along the seabed and she'd tumbled over and over as if she was in the spin cycle of a washing machine. When she felt certain she would drown, the wave had ejected her forcibly, and she'd managed to half swim, half crawl back to the beach.

At more or less the same time, a fisherman had pulled in a basking shark. Martine had seen its sinister shape on the sand as she staggered up the beach and somehow the two things had become combined in her mind – the shark and the washing-machine wave. Moments later she was in her mum's arms. Veronica, who'd been searching high and low for her, was so ecstatic to see her safe that she forgot to scold her. Not wanting to distress her mum further, Martine had thought it best not to mention the wave and how she'd nearly drowned, although she did vow to herself that she would never again swim in the sea if she could help it.

None of that had mattered until now because they'd left Cornwall the next day, and her parents had died before they could have another seaside holiday. As a result, nobody had found out about the one thing Martine had never confessed to another living soul because she didn't even want to admit it to herself. She was petrified of deep water.

2

In the six months she'd been in South Africa Martine had not once been to the beach because her grandmother rarely left the Storm Crossing area and wasn't the sort of person who would ever be caught covered in sunblock, reclining on a striped deckchair. For obvious reasons, Martine was quite content with this arrangement, so she'd been taken aback the previous evening when Gwyn Thomas had suggested that they get up at dawn and go for a walk along the Cape coast. Luckily it was far too cold to swim, so swimming wasn't an issue, which meant that Martine was much more enthusiastic about the idea than she would have been had it been summer.

She was even more pleased when they reached Uiserfontein shortly before eight that Sunday morning and she saw the ocean spilling out before her. The sun was a band of glittering gold splayed across a heaving wilderness of metallic blue. Purple heather grew right up to the shore. As she climbed out of the car, the sea breeze snatched at her scarf and the smell of the waves filled her nostrils.

It was definitely not warm and Martine was glad her grandmother had insisted she 'rug up' with a woolly hat, windcheater and gloves. Seagulls aside, there was no one around but a kite surfer out in the bay. Martine stood riveted on the dunes as he rode the waves like a charioteer. At intervals he'd disappear behind a swell and all that would be visible was his kite, a billowing parachute in candy-coloured stripes. He'd be gone for so long that she'd begin to think he'd fallen victim to the undertow, but then he'd come speeding out on the face of a breaker.

The wind whipped the waves into powdery plumes of spray, like the manes of white horses. They'd toss the man and his board into the air, and the kite would catch him and lift him even higher, allowing him to somersault and twist in effortless defiance of gravity. Then he'd float back down and slip behind another swell.

Out on the beach, the whistling wind made conversation difficult and Martine couldn't help thinking about the school trip again. Her swimming fears aside, it did sound fantastic. Miss Volkner had told the class that the Sardine Run was one of the great wonders of the natural world, as marvellous a migration as that of the wildebeest in East Africa, where every year over a million of the curly-horned beasts moved in an epic black sweep across the yellow plains of the Serengeti, evading lions, hyenas, the spotted gold streaks which were hunting cheetahs, and slow-blinking crocodiles in torrential rivers. On the Sardine Run, she said, it was not uncommon for shoals of sardines to be as much as fifteen kilometres long and three kilometres wide, and for the pods of dolphins which pursued them to be a thousand-strong.

Martine was looking forward to the dolphins most of all. She had only ever seen one dolphin in real life and that was at a grim aquarium she'd visited with her equally grim former school, Bodley Brook. In a peeling swimming pool, a trainer had coaxed it into performing dozens of tricks with beach balls and rubber rings. Some of the children had been invited to reward it with fish from a bucket – probably sardines – but Martine had kept her distance. When the dolphin approached the poolside she'd noticed that its mouth was curled at the corners in a permanent smile. Throughout the show, she'd had the feeling that the dolphin was smiling only because it couldn't help it – like a clown smiling through tears.

The dolphin memory reminded her of another animal she felt was being taken advantage of: her own white giraffe. The best thing about Jemmy becoming famous after the rescue was that he'd lost his currency to hunters. As the only white giraffe on earth, he was still very valuable, but not nearly as valuable as he had been when he was a mythical beast of legend. And he was not exactly of a size which would make it easy for a poacher to catch him and dye him a different colour for reasons of disguise.

The *worst* thing about Jemmy becoming famous was that everyone wanted to see him. Previously, he'd slept in his secret sanctuary during the day and only come out at night. Now, he went there at night and roamed the game reserve during the day, and Gwyn Thomas led White Giraffe tours around Sawubona in search of him. She had even ordered White Giraffe mugs and White Giraffe T-shirts.

Over the past few months, Martine and her grandmother's relationship had improved about a thousand per cent, but the White Giraffe tours were a bone of contention. Gwyn Thomas organized them very carefully so that Jemmy would not be stressed in the least, but Martine loathed the idea of camera-laden tourists gawking at Jemmy. She had made her feelings on the subject very clear. She'd begged and pleaded for the tours to stop and gone on and on about how sensitive and special Jemmy was, but her grandmother was adamant that the best way to ensure that the white giraffe stayed special was to allow people access to him in a controlled environment. Added to which, the game reserve needed the money he earned them.

'It's simple arithmetic, Martine. The more money we can make, the more animals we can save.'

And there was nothing Martine could say to that

because times were tough at Sawubona and she, too, wanted to save as many animals as possible.

A mitten-covered hand tugged at her sleeve. She realized that her grandmother was trying to get her attention.

'Honestly, Martine, I sometimes think your hearing's worse than mine. I haven't got my glasses with me. What's that on the beach up ahead? Is it a seal? Or is it just an oddly-shaped rock?'

Martine blocked out the sun's bright rays with her hand. She gasped. 'I think . . . I think it's a dolphin.'

Martine reached the dolphin first. Gwyn Thomas later commented that she would never have believed her granddaughter – hopeless at all sports bar giraffe-riding – was capable of moving at such a speed, had she not witnessed it herself. But Martine slowed for the last few steps so as not to alarm the dolphin if it was still alive.

It was, but if appearances were anything to go by, not for much longer.

Martine crouched by the edge of the water and two things happened at once. She looked into the dolphin's dark blue irises and had the curious sensation she was falling into them – into a place of wisdom beyond understanding and innocence beyond measure; and not only that, but that it wanted to communicate with her. Simultaneously, she put her hands on its shining grey body, expecting it to have a cold, rubbery feel, and found instead that it was satin-smooth and muscular. When she stroked it a bolt of electricity ran up her arms, just as it had when she'd first touched the white giraffe. She snatched her palms away as if she'd been scorched.

'The poor thing has beached itself,' said her grandmother, hurrying up. 'It's a real mystery why they do that, but it's happening more and more. Only the other week I was reading about 300 dolphins stranded on the shore in Zanzibar. Martine? Martine, are you all right? You're as white as snow. If this is too upsetting for you, you can wait in the car while I get help.'

Martine found her voice. 'What do we do? How do we save it? How will it breathe?'

'Well, dolphins are mammals not fish so they breathe oxygen like us, but shock and being out of the water are what kills them. We need to keep its skin wet. There's a bucket in the car. You're a lot younger and fitter than I am. Would you run and get it, and fetch my mobile, too. I'll call the marine rescue department. Isn't it amazing how that wretched phone is never handy when you need it?'

Martine stood up reluctantly. The dolphin was dying and it had as good as asked for her help. If she did as her grandmother requested it would take time – time that might mean the difference between life and death. If she attempted to save the dolphin herself she could start immediately, but there were two big hurdles. The first was that she'd never tried healing a dolphin before. What if she couldn't do it and she had wasted a crucial half hour which could have been used to summon the marine rescue people and the dolphin died and it was her fault? The second was that her grandmother didn't know about her gift. She did know about the Zulu legend which said that the child who could ride a white giraffe would have power over all the animals, but she had never seen any evidence of it and she didn't really know what it meant.

'It's a shame that any powers you've been given don't extend to keeping your room tidy, Martine,' she liked to joke.

Not even Martine knew what the legend meant. All she knew was that she had to find an excuse to get her grandmother out of the way.

'Martine, this *is* an emergency!' Gwyn Thomas reminded her.

A family of dog walkers spilled into view. They were moving down the creamy beach in the opposite direction, pulled by a trio of exuberant black Labradors.

'Those people might have a phone,' Martine suggested. 'It might be quicker if we ask them to call the marine rescue services.'

'Good thinking, dear. Why don't you run and ask them.'

'I can't,' Martine said. She hung her head in what she hoped was a bashful way. 'I'm shy. Please can I stay here with the dolphin?'

A germ of a suspicion crossed Gwyn Thomas's face. 'You're shy?'

'Yes.'

'I would have thought that this was one time when . . . Oh, never mind. Well, try to keep it calm while I'm gone.'

Martine waited until her grandmother was well on her way to the dog walkers before laying her hands on the dolphin's silky-smooth body again. Its skin was dry and warm. Once again, the electric current zapped her but this time she was ready for it. She kept her palms on the dolphin's side, and in her head she apologized to it for not knowing anything about the healing of dolphins. Nothing happened at first, but then her palms heated up to the point where they were almost sizzling, her heart felt full to bursting, and into her mind came a vision – not of tribesmen in animal masks and swirling smoke and great herds of buffalo and giraffe, as she'd experienced when she'd tried healing before, but of an island with white sand. And in the aquamarine waters which surrounded it, she saw herself quite clearly, swimming with dolphins.

'Is it dead?'

Martine jerked back to reality to find that her jeans were soaked through, as if she'd been waist-deep in water. The kite surfer was standing over her. 'Excuse me?' she murmured vaguely.

'Is it dead?' he repeated a little impatiently.

Martine shook her head, as much to snap herself out of her trance as in reply. She heard herself say, 'No, it was just resting. Would you mind helping me put it back into the sea?'

The kite surfer was powerfully built and he used the lines from his kite to assist him, but it took every ounce of their combined strength to pull, push and roll the dolphin into the ocean. Submerged in water, the dolphin made no attempt to swim. It sank slowly.

Martine's heart sank with it.

'I thought you said it was just resting?' the kite surfer said a little accusingly.

The dolphin gave an experimental twitch of its tail, then a more vigorous wiggle. It surfaced, tipped on its side and regarded Martine with inquisitive eyes. It flapped a fin, sent some cheerful squeaks and clicks in her direction, and was gone in a shining streak. When next she saw it, it was performing acrobatics in the far breakers.

The kite surfer chuckled. 'Funny thing about dolphins,' he said, 'ever noticed that you can't help smiling when you're around them?'

He picked up his board and departed with a friendly salute. Martine waded out of the icy water and wrung out the bottoms of her wet jeans, her hands tingling. She felt elated. Her gift had allowed her to help a wild dolphin. What else would it allow her to do? It seemed to be a gift of healing and communication. She didn't feel as if it belonged to her, though. She felt as if she was the caretaker of it. A sort of conductor.

Watching the dolphin dive gleefully over a wave, Martine found that the kite surfer was right. She couldn't keep from smiling. However, when her grandmother homed into sight, she hastily rearranged her expression.

'Well, that was a waste of time,' Gwyn Thomas reported as she strode up, bucket swinging. 'They had no phone so I did have to go to the car after all. Really, Martine, I think it might have been kind if you'd volunteered to do it for me. I'm not as fit as I used to be. Good heavens, you're soaking! What were you thinking of, going in the Atlantic in mid-winter? You'll end up with pneumonia.'

She did a double take. '*Where* is the dolphin?'

Martine pointed out into the bay. 'There,' she said, unable to suppress a grin.

'But how?' asked her grandmother, bewildered. 'I don't understand.'

Martine shrugged. 'The kite surfer came by and he helped me put the dolphin back into the sea. Then it just swam away.'

'Just like that, huh? It just swam away?'

'That's right.'

'Hmmm.'

Gwyn Thomas stared at her with a mixture of puzzled admiration and something else which Martine couldn't quite fathom, but which gave her a warm feeling inside. It was obvious that her grandmother wanted to probe further, but for some reason she resisted the urge. 'Come on, you,' was all she said, 'let's get you out of those wet things.'

They were almost at the car when Martine realized that, if she was soaked to the waist, she must have waded or swum in the sea during her trance. The odd thing was that she hadn't been afraid. She hadn't been afraid at all.

· 3 ·

To Martine, almost the best part about the whole dolphin rescue was the drive home. Her grandmother knew that something had happened; she just wasn't quite sure what. The invisible barrier between them, which had to do with the pain of past memories – mainly those concerning Martine's mum – dropped away, and the bond they did have, which was about a shared love of animals, deepened. Every so often Gwyn Thomas would mimic Martine saying, 'And then it just swam away!' and they'd both laugh.

That feeling of closeness lasted until precisely 5:47 p.m. when Martine came down from her room wearing jeans and boots and announced she was going out riding on the white giraffe.

'Not now, Martine,' her grandmother remarked casually, glancing up from her newspaper. 'I think you've had enough excitement for one day.'

'But I can't possibly go on the Sardine Run without saying goodbye to Jemmy,' said Martine, unable to comprehend that her grandmother might be serious. 'I *have* to see him, I just have to.'

'Then you should have done it earlier.' Gwyn Thomas lifted her newspaper as if to continue reading.

'But I didn't realize how late it was,' Martine said beseechingly.

Her grandmother was unsympathetic. 'Martine, it's already nearly dark and you know how I feel about you riding after sundown.'

Martine's blood began to boil. The ban on night riding was another big bone of contention between them. As far as Gwyn Thomas was concerned, the game reserve was simply too full of hunting predators after dark for riding the white giraffe at that time to be an option. She wasn't interested in Martine's explanation about how she was perfectly safe when she was on Jemmy's back because the other animals thought she was an extension of him.

'Besides,' continued her grandmother, 'you haven't even packed. No, don't look at me like that. I know you're disappointed but I promise I'll say goodbye to Jemmy for you. That's my final word on the matter. You're over-tired and if you don't get a decent night's sleep, you won't be in a fit state to enjoy the fantastic voyage Miss Volkner has planned for you. And that would be a real shame.'

Martine knew from bitter experience that when her grandmother used that particular tone of voice, argument was futile. But the idea of going away for ten whole days without riding Jemmy, or even saying goodbye to him, was too hideous to contemplate. She stewed about it all through dinner, pushing her roast chicken around the plate. Gwyn Thomas finally told her off for sulking. After that, Martine made an effort to sit up straight and be outwardly charming. Inside, she was hatching a plan. It had been months since she'd sneaked out after midnight to ride Jemmy, and she missed the exhilaration of those moonlit rides. Most of all, she missed the connection with Africa. Alone with the giraffe and the other wildlife, she'd felt as if she had opened a door on a hidden Africa, the Africa only a handful of people ever got to see.

Sitting at the table ladling gravy onto her crispy potatoes, Martine savoured the thrill of disobedience. She had always avoided being caught before, even when she was totally unfamiliar with the workings of Sawubona and her grandmother's routine. Now she was an expert on both. Now it should be simplicity itself.

Martine was almost giddy with anticipation. To divert her grandmother's attention, she turned the conversation back to the dolphin, asking her once more why a dolphin would drag itself ashore to almost certain death.

Relieved to have the tension broken, Gwyn Thomas

was more than willing to discuss the issue of dolphin beachings again, saying that she wasn't sure why they did it and could only imagine it was because something in the sea had made their life unbearable. 'It could be pollution or increased traffic in the oceans,' she said. 'Some parts of the sea have become virtual cities of ships, fishing trawlers and navy vessels, you know.'

Martine listened and tried to remember all the stories she'd heard over the years about the intelligence of dolphins, and how their mere presence could sometimes heal people from illness and trauma. She recalled the electric current that had passed through her when she touched the beached dolphin. Somehow, without words, it had appealed to her to help it. And somehow, without words, she'd agreed.

As a rule, Martine told her grandmother things on a need-to-know basis, and she had never confided in her about the silent dog-whistle she used to call the white giraffe. Consequently, she could now sit at her bedroom window blowing the whistle, without fear of detection, until Jemmy appeared at the skeleton tree near the waterhole.

When her grandmother's bedroom light went out, Martine took off her pyjamas and put on her jeans, boots, sweatshirt and windcheater. She removed her knife and torch from the survival kit she kept tucked behind the bookshelf and slipped downstairs. Jemmy was waiting for her at the game park gate, his white coat ghostly in the darkness. He lay down on the ground so she could climb onto his sloping, velvety back. 'Go, Jemmy,' she urged when she was on safely, and then he was up and galloping.

The winter wind blasted Martine's face but for once it didn't bother her. The rush of the illicit ride was too intoxicating. Riding in the daylight had its advantages – she was in a lot less danger and didn't have to sneak around for a start. But it did mean she had to ride more sedately. Her grandmother would have had a stroke if she saw how fast Jemmy went if he was allowed to. More importantly, it meant staying away from the Secret Valley, the sanctuary where the white giraffe had been taken as an orphan by the elephant who'd saved him from poachers.

It was the Secret Valley Martine was headed for tonight. For reasons she couldn't explain, she knew she had to see the cave which held the keys to her destiny before she left Sawubona. Unfortunately, it was not the easiest place to get to. The entrance was a crevice guarded by a twisted tree, draped with thorny creepers. The only way of negotiating the crevice was for Jemmy to gallop towards the tree at full speed and leap at exactly the right angle. She always found it difficult to stay on his back during the jump, and this time was no different. Vines and branches pricked, dragged and raked at her, and Martine could do little but bury her face in Jemmy's mane and cling on. She hoped the scratches weren't so bad that she'd be unable to explain them away in the morning.

Inside the valley, the fragrance of orchids still hung in the air, although they were no longer in bloom. A patch of star-scattered sky lent a bluey sheen to the dark of the grassy space. Martine slid off Jemmy's back and gave him a kiss of thanks. This was only the third time she'd been to the valley and she felt as jittery as ever about entering the creepy tunnel. Jemmy watched her go, ears flickering.

The narrow passage smelled musty and feral, as if a leopard had recently vacated it. Martine's torch cast a slender, wavering beam along its rough-hewn walls. After a few minutes, the tunnel widened and turned back on itself and she knew she was underneath the mountain once more. Clambering up the steep, mossy steps that led to the cave's antechamber, Martine felt annoyed with herself for not coming up with a plan to keep her jeans clean by, say, wrapping dustbin bags around them. She only had two pairs and both would be coming on the school trip in the morning.

Shortly before she reached the top, Martine turned off her torch. On her first visit, the bat colony which dangled with folded wings from the antechamber roof had gone berserk and got caught up in her hair. This time, fortunately, they didn't stir.

The 'Memory Room', as the ancients had called it, was before her. Martine switched on her torch as she entered the cave, and breathed in its weighty air. She loved the thickness of it. It was as if its very molecules were imprinted with the genetic codes of generations past. All around her were cave paintings capturing the lives and memories of a lost tribe of Bushmen, or San people as they were also known. Red, black and ochre sketches of great herds of wild animals, and men with bows and arrows, so vibrant that they could have been painted yesterday, seemed to spring to life as her torch danced over them. They galloped across the walls. Martine felt privileged to witness them. Coming to the cave, she always felt as though she was visiting her own personal art gallery.

She walked over to the paintings of the white giraffe. It was months since she'd last seen them, but she felt as if she carried them with her always. As if they were engraved on her heart. There were three pictures, but only one showed a child riding a white giraffe. The Bushmen artist had managed to capture Jemmy's exquisite coat exactly. It even shimmered the way Jemmy's did in real life.

So often had she revisited the cave in her head that at first she didn't register that there was something different about the line-up of images. She just stared at the wall in a daze. It was only gradually that she took in what she was looking at. Two new paintings had been added to the sequence!

Martine tried to work out whether it was possible for her to have missed them on a previous visit. She decided that it wasn't. They were slightly obscured by a pyramid-shaped rock, but she'd had the opportunity to study the other paintings twice, at length and at close range. On the second occasion Grace had been with her and *she* hadn't spotted them either. Or had she?

'The answers are right here on these walls,' the *sangoma* had told her, 'but only time and experience will give you eyes to see them.'

Martine touched the rock and felt its strange energy. It was wet. Her torch illuminated a trickle of water running down from a fissure. It provided an explanation of sorts; just not a very satisfactory one. Perhaps the paintings had been covered by a fine dust and a leak of rainwater had rinsed it away and revealed the image beneath. That was one possibility, anyway. Martine didn't buy it. She thought it more likely that Grace was right – only time and experience would allow her to see what she was meant to see.

In the first painting, twenty-one dolphins were lying side by side on a beach. Blood trickled from one dolphin's ear. The second painting was more of a pattern than a picture. It showed rings and rings of dolphins – more than a hundred of them by the look of it – surrounded by a large circle of sharks. There was something in the middle. Martine held up her torch and leaned closer. It was a swimmer. A swimmer surrounded by sharks and dolphins.

Martine's heart did an uncomfortable flip. She was caught in the middle of some ancient prophecy. The destiny that the forefathers had predicted or mapped out for her – she was never quite sure which – was in motion once more, carrying her with it like a leaf on a current. Martine wondered if it was possible to outrun fate. Her parents had tried it with catastrophic consequences, but maybe she could simply sidestep it. She would still go on the school trip but she would refuse to swim or go anywhere near the water, no matter what. Sharks were hardly going to climb up the side of the ship to get at her.

As if the forefathers were reaching out from beyond the grave, her torch fizzed and flicked. Martine, who had been trying to be brave from the moment she entered the claustrophobic tunnel, lost her nerve. She turned and fled. In her rush, she forgot about the bats and clattered down the rocky steps, torch beam swooping madly, startling them from their upside-down dreaming. Their silhouettes skittered across the rock walls like vampire wallpaper. Incensed squeaks, raised to the level of a cacophony by the echo, pursued her down the tunnel.

Back in the Secret Valley, Jemmy sensed her anxiety. He bolted almost before Martine was on his back, nearly unseating her as he crashed through the twisted tree. Clinging to his mane, Martine understood for the first time that she was never really in control of the white giraffe when she rode him; that she relied totally on the bond between them, on trust, on Jemmy's goodwill. If anything ever happened to change that, disaster would quickly follow. But, she told herself firmly, it wouldn't. So she leaned forward and let adrenalin course through her body and watched the dark shapes of a herd of browsing buffalo flash by.

When the white giraffe finally bounced to a halt in the trees near the waterhole, Martine slid to the ground and hugged him. His neck was wet with sweat. He put his head down and made his musical fluttering sound. Martine did her best to explain to him that she was going away for a little while, but that she'd be thinking of him constantly and loved him with all her heart.

Locking the game reserve gate behind her, Martine sprinted through the mango trees and perfumed gardenias. When she opened the back door, the silence of the house seemed to swirl out and envelope her. Perhaps because her nerves were still jangling from the wild ride, a sense of foreboding filled her. She stepped into the kitchen. The faint scent of roast chicken lingered. Moonlight fell in white streaks across the tiled floor. Martine stole past her grandmother's door and up the wooden staircase. Every creak sent her racing pulse into the stratosphere. When she reached her room, she didn't turn on the light but just sank onto the bed and exhaled.

She was unlacing her boots when she began to get the feeling that she wasn't alone. A stifled cough cut through the stillness. Martine leapt to her feet in fright.

A spectral figure was sitting in the wicker chair.

· 4 ·

A switch clicked and Gwyn Thomas's face came at her abruptly out of the darkness. The lamplight lent it a yellow cast, shadowing her brow and throwing the lines around her mouth and eyes into harsh relief. She looked like an eagle owl. Martine stood there feeling her intestines writhe like snakes and her stomach shrink into a hard, sick ball. She could almost hear the fragile bond between her and her grandmother shatter.

'Have you had a good time?' her grandmother asked lightly. 'Have you enjoyed yourself galloping merrily around in the moonlight, unconcerned that I might be lying awake not knowing which might maul, maim or gore you first – a lion, leopard, rhino or bull elephant? Afraid that the phone might ring and it would be the night guard to tell me that you'd fallen off and broken every bone in your body, or been bitten by a Cape cobra, or savaged by a male baboon, or ripped to shreds by a hyena protecting its young.'

As if to support her case, a lion roared in the starlight. 'Shall I go on?'

'I'm sorry,' Martine said inadequately. Somehow the knowledge that none of this was an exaggeration – that, any time she went out into the game reserve with Jemmy, particularly at night, she was taking the risk that one or more of those things could happen to her – made the words harder to bear.

Her grandmother's face was a mask of fury and disappointment. 'Well, I'm sorry, Martine, but sorry is no longer good enough. My first inclination when I found that you had disobeyed me was to pull you off the school trip . . .'

Martine held her breath. It would be ironic if her grandmother's punishment played into her hands by taking her off the school trip.

' . . . But that,' her grandmother continued, 'would be a slap in the face of Miss Volkner and everyone else who has worked so hard to put the voyage together. And I think it will do you the power of good to be away from Sawubona and the white giraffe for a while. You seem to have lost all sight of the fact that, although you have a special relationship with Jemmy, he is a wild animal and wild animals are unpredictable. To help remind you of that detail, I'm going to ban you from riding him or even entering the reserve for six weeks after you return.'

'No!' cried Martine. *'Anything* but that. I'll get up at five every morning and do the household chores; I'll wash all the dishes or do all the ironing; I'll even clean the sanctuary animals' cages for a month. But please don't take me away from Jemmy. He needs me and I can't live without him. I'll die.'

Gwyn Thomas started for the door. 'Don't be melodramatic, Martine. Jemmy will manage just fine without you and, at the rate you're going, you'll live a lot longer without him. The discussion is closed. A six week ban and that's final.'

In that instant, all the hurts long forgotten, all the times when her grandmother had seemed not to want her or snapped at her or sent her to her room, all her frustration over Jemmy being gawped at by tourists, came boiling to the surface of Martine's mind. Combined with this fresh injustice, they caused an explosion. 'I HATE YOU, GWYN THOMAS!' she screamed.

Her grandmother swung round as if to hurl a bitter retort, but caught herself just as swiftly. Her shoulders seemed suddenly to sag. 'We'll be leaving at eight sharp in the morning. Make sure you're ready,' was all she said. The lights-switch clicked and she was gone.

Darkness closed in on Martine. Somehow the noisiness of Africa's night creatures – the hunting lions, the crickets, frogs and night birds – which she found so thrilling usually, made the silence in the house more terrible. The cruel words lingered in the air. Martine was wracked with equal parts of shame and resentment. She tried, and failed, to picture two whole months without Jemmy: the school trip plus the six-week punishment. She was quite sure she'd be eaten up by loneliness – that the loneliness would devour her, millimetre by millimetre, like a flesh-eating bug, until there was nothing left.

It was almost morning before she fell into a restless sleep plagued with visions of circling sharks, and this time they were closer than ever.

Breakfast was a tense and tasteless affair of hard-boiled eggs and toast, after which she and her grandmother drove to the school in silence.

'I think you need to think long and hard about your behaviour while you're away,' Gwyn Thomas said as she lifted Martine's bag from the boot of the car. 'And when you come back, we'll have to discuss your future at Sawubona.'

They stood staring at each another for a long moment – Martine yearning so badly for her grandmother to take her in her arms and make her feel loved and okay and not like the worst person in the whole world that it was a physical ache in her chest. But Gwyn Thomas merely laid an impersonal hand on her shoulder.

'Goodbye, Martine,' she said. 'See you soon.' Then she climbed into her battered red Datsun and drove away.

It took all the self-control Martine possessed not to run after the car. Instead she walked pale and wretched into the rose-lined school courtyard, where the rest of her class were chatting and fooling around in the morning sunshine. Usually Martine loved the aroma wafting from the canteen, but today it made her feel nauseous. She began to wish that she hadn't forced down the boiled eggs.

'Cheer up, Martine, it might never happen,' called out Claudius Rapier, who was lounging at one of the rustic wooden tables, a can of Coke in his hand. His friends laughed raucously.

Martine gave him the most withering look she was capable of. She wanted to tell him that something *had* happened and that even if it hadn't, nothing put her in a bad mood faster than people telling her to cheer up. But she knew it wasn't worth it. In a war of words, Claudius always came out on top.

Claudius had been at Caracal Junior for little more than a term but already he was the self-appointed leader of the 'Five Star Gang', a group of the most popular kids in school. He'd replaced Xhosa Washington, who had transferred to a school in Johannesburg after his father, the local mayor, was jailed for his part in assisting Sawubona's last game warden to smuggle rare animals out of South Africa.

Like Xhosa, there was something princely about Claudius, but unlike the mayor's son, he wasn't muscle-bound. He was overweight – fat even – in a country full of athletes, but that didn't seem to bother him. He had the permanent serene smile of someone upon whom fortune had always smiled, and for whom money had always smoothed every path and made all things possible. He had long blond hair, curling up at the ends, and, in spite of the fact that he existed entirely on fast food (the family chauffeur brought a selection of it to him piping hot each lunchtime), clear gold skin with a slight flush to it. Life was one long joke to him.

'Hey, Martine,' he said again, nodding at her jeans, which were ripped at both knees. 'We know you're an orphan, but do you have to dress the part?'

Before she could answer there was a commotion at the table behind him. The enormous breakfast which he and his friends had been about to tuck into, a feast of bacon double cheeseburgers, jam donuts, chocolate-chip cookies, strawberry milkshakes and coffee lattés in Styrofoam cups, was now lying on the courtyard lawn, beneath the ketchup-covered newspaper they'd been using as a tablecloth.

'Who did this?' roared Claudius, as his friends leapt to their feet with cries of distress. Martine couldn't help giggling, but really she was as startled as he was. There was no wind and nobody near the Five's table. The closest person to it was Ben Khumalo, the enigmatic half Indian, half Zulu boy, but he was at least thirty yards away, studying a noticeboard pinned to the canteen door. He had his back to them and his body language was relaxed, as if he'd been there for quite some time. He took a pen from his pocket and wrote something on an A4 sheet on the board.

Claudius glared at him for several seconds before apparently concluding that Ben was too far away and too much of a wimp to have performed so audacious an act.

He reached for his mobile phone. '*Moenie,* panic *nie,* my friends,' he said grandly. 'Don't panic. We'll order some more.'

'Everyone on the bus,' boomed Miss Volkner. 'We're leaving in five minutes.'

'Well, thank you very much,' Claudius said loudly to no one in particular. 'Thank you, whoever you are, for ruining my morning.'

Martine couldn't be sure but she thought she saw Ben wink.

It was Ben who Martine chose to sit beside on the bus to Cape Town. She gave him a wan smile as she slid onto the seat, but didn't say anything. Ben never spoke at school, and she respected that. A lot of people thought Ben was mute – although some kids claimed to have once seen him having a perfectly normal conversation with his parents – and it made Martine feel good to share a secret with him, to know that whenever they were alone together, Ben talked to her quite freely, and that he spoke much more eloquently than anyone else she knew.

The teachers didn't mind that Ben didn't say anything because he had impeccable manners and always did his work well and on time, and Martine had never asked him why he didn't communicate with their classmates because it made perfect sense to her. Their conversations were all hot air. They talked about fashion and pop music and TV shows and the superficial, and sometimes just plain embarrassing, lives of the rich and famous. Ben didn't waste energy on words. He was a nature person like Tendai, happiest when he was outdoors. He was, thought Martine, a bit like a giraffe, mostly silent but no less extraordinary for it.

With a hiss of air brakes, the bus pulled slowly down the driveway and out of Caracal Junior's lynx-decorated gates. Tall pines slipped past the window. With no one to distract her, Martine sank quickly into a depression. Her grandmother's words went round and round in her head: 'When you return, Martine, we'll have to discuss your future at Sawubona.' What did that mean? Had she made up her mind overnight that she didn't want the responsibility of an eleven-year-old after all and decided she would just pack her off to a children's home in grey, rainy England? To boarding school? To foster parents?

And yet who could blame her?

Martine felt sick to her stomach when she remembered how she'd screamed like a demon child at her grandmother, 'I hate you, Gwyn Thomas!' She wished life came with a rewind button. If that was the case, she'd be feeling very differently now. She'd still be upset about not being allowed to see Jemmy, but maybe if she had apologized a bit more sincerely and promised faithfully never to sneak out at night again, her grandmother might have relented. She would have realized that keeping Martine and Jemmy apart for anything more than a week or two was like trying to separate Siamese twins.

Then, thought Martine, she and Gwyn Thomas would have parted with hugs and smiles and the special feeling they'd had after the dolphin rescue. Her grandmother wouldn't have been left believing that Martine hated her, when really the opposite was true. Martine loved her. She had just never found the right time to say it.

Her reverie was interrupted by a commotion at the back of the bus. Most of the kids were out of their seats. They were pointing at something outside and shrieking noisily.

'What's going on?' demanded Miss Volkner. 'We've hardly left the school gates and already you're up to no good.' She pushed between them. 'What on earth . . . ?'

Martine twisted round and was startled to see – through the dust-speckled window – Grace rushing after the bus, signalling for it to stop. She seemed to be carrying something. For a woman of her extravagant proportions, she moved with astonishing speed and, well, grace. Her billowing scarlet, orange and black African traditional dress made her an arresting spectacle.

Relief flooded through Martine. Grace might have a message from her grandmother. She levered open a side window. 'Grace!' she yelled. 'Grace!'

Miss Volkner raised her eyebrows. 'Do you know this person?'

'That's Grace,' Martine answered with pride. 'She's my friend.'

'Strange company you keep, Martine,' remarked Lucy van Heerden with a smirk. She tossed her silky blonde hair over her shoulder, and cast a disdainful glance at Ben. 'But then you always did like really peculiar people.'

Martine paid no attention to her.

'Be quiet, Lucy,' snapped Miss Volkner. 'I'm not sure why this friend of yours is pursuing the bus, Martine, but I'm afraid we can't stop to find out. If you've forgotten something, it's too bad. You'll just have to manage without it.'

'Oh, you have to stop, Miss Volkner,' implored Martine. 'You just have to.'

'I don't *have* to do anything, Martine. Try to understand that it's out of my hands. If we're not there on time, the boat will leave without us. Is that what you want?'

'I'll be really quick. Grace wouldn't have come unless it was an emergency. And she definitely wouldn't be running. What if something's happened at Sawubona?'

Miss Volkner pursed her lips. 'In the half hour or so that has elapsed since you left Sawubona, I very much doubt all the animals have escaped . . . '

Her voice trailed off. 'Oh, for goodness' sake, never let it be said I'm not fair. You have one minute. I mean it, one minute and that's it.'

She called to the driver and the bus stopped so abruptly that Martine was almost catapulted through the windscreen. The doors popped open. Martine jumped onto the verge, dew soaking her socks and trainers. Grace was waiting for her, still out of breath from her run. Her volcano-bright headscarf was unravelling and her rich brown skin glowed. She looked like a magnificent bird which had been subjected to some undignified ritual. She was holding a small rubbery plant with orange flowers.

'What's wrong, Grace?' asked Martine, speaking rapidly in the hope of getting information in the shortest time possible. 'Is everything okay? Has something happened at Sawubona? Have you been speaking to my grandmother?'

But Grace, straightening her headscarf, and checking the health of the plant, took her time answering. Vital seconds passed. Martine glanced over her shoulder and Miss Volkner tapped her watch. 'Be-Ware,' Grace said at last.

'Beware?' echoed Martine. 'Beware of what?'

'Tha boat fence. Watch out for tha boat fence.'

'I don't understand,' said Martine. '*What* boat fence?'

'That's it!' Miss Volkner interrupted. 'Time's up. Onto the bus THIS VERY SECOND or I'm removing your bags and leaving you behind.'

Grace thrust the plant at Martine. 'This here is a present for you.'

Martine took it uncertainly. 'Umm, thanks, Grace. What do you mean by . . . ?'

'I take it that you'd prefer to stay here?' Miss Volkner demanded, her voice shrill with exasperation. 'Driver, open the luggage compartment and we'll remove Martine's bag.'

Grace gave Martine a squeeze and a shove. 'Go, chile.

When tha time comes, you will know what to do.'

The bus was already moving when Martine leapt on board. The doors snapped shut. Grace's fiery plumage vanished in a swirl of dust.

Carrying the little plant, Martine walked the gauntlet of eyes down the aisle of the bus. She was bemused by Grace's warning and more than a little annoyed with Miss Volkner for wrenching her away before she could hear what the *sangoma* had come to say. It was obviously very important. Now she would never know. Now she would have to sail up one of the most treacherous coastlines in the world, unsure of what Grace had been trying to protect her from.

'Any other stops you'd like to make, Martine?' Claudius called. 'Should we pop into the game ranch? Or perhaps you'd like to pay a visit to all the other relatives and acquaintances you haven't seen recently? Don't mind us. We'll just come along for the ride.'

Martine could feel a beetroot flush spreading up her neck. She speeded up to get past her tormentor and her foot caught the handle of a sports bag. She tripped and the plant shot into the air. Martine almost did the same, but she managed to grab a seat-back and right herself. Claudius snatched the plant off the floor. He held it between his thumb and forefinger and regarded it with a comical expression of distaste. 'I didn't know you were a vegetarian,' he said to Martine. 'Hey, Sherilyn, have a bite of this!'

Before she could stop him, he'd tossed it across the aisle, where its gritty roots caught in Sherilyn's hair. Sherilyn gave a screech and batted it away. Luke caught it and threw it on, and after that it did the rounds of the bus, to the accompaniment of hoots and laughter. Martine tried pleading for its return but finally gave up and went to her seat, hot tears pricking the backs of her eyes.

'I don't know what's going on back there, but I've had about as much as I can take for one morning!' warned Miss Volkner from her seat beside the driver. 'If I hear so much as a squeak between here and Cape Town, we're turning the bus around and going back to Caracal Junior and you'll all spend the rest of the month in detention.'

Martine sat down beside Ben, avoiding his gaze. The gruelling morning had been too much for her. A few tears escaped and splashed onto the leather seat. Embarrassed, she rubbed her eyes roughly. When she opened them again, Ben was holding out a faded red bandana. Martine took it from him gratefully. She held the soft cloth against her face and somehow the clean cotton smell of it and Ben's simple act of kindness made her feel better almost immediately. She went to give it back to him but he shook his head. Instead he handed her the two leaves and thread of root which were all that remained of Grace's plant. Martine tried to thank him but he had already turned away and seemed to be absorbed in his book.

As the bus sped along the highway and the savannah gave way to the sharp-edged mountains and mist-wreathed forest cabins of the wintry Cape land-scape, Martine tried to make head or tail of the events of the past eight hours. First the image on the cave wall and now Grace with the incomprehensible warning about a 'boat fence'. What *was* she talking about? And why would she give Martine a plant for a present?

She opened her hand and studied the scrap of green. The thin leaves oozed a milky sap where they'd been torn. With the plant destroyed there didn't seem much point in keeping them, but she couldn't bear the thought of throwing away a gift from Grace. She wrapped the leaves in Ben's bandana and found a space for them in her survival kit. The waterproof pouch had been a gift from Tendai for helping him find two missing leopard cubs. She planned to keep it around her waist for the duration of the school trip. She knew she'd probably be teased about it, but she'd made up her mind not to care.

'Most people keep their survival kit in a drawer in their house, or in a locked box in their garage, or some other place where they're probably never going to have an emergency,' Tendai had told her. 'They think they will be able to see an emergency coming. Unfortunately, that almost never happens. Keep your survival kit with you for when you most need it, little one – when you need to survive.'

The Zulu had helped her pick out what to take on this particular trip. As well as her pink Maglite torch, Martine had some matches she'd waterproofed with candle wax, her Swiss Army knife, a coil of extra-strength fishing line with a hook fastened to it, three corked bottles containing Grace's special preparations for wounds, headaches and upset stomachs, a whistle, a piece of root ginger she could chew on if she felt seasick, and a tin lid with a hole in it for signalling aeroplanes.

'Surely I don't need all these things,' she'd said to Tendai. 'I mean, why would I need to signal an aeroplane?'

But Tendai replied that that was the whole point of a survival kit. You took things for every eventuality. Chances were you'd never need any of them but if you did, you wanted to be sure that all bases were covered.

By the time the cloud-scattered crags of Table Mountain came into view the kids on the bus were singing African songs, and the spirit of freedom – the feeling that by going off on a sea adventure, they were somehow playing truant – was infectious. But Martine still couldn't shake the sense that something darker lay ahead. She put a hand on her survival kit. She had a bad feeling she was going to need it.

In a matter of hours, Martine's misgivings had been banished by the powerful, salt-laden winds of the Cape and the sheer visual wonder of the sapphire-blue sea which pounded its shores. It helped, too, that she hadn't had a moment to think. After a tour of the penguin colonies of Simon's Town, home to South Africa's largest naval base, and a lunch of mango juice and smoked snoek paté batter-bread sandwiches, Miss Volkner had sprung a surprise on them. Before boarding the ship for the Sardine Run, they were going to 'Shark Alley' to watch tourists cage diving with Great Whites.

Shark Alley! Even the name made Martine shiver. Her gut reaction when she'd heard the news was to pretend she'd come down with food poisoning. That way, there'd be no danger of her nightmares coming true. That way, she was unlikely to end up in the choppy blue bay, encircled by sharks. Then it occurred to her that feigning illness at this stage of the journey, before they were on board the main ship, would result in her being sent back to Sawubona to face her grandmother, and even the sharks seemed preferable to that.

Barrelling over the white-capped sea a little while later on a deep-sea fishing boat named *Prowler IV,* Martine was glad she hadn't given in to her fears. She told herself they were ridiculous. It's not as if every dream she had came true. Once she'd dreamt that she'd forgotten to put on her uniform and only realized her mistake when she walked into assembly at Caracal Junior, and, to the best of her knowledge, that had never even come close to happening!

As for the image on the cave wall, well, perhaps it only meant that she'd be spending a lot of time surrounded by sharks and dolphins. Which she would. Perhaps the Bushmen had simply neglected to draw in the boat. Martine decided to stop fretting and enjoy the day. After all, what could go wrong? Safety checks on *Prowler IV* had been stringent. Stinging pellets of spray peppered her face each time the boat hit a wave, but short of being bodily hurled overboard there was very little chance of her ending up in the sea.

Geyser Rock was home to a colony of around 40,000 Cape fur seals and several hundred Jackass penguins. The seals flopped around the rocks, barking and moaning and posing for pictures, their whiskered snouts turning this way and that. Their bodies shone like bronze in the pale sunshine.

'Gourmet food for sharks,' joked Greg, *Prowler*'s skipper, a freckled South African with a bushy ginger beard. 'This is like restaurant row for Great Whites.'

Martine felt a twinge of sadness at the thought, but she understood that, if too many seals were competing for space, mates and food, it would devastate their colony. The seals needed the sharks as much as the sharks needed the seals.

As a result of the feast available to them, huge numbers of Great Whites congregated in the shallow channel between Dyer and Geyser Islands, and tourists came from all over the world to cage dive with them. Martine wasn't too sure what cage diving involved, but Greg explained that it provided an opportunity for everyone from nature lovers to adrenalin junkies to get up close and personal with the killers of the deep. There were different ways of doing it, but one of the most common was to use a cage made from galvanized steel mesh, 12mm thick. Three or four people climbed inside and the cage was lowered into the midst of feeding sharks, often only a metre or so beneath the surface.

Conservationists, Greg said, were divided over cage-diving. Some thought that it altered the behaviour of sharks, increasing the risk of them attacking humans close to beaches, but others, like Greg, who was passionate about sharks, hoped that by showing sharks in their natural habitat, more people would realize how incredible they were. Movies like *Jaws* had given them a bad name, but some sharks ate only plankton and it was rare for even Great Whites to prey on humans. Most shark attacks happened when sharks mistook surfers or swimmers for seals or fish.

Greg broke off his talk to manoeuvre *Prowler* alongside a smaller boat which was already moored in Shark Alley. There were ten tourists on the deck – three Japanese businessmen, two Germans, and a party of friendly, talkative Americans, all of whom had film star teeth. They'd spent the morning touring the islands and were very cheerful. They came aboard *Prowler* – which was now pretty crowded – and drank mugs of coffee and *rooibos*, the Afrikaans name for red bush tea, to fortify them for the cage diving experience. Martine sat chatting to Norm and Mary Weston, a couple from Florida, who were on a vacation to celebrate Norm's retirement from the staid world of vacuum cleaner sales.

'We're making it our mission to do all of the things we were too chicken or too poor to do when we were young,' Mary told Martine with a wink. 'Norm said, 'Why don't we go swimming with sharks?' And I said, 'I tell you what, darling, I'll let you swim with sharks if you let me go bungy jumping and whitewater rafting.' So we made a deal!'

Martine enjoyed talking to them and admired their spirit of adventure, but when Norm donned the thick wetsuit, boots and gloves which would protect him from the freezing temperatures of the winter water, she could tell that behind the bravado Mary was extremely anxious. The sun had been swallowed by a bank of woolly cloud and the sea was more grey than navy. It did not look inviting.

Greg, meanwhile, was busy pouring 'chum', a mixture of ground-up fish heads and other foul-smelling, bloody ingredients, guaranteed to lure sharks to the boat, into the sea. He helped Norm and three other men into the cage, and they gasped and whooped as trickles of seawater made contact with their skin. Once the sharks appeared, the tourists would be lowered beneath the surface and would breathe through hoses fed with air from the boat. Behind his goggles, Norm's face was alight with anticipation. He looked twenty years younger than his sixty-five years.

'Over there!' Scott Henderson shouted, and everyone rushed to his side of the boat, where a swishing black shadow was rising slowly from the deep. It was so enormous that Martine thought at first it was a whale, but as it neared the surface the unmistakable outline of a shark became visible. Without warning, it burst from the sea. The children and tourists reeled back. For one terrifying moment it hung in the air, so close to the boat it seemed it would land in it, and Martine saw at close range its flat grey snout, corpse-like eyes and crooked rows of needle teeth. Then it belly-flopped back into the ocean, sending a gruesome shower of chum and icy water their way.

Other Great Whites quickly joined it and soon there were as many as eighteen sharks surrounding the boat. Their fearsome jaws snapped at the fish-heads floating close to the cages. Martine could make out Norm, secure behind the steel mesh, snapping away with his underwater camera.

All at once, he stopped taking photographs and became agitated. There seemed to be a problem with his air hose. The boat assistant ran to start the machinery to raise the cage and Greg rushed to help Norm. Even before the skipper reached him, Norm had opened the lid of the cage and was attempting to clamber out.

'Slow down, Norm,' warned Greg, leaning out over the water. 'The sharks are in a feeding frenzy. You'll be okay but you need to let me help you.'

Norm smiled bravely. He put a foot on the edge of the cage and reached for Greg's freckled hand . . .

Later, when Martine tried to piece together the events of that afternoon, the thing that struck her was that it was true about accidents happening in slow motion. In reality, obviously, they took place in a split second, but that wasn't how they felt at the time. One moment

Martine was watching Norm balance on the edge of the cage like a black-winged crane, reaching for Greg's hand; the next, time had slowed to a crawl and she was watching as the American, unsteady from lack of oxygen, missed Greg's fingers and fell backwards into the churning grey sea.

The wheeling gulls matched Mary's screams.

Norm landed with a terrific splash, temporarily scattering the sharks. The scene took on a surreal quality. It didn't seem possible that the smiling man with whom Martine been sharing coffee and biscuits barely half an hour earlier was now flailing about in the bloody water, fighting for his life. But this was no movie. The largest of the Great Whites, a prize specimen of about twenty-two feet – Greg had told them that it probably weighed close to 7,000lbs – had already changed direction and was on its way back to see if Norm was edible. The boat was a madhouse, with Greg appealing for calm while his assistant hung over the edge with a boathook. He planned to bash the shark on the nose, its most sensitive part, if it came within range.

The menacing shadow circled Norm twice. The pinched snout of the shark poked above the water and its mouth opened briefly as if it were testing to see how much of him it could bite off in one go. It was then that Martine seized her chance. She focussed her green eyes on the shark's sunken grey ones, summoned all the furious energy she could muster and directed it at the shark in a conscious stream, the way she'd once done with a rottweiler dog. She willed it to leave Norm alone, to find something its own size to terrorize or, better still, to consider a diet of plankton.

The shark's head dipped beneath the surface. The assistant threw the boathook, but it fell wide and drifted away on the current.

'STOP!' Martine yelled at the shark in her head. 'STOP!'

But the Great White was already in motion. It was like a torpedo, sleek and deadly, shooting towards the stricken man. As it approached, its jaws stretched wide and its rows of serrated teeth were plainly visible. In seconds, Norm would be missing an arm, his head or even his torso.

'STOP!' Martine yelled silently.

The shark veered away with an irritable flick of its tail. It vanished into the camouflage of the sea. The waves created by its passing shoved Norm hard against the side of the boat, where willing hands hauled him from the water.

Mary fell on him with kisses and cries of thanks. 'When you said you wanted to swim with sharks, I didn't think you meant you'd be doing it outside the cage!' she scolded her husband in a trembling voice, but it was said with humour and a lot of love.

A warm glow spread through Martine. She gave an involuntary cheer, but nobody noticed in the general bedlam. Everyone was talking at once as they tried to work out why the shark had changed course.

'At the last second it figured out that you weren't a seal, Norm,' reasoned a mightily relieved Greg, as he rushed about getting hot towels and sweet tea for his shaken client. 'Humans are just not natural prey for sharks.'

'Well, I sure am glad about that,' Norm said as the colour returned to his cheeks. 'Now, at least, I get to dine out on the story.'

In midst of all the chaos, something made Martine look up. While everyone else on the boat was focussed on the Westons' reunion, Ben, sitting cross-legged on the roof of *Prowler*'s cabin, was focussed on her. He was smiling.

7

The following morning Martine lay on her stomach on her bunk in the *Sea Kestrel* watching a porthole-shaped dawn divide the ocean into sections of pink, apricot and blue. There was not a trace of land on the horizon. At some point during the night, Africa had slid away, taking Sawubona, Jemmy, and Martine's only connection to a home of any kind, away with it. She was adrift once more, as she had been after her parents' death. A stranger in a strange, watery wilderness, unsure of what lay ahead.

And how did she feel about that?

Well, so far, much better than she'd expected.

Overnight her mood had lifted. It was reassuring to know that the shark encounter predicted by both her dreams and the cave paintings was over, especially because it had all ended happily. It was Norm in the pictures. She even had an explanation of sorts for Grace's 'boat-fence' warning, because the steel mesh of the cage could be said to resemble a fence. The sharks had returned to haunt Martine's sleep again, but that was hardly surprising given that she'd almost seen a man swallowed alive by one!

The important thing was, she didn't have to worry about sidestepping destiny anymore, particularly since she had resolved that for the entire ten days of the voyage, nothing and nobody was going to get her into the water. She still felt bad about the row with her grandmother and she was still concerned about her future at Sawubona – life without Jemmy wasn't worth contemplating – but with no way of communicating with anyone (Miss Volkner had banned mobile phones on the ship because she wanted the class to 'lose themselves in nature'), there was nothing she could do about it until she returned to Cape Town.

To help them recover from the trauma of Shark Alley, Miss Volkner and Mr Manning, the conservationist accompanying them on their voyage, had taken the class for a seafood dinner at a harbourfront restaurant in Simon's Town. Afterwards, they'd walked through the pretty, historic streets to the docks and there she was – the *Sea Kestrel* – all lit up like some magical cruise-liner. Boarding under the moth-swirling harbour lights, with the seaweedy air teasing her nostrils, Martine had begun to appreciate how fortunate she was. She'd caught Ben's eye and it was obvious that he felt the same way.

There were twenty clean but basic cabins on the ship, with two bunks apiece. Martine was sharing a cabin with Sherilyn Meyer, a close friend of Lucy's. Sherilyn was nice enough, but a bit helpless. She had a phobia about all creatures with more than two legs. Before getting into her bunk that first night, she'd made Martine crawl around the floor checking for spiders. Martine hadn't really minded because Sherilyn's other concern – that she might get seasick – meant that Martine got to have the top bunk she was coveting, but she was thankful when the South African girl was at last satisfied the cabin was a bug-free zone, and she was able to climb between the sheets and fall into an exhausted sleep.

It had been a very, very long day.

When the red ball of sun freed itself from the smoky blue ocean, Martine slipped carefully off her bunk, showered as quietly as she could manage and went in search of sustenance. It was still early and, apart from a couple of crew smoking outside the engine room, there was nobody about. She passed a galley hatch, from which copious quantities of steam and the smell of frying bacon issued.

'Ah, a hungry sailor!' said a voice. Its owner sounded

as if he gargled regularly with beach sand. 'Step this way for an Indian Ocean breakfast!'

Martine squinted between the stainless steel shelves and dangling copper pots and saw a lively African face. A hand came out and gripped hers. 'Alberto,' said the gravelly voice. 'How do you do, Miss Martine?'

'Uhh, good morning, Alberto,' responded Martine. 'I'm very well, thank you. Have we met before?'

Alberto indicated that she should enter the galley through the main door. Martine walked into a cooking area where a diminutive African with a white cap of hair and remarkable, wrinkle-free skin was juggling sizzling pans of bacon, spiced potatoes and eggs with octopus-like dexterity. Without pausing to consult her, he lifted Martine with his small, strong hands and sat her on one of the stainless steel benches. A mug of milky coffee came her way, followed by a bacon and fried banana roll. It was not a combination of flavours that Martine had ever considered, but the crispy bacon combined with the caramel taste of bananas fried in butter was addictive. No sooner had she eaten one than she wanted another.

'Are you Mozambican?' she asked the chef in between mouthfuls. 'What tribe are you from?'

'I am Tsonga,' Alberto replied at last. 'The Tsonga are island people, living mainly in the Bazaruto Archipelago off the coast of Mozambique. And you are the girl in the story, no? The one who can ride a white giraffe.'

Martine could never get over how far news travelled on the 'bush telegraph'. African tribes and big, extended families had spent generations communicating with one another across vast swathes of savannah, desert or mountain ranges, and their conversations seemed to travel almost on the wind. Then again, several newspapers had carried photographs of her and Jemmy, so it was possible Alberto had simply read about her and might never have heard of the Zulu myth.

She took another bite of her bacon and banana roll, savoured it, and then said evasively, 'What do African islands look like, Alberto? Do they have thick bush on them and thorn trees, or are they white with palm trees?' She was thinking of the island calendar in Grace's living room which showed the Caribbean home of her father and his ancestors.

'All I know is that when I return from a long voyage and I see my home island, Benguerra, my eyes feel peaceful,' Alberto replied.

Martine understood what he meant. She experienced the same sensation whenever she passed through the gates of Sawubona. But the Bazaruto Archipelago was nothing like the golden waving grassland, thickets of acacia, and herds of zebra and elephant in the place that made her own eyes feel peaceful. Alberto conjured up images of palm-fringed islands scattered, like snowy teardrops, across a turquoise lagoon. In centuries past, he said, when it was the bountiful Southern tip of the trading routes of Arabia, the Queen of Sheba had made the islands her personal playground.

Martine knew nothing about the Queen of Sheba and didn't like to appear ignorant by asking where Sheba was or if, in fact, she had ruled over it. But it turned out that she wasn't the only one who was unclear about the queen's origins. Alberto said that, while most Africans believed the ancient kingdom of Sheba to have been close to the horn of Africa, where Eritrea and Ethiopia were now, others were convinced it was in the Yemen in Arabia.

Martine liked the notion that the queen was African royalty, and pictured her as a striking ebony woman with the high cheekbones that occurred among the tribes of north-east African nations. She'd have been dressed in robes edged with precious jewels, and seated on a throne mounted on the prow of a great sailing ship. In between visiting King Solomon to test his wisdom, as she was reported to have done in Biblical times, she'd have floated around the Bazaruto Islands, eating oysters and pink lobsters and buying gold.

The Portuguese came next, in the 16th century. Alberto rolled his eyes a little when he talked of them and it was clear that he was not a fan of the way they had colonized his country, gobbling land, setting up ivory trading posts and penal colonies, and making a fortune harvesting the oyster beds around the Bazaruto Islands, which yielded some of the creamiest pearls on earth. Legend had it that the captains of ships sent to transport precious cargoes of gold, pearls and beads, hurled the odd casket overboard, in locations marked on secret maps, in the hope that they might one day be able to return for them. And that since they rarely did, treasures beyond imagining lay buried under the seas around the islands.

Modern life on Benguerra seemed to consist of prawn feasts and trees laden with cashew nuts, marulas and monkey oranges. Alberto talked proudly of how the Tsonga had remained more or less untouched by the decades of invaders, civil war and strife which had affected the rest of Mozambique.

'During the war, we would sit under the palms on our islands and watch the flashes of rocket fire on the mainland light up the night skies, and our hearts would break for our brothers and sisters. Even now, we hear stories of hunger, disease and murder in the cities, but we know nothing of such things on Benguerra. If today you leave your camera on the beach, tomorrow somebody will find it and bring it to you. The smallest children can walk anywhere on the island by themselves. We don't have locks on our doors. We say to our neighbours, "Come, everything we have is yours." '

To Martine, it sounded like paradise, although like all paradises it had its little drawbacks. In the summer months, the heat and malaria-carrying mosquitoes were torture, and Alberto's home island was famous for having enormous numbers of snakes.

'These are small things,' the chef said. 'Truly we are blessed to live in such a wonderful place. But you know, even special places can change. With the islands becoming so popular, many outsiders are coming in, and some of our young people are moving out. They get tired of the old ways and want to move to the towns, where they think they will find more money and more fun.'

'I wish *we* were going to the Bazaruto Islands,' Martine

said. 'We're only going as far as Inhambane, in the south of Mozambique, where we're supposed to help count the population of dugongs, and then we're returning to Cape Town.'

Alberto gave a throaty laugh, revealing a little red gemstone set in one of his front teeth. It flashed like fire in the galley lights. 'That is true,' he said. 'We are not going to Bazaruto. But you never know in this life.'

8

The one thing the class had been told over and over was that the Sardine Run was unpredictable. It was a natural phenomenon and natural phenomena were not in the habit of organizing their timetables to suit school trips, or reporters with deadlines, or tourists on expensive Sardine Run package tours. The sardines responded to subtle changes in water temperature and if the temperature didn't spur them to make a move, sometimes they didn't 'run' at all. Every day Mr Manning radioed the Sharks Board in KwaZulu-Natal to check if there were any sightings, and every day he came away disappointed.

His disappointment was nothing compared to that of the children. They'd heard so much about the Sardine Run that their expectations were sky high. The majority of them had not bothered to read Miss Volkner's notes on the voyage and had imagined themselves on a cruise ship like the famous *QE2*, with sun-loungers and jacuzzis, and plenty of time to nap beside the pool in their swimwear. Even those who had glanced through the notes had thought of the trip as a vacation from schoolwork.

The reality was a little different. The *Sea Kestrel* had more in common with a fishing trawler than a luxury liner. There were no sun-loungers, drinks with umbrellas in them, seafood buffets, or other cruise ship luxuries. There were bare boards and bare essentials only. As for getting a holiday, the children found that the opposite was the case. Caracal Junior was an eco-school, which meant that there was a strong emphasis on the environment in lessons, and Miss Volkner and Mr Manning were determined that not a moment of the ten-day voyage would be wasted.

From morning till night, the class were kept busy with conservation projects. They identified migrating sea birds, or collected jars of sea water and examined their contents under microscopes for traces of things like phyloplankton.

'Phyloplankton is phosphorescent,' explained Mr Manning. 'That means it glows in the dark. It looks like fairy floss under the moonlight. Dolphins and whales swim through it and it coats their bodies like a film. If you see them playing in the waves at night, it looks as if they're outlined in silver.'

Martine was so entranced by this that she spent the next few evenings running back and forth on the deck to check if there were any fairy-flossed dolphins leaping alongside the ship, but none appeared.

She cornered Mr Manning one afternoon to ask him why dolphins and whales beached themselves. Mr Manning was not a man who did anything speedily and it took him a while to answer. He removed his spectacles, which had a chipped lens and a broken arm he had mended himself with yellow insulation tape, and wiped sea-spray off the lenses.

'To be honest, Martine,' he said, 'it's a bit of a mystery. Sometimes it has an obvious cause, such as dolphins being wounded by fishing gear, or bite wounds from sharks, or being ill. But when large numbers of dolphins and whales are involved it's not that simple. Alberto was telling me that, in the Bazaruto Islands, dolphins have beached themselves on the thirteenth day of each of the past three months. Isn't that peculiar? Some Tsonga believe that it's because the dolphins have become drunk on rainwater, and around the world other cultures have their own ideas. But many scientists are now coming round to the theory that one of the main causes is sonar.'

'Sonar? You mean the thing ships use to communicate with each other?'

'Exactly. SOund Navigation and Ranging is its full name. It was invented in 1906 by a man called Lewis Nixon as a way of detecting icebergs, and then modified by a French physicist and a Russian engineer for use in detecting submarines during the First World War. These days, of course, sonar is used extensively by the Navy for military purposes, and many other people and organizations for all sorts of other things. For instance, fishermen use it to find shoals of fish.'

The *Sea Kestrel* was steaming through the waves in response to a supposed Sardine Run sighting, and Martine and Mr Manning moved back from the railings to avoid the flying spray. 'I don't understand,' said Martine. 'Why would that cause dolphins and whales to want to escape the sea?'

'Ah, well, you see whales and dolphins use a kind of sonar to locate prey and find their way around the oceans. It's known as echolocation. Scientists fear that the Low-Frequency Active (LFA) sonar used by the Navy disorientates and confuses them. It sweeps the ocean like a sort of floodlight and the sound it gives off can carry up to 100 miles and be as loud as a fighter jet at take-off. In some cases, it can cause whales to surface too quickly, leading to a fatal condition similar to the bends in human beings. They get gas bubbles in their organs. Their brains bleed.

'Sometimes the sonar is so deafening that it bursts their ear drums. A few years ago, LFA testing in the Bahamas was found to be responsible for the stranding of sixteen whales, seven of which were found dead. There have been numerous similar incidents across the planet, often when there have been naval exercises in the area. The total number of cases runs into thousands.

300 hundred dolphins in Zanzibar, 130 pilot whales in Tasmania, 68 dolphins in Florida . . . '

He polished his glasses again. 'This is not a very cheerful subject, is it? Why are you so interested in it, anyway? Have you seen any beached dolphins?'

Martine gave him an angelic smile. She was not about to tell the conservationist about her experience with the dolphin in Cape Town. 'I just love dolphins.'

'Then I'll tell you some nice things about them,' Mr Manning said. 'Their pointed snout is called a rostrum. Did you know that? And have you heard that dolphins know each other's names? Isn't that wonderful! Each one of them has its own signature whistle.'

Martine was intrigued but before she could ask another question, a cry went up, 'The Sardine Run! We've found the Sardine Run!'

Every person not engaged in the sailing of the ship converged on the starboard edge, but there were no sardines to be seen. Instead it was as if the *Sea Kestrel* was entering a bizarre weather system. Oddly-shaped clouds were scudding across the sky and tufts of spray were kicking up randomly.

'This is the Sardine Run?' said Luke, distinctly unimpressed. 'This is what we've come all this way for? The sardines aren't even visible.'

'Be patient,' counselled Mr Manning. 'Wait till we get up close.'

'Mind if I take a nap?' Luke said under his breath, and Lucy sniggered.

Martine stayed staring hopefully ahead, watching for dolphins. The ship forged through the waves. At length, the curious clouds resolved themselves into birds – hundreds and hundreds of Cape gannets and cormorants – all dive-bombing the sea. Then she spotted the sardines. Seen from above, they looked like an immense silver oil-slick. So dense was the shoal and so closely did the flashing fish swim together that it was as if they were being directed by an invisible conductor. A whale sliced slowly through the middle of the silver symphony, chomping sardines as it went.

The dolphins came next, several hundred of them. They converged on the shoal at blinding speed and worked like sheepdogs to corral a mass of sardines into a tight ball, on which they proceeded to gorge themselves. 'That's what's known as a "baitball",' explained Mr Manning, who was practically levitating he was so excited.

The children were awestruck. Even Luke and Lucy were silent with wonder. Martine realized that her mouth was hanging open.

The *Sea Kestrel* anchored within sight of the beach, although the sand could not be seen for the crowds pouring down to the water. As the sardine shoal entered the shallows, the human tide tore into the sea, shouting and squealing, to fight over the feast with the birds.

There were children with plastic buckets, men with nets, pots, pans and even wheelbarrows, and women scooping sardines into the skirts of their dresses and handbags. It was pure frenzy.

Then, just as suddenly as it had started, it was over. The sardine shoal dropped out of sight and the whirling birds moved on. Only the dolphins remained, sated now but still milling around the ship as if they were waiting for something.

'Martine,' said Mr Manning, 'could you do me a favour and fetch my binoculars from the prow? I left them on the bench close to where we were talking.'

Martine was too overwhelmed to reply but she nodded and wandered unsteadily towards the front of the ship, trailing her fingers along the rails. She was halfway there when she noticed that some thirty dolphins had separated from the pod, and were moving along the side of the *Sea Kestrel* in the same direction she was. When she reached the prow, they congregated below her. The ship was at anchor, so Martine put the binoculars to her eyes and leaned over the rail to study them. She wondered what they were up to.

The dolphins were fuzzy through the lenses of the binoculars, but she adjusted the focus and their grey faces and pink mouths popped into view. Every one of their faces was turned upwards, and they were all clicking and whistling at once. Martine took the glasses from her eyes to see who or what they were chattering to, but no one was there. They appeared to be talking to her!

'What do you want?' Martine called down to them,

bending over the railings. 'What are you asking me?'

Aware that she was keeping Mr Manning waiting, she began to stroll slowly back to the other end of the ship, keeping her eyes on the dolphins. To her amazement, they followed her again. She was so absorbed that she didn't see Mr Manning until she slammed into him. Several of her classmates were gathered around him, staring at her with envious disbelief.

'Extraordinary!' Mr Manning said. 'This is my eighth Sardine Run and I've never seen anything like it. It's almost as if you were a sort of dolphin Pied Piper. I mean, why would they follow you like that?'

Out of the corner of her eye, Martine saw the dolphins slip beneath the sea's rocking blue surface.

'I think it was coincidence,' she told him. 'There were some fish jumping around the prow and the dolphins just happened to go there at the same time as I went to get the binoculars. Then they returned at the same time too.'

'Yes,' said Mr Manning doubtfully. 'Yes, I suppose that must be it.'

9

L ate afternoon on their fifth day at sea, the wind began to make a keening noise like a pack of wolves. By dinner time, every heave of the ship sent crockery and knives and forks smashing and clashing, and orange fish soup stains were splattered across the tablecloths. It was hard to walk, let alone keep the food which had gone down from coming up again, and not everybody made it through the meal. Sherilyn was the first to go, triggering an exodus as she raced green-faced for the exit, after the rolling ship and the discovery of a squid eye at the bottom of her bowl proved too much for her.

Soon there were only a handful of children at the

tables. Above their heads, light bulbs tinkled in their holders and misshapen monster shadows chased one another around the walls. Martine, who felt fine, didn't fancy being trapped in a cabin with a seasick Sherilyn, nor did she want to hang around the recreation room where Claudius could be heard regaling anyone who would listen with stories about the time his family, who owned an ocean-going yacht which had once belonged to a Greek billionaire, had sailed through a hurricane in the Cayman Islands, 'The waves were sixty feet high! My father said, "Son, your hand's steadier than mine, so you take the wheel while I plot a course to keep us ahead of the storm's eye…"'

Grimacing, Martine ducked out of the door and turned left along the swaying corridor to the galley. She was just in time to see Ben disappearing down the stairs to the engine room, and she smiled to herself. This had become their ritual. Every evening after dinner, when everyone else was watching DVDs or playing board games, she and Ben were in separate parts of the ship talking to the crew.

Ben's father was a sailor and Ben adored boats and anything to do with the sea, so Martine knew that he'd be learning how the *Sea Kestrel* worked. She, meanwhile, had become firm friends with Alberto, bonding over daily breakfasts of bacon and banana rolls and after-dinner treats of crème caramel dessert or coconut cake.

On her third night on board Martine had been unable to sleep because, at dinner, Miss Volkner had told her that she absolutely had to join the rest of the class when they were snorkelling and searching for dugongs in Mozambique. She wasn't interested in excuses. After that the conversation at the table had moved on to shipwrecks and the many reasons ships sunk, so that by the time Martine reached her bunk all she could think about was the washing-machine wave engulfing her and water pouring into her nose and mouth.

She'd tossed and turned for what seemed like hours before giving up and creeping quietly out of the cabin, taking care not to rouse Sherilyn. Alberto wasn't in the galley but she'd found him up on deck, smoking and looking out over the inky sea.

'You look very troubled for one so young,' was the chef's comment.

Martine denied it at first, but after a long pause she said, 'Alberto, were you ever afraid of the ocean or even just, you know, of deep water?'

The chef smiled ruefully. 'Many times I have been scared on the dhows, the sailing boats which we use in the Bazaruto Islands. Many, many times. As a boy, especially. But my grandfather was a fisherman. One night a cyclone swept through the islands of Bazaruto, uprooting palm trees and whipping up waves as big as houses. The dhow he was on overturned, leaving him and four others in the sea, but the dolphins – *mathahi* we call them in our language – they surrounded them and protected them from the sharks. After this time I was afraid no more.'

He studied Martine kindly. 'The *Sea Kestrel* is a big, solid ship,' he said, in case she thought otherwise. 'It would take a bomb to sink her.'

They'd gone down to the galley after that and Alberto had made her a mug of malted Milo, which he'd heated in a pot on the stove. Martine had felt a bit shy because the chef was a virtual stranger and yet there she was in her pyjamas, about to tell him things she couldn't even admit to her grandmother. But she knew instinctively he wouldn't think any less of her for them.

When the hot, sweet Milo gave her courage to speak, she said, 'I don't know what's wrong with me, Alberto. At Sawubona, the game reserve where I live, I've ridden my giraffe at night with lions, hippos and buffaloes. I've almost been bitten by a Cape cobra, escaped from poachers with guns, and been in underground caves with bats. Yet I've never been as afraid of any of those things as I am of deep water. I loved the Sardine Run and I especially loved the dolphins, but I just don't feel at home on the ocean. I was okay when I thought I wouldn't have to go in the sea, but this evening Miss Volkner told me that I absolutely have to go snorkelling when we reach Mozambique, and I'm scared that something will go wrong and I'll drown because I'm a terrible swimmer. Alberto, I'm the worst swimmer in the whole school.'

'I would be afraid of a giraffe if I saw one,' Alberto replied, somewhat confusingly.

Martine was puzzled. 'Why? Giraffes are the gentlest animals in the world. They'd never dream of hurting anyone. Not unless they were trapped, or threatened, or protecting their young.'

'I'm sure you are right but I have never been close to any wild animal, apart from whales, dolphins and

275

dugongs, and I have never been in a safari park. I would be afraid because it is all unknown. You are afraid of the sea because you don't understand it. It is not familiar to you. So you shall know about it.'

On the night of the storm, Martine sat on the stainless steel bench in the galley, swinging her legs and listening to Alberto talk about what she thought of as 'island-craft.' Tendai had taught her bushcraft – vital tips and tricks to help her understand and survive the natural laws of the African savannah, and in some ways the chef did the same for the marine environment of his homeland.

'On Benguerra,' he said, bracing his legs against the rolling of the ship, which seemed to be worsening by the minute, 'the children of fishermen learn from their earliest days to catch fish in many different ways, because their fathers believe it will teach them to know the sea's secrets and be grateful for the gifts that it provides. So they send each child out to catch his or her own pilot fish, a small fish which hitches rides with large fish like they are buses. When they find this pilot fish, they tie a fishing line around it and send it out to sea. When it attaches itself to a big fish, they reel it in, eat the big fish and set the little one to work again!'

Alberto liked to hear about life on Sawubona as well, so Martine told him about Tendai and about Grace's traditional medicine and her wonderful cooking. Alberto's local witchdoctor, a young male *sangoma,* was very different to Grace. According to the chef, he spent more time in a football shirt than a feather headdress, and had never been known to say no to a lethal moonshine called palm wine. Alberto told her a story about a villager who'd once gone to him with a skull-splitting headache. The footballing witchdoctor had started the treatment by putting a large pebble into his fire. While it was heating up, he blended herbs in a bowl made from a special wood and engraved with a cross, then added water. When the stone was red-hot he dropped it into the bowl, causing the water to boil and turn green. After making a series of tiny incisions in the man's forehead, the witchdoctor rubbed in a little of the herb potion and sent him home with the remainder in a bottle and the wooden bowl on his head.

'From that day on, no more headaches,' Alberto said with a grin.

Martine expressed what she hoped was the right amount of respectful admiration, while privately thinking that Grace was clearly a better traditional healer by miles, since her remedies were not based on hocus-pocus like putting bowls on people's heads, but had been tried and tested by all the grandmothers going back hundreds of years. She cast a critical eye over Alberto's smooth brown forehead. 'Do *you* go to the witchdoctor for headaches?' she asked.

Alberto chuckled. 'No, I prefer to take an aspirin.'

He was interrupted by a thunderbolt so ear-piercing it

sounded as if the *Sea Kestrel* had collided with an iceberg. The ship bucked wildly. Martine flew off the stainless steel bench and hit the tiles with a painful smack. A split second later, a stack of plates sailed off a shelf and shattered against the bench in the exact spot where she'd been sitting. A confetti of sharp ceramic chips showered spikily down on her head. Alberto helped her up, dusted white flecks of plate from her hair, and checked her for cuts and bruises, but he was no longer laughing.

'Miss Martine,' he said darkly, 'this is like the cyclone that nearly stole my grandfather. I have work to do to secure the galley. You must go now and stay close to your friends and your teachers.'

The ship was tossing violently and both he and Martine were holding onto the bench for support. Martine felt a mounting sense of alarm. Unbidden, the shark and dolphin cave painting came into her head. What if she'd been mistaken and the picture had not been about the Sardine Run or the incident at Shark Alley? What if the prophecy was yet to be fulfilled?

She said to Alberto, 'What makes you think this is a cyclone? Surely it's just a bad storm, and you told me that this was a big, solid ship. You told me it would take a bomb to sink her.'

Just then, the siren began to wail.

10

In the corridor, frightened children in puffy orange lifejackets were streaming up to the deck. Some, like Sherilyn, were a ghastly colour. They wore pyjamas with the buttons done up wrong and dressing gowns with trailing cords and one boy had on a lone leopard-print slipper. Others had flung on mismatched clothes in clashing colours and had sticking-up sleep hair. Only Lucy, immaculate in a white tracksuit with a red trim, looked as if she was on her way for a lesson at the tennis club. Most of the girls were crying.

Miss Volkner and Mr Manning were doing their best to keep everybody calm by telling them that this was nothing more than a routine safety procedure and they'd be back in their bunks in no time.

'Walk, don't run,' ordered the teacher, trying to make herself heard above the racket of the siren. 'No, Boysie, you can't bring your suitcase. You want what? Yes, you can bring Pooh Bear.'

Martine darted unnoticed through a side door. Her survival kit had been around her waist for the entire duration of the trip, as she'd promised Tendai it would be, but she'd taken it off to shower before dinner and had forgotten to put it back on again. In the event this was a real emergency, she wanted it with her.

The siren's insistent blare had shut off and the cabins were eerily quiet. Martine was reminded unpleasantly of a ship disaster film she'd watched with her parents. She took the survival kit from behind the locker where she'd hidden it and tied it securely around her waist. Then she put on a windcheater. As a sort of tribute to Grace, she'd put the forlorn remnants of her plant in a blue mineral water bottle Alberto had given her. The bottle had toppled over and was lying in a puddle on the floor. Martine wrapped the leaves in Ben's bandana again and added them to her survival kit. She felt a little silly doing it, but there was something about the wisp of plant that made her feel connected to Grace and Sawubona. The last thing she did was take off her shoes. She always felt better barefoot. She was on her way to join her classmates when she heard voices coming from the recreation room.

'But don't you think we should go up to the deck?'

Luke was saying. 'What if it's serious? What if the ship is sinking and we miss getting on the lifeboat? And anyway, won't they take a roll call?'

Claudius laughed. 'Please tell me you're kidding. You are kidding, aren't you? This is a drill, that's all it is. Or maybe it's just some teacher who knows nothing about the sea getting into a panic over a breeze and a bit of rain. This is nothing compared to some of the storms I've been through on our yacht. There's no way I'm going out there and getting drenched to the skin for nothing. I'm going to stay where it's warm and dry and watch a film.'

'Look, I'm sorry but I have to go check on Lucy,' Luke said apologetically. 'Even if it is only a drill, she'll still be scared.'

'Hey, no hard feelings,' Claudius told him. 'See you in ten minutes.'

Anxious to avoid being seen by either boy, Martine skipped nimbly up to the deck. She was almost flattened by the force of the storm which lunged at her out of the night. In seconds, her jeans were soaked through. Luke pushed past her, shielding his face from the onslaught. He leaned into the wind and headed for the prow, where the rest of the children were gathered in a dripping bunch, outlined against the torrid sky. They appeared to be receiving emergency evacuation instructions from a couple of crew members. Lucy threw her arms around her twin and handed him the lifejacket she'd been keeping for him. Even through the rain and from a distance, Martine could see how ecstatic she was to see him, and she thought how great it must be to have someone who loved you unconditionally no matter what. That made her remember Jemmy and she was glad that at least one creature on earth loved her that way.

Unconditionally.

Miss Volkner and Mr Manning emerged from the doorway behind Martine. 'You've checked every cabin?' Miss Volkner was saying. Her red curls waved madly in the wind. 'You're absolutely sure there's nobody left below deck?'

Martine wondered what had become of Claudius. As much as she disliked him, she knew she should tell Miss Volkner he was planning to stay in the rec room for the duration of the storm. But before she could say anything, the teacher let out a startled shriek, 'Martine, *where* is your lifejacket? Where are your shoes? Lord, give me strength. What are you doing here? Why aren't . . . ?'

The rest of her tirade was drowned by the screech of splitting metal. Jake Emery, who had been leaning over the edge of the ship, transfixed by the raging sea, jumped back, a horrified look on his face. A section of rail had torn loose and was swinging like a gate in the gale.

Grace's words came back to Martine. 'Beware of the boat-fence.'

The boat-fence! Of course! It was the railing around the ship. How could she have been so blind? How could she have missed something so obvious? The railing was going to be the cause of a catastrophe.

Martine started forward but Miss Volkner grabbed her by the arm. 'Oh, no you don't,' she cried. 'You're not going anywhere until you've got a lifejacket on.'

Martine tried to twist away but Miss Volkner was surprisingly strong. 'The guard rail,' Martine screamed in the direction of the kids near the prow, cupping a hand over her mouth. 'Get away from the guard rail!'

But the wind and the roaring sea swallowed her words and the only one to look her way was Ben.

The ship pitched sharply. Miss Volkner lost her balance and was forced to let go of Martine to save herself. The children near the railing went down like dominoes. Through slanting sheets of rain, Martine saw Ben start towards her. She blinked and he was gone.

She blinked again but he was definitely gone.

Concerned that he might somehow have fallen overboard, Martine leapt out of range of Miss Volkner's clutching fingers and started running along the slippery deck, ignoring her teacher's enraged shouts. The pelting rain stung her face. Beneath her feet, the ship rolled and shuddered, and foaming crests of waves shot so high above the sides of the ship they might have been tsunamis. Two sailors were untying the lifeboat. That's when the severity of the crisis really came home to Martine. If the storm didn't abate soon, she could end up living her nightmare.

She rounded the ship's funnel and stopped short. Two figures, one large and one much smaller, were wrestling in darkness, lashed by the driving rain. Claudius and Ben!

'Give it to me, you little runt,' panted Claudius as he wrenched at Ben's lifejacket, trying to pull it off by brute force.

Ben wriggled out of Claudius's desperate grip and held up a hand in a gesture of surrender. There was a faint smile on his lips. The look he gave the bigger boy spoke so many volumes that it rendered Martine, who'd been about to intervene, temporarily paralyzed. Mainly it was a look of pity. It was a look that said, 'If you want this lifejacket so much that you're prepared to do this terrible thing, you need it much more than I do.'

Then he unzipped the orange vest and handed it to Claudius.

Claudius snatched it from him without a word, pulled it on over his tubby frame, and stumbled away into the rain-swept night. Martine went up to Ben. She was sickened by what she'd seen. She wanted to rush after Claudius and pound her fists against his meaty back, or rant to Ben about how evil he was, but she knew Ben wouldn't appreciate either. So she just said, 'Don't worry, I don't have a lifejacket either,' which she knew was a bit lame because why would it be of any comfort to him that she, too, was without a safety vest?

The same thought must have occurred to him because his mouth curled up at the corners and he replied, 'Well, that's okay then!'

Another tsunami-like wave rose into the night, its crest glistening like shaving foam. Martine remembered that she was supposed to be trying to move everyone away from the railings. Hurriedly she told Ben about Grace's warning and together they pushed into the teeth of the gale. Their progress was slowed by the sheer volume of water swilling around their ankles.

They were within reach of their classmates when the ship dipped so steeply it seemed certain it was going to upend. One moment Martine was straining to stay upright on the waterlogged deck, the next, the deck wasn't there. The momentum of their run carried her and Ben helplessly forwards and they collided with the tangle of bodies. There was a screech of tearing metal and the entire rail gave way. Next time Martine looked, some of the children didn't seem to be there any more.

Before she could fully comprehend what was happening the deck was dropping away again. Once more Martine had the feeling that time had slowed to a crawl. First she grabbed at a steel post in a bid to save herself. It came away in her hand. Secondly she took in that the din on the boat – the slashing rain, the roaring sea, the screams and yells – was hurting her ears. Finally, Martine noticed that the two girls in front of her, the last line of resistance between her and the witches' cauldron of ocean, had lost their grip on the slippery edge and were on their way overboard.

Then time speeded up again and she was plunging after them, tumbling headfirst into the darkness, and the seething, sucking sea was reaching up to claim her.

11

*C*oncrete. That's what went through Martine's mind. When you hit water from a great height, it feels like concrete. It almost winded her. The icy shock of it blasted the remaining air from her lungs and before she knew it she was spinning helplessly into the jet-black deep, dropping like a human anchor until she was sure she'd hit the ocean floor, 10,000 leagues under the sea. Then, just as suddenly she was shooting up again, flailing, spitting saltwater, gasping for breath.

Already, the ship was further away than she could ever have believed was possible, but it was still within reach. She could see people scurrying around the deck. They were throwing lines and lowering a lifeboat. A weaving searchlight illuminated pale heads bobbing in the surrounding sea. Martine struck out in their direction but her clothes and the survival kit weighed her down and restricted her movements, and she could have been a cork on a rapid for all the impression her efforts made on the treacle-black waves. She went to unbuckle the pouch but something stopped her. 'Keep your survival kit with you for when you most need it, little one,' Tendai had told her, 'when you need it to survive.' He hadn't said anything about what to do if the kit supposed to save you was dragging you down to the bottom of the sea, but there was no denying that this was a survival situation if ever there was one.

Martine was panic-stricken. She yelled for help, but it was a feeble yell because she was beyond the arc of the searchlights and she knew with nauseating certainty that they wouldn't be able hear her on deck; that if she couldn't reach the boat before the waves obscured her, she'd be left alone in the raging ocean in the middle of the night, waiting to drown or be eaten by sharks.

Fear lent her energy. She started to swim again. To distract herself, she did her best to imagine she was competing in the school gala, but that only reminded her of how she always came last. So she put her head down and concentrated instead on doing one stroke at a time. When she judged she must be nearing the lifeboat, she stopped and trod water. Her chest constricted with shock. The ship was a fast-shrinking square of light on the horizon! Martine wiped the salt water from her eyes and, when a swell lifted her up again, squinted into the darkness. But there was no mistake. The current and the huge waves had swept her away. At least a mile lay between her and any hope of rescue. She was on her own.

Battling to stay afloat, Martine started to cry. Breaking down went against everything she knew about survival, the most crucial part of which was staying calm and not giving up, but she couldn't help it. It would take a miracle to save her now. Already, she was completely exhausted. She'd swallowed gallons of seawater and she was so cold she didn't know which was going to get her first, hypothermia or the sharks that lurked in the depths below. She could imagine them circling in preparation for charging at her the way the Great White had hurtled at Norm in Shark Alley, their deep-set, dead eyes on her flapping white limbs. She tried to paddle more slowly and to tuck her legs up, to minimise the area of flesh they had to attack, but all that happened was that she sank.

Terrified, she clawed her way to the surface. She was almost there when there was an explosion of bubbles and a shining streak passed her – a sort of oceanic shooting star. Then it swooped the other way. Martine tried to focus, to see it through the darkness and rain, but the whale-tail strength of the waves shoved her back and forth and she caught only glimpses of a long, swiftly moving shape, glowing with some unearthly light.

Instinct told Martine that if she could only reach the shining thing it would mean survival. But she kept sinking. No matter how hard she struggled, it stayed tantalizingly out of reach. And with every passing second the chill was numbing her limbs, making the sea seem heavy, as if she was swimming through snow. She was so tired that she knew she wouldn't be able to fight for much longer. Soon she'd have to stop paddling and then . . .

The edges of Martine's vision wavered and darkness closed in.

It was Cornwall she remembered first. A spring day on Porthmeor Beach in St Ives, before the summer madness when the tourists came. Martine had been standing on the apricot sand, reaching for a honeycomb ice cream mum had bought her, when a fat seagull had swooped down and snatched it. But her dismay had quickly turned to laughter. While the seagull was gloating over its spoils on a nearby rooftop – sending ear-piercing screeches in their direction – another seagull had reached over and swallowed the cone in a single gulp! By then Martine and her dad had decided that it was too chilly for ice cream anyway, so the three of them had spent the rest of the afternoon scoffing warm scones heaped with strawberry jam and clotted cream in a cosy harbour café, watching the tide spill in around the rainbow-painted fishing boats.

Martine remembered it as a day of perfect happiness.

Other memories followed, flickering through her head like a well-loved home movie. There was the magical night on the game reserve when she'd woken from a dead faint to find the white giraffe towering over her, his coat shimmering like sun on snow, his silver patches tinged with cinnamon; the exhilaration she'd felt the first time she rode him – the way they'd swept across the moonlit savannah, Jemmy galloping with a rocking-horse stride.

Next, and as vividly as if it was happening then, Martine felt electricity crackle through her just as it had when Grace placed a hand on her forehead on the day she arrived in Africa. 'The gift can be a blessing or a curse,' the *sangoma* had warned her. 'Make your decisions wisely.'

The scene changed and Martine relived the horror of the fire and the last time she saw her parents, when her father had hugged her goodnight and told her he loved her. She'd been about to go into her bedroom when he'd said, 'You have to trust, Martine. Everything happens for a reason.' And afterwards she'd thought how odd it was that he should say it then, at that precise moment.

Last – and as if she was watching from above – she saw herself as a baby. She was in her mother's arms in the living room at Sawubona. Mum was holding her up to the window so she could glimpse the animals – lions beside zebras, leopards beside springbok, baboons beside warthogs – lined up along the game fence, their eyes trained on the house. 'See that, beautiful girl,' Veronica murmured. 'That's your destiny.'

Then, almost imperceptibly, she had added, 'But not if I can stop it.'

Gradually Martine became aware that she was being raised to the surface of the sea by something immensely strong and yet infinitely gentle, like angels' wings. A blast of stormy air hit her face and shocked her back to life, and then she was coughing up seawater and sucking oxygen into her burning lungs. She was draped across something solid and slippery. For a minute she lay there, grateful for the opportunity to rest and breathe and be partially out of the freezing water. Then the solid thing moved. Martine, who'd been idly speculating she had happened upon a piece of floating wreckage or, miracle of miracles, the lifeboat, nearly passed out with fright. She struggled upright. The clouds cleared from her vision and she realized that she was holding onto a large dorsal fin.

A shark! She was sitting on a shark!

Then a nose poked above the water and emitted a few clicks and squeaks, and Martine was filled with an intense relief. In spite of her predicament, she laughed out loud. She'd been rescued by a dolphin. All of a sudden it didn't seem so bad that she was in the middle of the ocean in the middle of the night, with the ship long gone. She wasn't sure what was going to become of her now, but whatever it was it had to be better than being snacked on by sharks.

Even as she was congratulating herself on this piece of good fortune, a movement in the blue-black water caught Martine's eye. A dorsal fin cruised slowly by. She tried to see it clearly. Surely it was another dolphin? Surely it was a friend, come to join her saviour? But the dorsal fin began to circle and soon it was joined by a second fin and a third, fourth, fifth and sixth. In a matter of minutes, she and the dolphin were ring-fenced in a deadly shark corral. Martine was already shaking with cold and exertion, but now she began to shiver so violently at the thought that she might, after all, be torn apart in a feeding frenzy of Great Whites (Greg's talk about their many good qualities had failed to reassure her) that she was worried she might slip off the dolphin. And anyway, what was to prevent her newfound friend from darting away to save itself, abandoning her to her fate? But the dolphin stayed with her, although it made squeaks of alarm at the encroaching sharks.

Suddenly the sharks melted away. Nothing happened for a moment and then, over the sighing of the sea, Martine heard a tremendous splashing. What she saw next took her breath away. Through the wild waves came what must have been 100 dolphins, their silhouettes outlined in silver. They were leaping, dancing and cavorting, and their silvery arcs, freeze-framed against the midnight ocean and the scudding storm clouds, were beyond beautiful. Martine sat perfectly still, awed by the spectacle. As they drew nearer, she could hear them communicating with one another and it sounded to her like music; like singing. And whether or not it was her imagination, she fancied they were singing in Xhosa, because their clicks were not dissimilar to the lovely clicks made by African singers she'd heard. And that, strangely, calmed her and made her feel that somehow, some way, she'd be all right.

The dolphins surrounded Martine in their dozens and opened their smiling mouths and squeaked and whistled, almost as if they were greeting her. That was amazing enough, especially because they allowed her to reach down and stroke their satin skins, but then Martine noticed that several of the dolphins were transporting passengers. The other kids! Most seemed barely conscious. A couple cast desperate glances in her direction, blinked in acknowledgement and resumed their frozen postures on the dolphins' backs, sobbing quietly.

Martine counted five figures, but as far as she could tell, Ben wasn't among them. What if he hadn't been saved? What if he was lost at sea? What if he was gone forever? She tried to imagine life without the boy who, in the shortest possible time, had come to mean so much to her, and was taken aback by the pain that suddenly speared her heart. After all, it's not as if she really *knew* him. Ben wasn't someone it was easy to get to know. She always had the impression that he was watching the world from some peaceful place inside himself.

Martine was so busy agonizing over Ben and whether or not she could have interpreted Grace's clue sooner and prevented the whole disaster that she didn't notice a new dolphin entering the ranks of those around her until it actually nudged her foot. Ben was slumped on its back. By the look of him, he was drowned, or very close to it.

'Ben!' cried Martine hysterically. 'Ben, wake up! Oh, please be alive. Please be alive.'

When he didn't respond, she shook him hard. She was so afraid that this was to be her fate – to lose everyone she ever cared about – that she forgot everything she knew about First Aid. Ben sat up, startled, his eyes glazed. She could see him trying to make sense of the scene around him. Perhaps he, like her, had dreamed he was somewhere else. Slowly his expression began to register the same incredulity Martine had experienced as he took in the fact that not only was he surrounded by dolphins; he was on the back of one. Then he saw Martine herself. Wordlessly he reached for her hand. He made no effort to disguise how frightened he was, nor how happy he was to see her, and that made Martine cry again, and for a while they just rode along like that, holding hands.

After a while Martine felt shy, which she knew was ridiculous under the circumstances, but she let go of his fingers and said, 'What time do you think it is?'

Ben managed a weary smile. 'Why, have you got an appointment?' But he went on quickly, 'We can probably work it out. It was about nine-thirty when the siren went off, and we've probably been in the water for two or three hours. Judging by the position of the moon, I'd say it's between midnight and one in the morning.'

Martine fell silent again and the two of them concentrated on staying awake so they could watch over the others. After a while the numbing cold and the easy rhythm of the dolphins and the endless, rolling ocean, almost flat now that the storm had passed over, had a soporific effect. They began to murmur to themselves about mirages they glimpsed of palm-fringed islands, or steaming bubble baths, or rescue parties bearing mugs of hot chocolate and thick, soft blankets, so that when a lighthouse did actually loom into view – atop a hulking dark outline of land, ragged with palms – they thought it was just another mirage.

The dolphins slowed and stopped. When their passengers didn't respond, they deposited them unceremoniously in the shallows. And even when the seven frozen figures felt solid sand beneath them, even then they couldn't believe it was real, because the rocking motion of the sea had infused their bodies, and they still felt as though they were floating. It was all any of them could do to crawl beyond the fringe of surf, which they did without speaking, the stronger ones helping the others. Then they collapsed on the darkened beach.

Martine's muscles were so sore and wobbly that those final few steps were the most arduous of the night. The air was fragrant and balmy, but the chill had penetrated to the very marrow of her bones and her teeth chattered uncontrollably. When she could go no further, she toppled onto the pillowy sand. Ben dragged her a bit further, beyond the tide's reach, and then he flopped down a few feet away from her. As weak as he was, there was something about his presence which made Martine feel protected. Moments before she lost consciousness, she whispered to him, 'Ben, weren't you afraid of dying?'

'No,' he said quietly. 'I was afraid of not living.'

Martine fell into a sleep which was closer to a coma, with the palm fronds rattling like wind chimes in the breeze and her head full of the dolphins' song.

· 12 ·

M artine woke to the soothing swish of sea and the sun on her skin. It flowed into her grateful bones like hot honey. She tried opening her eyes but her lashes were crusty with dried salt and at first all she saw was a beach strewn with untidy heaps of clothes and a few life-jackets. Then one of the heaps started snoring. Claudius! Martine couldn't believe it. As if she hadn't been through enough. What had she done in her life to deserve being stuck on a desert island with Claudius?

Further down the beach, Sherilyn was lying on her back, wearing pink pyjamas. Her mouth was open. Her fluffy, polka-dotted dressing gown was gone. On her left was Jake Emery, his lanky, athletic limbs curled into a foetal ball, and on the other side was Lucy Van Heerden, her pale blonde hair splayed over the sand. A large orange crab was making a home in it. Martine debated whether to remove it, but couldn't summon up the energy. Further along the beach lay the sprawled figure of an African boy. Martine's eyes wouldn't cooperate enough for her to be sure, but it looked like Nathan Nyathi. He, too, appeared to be asleep. Her gaze shifted to the last item of clothing and she saw that that was all it was, an item of clothing.

Ben! Where was Ben?

Some of the terror of the previous night returned to rob Martine of what little reserves she had. She scrambled to her feet and stood rocking, her head swimming. The beach felt as unsteady as the deck of a yacht. Gradually the dizziness passed and she took a few steps, wincing at the stiffness in her muscles. Her lips, too, were cracked and swollen. She had a raging thirst. Her jeans and top were still damp on the side where she'd slept on them and her hair was matted with gritty sand. Her stomach growled loudly. She longed for a shower, a coffee, and two or three of Alberto's bacon and fried banana rolls, but those were clearly out of the question. Ben, she had to find Ben.

She began to walk along the beach, and it was only then that her mind unfogged sufficiently for her to take in her surroundings. The sand stretching out before her was of the purest white, though the early morning sunlight gave it a rose glow. It was so clean that it squeaked underfoot as if mice or a litter of puppies were nestling beneath it. Palm trees followed the long, lazy curve of the bay. The turquoise sea was as translucent as bath water. Martine could see a big blue starfish drifting along the bottom of it. In the distance, she could hear the dull crashing of waves, but the water in the bay was tranquil and idyllic, suggesting it was ringed by a coral reef.

But it was the island itself that really got Martine's attention. It didn't look like the sort of island one saw in photographs of Mauritius or the Caribbean. It was a mix of mountainous sand dunes, regular African bush and lush, low-lying greenery, as though the deserts of Arabia had been joined up with Sawubona. A lighthouse was perched on the highest point. There were no obvious signs of human habitation, but the lighthouse was very encouraging. Martine had a dim recollection of coming round briefly at some point during the night and seeing a yellow beam flashing from its tower. If there was a lighthouse with a working light, surely that meant there was a lighthouse keeper?

Martine reached the end of the beach without seeing any sign of Ben. She was staring up at the Everest of rippled chestnut sand, trying to pluck up the courage to return to her fellow castaways and appeal to them to form a search party, when he came tripping over the top of the dune. His black hair was wet and shiny and he was wearing frayed denim shorts, which he'd manufactured somewhat haphazardly from his jeans. Shirtless, he looked slimmer than ever, but his arms were strong and his chest and stomach were ridged with muscle. With his burnt caramel skin, he looked as if he belonged to the island; as if it was his natural home.

'Breakfast,' he called to Martine when he saw her, dipping his chin at the stack of green coconuts he was holding in his arms. He slid the rest of the way down the dune and dropped them at her feet. 'Only one small problem – I haven't been able to find a way to remove their outer husks. They're very tough and fibrous and bashing them against rocks barely makes an impression.'

Martine was so taken aback by the sight of him – particularly since he looked and spoke like a boy on his summer holidays and not like the survivor of a harrowing ordeal – that she was silenced. A concerned frown came over Ben's face and he had to ask her twice if she was okay before she managed to get out, 'I have a knife . . . maybe we can use the knife to cut off the husks?'

Then it was Ben's turn to look astonished as he realized that, not only was she still wearing her pouch, it was a survival kit. He watched wide-eyed as she turned out the contents for him to see, showing him the matches, Swiss Army knife, fishing line, compass and Grace's potions. Everything had stayed clean and dry in the waterproof pouch but the leaves were badly wilted. Their days were numbered.

Ben couldn't believe she had carried them all the way from Cape Town. 'Are they important? We might be able to save them.'

'What are we going to save them with? Coconut milk?'

Ben laughed. He'd cut the husk off the first coconut and now he pierced three little holes in the top of it and handed it to Martine. 'Drink this and I'll show you.'

Martine had never appreciated any liquid more, although it wasn't as coconutty as she was expecting and was really quite sour-tasting and fermented. Still it was wonderfully soothing to her cracked lips and parched throat. When she was done, she broke the brown-bristled shell against a rock. The moist coconut meat inside was sweet and moreish. With every mouthful, she could feel the energy returning to her limbs.

Ben nibbled at his while he worked at de-husking the remaining coconuts. Martine watched, wondering how he'd managed to scrub up so well in the sea. She felt very self-conscious beside him. Her salt-stiffened hair was sticking up like a punk-rocker's Mohawk and she was quite certain she smelled like a day-old haddock. She was very relieved when Ben put the coconuts in the shade and said that he had something to show her. She followed him up the high dune with difficulty, the soft sand sinking like snow beneath her feet, her muscles protesting.

Over the other side, the ground was firmer. Ben led her through palm groves and trees draped with tropical creepers, walking with an enthusiasm she was far from sharing. She plodded behind him, feeling breathless. Her head hurt. Colourful birds skittered through the leaves, but Martine barely noticed them. She was remembering what Alberto had told her about all the snakes on the Mozambican islands.

'Ben, I don't understand why you're so cheerful.' She was unable to keep the frustration out of her voice. 'We nearly died last night, and now we're marooned on an island in the middle of the Indian Ocean. It's a disaster and you're acting like we're on vacation or something.'

'I'm not happy because we nearly died last night, I'm happy because we're alive this morning,' Ben explained. 'I'm happy because the dolphins saved us, which is sort of a miracle, and because we've already found two of the things we're going to need to survive. Obviously, I'd rather be eating breakfast on the *Sea Kestrel,* but whatever happens now it'll be an adventure. A real adventure.'

'You said we've found two of the things we need to survive. We've found food. What's the other thing?'

They'd reached the edge of the trees. Ben stepped aside. Before them, fringed with reeds, was a small lake. 'This,' he said.

'Is that really . . . ?' Martine was reluctant to put what she saw into words in case it, too, turned out to be a mirage.

'Clean water? Well, no, not exactly, but it is fresh water. Just to be on the safe side, use the bandana to strain it into one of the gourds from that monkey apple tree before you drink it, but I'd say it's pretty pure. It's definitely pure enough to bathe in. You'll need to be careful, though. Mozambique has lots of freshwater crocodiles and this kind of habitat is perfect for them.'

Martine, who'd been so eager for a drink and a bath that she'd been poised to leap into the shallows, fully-clothed, decided that cleanliness was not a priority after all. She'd had enough problems with sharks; she didn't need new nightmares about crocodiles. 'Maybe I've had enough of being in water for the time being ... ' she began.

She stopped. Ben was holding his nose.

'Okay, I take the hint,' she said crossly, 'but if I get attacked by a crocodile, you're going to have to answer to my grandmother.'

As soon as the words were out, it hit her that she'd been so preoccupied with searching for Ben and thinking about how hungry she was and how much her head hurt, she hadn't taken in that there was no guarantee she would see her grandmother or her beloved white giraffe ever again. It was heart-breaking to realize that her grandmother's last memory of her might be of their fight, and that Jemmy would never understand that something had happened to prevent her returning to him. He'd think she'd abandoned him.

Ben saw the anguish on her face and his own sobered. 'Listen, if there's a way off this island, we'll find it, I promise. You *will* see your grandmother and Jemmy again, and I *will* see my mum and dad. But I have a feeling that the dolphins have brought us here for a reason. It's up to us to figure out what that reason might be.'

· 13 ·

Twenty minutes later Martine was drying off in the sunshine at a respectful distance from passing crocodiles and marvelling at how rapidly she'd recovered from the previous night's trauma once she'd had a drink of water and washed the salt and grit from her hair, when there was a blood-curdling screech.

Ben came running out of the trees. He'd climbed up to the lighthouse while she was bathing. 'Do you think one of the girls is in trouble?'

'Oh, I think Lucy probably just found a crab nesting in her hair,' said Martine.

Ben gave her a quizzical look, but didn't ask how she was so sure.

Martine used a gourd to trickle water onto Grace's wilted leaves. She'd found a home for them and the thread of root which bound them together in the fertile soil near the lake. On the one hand there didn't seem much point in trying to revive them, but on the other hand they were symbolic of Grace and Sawubona. It was as if a little piece of both was here on the island with her. That made the scrap of plant as important as her survival kit.

She felt like a new person after her wash and a few gourd's full of water. Her headache had gone. She'd used the knife to cut her jeans into shorts like Ben's, and washed her T-shirt and sweatshirt. They were still a little soggy but the sun was so warm she didn't mind.

As they wandered back to the others, Ben told her about the lighthouse, which was derelict, although solar panels and a timer kept its beam working at night. Alas, there was no friendly lighthouse keeper and no working radio. The only useful thing he'd discovered was a piece of broken sign. It was written in Portuguese but in the centre was a partial word in bold letters, 'BAZ . . . '

'Bazaruto!' breathed Martine. 'I bet you we're on one of the Bazaruto Islands in Mozambique. We were about 100 miles from them at lunchtime yesterday so I guess it's possible. Alberto told me that there are six main islands and some tiny ones, but that they're not all inhabited. Trust us to have landed on an abandoned one.'

At the beach, they collected the coconuts. Ben counted out five.

'Are you really going to give one to Claudius after what he did to you?' Martine asked, unsure whether to be impressed or disgusted.

Ben shrugged. 'It's only a coconut.'

'But you could have drowned without your lifejacket.'

'Yes, but I didn't,' was Ben's reply, and Martine could tell that it was his final word on the subject.

Their fellow castaways were in a huddle on the beach, red-eyed and bedraggled. Lucy was shuddering and inspecting her hair, strand by strand, for wildlife. Sherilyn was so distressed she was practically sitting on Jake's lap. A large orange crab was moving ponderously off towards the sea.

'Well, if it isn't Robinson Crusoe and Girl Friday!' Claudius drawled, but not before Martine caught the flicker of shame or perhaps fear (fear of exposure, she was sure) that passed across his plump gold cheeks. She couldn't look at him directly. It made her too angry. Ben might have been able to forgive and forget, but the sight of a rain-lashed Claudius trying to rip Ben's lifejacket from his body was not something she was going to forget in a hurry.

'Where have you been?' Nathan asked. 'We were starting to worry.'

'Were we?' Jake muttered.

Martine ignored him. 'We've brought you some breakfast,' she said by way of a reply, and she and Ben dished out the coconuts.

Squeals of delight greeted this news. Even Claudius managed a grudging, 'Thanks'. There were sucking noises as they swallowed down the milk, followed by a horrible hawking from Claudius as he spat it out. 'Ugh!' he said, wiping his mouth. 'That's revolting. Where's a soda fountain when you need one?'

He hurled away the coconut and it struck a rock and split open. The remaining milk leaked onto the sand. Grit covered the white meat.

Martine shot a look at Ben, but his face was impassive.

'Claudius, mate, that's not cool,' scolded Jake. 'One of us could have eaten that.'

'Get a grip, Jake,' Claudius said impatiently. 'We'll probably be off this island by dinner time. Provided the *Sea Kestrel* didn't sink—'

'Don't say that!' shrieked Lucy. 'What if Luke has been shipwrecked? What if our friends have all drowned?'

'—which is *highly* unlikely, as the captain would have sent a mayday call for assistance. As soon my father hears I'm missing, he'll launch the biggest air and sea rescue ever undertaken in Southern Africa. We'll be tucking into bacon double cheeseburgers in Maputo in under twenty-four hours. Two days, tops. All we have to do is survive till then.'

His friends looked encouraged, but not entirely convinced.

'What if we're not?' demanded Lucy. 'Have you thought about that? My brother will be going nuts wondering what's happened to me. You should have seen the look on his face when I slid off the edge of the *Sea Kestrel*. If I live to be a hundred I'm never going to forget how the sea looked like boiling black oil from above, but it felt like swimming in a freezer, and how hard it was when I hit it. I thought my back was broken or my head had split open or something.'

There were murmurs from the group as they relived their own nightmarish falls.

'If it weren't for the dolphins, we wouldn't be here right now,' Lucy went on. 'And that's great except that now we're stranded on some desert island in the middle of nowhere. If nobody finds us we'll probably starve to death.'

'It's hard to get lost these days,' Claudius assured her. 'The coastguard has very sophisticated search and rescue equipment.'

'I'm thirsty,' Sherilyn whined.

'So am I,' Nathan sympathized.

'We found fresh water,' Martine told them. 'There's a lake in the valley on the other side of the dunes. Also, Ben went to look at the lighthouse. The bad news is that, although it's a working lighthouse, it runs on solar panels. It's not operated by anyone. The good news is that while he was there, he found a piece of a sign. We think we're on one of the uninhabited islands in the Bazaruto Archipelago.'

'The Bazaruto Archipelago?' Lucy repeated. 'That's a huge tourist destination. Some friends of ours stayed at a luxury lodge on Benguerra Island. That means we're really, really close to civilization. The tourists who visit the islands go deep-sea fishing and cruising and snorkelling all the time. That's fantastic news. That means we'll definitely be rescued.'

'What did I tell you?' said Claudius with a confident grin. 'And since that's the case, I think Crusoe and his friend can find somewhere else to hang out until the rescue boats come. We don't get along with them at school. I don't see why we should have to put up with them on an island as big as this one.'

'But they brought us food,' objected Sherilyn.

'We did say thank you,' Lucy pointed out.

Martine was spitting mad, but she tried to follow Tendai's survival advice about not acting impulsively or making rash decisions. 'Don't you think we should stick together?' she asked, looking to the others for support. 'We're in a survival situation and we should really be helping each other.'

'I'm not being funny,' Lucy said, 'but have the two of you seen a mirror recently? You don't look as if you could cross the street safely by yourselves, let alone help anyone else. Ben doesn't even speak. I agree with Claudius.'

'So do I,' put in Jake.

Nathan and Sherilyn pretended that their mouths were suddenly full of coconut.

'That's settled,' announced Claudius. 'We'll call you when the search party gets here. Until then, stay away from us.'

· 14 ·

As soon as they were out of earshot of the others, Ben said, 'Phew, that's a relief.'

He set down the crab. Much to Sherilyn's horror, he'd scooped it up with his bare hands as they'd left.

'What do we do now?' asked Martine, biting her lip. She was as glad as Ben to be away from the others, but she found it difficult to share his holiday spirit. Tendai had drummed into her that a group of lost kids had more chance if they stayed together, and the first thing this group had done was split.

She was also quite shy. In the two months that Ben had been her unofficial best friend, she'd never actually done any best friend things with him, mainly because she only really saw him at school and he never talked there. Plus, she was not exactly up to speed with best friend etiquette, never having had a best friend before apart from Jemmy.

'I think Claudius and Lucy are right about one thing,' Ben said. 'It's very likely that we'll be rescued, if not by the coastguard then by a tourist boat or some local fishermen. But we can't count on it being a day or two. It might take a couple of weeks, or even a month. We need to survive until then.'

A couple of weeks, or even a month. The reality of their situation hit Martine and a curious thing happened. A calmness came over her. She thought about Grace and the Bushmen paintings on the cave wall, 'Only time and experience will give you the eyes to see them,' the *sangoma* had predicted. Martine had seen them when she was supposed to. That meant that, whether she liked it or not, this was her destiny. This African island, with its fairy-flossed dolphins and squeaking white sand and clear, azure waters. And she owed it to Grace, who had counselled her on her gift, and Tendai, who'd spent hours patiently teaching her the secrets of the African landscape, as well as to Jemmy and even to her grandmother, to return safely to them. She had to wake up, be positive and prepare herself for whatever came next.

She smiled at Ben. 'Should we start by making a shelter?'

His eyes lit up. 'Do you fancy building a fort up at the lighthouse?'

311

Before leaving the beach, Martine filled her sweatshirt with coconuts and helped Ben search for more crabs. They found five large orange ones and a blue and white one with a shell like a willow-pattern plate. 'Sorry, fellas,' Ben said as he bundled them into his windcheater, pincers waving threateningly.

They didn't have a container so they stopped at the lake and drank as much water as they could. The long climb to the lighthouse meant scaling the high, honey-coloured sand dunes. It was torture. Every stride Martine took created a mini-avalanche, causing her to slip two or three steps back. The sand fell away in sheets. The coconuts seemed to increase in weight as she went. Halfway up, one of the crabs crawled out of a hole in Ben's windcheater, which he had slung across his shoulders in a makeshift rucksack, and crushed his earlobe with its pincers.

'Ow!' he yelled, as his ear turned crimson. 'Ow!' He detached the crab with difficulty and returned it to the windbreaker, telling it that it would be the first to be eaten for dinner if it wasn't careful.

When they did reach the lighthouse, it was worth it just for the view – all Sahara-type dunes, green valleys and white beaches. Seen from above, the turquoise water was streaked with splashes of jade and ultramarine blue. The island itself was triangular in shape. Two sides of it were protected by reef, but the third was pounded by rough seas. Red cliffs reared over a rocky coastline, curving round to a calm bay.

The lighthouse had the year 1902 etched above its

entrance. The tower was more or less intact, but the building attached to it was in ruins and missing most of its roof. The concrete floor was cracked and the steps crumbled beneath their feet. Entire pine trees grew out of yellow fissures in the walls. Red hot pokers nodded in empty doorways. Pine needles whispered in the breeze.

Martine and Ben walked from room to echoing room, establishing which was the most habitable. Every window framed a spectacular vista, although the glass was shattered or gone. A smudge of an island – little more than a sandbar – was just about visible through the midday haze. Martine wondered if it was Death Island. One of Alberto's tales had been about a penal colony on Santa Carolina, centuries earlier. He claimed that at low tide the jailers used to take prisoners to Death Island, a tiny shell sandbar, and tell them that if they could swim the eight kilometres or so back to the mainland – a stretch of water cursed by vicious cross-currents and even more vicious sharks – they'd be exonerated. Needless to say, few did. At high tide the sea completely covered the island, and those who were unable to swim simply drowned.

Martine shuddered at the thought of lives so ruthlessly squandered.

'Ghosts?' Ben asked, and she nodded without saying anything.

They decided to sleep under the stars in the raised living area of what would have been the operating centre of the lighthouse, beside the room with the largest section of roof intact. That way if it rained they could quickly seek shelter. The room would also be useful for storing food during the sweltering days. Ben dragged a couple of rocks across the doorway and set the crabs free to roam around in the shade.

It was when the two of them started to stock their new home that they found they had skills which complemented one another. Martine had learned bushcraft techniques from Tendai and a little bit of islandcraft from Alberto, and Ben had learned how to tie knots and the basics of marine survival from his sailor father. So, for instance, while Martine knew that maintaining body heat in a survival situation was vital, and that one simple way to achieve that was to sleep off the ground, Ben was able to construct the low beds that she envisioned in her head, using a combination of bamboo and palm fronds. He tied them together with reef knots, aided by the strips of bark Martine had collected with her knife.

Of course, none of these things were exactly handy, and they required a further three gruelling trips down the dunes in the heat. While they were gathering bamboo, they discovered that there really were crocodiles. Ben had to do a long-jump-style leap to escape from the jaws of a gargantuan male.

On their last trip up the dunes, they carried four gourds of water, although admittedly they were only half full when they reached their destination. Martine was disappointed that the monkey oranges and cashew nuts Alberto had spoken of were not yet ripe because it was winter. She was absolutely ravenous, and had no idea how they were going to pluck up the courage to cook the innocent scuttling crabs.

While Ben built the beds, Martine tied a bundle of twigs together like the African women did at Sawubona, and swept the floor, choking on the thick dust. Then she gathered kindling and built a fire the way Tendai had taught her, making sure that there was plenty of space between the logs so the fire could 'breathe.' By that time the sun was setting and they climbed up into the old lighthouse tower and had a 360 degree panorama as the ocean turned seven shades of red. There was no sign of the others. Half an hour after the sun slid into the sea, it was dark. Martine, who'd been used to endless summer evenings in England, could never get over the guillotine speed of nightfall in Africa, or the impenetrable blackness of it.

With the 'switching off' of the sun, the temperature plummeted sharply. Night birds and bushbabies began to call and cry out softly from the trees. Martine and Ben picked their way carefully down the lighthouse's steep spiral staircase. In their absence, the fire they'd built had burned down to coals and the warm glow of them lent a homely feel to their living area. They put more wood on it and sat close to toast their arms and legs, which were aching after the assault of the past twenty-four hours.

At length, Ben gave an unhappy sigh and went off to deal with the crabs. His father had taught him how to end their lives humanely, but he was still very reluctant to do it. However, without food their own days would be numbered.

'I thought you were a Buddhist,' said Martine when he

returned. 'Don't Buddhists believe that all living things are sacred, and that nothing should be harmed or injured in any way, not even mosquitoes?'

'Haven't you heard the Buddhist story about the crab?' Ben asked, placing the crabs on the edge of the coals. 'They're pretty crafty. Once upon a time there was this crane living beside a pond packed with fish. Every day he ate until he was stuffed but he found that no matter how many he gobbled, he was never satisfied. He became convinced that if he could somehow eat every single fish in the pond, he'd be truly content. First, though, he had to get them all out of the water. So he told the fish that he knew of another, much more beautiful pond, where he'd be more than willing to carry them. One by one, they believed him, and one by one, they climbed into his beak and were eaten. Eventually, he was so full he could hardly fly but then he noticed he'd left behind a crab. He couldn't bear the thought of such a delicious treat going to waste so he offered the crab a ride to the pond.

'But the crab was smart and told the crane that he knew all about his tricks with the fish and that he had no intention of being devoured. However, he did like the idea of being transported to a special pond. He agreed to go on condition that he could ride on the crane's back, with his pincers around its throat. They were almost at the pond when the crane's greediness got the better of him and he tried to trick the crab into getting down off his back so he could eat him. The crab was so angry that he cut off the crane's head with his pincers, just slicing it off "like a knife through butter!" '

'Charming,' said Martine. 'Maybe I won't have crab for dinner after all.'

Ben grinned. 'That's all right. More for me. Actually Buddhism does allow the eating of meat; we're just not supposed to cause pain. I'm a bit of a mix, though, because I'm also half Zulu and some Zulus believe that fish are from the snake family and that the eating of them is forbidden. But Dad is a sailor and sailors love fish and the sea, so we go fishing together and we eat what we catch. Mostly, though, we do try to eat food that doesn't hurt animals. Buddhists believe that animals are equal to people, although the crabs probably wouldn't take my word for that.'

The night had a winter nip to it and they bent as near as they could to the fire. When the crabs were cooked they used a rock to pound the shells and ate the fleshy white meat with crystals of sea salt they'd found in a dried up rock-pool, followed by more coconut for desert. When the last morsel was gone, they sat in companionable silence and listened to the sounds of the island – the squabbling bushbabies, the whine of the occasional mosquito and the far away hiss of the sea. Behind the windowless frames of the lighthouse, the sky was a curtain of stars.

It wasn't long before Martine's eyelids began to droop with exhaustion. She lay down on the low bamboo frame, rested her head on a pillow made of palm leaves, and fell asleep thinking it the most comfortable bed she'd ever slept on.

15

Over the next two days, Ben and Martine explored every inch of the island – except, of course, the beach where the others were camped out, which they'd named Runway Beach because that was where they'd landed. Martine found it hard to get used to the mix of tropical and African scenery, although there was no denying it was beautiful. There were great, gnarled marula trees alongside coconut palms and hibiscus flowers, and crinkled brick-coloured cliffs towering over rocky beaches or snowy sands over which translucent crabs scampered. And surrounding it all was the sea with its fizzing shades of washed-out blue, like ink dropped on watercolour paper.

At the top of the wind-rippled dunes, they found hundreds of heavy white shells, fossilized and catacombed with minuscule holes. Ben made up a funny story about them being carried there by a prehistoric bird as big as an ostrich. There were also black clay and glass beads which they supposed had been left by the Arab and Portuguese traders, and on the beach itself there were Pansy shells – white, eggshell – delicate creations etched with the petals of a flower. Just around the peninsula, near the end of the cliff, were a stack of rocky shelves, overlooking a picturesque bay. They were not deep enough to be proper caves, but they were secluded and provided welcome shelter in the heat of the day.

The shelves proved a fine lookout point, but the two whole days passed without a single sign of humanity. They did see a couple of planes, but those were commercial aircraft flying so high they were mere specks across the sun, and Martine's tin lid signal would not have been visible to them. From the lighthouse it was possible to see that their classmates had written a huge SOS on Runway Beach, using dark rocks that showed up against the sand, in anticipation of the arrival of Claudius's father. They had also constructed a crude shelter from sticks and palm fronds, although every time the breeze wafted it collapsed. Once they saw someone – it might have been Jake – kicking it in fury.

At night-time the temperature hovered around zero degrees Celsius, but in the afternoons it was scorching hot.

'If this is winter, I don't think I'd like to try Mozambique in summer,' remarked Martine on the third afternoon, fanning her face with a palm frond. She had found a clump of aloes near the lighthouse and was using the gel from the leaves to calm her sunburn.

Ben was fishing on the rocks near the sea's edge, using the line and hook from the survival kit and crab entrails for bait. He had caught two bream, which he'd put in a shaded rock-pool where they could be easily retrieved later, and he was trying for another. But he was distracted. The water-level had dropped with the departing tide and the tip of a wreck had appeared on the edge of the reef. Ben was sure it was a Portuguese galleon. It reared above the crystalline waters.

'I've always wanted to look inside a real wreck,' he said wistfully. 'Imagine the stories it could tell. Imagine the history it's seen. It might even have been a treasure ship. There could be caskets of pearls and gold. Better still, they might contain old journals or maps. It's very unlikely because lots of other people would have investigated it before us, but you never know. We might find something that they missed. Oh, I can't wait to get home and tell my dad about it.'

Martine was fascinated by the wreck herself but she shivered at the thought of tackling the currents again. Bathing on the edge of the lake, or paddling in the clear island shallows, which were as non-threatening as Caracal Junior's swimming pool, was one thing, but never again would she put herself in a situation where there was even a remote chance she might be circled by sharks or fighting to breathe in deep, dark water. The ordeal of the storm was still too fresh in her mind. Her fear of the sea had become a virtual phobia. The wreck was on the edge of the open ocean. Who knew what lurked in the churning depths around it.

'Will you come with me?' Ben asked eagerly. 'I know it's a long way out but we'll be fine if we're together.'

Martine flushed. She wanted so badly to say yes to her friend because she knew how much it would mean to him, but it was impossible. 'I'm sorry,' she said. 'I just can't.'

Ben thought she was probably still traumatised by the storm so he did his best to hide his disappointment. 'That's okay,' he said. 'I understand.'

He went to cast his line again and a movement in the water caught his eye. 'Hey, look! The dolphins are back.'

Martine returned the fishing equipment to her pouch and then she and Ben waded into the bay. At first, the dolphins seemed too busy to notice them. They darted about like quicksilver in pursuit of invisible shoals, so lithe and graceful that it was almost as if upon entering the water they, too, became liquid. On surfacing, they exhaled in soft puffs.

Gradually, their inquisitive nature got the better of them and they swam nearer and nearer. One was bolder than the rest. He separated himself from the pod and sidled up to Martine. There were three V-shaped grooves on his dorsal fin and she recognized him as the dolphin who'd saved her on the night of the storm. He showed off a little, approaching her shyly and then gliding away to turn a few artistic backflips and somersaults. When at last he settled for lying on his side close to Martine, she tickled his chin and the area around his blowhole and pectoral fins. He enjoyed that so much that he rolled belly-up and allowed her to stroke his speckled tummy. His eyes were half-shut in ecstasy. He lolled in the water as if it were as supportive as an armchair.

Ben had seen plenty of dolphins on boat trips with his father, but until the night of the storm he'd never touched one. He, too, had been surprised by the satin-smooth texture of their skin. He also wanted to know how Martine had recognized her dolphin so easily, so she told him what she knew about dolphins' dorsal fins being as unique as giraffes' patches and human fingerprints. That jolted Ben's memory and he recalled that the dolphin who'd carried him had had cookie-cutter-shaped holes in her fins. Shortly afterwards, he spotted her.

'We're not going to hurt you,' Martine told the dolphins. 'You saved us and brought us to this place. We only want to get to know you.'

The dolphins picked up on the gentleness in her voice and her saviour-dolphin's willingness to accept her touch, and their last shred of reserve melted away. They came crowding around with rough trills and whistles.

Their dorsal fins were relatively easy to tell apart, so Ben and Martine decided to name them. Martine called her boisterous dolphin Sun Dancer, because of the way the light glinted on his back as he leapt. Ben christened his dolphin Cookie and another Honey because she had a golden tint in her silver-grey skin. Patch had white splotches on his back – the result of sunburn or battle-scars from a shark attack; Mini was small and elderly – a grandmother dolphin; Rain Queen appeared to be Sun Dancer's wife and Little Storm their baby; and then there were Ash, Steel and Thunder, three bright-eyed boys. They were also named after their colours, but it was their dorsal fins and cheeky faces which provided the real clues to their identity.

Ben had collected a few strands of sea grass and was playing a game of tag with Cookie, so Martine floated in the translucent water, eyes half-shut, and let the sunshine and the presence of the dolphins infuse her being. There were so many exquisite, ingenious and loveable animals on the planet – giraffes for starters – but dolphins, she felt, were different. They were like the chocolate of the animal world. You couldn't get enough of them.

Soon she sensed one of the dolphins approaching. She opened her eyes and saw that it was Little Storm. She stretched out her arms and opened her palms to show him there was nothing harmful in her hands. But the baby dolphin was wary. After each timid advance, he would swim away. He whistled at her a couple of times and Martine tried whistling softly back, experimenting with a song her father had taught her: 'Amazing Grace'. Little Storm mimicked her, and she could have sworn that he'd learned a couple of notes of it. Either way, it seemed to soothe him. He swam up to her and laid his face in her palms, and they floated in the buoyant water looking at one another. For Little Storm, it was a gesture of supreme trust. For Martine, it was unforgettable.

Later, as she and Ben paddled to the shore, Martine said, 'We should name this bay so it can be our special place even after we leave here.'

'Why don't we call it Dolphin Bay?' Ben suggested.

So Dolphin Bay it was.

That evening, Ben cleaned, gutted and filleted the fish from the lake, and Martine picked a few banana leaves in which to wrap them while they cooked, as she'd often seen Tendai do. Unfortunately, the bananas themselves were not yet ripe. They built a new fire and warmed up while they waited for it to burn itself out and turn the wood into coals. Only then did they put the fish on.

Laying her damp survival pouch near the fire to dry, Martine was reminded of her classmates who didn't have matches and faced a third long, cold night, probably without dinner. That made her feel guilty, even though there was no real reason she should since it was she who had attempted to keep everyone together. Earlier that day, while she and Ben were laughing and fooling around with the dolphins, Martine had spotted a couple of figures watching them from the palm trees. When next she'd turned her head, they'd gone. She'd told herself that they could be having fun as well if they'd chosen to, but it was hard not to feel bad.

'I feel guilty, too,' said Ben, guessing her thoughts. 'But I'm trying not to.'

Their supply of firewood was running low, so they left the fish to cook while they went out to find more. They gathered anything combustible they could find and put it into a single pile. For the first time since leaving Sawubona, Martine felt something close to happiness – or at least as happy as it's possible to be when she didn't know when, or if, she'd see Jemmy again.

Her mum and dad would have been proud of how she was adapting, managing, surviving. She hadn't given a thought to being rescued for hours. Being on the island and around dolphins had certainly made her feel differently about things. She was forced to exist in the moment. To take each day as it came. Hopefully some of it would rub off, so that when she did eventually get back to Sawubona, she and her grandmother would work everything out. They would hug and make up. It would all be okay.

When she and Ben had collected enough kindling, they climbed back up to the lighthouse under the blazing white light of a full moon. Far below them, the ocean spilled out like a wizard's cloak, dark blue and speckled with sparkles. The smell of barbecuing fish wafted through the air.

'I wonder what the others are doing?' Martine said, her words muffled by the armful of timber she was carrying. 'I bet you anything *they* haven't managed to catch any fish. I wonder what they're planning to eat tonight?'

Ahead of her, Ben stopped so suddenly that she ran into him. He put down his wood. 'I think we're about to find out,' he said.

Jake and Nathan were sitting in front of the fire in the lighthouse, white flecks of fish dotted around their mouths. Sherilyn's cheeks were so stuffed that she resembled an especially greedy hamster. Lucy and Claudius were reclining on the low bamboo beds. They looked as though they were waiting to be fed grapes.

Jake was the first to spot the aghast faces at the door. 'Hi guys!' he said. 'Thanks for the great dinner. We really appreciate it. Who knew you could cook like that?'

Sherilyn spluttered something unintelligible.

'Even I have to admit that it was pretty good,' Claudius added more coherently. 'Full marks. And this is even better . . . ' He reached under the bed and pulled out the survival kit.

'Leave that alone!' cried Martine. She went to fly at him, but Ben's hand shot out and grabbed her wrist and he held her there, struggling.

'Oooh, temper, temper,' mocked Claudius, and the others laughed. He unzipped the pouch and began pulling out its contents. 'I've been having a rummage through this and it's unbelievably useful. Were you a Brownie in a past life, Martine? Look at this – a knife, matches, fishing line . . . Everything anyone could need on a desert island.

It's almost as if you knew you'd be ending up on one.'

'Give it back to me,' demanded Martine. '*Please.*'

Claudius gave a dramatic sigh, as if the decision were out of his hands. 'Sorry, Martine, no can do. This stuff is very handy.'

Nathan seemed embarrassed but he didn't say anything.

'*Ja,*' said Jake, 'you didn't share with us, so why should we share with you?'

Martine was outraged at the injustice of this accusation. She and Ben had worked like Trojans to create a warm shelter and catch fish for their dinner, and now the others were going to reap the benefits of their labours. It was so unfair. She looked to Ben for support, but none was forthcoming. If anything, he seemed ever so slightly amused.

'You were the ones who didn't want anything to do with us,' she reminded Jake. 'We did want to share stuff with you but you told us to stay away.'

'Yes,' agreed Claudius, 'but you didn't mention that you happened to be carrying a Girl Guide pouch. If you had, we might not have been so hasty.'

Martine was fuming. She lunged at him in a last-ditch attempt to snatch her survival kit, but Ben was too fast for her and he pulled her out of the lighthouse and along the path.

'Let go of me,' said Martine, panting. She wriggled out of his grasp and stood glaring at him. 'Why didn't you *do* something? How could you just let them get away with taking everything from us – our food, our shelter, our survival equipment? What are we meant to do now? Why do you have to be so nice all the time? You're ten times faster and fitter than Claudius. You didn't have to give him your lifejacket on the ship. You could have saved my survival kit if you'd tried. But no, you did nothing. What's worse, you wouldn't let me do anything. Don't you know that sometimes you have to fight for what's right?'

Without a word, Ben began to walk away.

'That's right, just run away,' Martine said scornfully. 'You can't even stand up to a girl. It's true what everyone says about you. You are a wimp. You're pathetic.'

Ben froze in his tracks. He turned around slowly and the lighthouse beam fell on his face. Martine saw the terrible hurt in his eyes.

'What did you want me to do?' he asked quietly. 'Did you want me to hit him? Did you want me to attack Jake or Nathan or even Lucy? Why? Because they were hungry and ate a bit of fish? Because they saw an opportunity for some easy shelter and took it? The sea is full of fish and the island has plenty of shelter. When did fighting ever solve anything?'

Martine didn't answer. She felt as if she was standing outside her body looking down on herself. She knew she was behaving badly but she was powerless to do anything about it.

'I *do* fight,' Ben continued in his soft, steady voice. 'I fight every day to be allowed to be who I am. I just don't do it with my fists, or with words the way other kids do.'

Then he strode away down the dunes and was swallowed by the night.

16

It was an odd experience to be utterly alone. Martine felt like a pinprick in a vast, star-speckled universe, standing in a landscape as alien as the mountains of Mars. Every reference point she'd ever had was gone. Her mum and dad were dead. The new life she'd built for herself was an ocean away. Her new family had been torn apart. In a matter of a week, she had fallen out with her classmates; been unkind to her best and only human friend, a boy who had only ever been kind to her; and told her grandmother that she hated her. As a result, the loneliness she had been so scared of at Sawubona had come to find her here, in the loneliest place of all.

Martine felt a lot of emotions but the main one was shame. She wished that Grace was around to envelop her in a mammoth hug and say something wise, or that Jemmy was nearby to nuzzle her and make his musical fluttering sound, but another part of her felt that she didn't deserve a hug or a nuzzle. She listened, hoping to hear Ben's footsteps. But there was only the whisper of waves and the sad whine of the wind, which lifted grains of sand and stung her with them. She wanted to cry, but she knew that crying wouldn't help. People who felt sorry for themselves in survival situations tended not to last very long. She needed to get her head together and prepare for the long night ahead.

After a lingering look at the lighthouse, where the dancing light of the fire set the walls and windows aglow, she set off down the dunes. Her plan was to make her way to the rocky ledges above Dolphin Bay on the far side of the island. There she would be shielded from the worst of the weather and, with any luck, out of the reach of passing snakes or scorpions.

The part of the journey Martine found most unnerving was the walk through the copse of trees near the lake, where blustery sea winds threw leaping-panther shadows. She was too heart sore to be truly afraid, but she was definitely relieved when her toes sank into the squeaking sand of Runway Beach. It took another fifteen minutes to reach Dolphin Bay, and her muscles were quivering with tiredness by the time she climbed the slick rocks of the cliff. She was starving, too – not that she could have eaten a thing.

The ledge she chose smelled of bird's nests and fish bones, but it was dry and sheltered. Martine sat on the edge of it and gazed out at the moon and the glittering sea beneath it. There was some comfort in knowing that the same moon would be shining on the white giraffe and the other animals at Sawubona. And, of course, on her grandmother, who would probably be finishing dinner around now.

But Martine's other life, life at Sawubona, seemed a million miles away. She tried to remember how things were before they got so mixed up – before she upset everyone she cared about. That got her thinking about how small and petty the causes of arguments were. Mostly they came down to one person believing that they were more right than somebody else, or another person wanting what someone else had.

That's what had happened tonight.

She lay down on the rock but the hard, chilly stone made sleep impossible. She sat up again and that's when she heard it – a cough. It came from the next ledge, she was sure of it. Ben! Immediately Martine felt better. Even though they weren't speaking – even though Ben probably thought her the most monstrous girl he knew, it was good to have him near by. She wondered if he was as cold as she was and was jolted by an awful thought. Ben had no warm clothing with him. When they'd been gathering wood, he'd been bare-chested and in shorts, because she'd teased him about the goosebumps all over his body. And after the row at the lighthouse, he'd been so concerned about preventing her from getting into a fight that he hadn't thought to grab his T-shirt and windcheater as he went. Martine knew that if she was freezing in a T-shirt and sweatshirt, Ben would be feeling even worse.

For half an hour, she plotted and schemed about hiking all the way back to the lighthouse and snatching her survival kit or, failing that, a red hot ember which she could use to start a fire. Then she remembered something. During one of her attacks of guilt over their fellow castaways, she'd taken a couple of matches from the pouch with the intention of giving them to anyone except Claudius if the opportunity arose. But it never had.

She dug in her pocket. They were still there.

Minutes later, Martine was foraging along the shoreline in pitch darkness in a bid to find dried palm fronds, coconut husk, pieces of driftwood or anything else that might burn. It was horrible rummaging around blindly, not knowing whether a scorpion was about to sting her or a vengeful crab was waiting to crush her fingers with its pincers – she kept thinking of the crab in the Buddhist story, slicing off the crane's head 'like a knife through butter', but she persevered until she had two big piles of wood. Then, using her sweatshirt, she transported them back to the ledges.

Ben was curled up on the edge of the fluttering moonlight, bare shoulders against the bare rock. He was asleep. Goosebumps covered his body and his lips looked blue. As quietly as possible, Martine stacked the logs the way Tendai had shown her and lit the kindling. The flames crackled into life. Ben never stirred, but as the driftwood began to smoulder and the heat spread his skin regained its smoothness and he stopped shivering. Martine made one more trip down the rocks for extra wood, which she stacked close by. Only when she was satisfied that the fire would burn for most of the night did she return to her own ledge. She built herself a smaller version of Ben's fire and lay down beside it, tired to the bone. Not even the unforgiving rock could keep her from sleep.

It rained all morning. Martine sat under the overhang, watching the still, empty sea. Alberto had told her that in his youth it had never rained in the winter, but that this year there had been floods. She neither heard nor saw Ben. Around midday, she couldn't stand the suspense any longer and poked her head around the rocks. He was gone, although he had taken care to sweep the ash, coals and unburned bits of wood into a pile so that when he returned the embers beneath would be hot enough to restart the fire. Martine took that as an indication that he'd appreciated her efforts, but not that he'd forgiven her.

At lunchtime the rain stopped and the sky turned a milky blue. The birds celebrated with a burst of song. For a multitude of reasons, Martine did not want to encounter the lighthouse thieves, so she stayed in her shelter until hunger drove her out. Even then, she merely dashed to the nearest coconut palm for a couple of coconuts and dashed back. Removing the husks without the knife was a trial. Martine spent nearly an hour using a sharp rock to liberate the white flakes inside. But all she got for her trouble was a stomach ache. It didn't fill her up. She ventured down again to the rock pools and scooped up a tangled pile of slimy seaweed. After several failed attempts to cook it on the fire, she ate it as it was. It was salty, rubbery and completely vile, but it cleared her head and made her feel less tearful.

Mid-afternoon, the dolphins appeared in the bay and she decided to go down and talk to them. They would cheer her up. They would make her believe that absolutely everything was going to be all right. That Ben would be her friend again. That Gwyn Thomas wouldn't always be annoyed with her and wouldn't send her away from Sawubona. That she would see Jemmy again.

She was standing in the frothy fringes, adjusting to the water temperature, when she noticed that the departing tide had uncovered the wreck and it reared once more from the sea which had conquered it. It seemed to beckon to her. Miss Volkner had told the class that no less than eleven Portuguese galleons had been dashed to pieces on the rocks along South Africa's Transkei coast between the mid-16th and 17th centuries, and that many were thought to be treasure galleons. Ben had thought that this wreck might be one too, but now she would never know. She had turned down the chance to go out to it with him, and investigating the old galleon without him would be both pointless and insane. That was the thing about having a friend. You could do things that weren't really possible on your own. Friends made you brave. Friends made things fun.

Of course, fun was going to be in short supply from now on.

Unless . . . Martine swallowed hard. Unless she did something to win back Ben's trust. Something like . . . But no, it didn't bear thinking about. Venturing out alone to the reef, where the only thing holding back the full ferocity of the Indian Ocean was a fragile wall of coral, was not a risk worth taking. There was no telling what treacherous currents swirled around its edges, or what sea monsters lurked in the rusty carcass of the wreck.

But the thought wouldn't go away. Ben had been so incredibly excited at the prospect of finding a casket containing old journals, maps or bits of treasure. 'It's very unlikely,' he'd said, 'but you never know. We might find something they've missed.' Perhaps *she* could find something. Then she could present Ben with a ship's compass or a gold coin as evidence that his friendship was so important to her that she'd been prepared to overcome her worst fears to get it for him. Surely that would be enough to restore his faith in her?

But at the back of her mind two things kept nagging at her. What if she got into trouble in the water and nobody knew where she was? Worse still, what if the rescue boats came and nobody could find her, and they thought she was dead or lost at sea, and they went without her and she was left alone on the island forever? What then?

· 17 ·

The first sign that swimming out to the wreck might not be the best idea she'd ever had came when the dolphins kept blocking her path to it. They lay on their sides and squeaked and looked impossibly cute. They turned their bellies to the late afternoon sky and did dolphin backstroke. They did rolls and acrobatics and half a dozen other tricks.

Initially Martine interpreted it all as a game, but when the end result of everything they did was to prevent her from swimming in the direction of the reef, she became convinced the dolphins were trying to tell her that there was something dangerous there. Either that or they had become drunk on rain water, as the Tsonga believed they sometimes did.

'What are you trying to tell me, Sun Dancer?' she asked. 'What's wrong, Patch and Honey? Is there something bad out there? Are there sharks out there?'

Before wading out to the dolphins, Martine had made a trip to the lake to fetch a couple of reeds. In times gone by, warriors and hunters had used reeds as makeshift snorkels in order to cross rivers or approach enemies or animals undetected, and she was going to attempt to do the same while searching for treasure. She'd broken the reeds into pieces of varying lengths. After a brief experiment in the shallows, she'd chosen a medium-length one. Periodically, she scanned the beach for Ben in the hope that he'd come rushing over to stop her and to tell her that what had happened the previous night was a silly misunderstanding, and that *of course* he'd be her friend again. But the beach stayed empty.

While she'd been at the lake, a stiff breeze had picked up and now she watched as a wave from the open sea dashed against the reef, sending an avalanche of spray across the wreck. Martine's nerves combined unhappily with the stew of seaweed and coconut in her stomach. One false move and she'd be swept into the ocean.

She started to swim for the galleon, but again Sun Dancer blocked her way. The other dolphins crowded round her and, sad and frightened as she was, she couldn't help smiling. They had a way of looking at her that was very wise but also very childlike and cheeky. She suddenly realized that, far from being isolated, she was surrounded by animals, and that they would always accept her the way she was. That, even if every human being she knew gave up on her, or was angry with her, she would still have her gift.

It was a heartening thought and it gave her the courage she needed to kiss Sun Dancer goodbye, push him gently but firmly aside, and swim for the reef. Nevertheless, she found it disturbing that the dolphins refused to accompany her. It was almost as if there was an invisible line in the bay that they knew not to cross. Martine herself crossed that imaginary line with trepidation.

The wreck was much further than it had seemed from the beach, and Martine had to cling to its rusting side and rest for several minutes when she finally reached it. When she saw how close she was to the tumultuous waters of the Indian Ocean, her fear returned. At intervals, spray splattered the wreck and a powerful current tugged at her limbs. The insanity of her mission came home to her. Surely there were easier ways to win back Ben's friendship?

Still it seemed a shame to turn back, so she tested the reed again to be on the safe side. It was quite effective. It would have been nice to have a mask, but the water was so clean and the fish so brilliantly coloured it didn't matter.

As far as she could tell, the galleon had run aground on the reef and sunk right where it was. Martine wondered what had become of its crew. She understood all too well the terror they must have felt as white water plumed from the bottom of the boat. There would have been mayhem on board as men, doubtless the worse for wear on rum and without lifejackets, were swamped by the in-rushing sea. Had their caskets of pearls and gold – if indeed that's what they were carrying – gone down with them? Had they made it to shore? Had they ever been rescued? Or had their skulls become homes for fish and, over time, become one with the brain-like coral?

These macabre thoughts were pushed from her head by the otherworldly beauty of the reef. There were blue starfish and red and white ones; fat-lipped parrot fish in glorious shades of mauve, pink and purple; angel fish with yellow and black stripes; and a sprawling octopus which looked like a jellified cartoon ghost. Best of all, there were half a dozen turtles. They were a deep-brown with patterned cream grooves and they sailed lazily through their undersea world with their stumpy legs waving. It seemed impossible that such cumbersome creatures should float, but float they did, their prehistoric heads comically surveying their surroundings.

Slowing every now and then to suck in oxygen through her reed – which was easy enough so long as it remained perfectly upright, but punished her with mouthfuls of salty water when it didn't – Martine glided through the rainbow aquarium. She was surprised to find she was enjoying herself.

At a certain point, shafts of gilded light illuminated the jade depths and she guessed that the sun would soon be setting. She was about to give up her quest and return to the surface when a metallic glint caught her eye. She took a big gulp of air from the reed and dived down to it. As she neared it she saw that it wasn't the sunken treasure it had appeared to be from a distance, but a link in a thick cable. There was nothing old-fashioned about the cable. It was very modern and appeared to be very new.

Martine knew she should be getting back to the beach, but was reluctant to leave without investigating further. A cable suggested communications or electricity and there was always the possibility that it might be connected to something that could lead to them getting off the island. That would impress Ben as much as any treasure would have done. She returned to the surface for more air and swam down again. As she drew nearer to the cable, she spotted another metal band, then another and another. There wasn't just one cable; there was a whole grid of them! A virtual latticework of clear plastic tubing was snaking its way under the sea, tapering into the blue distance.

Martine was about to give one of the cables a tug when a manta ray came flapping towards her. Its black, diamond-shaped wings billowed out like a highwayman's cape. Martine knew that manta rays rarely harmed humans but its size was intimidating and she moved to one side so as not to be in its path. It changed direction and headed straight for her. She shifted again, but it kept coming. The closer it got, the less friendly it looked and the more it resembled a Stealth bomber jet she'd seen on the news in England. Its wings filled her whole vision.

Then it cannoned into her like a charging bull.

'Bl-bl-uhggh,' spluttered Martine as she was propelled to the surface, gagging on seawater. 'Bubblug-h-uhh . . . '

An instant later, there was a muffled, undersea explosion. The force of the blast had a water-cannon effect, flinging Martine upwards and outwards; but the ray caught the full impact. Bits of cartilage, tissue and manta ray skin rained down on the sea like lava.

Martine screamed.

Ben burst from the water beside her, frightening her almost as much as the explosion had done, 'Martine! Martine, speak to me. Are you okay? Where are you hurt? Here, hold on to me.'

Martine was in shock. She couldn't believe that a living creature had been blown apart right before her eyes. She couldn't stop shaking. Her ribs, where the manta ray had barrelled into them, felt as if they'd been through a crusher. 'B-Ben,' she finally got out, 'w-what are you doing here?'

'I saw you swimming out to the wreck and I followed because I was worried about you. But never mind about that now. Did you see what caused the explosion? Was the wreck booby-trapped? Did you touch something?'

'No. I mean, I don't know. I found these cables on the sea-bed and I was on my way to take a closer look at them when this manta ray knocked me sideways. It sort of came after me. Then there was just a bang and a blur of red and white. Oh, Ben, the poor ray. What happened? Was it a bomb?'

Ben was treading water, taking as much of Martine's weight as he could. Blood trickled from a gash on her upper arm, mushrooming into the water and then dissolving into nothing. Above the horizon, a washed-out sunset indicated that they had perhaps half an hour before the African night descended. 'It sounded like an underground mine of some kind,' he said darkly. 'We need to get you back to the beach fast. Do you think you can swim?'

A sudden, unnatural wave rippled across the surface of the sea inside the reef, which had become glassy again as if the blast had never happened.

'What was that?' panicked Martine, clutching at Ben's arm, and then they heard it, the snap of sails and the slap of a boat hull against water. A dhow appeared from around the other side of the island, bounding over the rolling waves.

'A rescue boat,' cried Martine. She raised an arm painfully and opened her mouth to shout.

'No!' Ben warned. 'Those might be the men who laid the mine. Dive deep *now!*'

The wind was strong and the dhow was approaching the mouth of the reef at speed. Martine had time for only one gulp of air before Ben pulled her beneath the surface. Seconds later, the sea boiled white and the dhow's rudder flashed over their heads. Had they moved any slower it would have smashed into them.

Ben swam strongly for the wreck, Martine behind him. The fading of the sun meant that the hulk of the galleon was barely visible underwater. It seemed a long way in the greeny dark. Martine had lost her reed in the blast and her lungs were on fire by the time she felt the ship's grainy side beneath her fingers. She and Ben surfaced cautiously and gasped for breath as quietly as they could.

The dhow had anchored and its sails were down. There were four Africans on board. Two were clad in shirts and trousers; the others were in wetsuits.

By now, a gloomy twilight shrouded the bay, and one of the divers produced a spotlight. He held it up with his right hand and pointed at the sea – which was gory with the remains of the ray – with his left. He said something in a dialect Martine didn't understand.

Ben strained his ears. 'He's saying that something big has died,' he translated. 'Probably a shark or a ray, but not a human being.'

The taller of the two men in shirt and trousers barked aggressively at the diver. He seemed to be questioning this verdict. The diver handed him the spotlight and picked up a spear-gun, and then he and the second diver flipped backwards off the boat. They entered the water with barely a splash. Ben and Martine looked at each other in trepidation. If the divers checked the wreck, they'd be discovered.

'Quick,' whispered Ben, 'up here.'

He clambered onto a ledge about as big as a shoebox and pulled Martine up beside him. They clung to each other for balance. Blood seeped from the graze on Martine's arm, trickling down her bicep. Salt had penetrated the wound and she winced at the sting of it.

The divers appeared in the water below them, the torches on their helmets lighting up the nooks and crannies of the galleon. A tickle came into Martine's throat. Her face turned red and her eyes began to water. The divers separated. One swam out through a hole in the ship's side to check the reef; the other swam directly beneath them. The tickle in Martine's throat was excruciating. Her whole face contorted with the unbearable itch of it. Finally it erupted in a combination cough-sneeze. The sound ricocheted around the wreck.

The diver's head popped out of the water. He had a spear-gun in his hands, cocked and ready to fire. He shouted through the echoing hull to the men on the dhow, apparently asking if they had heard anything.

Their reply was accompanied by laughter. From the sounds of things, they were making jibes about him hearing the voices of long-dead sailors.

The diver scowled. He was so close they could have bent down and touched him, but he was preoccupied with examining the underbelly of the wreck and it never occurred to him to look up. Satisfied that there was nothing more hostile there than a shoal of striped fish and a single bemused turtle, he tucked the spear-gun in his belt and sank beneath the water. There was a snap of cloth as the dhow's sails billowed. A minute later, Martine and Ben were alone with the wind and sea.

They swam back to the shore in darkness. All the way there, Martine kept thinking about what might have happened if Ben hadn't shown up. She could have panicked after the explosion and tried to get back to the beach before she was ready, got cramp and sunk to the bottom of the sea. She could have been kidnapped, or even shot with a spear-gun. She tried to thank Ben and to apologize for hurting him but he hushed her, telling her to save her energy for the swim. Halfway across the bay, the dolphins came fussing round. Martine hung gratefully on to Sun Dancer's dorsal fin and was given a ride in.

As she clambered tiredly up the cliff, it occurred to her that she need never be afraid of deep water again, because what, in the ordinary course of events, could possibly be worse than falling into a stormy sea from a great height, half-drowning in tsunami-sized waves, being circled by sharks, battered by a manta ray, and almost being blown to bits by an undersea mine? After this, the swimming pool at Caracal Junior would feel as safe as a bathtub.

Half an hour later, they were sitting by a fire on Ben's rock ledge, drying a slimy, unappetising heap of seaweed for dinner. It hissed and spat while Ben cleaned the graze on Martine's arm with fresh water he'd fetched earlier that day from the lake, binding it loosely with his red bandana. They were both deep in thought. The same thing was going through both their minds: What should we tell the others?

Should we tell the others?

Martine broke the silence. 'The ray saved my life,' she said suddenly. 'Somehow he knew what was going to happen. So did the dolphins. They tried to stop me.'

'What kind of people would plant an undersea mine in an area with so much marine life?' Ben said, with uncharacteristic anger. 'The ray must have swum into some sort of trip wire and detonated it. Somebody or some organisation has gone to a lot of trouble to make sure that something underwater stays untouched or undiscovered. The dhow was on the scene within minutes of the explosion. That means it was probably anchored, or sailing nearby. But what was the mine protecting? The cables or the wreck? Maybe there is buried treasure there after all.'

They were eating shrivelled kelp and pulling faces at the foul saltiness of it when a figure appeared at the far end of the beach. It was moving swiftly through the darkness, as if the person was running at tremendous speed.

Ben sighed. 'What now?'

Martine rolled her eyes. Whatever it was, it couldn't be good. As the figure neared the foot of the cliff, they saw it was Lucy. Her hair was flying in the sea wind. She scaled the slippery rocks and pulled herself weakly up onto the ledge. When she stepped into the firelight, Martine saw that she was a wreck. She bore no resemblance to the well-groomed, tennis-club girl she'd been on the ship. Her hair hung in rats' tails, her white tracksuit was filthy, and her eyes were spidery squiggles of red.

'It's Claudius,' Lucy said in a small voice. 'There's been an accident. We need your help.'

18

Claudius lay unconscious on the sand, so colourless and lifeless in the glow of the torch that if it weren't for the red weals on his belly, he would have blended into it. His face, lips and neck were swollen. His breathing was shallow and laboured. A short distance away from him was the Portuguese man-o'-war responsible for his condition, its top a clear, gas-filled bubble, its tentacles trailing like purple-blue spaghetti almost the width of the beach. It looked too pretty to be dangerous.

Jake was pacing up and down, periodically squatting beside his comatose friend, saying, 'Claudius, mate, you stay with us, you hear?'

Sherilyn was even more of a mess than Lucy. She was sitting on the sand in her crumpled pink pyjamas, wringing her hands. 'We're going to die here,' she said plaintively. 'I'll never see my mum and dad again. This island is going to kill us and all they'll find is our bones.'

The only person doing anything constructive was Nathan, who was going back and forth to the ocean's edge like an automaton, filling a gourd with seawater and trickling it over the weals on Claudius's stomach in an attempt to soothe the inflammation. Martine remembered her dad telling her that vinegar or urine were the best treatments for jellyfish stings, but the man-o'-war was a different species and had a reputation as one of the most venomous creatures in the sea.

'We thought because your dad was a doctor, you might know some first aid or something,' Lucy said in the same small voice to Martine. 'We've tried everything.' Shamefaced, she handed over the survival kit. 'We even tried pouring some of the stuff you had in bottles over the red patches but nothing worked.'

Martine could have wept. Grace's lovingly made potions had been wasted in the sand. The fishing hook and line was missing. Other items were covered in grit. She zipped it up so she didn't have to look at it, and knelt beside Claudius. As they'd run over, she'd felt many conflicting emotions about her tormentor, few of them good. She'd been quite sure that he was being a hypochondriac; that they'd get all the way across the island to find him faking some medical drama just so he could be the centre of attention. But those feelings and

348

doubts left her as soon as she saw him. It was obvious he was critically ill. He was straining so hard to breathe that the veins were practically popping from his neck and his pulse was so weak that Martine had difficulty finding it.

She tilted his head back to ensure his airways were clear, and stood up. 'There's nothing I can do,' she said. 'There's nothing any of us can do. He's had a severe allergic reaction to the sting. I think he's gone into anaphylactic shock. Unless he gets to a hospital fast, he'll probably die.'

Lucy went almost as pale as Claudius, Nathan threw his gourd into the sea and Jake swore softly. Sherilyn burst into tears again.

Ben said, '*You* can help him.'

Five mouths dropped open – Martine's, because she was so stunned to hear Ben break his silence in front of their classmates, and the others, because in the entire three and a half years they'd known him, he'd never uttered a syllable.

'What did you say?' Lucy said incredulously.

'I knew it!' Jake cried. 'I *knew* you could talk. I knew it was an act.'

'Shut up, Jake,' snapped Lucy. 'Claudius is about to die and all you can think about is yourself. Ben, what do you mean about Martine helping him? Martine, if you know a way to save him, do it. I know he's given you a lot of grief. We all have. I'm sorry about the lighthouse and I feel really bad about your survival kit. But can't you forget about that for now? If you help Claudius we'll make it up to you, I promise.'

349

'It's not that,' Martine told her. 'None of that matters now. Claudius needs treatment only a hospital can give him. He needs allergy medication or some antidote to the man-o'-war venom, and if his heart stops he's going to need to be resuscitated to get it going again.'

'What about that black magic thing you do?' Jake demanded. 'What about that thing you did with the goose at the Botanical Gardens in Kirstenbosch?'

Martine looked at him. She'd once healed an Egyptian goose with a broken wing during a school visit to the botanical gardens in Cape Town, but it was not a happy memory. The part with the goose was, but afterwards the group of kids who'd witnessed the healing – of whom Jake was one – had chased her with sticks, chanting, 'Witch! Witch! Witch!'

She snapped back to the present. 'I don't do black magic,' she told Jake. 'It's the opposite of black magic. Sometimes I help animals a little, that's all. I can't help people.'

'Yes, you can,' Ben repeated. 'You *can* help him.'

There was such conviction in the way he said it that Martine, conscious of what Ben had done for her that afternoon, knelt down beside Claudius without another word and laid her hands on him. Almost immediately her palms began to heat up, just as they had done with the goose and the dolphin, and she could feel a powerful energy flowing through her. But there was a problem. The energy went as far as Claudius's skin and then stopped as if blocked by an impenetrable barrier. Martine concentrated harder, but there was no improvement in Claudius's condition. If anything, he grew even paler and his breathing became more ragged. That's when she knew for certain that her healing gift was for animals and not for people.

So she thought about Grace instead and the wisdom of the grandmothers through the ages, trying to fathom what they would do if they were her. She remembered the night that Grace had come to her in the Memory Room in the caves at Sawubona and had given her a crash course in traditional medicine. Was there anything she had learned then that would help? Grace had spoken a lot about toxins and venoms, but there seemed to be hundreds of variations – poisons that attacked nerves or cells, or clotted blood, or shut down the immune system. It took years of *sangoma* study to get to grips with the antidotes. Martine had a couple of hours at most to find one for Claudius. Meanwhile, his hands, feet and face were swelling to elephantine proportions.

Grace had told her on the day she stopped the bus that when the time came she would know what to do, but Martine didn't. She didn't have the faintest idea.

She concentrated harder. Soon she began to feel light-headed and peculiar. The scene at the beach swam away and she saw smoke and Africans in animal masks and then, out of nowhere, a mental picture of Grace's plant sitting in the blue mineral water bottle in her cabin on *Sea Kestrel* came into her head.

The beach scene, with its deathly-still patient and circle of frightened faces, came rushing back to Martine. 'Is there another name for a man-o'-war?' she asked.

They stared at her blankly.

'Oh, please think. Does it have another name? Do they call it anything else?'

'Umm, uh, a bluebottle,' Jake answered. 'Some people call it a bluebottle.'

'The leaves,' she said to Ben. 'We need Grace's leaves.'

He was gone before she had finished the sentence.

19

Martine sat with her knees scrunched up, watching Claudius's chest rise and fall. For months, she'd thought him one of the most arrogant, unpleasant boys she ever had the misfortune of meeting. Now, as day broke muted and grey across a motionless sea, all she could think was how good it would make her feel if he woke up.

Little by little, Martine realized, the island was changing them. The evening before, Lucy, who'd never previously exhibited the slightest interest in anything other than fashion accessories, shopping and herself, had worked as hard as the boys to construct a shelter to protect Claudius from the elements, and then she had insisted on taking the first shift to watch over him, sitting up all night long before waking Martine shortly before dawn. Now she was asleep, spread-eagled on the sand, snoring faintly.

Even Sherilyn had pulled herself together enough to help gather firewood in the creepy-crawly-haunted darkness. But the biggest change was in Nathan, who was a city boy through and through and had always gone out of his way to avoid contact with wild beasts and the outdoors. At school, he was obsessively neat and had never been known to have a wrinkle or stain on his uniform. And yet he had volunteered to rise when it was still dark and go with Ben to try to catch fish without a hook or line. An embarrassed Jake had confessed to losing Martine's fishing equipment the first time he used it. He and his friends had eaten nothing but coconut for days. So Ben and Nathan were going to try an old islanders' trick to get some.

One of the Mozambican sailors on the ship had told Ben that, in the absence of line, island fishermen would sometimes crush the leaves of the lulla palm, spoon the juicy mixture into a rock pool and wait for the fish to become intoxicated. Meanwhile, they would block the fishes' exit to deeper water. When the fish were rolling drunk, the men would simply scoop them into a net, using sand to protect their hands from the spiky gills.

Since they weren't sure which, if any, of the species of palms that grew in groves on the island were lulla palms, the boys were going to take sample fronds from each and hope that the lulla was among them.

'We don't have a net,' Ben said, with a sly sideways glance at his assistant, 'but Nathan has already offered to give up his shirt!'

Nathan's squawks of protest could be heard halfway down the beach.Martine waved them off and returned to her unconscious patient. It had been a traumatic night. Ben had taken over an hour to find Grace's plant, because he'd been up at the lighthouse when she'd planted it at the lake, and he'd had great difficulty locating it by torchlight. By the time he reappeared with the leaves, Martine had got cold feet about squeezing their milky sap directly onto the weals on Claudius's stomach and legs. Then again, doing nothing could be disastrous. It was Nathan who eventually convinced her to take a chance on the leaves by suggesting the group make a pact. They would each put a hand on Martine while she was administering the sap so they all shared responsibility for the outcome. So that's what they did.

To begin with, the outcome had been as bad as it could possibly be. The weals on Claudius's skin had turned a horrendous colour in the firelight, and he had writhed and moaned in his unconscious state. Martine was quite sure she'd killed him. But after ten minutes or so the high colour faded and the weals had slowly begun to shrink. Over the next couple of hours, the swelling around his neck and face went down and his breathing became more regular. But he had remained unconscious throughout the night.

Now Martine was alone with him. Lucy and Sherilyn

had managed to sleep through Ben and Nathan's fishing preparations, and Jake, who was restless, had gone to the lighthouse to bring down anything that looked as though it might be useful until they could move Claudius. They were all trying to put a brave face on, but an air of desperation had hung over the group the previous evening. Nobody wanted to say out loud that they had been on the island for coming up to five days and they had not seen so much as a glimmer of a search party, tourist or fisherman. And with Claudius at death's door, Martine and Ben had decided that it wasn't a good time to mention undersea mines and spear-gun carrying divers at the wreck.

Martine wondered what was going to become of them. They were all so certain they were going to be rescued. But what if they weren't? What if the men on the dhow came ashore first? What if Claudius never came out of his coma?

It seemed to her that there were a lot of 'what ifs' on the island, and none of them were pleasant.

All at once Claudius's eyes flew open as if he'd been startled awake. He stared around in bewilderment. 'Mum!' he blurted out. 'Mum!'

'Claudius, it's me, Martine. You're still on the island.'

Claudius took in the reed shelter and the white sand and palm trees visible through the entrance and took a ragged breath. In a strange, raspy voice, he mumbled almost to himself, 'It looked so pretty in the water. I was swimming and I tried to catch it. It was like touching fire, only I couldn't get away from it. I was all tangled up in it. I felt as if I was being burnt alive. I was screaming at Jake because he was too scared to take it off me, and then I couldn't feel my legs any more.'

'It's okay,' Martine said, shaken. 'It's okay. You've had an allergic reaction to a Portuguese man-o'-war sting, but you're safe now. You're going to be all right.'

She tried a smile, and even that was an odd sensation because Claudius was not someone she'd ever imagined smiling at. 'Would you like some water?'

He nodded and she held a gourd to his lips and, with some difficulty, supported him as he drank. He lay back down again, facing the wall of the shelter, and was quiet for a long time. Martine thought he'd gone back to sleep and she dozed a little herself. She was awoken by a hoarse, 'Why?'

'Why what?' Martine asked sleepily, although she already knew what he meant.

Claudius rolled over. His cheeks were sunken and his skin tinged with yellow. 'Why did you do it? Why did you help me after the things I've done to you and Ben?'

There was no easy answer, so Martine just said, 'You were very ill. Anyway, it wasn't really me who helped you. It was Grace. She's a traditional healer. She gave me the plant which cured you.'

'Well, she shouldn't have!' Claudius burst out, his voice strained and unsteady. '*You* shouldn't have. I don't deserve to be cured. I wish the dolphins had never saved me. I wish I was dead. You saw what I did to Ben on the ship. I'm a coward.'

Martine had spent a lot of hours thinking much the

same thing, but when Claudius said it himself, she saw that Ben was right. He deserved pity not contempt.

She shook her head. 'We've already forgotten about that.'

It was a lie, but if ever a lie could be justified it was now. 'Everybody does silly things when they're frightened,' she consoled him. 'Anyway, you're not a coward. You were the least scared person on the *Sea Kestrel* at the start of the storm. I heard you telling Luke you were going to stay below deck and watch a film while everyone else was panicking up above. And you helped your father sail your yacht through a hurricane in the Cayman Islands. That takes real guts.'

Claudius said brokenly, 'It isn't true about the yacht, you know.'

'What isn't true? You mean you don't really have a yacht?'

'*Ja*, we have a yacht. And not just any yacht, we have a yacht which once belonged to one of the richest men in Greece. No, I mean it's not true about the hurricane, or about my father asking me to take the wheel. My dad doesn't know one end of a yacht from another, and even if he did, I'm the last person he would trust with it. I did see a hurricane when I was in the Cayman Islands, but it was on the news in our hotel room. Our windows were lashed by wind and rain and the palm trees were bending double, but we were never in any danger. The eye of the hurricane never came within fifty miles of us. A father and son came on the television and talked about how they'd battled the storm in their little boat, and the father was so proud of his son's heroism I decided to pretend that their story was mine.'

He looked away. 'I spend a lot of time watching TV in hotel rooms when my mum and dad are out at cocktail parties with their rich and famous friends. Those kinds of people don't like kids around, especially fat ones.'

Martine pictured her own life at Sawubona – the campfire breakfasts with Tendai where he would talk to her about bushcraft and Zulu legends; the newly-cut-grass scent of Jemmy and the feel of his whiskers when he nuzzled her; the homely evenings with her grandmother when they'd celebrate the successful rehabilitation of a sanctuary orphan with a special African dinner. She realized then how fortunate she was. Yes, she'd lost her parents, but they'd given her more love than many people had from families who were with them for a lifetime. And her grandmother constantly showed Martine that she cared with actions, even if she couldn't always do it with words.

'Is that why . . . why you're not very nice to us?' she asked Claudius. 'Because you're unhappy?'

'Is that why I bully you, you mean? You can say it. No, I give you a hard time because you're the opposite of me; because I envy you. Because your life seems so simple, and because you don't seem to want, or need, anything apart from your white giraffe and your friends at Sawubona. Because even though Ben doesn't speak, it's obvious that you're there for each other. You *care* for each other.'

Martine was stunned. 'Look,' she said, 'my life might

seem perfect to you, but you wouldn't believe how many people I've managed to upset or disappoint over the past few weeks. I've even hurt Ben – the nicest person I've ever met. But, earlier this year, when the white giraffe was stolen because of something dumb I did, somebody told me it's never too late to fix things.'

Claudius gave a tired laugh. 'I'm not sure about that. Anyway, now that you know the truth about me, you can take your revenge. Go on. Tell everyone what a loser I am.'

Nathan's dark head came round the door of the shelter. He thrust forward a bamboo pole with five fat fish speared on it. 'Ta-dah!' he trumpeted. His eyes widened when he saw that Claudius was conscious. 'Is everything okay in here? We heard voices.'

'Everything's fantastic,' Martine assured him. 'Claudius has just woken up. He was wondering if anyone has had a chance to go to McDonald's yet? If not, he says some coconut milk and a fish barbecue breakfast would be perfect.'

20

The revival of Claudius changed everything. There was no longer any separation between the seven of them, and nobody suggested that there should be. It was agreed that they would all sleep on the beach until Claudius was well enough to climb the steep dunes, and then they would all stay together in the lighthouse.

Martine had spent a good proportion of her school days in solitude, and had never been involved in any team sports (vacancies on netball and hockey teams at school had an uncanny way of being conveniently full when she applied to join them), so it was a novel experience for her to be part of a group, especially since she was a very appreciated part because of what she'd done for Claudius.

'It's not me you have to thank; it's Grace,' Martine kept saying to everyone. 'She gave me the plant.'

'Yes,' said Sherilyn, 'but you guessed what the leaves were for. You kept them alive. I mean, when you put them in that bottle in our cabin, I thought you were a fruitcake.'

One of the first things Martine discovered about being in a group was that, while at school you could fool yourself into thinking you knew people really well because you saw them every day, you never actually knew them until you had to live with them.

Take Sherilyn. Martine had always thought of Sherilyn as being nice but a bit dim, and had taken it for granted that she came from a cereal-box-perfect family living behind electric gates in a suburb packed with other cereal-box-perfect families. Yet she couldn't have been more wrong. It turned out that Sherilyn's actress mum had walked out of the house when Sherilyn was one and her brother and sister were two and three, and hadn't been seen since. For the past seven years, Sherilyn had been living with her dad, siblings and Thai stepmother in one of Storm Crossing's most bohemian, multi-cultural neighbourhoods.

As a consequence of her step-mum's influence, she had become quite a good cook. Nobody had found that out until now because Sherilyn had spent a lot of her time on the island homesick, weeping and trying to escape from crabs and insects. Also, for the most part, there hadn't been any food for her to cook or any fire for her to cook with. Now she had both. Claudius's near-death experience had made her pull herself together and she was determined to contribute. There was limited fare on the island but Sherilyn worked wonders with what there was. It was she who recognized the grizzled old tubers in a store-cupboard in the lighthouse as cassava, a root vegetable. Jake improvised a pot for her using bulb protectors from the lighthouse. She boiled the cassava and mashed it and served it up on banana leaves, accompanied by fish cooked in coconut milk and flavoured with wild chillies, herbs and green lemons. They ate it with their hands and somehow that made it extra tasty.

The fish were provided by Nathan and Ben, their chief fishers. There wasn't too much to discover about Nathan, who was sweet but dull and would probably grow up to be an accountant, but he was very likeable and a good person to have around. He was never going to be a nature-lover, but he did enjoy fishing, and once, when he and Ben had come across a bees' nest in the hollow of an old tree, he'd unexpectedly revealed that his uncle was a beekeeper. Before anyone could stop him he was smoking the bees out of their hole. He earned a great, dripping wedge of honeycomb and two stings for his trouble.

Lucy, meanwhile, had recovered her airs and graces – something Martine found weirdly comforting. She spent a lot of time lying in the sun complaining about the stains and rips in her white tracksuit, and being nostalgic about Luke. She was nice (well, nice-ish) to Martine, but not exactly industrious. Most of her energy seemed to have been expended on the night Claudius fell ill.

'I'm so bored,' she told anyone who would listen. 'I miss TV, I miss music, I miss my room. I miss Luke and my mum and dad and my bed and soap and toothpaste and shampoo and coffee and chocolate. *Boy*, do I miss chocolate. But mostly I'm just bored. Bored, bored, bored.'

Jake had set himself the task of maintaining the giant SOS (large enough to be seen by passing aircraft) on Runway Beach. He did everything that was asked of him, effortlessly gathering great piles of wood, but he kept himself to himself. To varying degrees, they all went through parts of every day where they hated their island prison, lovely as it was, but Jake agonized most over the rugby training he was missing. He made a crude rugby ball out of coconut husk and bark, and whiled away the hours kicking it over palm trees and doing press-ups so that he'd be match-fit when he eventually returned to Storm Crossing.

Not surprisingly, Ben was the subject of much interest. Jake had not yet forgiven him for 'deceiving everyone', as he saw it, by making them think he was mute, and Lucy, who had always ridiculed him as a tree-hugging nutcase, now had to live with the remembrance of how she had treated him. But everyone was fascinated to hear his story. Not that he gave them much information. When Sherilyn asked him the question they all wanted the answer to, namely, why had he never spoken at school, Ben replied simply, 'I didn't have anything to say.'

But after years of being an outcast, he, like Martine, couldn't help but enjoy being included or asked for his opinion or help, which he frequently was. Of everyone, Ben had adapted best to island life. It was as if he was born to it. It made Martine proud to see the envious faces of kids who had always bullied or belittled him, when they saw him swim, fish, or build beds or shelters.

'Where did you learn all that?' Sherilyn wanted to know.

'All what?' Ben said, and then pretended he had an urgent appointment with Nathan on the other side of the island.

Over the next three evenings, the seven of them came together around a fire on the sea shore, and everyone except Claudius talked about the things they had in common – the dolphins, or their feelings on the night of the storm, or how desperately they missed their families, or how terrified they were of never being found, or whether or not they would do things differently when they left the island. Topics like pop music and the bizarre behaviour of celebrities, favourites at school, seemed trivial after what they'd been through.

Claudius was still too weak and listless to participate. If someone addressed him, he would nod, or shake his head, or give a one sentence answer, but most of the time he just stared into the flames.

'I never thought I'd say this,' Ben commented privately to Martine, 'but I miss the old Claudius. The spirit of him, anyway.'

Only Martine knew the root cause of Claudius's blues.

When they were alone together on the second day of his recovery, he'd mumbled something about hating himself for letting everyone down.

'I told everybody that my father would have us out of here in forty-eight hours,' he confided. 'I told them it was hard to get lost these days. I got my friends' hopes up. Now we could be stranded here for months.'

'Nobody blames you for that,' she assured him. 'Tendai always says it's important to be positive in a survival situation. Anyway, it was you getting sick that brought us all together. Don't worry. We'll be rescued soon.'

Inside she didn't feel nearly as confident as she sounded. She couldn't stop thinking about something Ben had said earlier. 'Martine, I have a really bad feeling about this island. I don't think it's a coincidence that the only boat we've seen in nearly a week is one that came to investigate an explosion. There is a reason people are staying away. There's something wrong with this place.'

It was Jake who came to tell them that the dolphins were behaving strangely.

'I was practising sprints at Dolphin Bay and they came right up to the shore. I thought it was cool that they were watching me, but then they started milling around and acting all confused. You'd better come see what's going on.'

It was late afternoon. Everyone but Claudius, who was

still too weak to leave his bamboo cot for more than a few hours at a time, ran the length of Runway Beach. They rounded the peninsula and were confronted with the most heartbreaking sight. Twenty-one dolphins were splayed across the white sand in golden sunlight. Something had driven them to flee the sea. The tide was going out and they were stranded, waiting to die.

Martine couldn't believe what she was seeing. It was the image in the cave painting, right down to the number of dolphins. The second prophecy had just come true.

But it was worse. These were the dolphins who had saved them from the ocean's wrath. They had become friends. They had names. Sun Dancer, Rain Queen, Patch, Honey, Thunder, Ash, Steel and Mini and, most distressingly, Little Storm – they were all there.

Everyone turned to Martine for answers. 'What do we do? How do we save them?' they clamoured.

Martine didn't know how to respond. Even supposing they were able to keep twenty-one dolphins from dying of shock and over-heating, which she doubted, there was no earthly way that they were strong enough to carry any dolphin apart perhaps from Little Storm to the water's edge. Not with the tide going out. The sea was retreating so quickly that it was already more than twenty feet from the nearest dolphin. Soon it would be a quarter of a mile away.

She wanted to shout back, 'Why are you asking me? I'm not a doctor or a vet. I'm an eleven-year-old kid. Yes, I have a gift, but I don't know what it does, or what it's for, or how to use it properly!'

But that wouldn't help the dolphins. Plus, she was not about to admit to having a gift. So she just said, "There's only one thing we can do and that's try to keep them wet and cool until the tide turns and we can push them back out to sea."

'How long will that take?' Lucy asked. 'I mean, are we talking one hour? Two hours?'

'Twelve hours,' Ben told her.

Sherilyn gulped. 'Twelve hours? We're meant to keep them wet and cool for twelve hours?'

'Well, we just can't,' Lucy declared flatly. 'Simple as that. We'll be dead as well.'

'We can try,' Nathan said, but without much conviction.

Martine glanced at Ben. Precious minutes were being wasted while they argued.

'These dolphins saved our lives,' Ben reminded them.

'*Ja*,' agreed Jake, 'and if it was a matter of keeping them wet for an hour or two, I'd be the first to do it. But get real, guys. You're asking us to keep twenty-one dolphins wet for a whole day.'

'Exactly!'

They all jumped. Unnoticed, Claudius had come up behind them. He was swaying slightly and his skin was still more yellow than gold, but there was something of his old charisma in the set of his shoulders. 'That's what you do when someone, or something saves your life,' he told Jake. 'You save theirs right back. Come on everyone, you heard Martine. We need to keep the dolphins wet.'

21

It was extraordinary to witness how much one not-very-well boy could do to galvanize a group. Before anybody could object, Claudius had organized Jake to run to the lighthouse and Runway Beach to collect every bulb, pot or container capable of holding water, plus some palm fronds to shade them all. Ben and Nathan were sent to gather firewood and catch fish, because, Claudius said, they would need all the energy they could get to make it through the night. Lucy and Sherilyn were dispatched to gather up the honeycomb, coconuts, spare clothing, and chunks of aloe. Martine hoped that the aloe leaf gel would help soothe the dolphins' exposed skins and prevent them from cracking.

She and Claudius stayed behind to dig holes in which to tuck the dolphins' pectoral fins, which would help keep them upright and comfortable. Then they spread great armfuls of seaweed over the dolphins to keep them from literally cooking in their own blubber. Martine went from one to the next, putting her palms over their hearts and feeling the tingle of electricity in response. They gazed up at her with their limpid, knowing eyes as if they trusted her to help them, and that terrified Martine because she was afraid she might not be able to.

And as she walked and murmured to them, not really knowing what she was saying, she became aware that what had started as a feeling of anguish when she saw the dolphins in distress, was gradually consuming her heart. It was as if they were extensions of her. When she looked into Little Storm's eyes, she saw that he recognized something she herself had never understood until that moment. That she felt his pain. She took on the burden of it.

Claudius was unaware of these internal revelations as he followed her, pausing in between dolphins to scoop up water from the departing sea with containers he'd improvised from a large shell and a coconut.

'Thanks for what you did earlier,' Martine said, as she watched him pour water onto Rain Queen's head, taking care to avoid her blow hole. If water went into the blow hole she used for breathing, she could drown.

Claudius's mouth twisted. 'No, thank *you*,' he replied. And she knew he wasn't talking about the dolphins.

When she reached Sun Dancer, Martine cradled the dolphin's silver-grey head in her arms and kissed him. Fighting back tears, she said softly, 'Please, Sun Dancer, find a way to tell us how to help you.'

'What do you expect – that he's suddenly going to start talking like Flipper?' Claudius jibed with a flash of his old sarcasm. But he knew straight away that he'd been insensitive and tried to make amends, saying, 'You really love them, don't you?'

'Yes, I do. Why, how do you feel about them?'

Claudius gave Sun Dancer's back an experimental stroke. 'I'm not sure. I haven't been around them as much as you. I just know that saving them seems like the most important thing I've ever done in my life. I care about that more than I care about getting off this island.'

But saving the dolphins was, as Jake had predicted, backbreaking work. They split into two groups and worked in shifts. Martine, Jake and Lucy took the first shift because Nathan and Ben were still out fishing. Each of them had responsibility for seven dolphins. They had to apply aloe gel to their skins, pour seawater over them and then drape them with seaweed. The most tiring part was the trips to the lake for fresh water, or to the edge of the crashing waves around the peninsula, a stony beach they'd named 'Danger', to fill the various containers Jake had found. Every hour, they switched, and slept, ate or stared into space while Ben, Nathan and Sherilyn took a turn with the dolphins. Then they'd rotate.

Claudius didn't have the stamina of the others, so it was his job to keep the fire blazing, time the shifts, motivate everyone, and attempt to cook meals, which he did extremely badly – so badly that it was decided after a disgusting lunch that at mealtimes he should take over Sherilyn's duties with the dolphins while she cooked.

As night drew in, a wicked wind whipped up the surf and the temperature plunged. They were on Danger Beach filling the containers when Ben suddenly stopped what he was doing, straightened and said, 'Did anybody hear that?'

Everyone fell silent. A wave crashed and the sea was temporarily hushed. The sound came again – a distinct ping. They waited a few seconds and it happened once more.

'That's the sound I heard when I was doing my exercises,' said Jake. 'A pinging noise. I thought it was a bird, or some weird fish or other.'

'It's sonar,' Ben told him.

'Sonar!' cried Martine.

Ben raised his eyebrows. 'Yes, sonar. When my dad was in the navy he took me to see the testing of a new transmitter, and I'd know that noise anywhere. Basically, a transmitter sends out pulses of sound that bounce off submarines and other objects in the ocean and are detected as returning echoes. That's what the ping is. But why would anybody test it out here? If we can hear it, it's probably Low-Frequency Active sonar, which is used by the navy.'

'A lot of scientists believe that LFA sonar's one of the main causes of dolphins and whales getting stranded,' said Martine, remembering her conversation with

Mr Manning during the Sardine Run.

'If scientists know that, why do the navy still use it?' Sherilyn asked.

'Grown-ups don't always fix the obvious things,' Nathan told her.

'That's because they're so busy telling us not to eat too many sweets, or run in the house, or talk to strangers, or stand under trees when there's lightning, they don't have time,' Lucy remarked.

There was quiet as they listened again for the pinging noise, but it had stopped.

'That's a pity,' said Jake. 'If there's sonar, maybe it means the navy are about and if the navy are about, they might save us and take us back to Cape Town.'

Everybody glared at him and he had the grace to look ashamed. 'I'm just *saying*...' he said defiantly. 'Of course I care about the dolphins.'

22

To be fair, Jake more than pulled his weight during the endless night that followed. It was so cold and the ritual rinsing of dolphins' skins so mind-numbing that half the time Martine wasn't sure if she was awake, asleep or hallucinating. She worried that the unaccustomed pressure could damage their kidneys, livers and hearts, so she focussed what little healing power she could summon on those organs. Once an hour, she moved from dolphin to dolphin in the fire-lit darkness, running her hands along their abdomens and bellies in such a subtle way that not even Ben noticed.

To take her mind off her muscles, which soon grew

sore to the point of screaming, she allowed her thoughts to drift to Sawubona. There was a giraffe-shaped hole in her heart where Jemmy was supposed to be. She wondered what he was doing now, and whether he missed her as much as she missed him. She wondered if she'd ever again have the chance to ride him up to onto the escarpment on a starry night, as she'd done before Gwyn Thomas stopped her from riding after sundown, and to lie with her head on his withers and her feet on his hindquarters, losing herself in Mars, the Southern Cross and the Milky Way. On those nights, she'd felt cloaked by Africa, almost as if the mother spirit of the landscape had cast a protective veil around her shoulders.

She missed Grace's wisdom and Tendai's bass-drum laugh and, increasingly, she missed the evenings with Gwyn Thomas. Sometimes her grandmother was worn out from a hard day on the reserve and they'd just sit quietly together after dinner, listening to the radio or reading books, but at other times she'd tell Martine tales of the history of Southern Africa – of rivers running red with the blood of spear-throwing Zulus and *Voortrekkers,* the early white settlers; of epic, malaria and blackwater fever-wracked journeys by oxwagon; of tribes displaced by the whims of politicians in Europe; of men driven mad with greed for gold and diamonds.

She talked, too, of Martine's mum and dad, and those were the stories Martine cherished most. 'Your mum always said that she knew David was the man for her when she watched him wade into the middle of a torrential river to rescue a baby monkey clinging to a fragment of rock,' Gwyn Thomas had told her with a smile.

David Allen was an Englishman, in Cape Town for a medical conference, and for both him and Veronica it was love at first sight. They'd been married at the game reserve, three months after David waded from the river with the dripping baby monkey, and David had moved to South Africa to be with his new bride. He'd found a job at a famous hospital, and for a while the future had looked perfect.

Until fate had intervened. Or, at least, until Grace had told Veronica that her baby – born on New Year's Day, a year after their wedding – had a gift with animals. The *sangoma* warned her that the gift would carry an awesome responsibility, and that Martine's destiny was unalterable. Those words had changed everything.

'Martine. Martine!'

Martine shook herself. Nathan was standing in front of her. 'You can rest now,' he said. 'You look as if you need it.'

In the end, the actual saving of the dolphins was almost an anti-climax. The tide came in shortly before four-thirty a.m. and left foaming outlines around the dolphins, who by then were as weak as their carers. The water took an age to inch high enough up the beach to actually lift the dolphins off the sand, and by that point nobody was capable of doing anything but encouraging them to swim out to sea.

The dolphins moved tentatively at first and then with increasing fluidity and speed. Martine's chest was tight with emotion as she watched them go, especially when Sun Dancer wheeled back and clicked to her before leaving.

'We did it!' whooped Jake. Everyone came together for a group hug which, despite their wet, clammy skins, was somehow the warmest Martine had ever had. Then they collapsed in hysterical laughter on the sand.

'That's it,' said Lucy. 'I'm officially on holiday. I refuse to lift a finger between now and when we leave the island. I don't care if we're stuck here for a year.'

'How is that different to usual?' Claudius asked drily, and even Lucy had to giggle.

All of a sudden Sherilyn said, 'Oh, no!'

Nathan groaned.

'What is it?' asked Martine. She sat up and squinted into the sunlight. Mini was on the fringe of the surf. It was plain she intended to beach herself again.

Martine was distraught. The weight of the dolphins' suffering returned to crush her again. 'Maybe she's so traumatized she's lost the will to live. That happens to some dolphins. No matter how many times they're returned to the sea, they keep trying to escape it.'

'Come on, everyone,' Claudius said tiredly, 'back to work.'

'I can't,' Lucy whined. 'I just can't.'

'Get up off your lazy bum and come and help,'

Sherilyn ordered much to everyone's astonishment, and Lucy, to her credit, did just that.

Three times they pushed Mini out to sea and three times the dolphin returned. Finally their strength really did run out. The marathon night had taken its toll.

Mini dragged herself onto the beach one final time and Martine went to sit beside her, to try to comfort her in her last moments. 'Don't you want to be in the ocean any more?' she asked despairingly. 'Don't you want to be with your friends?'

She was stroking Mini's head when she noticed something jutting from the dolphin's mouth. She removed it carefully. It was a section of clear cable.

Martine's hands began to shake. 'Ben,' she called, and he was by her side in an instant. He took the cable from her and examined it closely, and they both looked over at Mini. The grandmother dolphin's eyelids slid shut and she heaved a big sigh.

'No, Mini, you're not allowed to die,' Martine sobbed, but it was already too late.

Sherilyn came over and tried to console her, but Martine was beyond consolation. Someone, or something, had killed Mini as surely as if they had shot her, and she was not going to rest until she found out who, or what, had done it.

'I think you're right,' she said in a low voice to Ben when Sherilyn stepped away to talk to the others. 'There *is* a reason why people are staying away from this island. It's cursed, or protected, or there's a secret here. There *is* something wrong with this place. And what do the cables have to do with anything?'

'I don't know,' Ben said. 'But I know we're not going to be able to find the answers on our own.'

23

'Who do you think the men are?' Nathan said. 'MI5 spies? Foreign mercenaries plotting a coup?'

They were up in the lighthouse, thawing out around a roaring fire. They were filthy, smelly and so sleep-deprived they practically needed matchsticks to keep their eyelids open, but the discovery that the sea around the island was a virtual minefield, and that they were not alone at all but so close to 'civilization' that men in dhows could be on the scene in minutes, had temporarily re-energized them.

'We're not sure,' Ben told him. 'They could even be pirates.'

'*Pirates?*' Lucy said skeptically. 'Are you making this up? Did they also have eye-patches and cutlasses and a black flag with a skull and crossbones on it?'

'Modern pirates aren't like that,' Nathan informed her. 'I saw a documentary on them. They prey on tourist boats and cargo vessels in isolated locations just like this one, and are so bold they'll swarm aboard in broad daylight and rob people at knifepoint. They're ruthless.'

'*Oh. My. God!* So, along with being half-drowned and marooned on an island, we're now going to be murdered by pirates?'

'Well, we don't have anything to steal,' Ben said, unable to hide a smile, 'so I don't think they'd be too interested in us, even if they are pirates. It's more likely that they're treasure hunters who've booby-trapped the wreck to keep other fortune seekers away from it, or that they're working for the organization that laid down the cables. If we're right and Mini *was* trying to tell us that there's a connection between the dolphins beaching themselves and the cables, then we need to find out what the cables are for. Especially if it turns out that the undersea mine was protecting the cables and not the wreck.'

'Why don't we take a closer look at them?' Jake suggested.

'What, and get blown to pieces like the Manta Ray?' exclaimed Lucy. 'No thanks.'

'What about the sonar?' asked Martine. 'Do you think the men we saw could be involved with that?'

'Sonar can travel for miles, so the transmitter that's

being used could be anywhere,' Ben said. 'Some navy might be testing in the middle of the Indian Ocean. Maybe we should concentrate on the divers, because they and the cables are our only clues. The fact that they responded to the explosion so rapidly means that they must be based reasonably close to us, possibly on another island – although not close enough to know that we're here. Unless it was just chance and they happened to be sailing nearby.'

'What happens if they do notice we're here?' fretted Sherilyn. 'Are they going to come to the island and shoot us with their spear-guns?'

Claudius made a scary face at her. 'No, they'll just kidnap us and hold us for ransom.'

'Well, that's a real comfort,' Lucy said sarcastically, and Martine smothered a giggle. Claudius was definitely on the mend.

'The one thing I keep thinking about is how proud Alberto was there was no crime in the Bazaruto Archipelago,' she said. 'He told me that the islanders don't even have locks on their doors and that the smallest child can walk anywhere by themselves. He didn't say anything about pirates or undersea mines. So maybe there's an innocent explanation for all of this.'

'We're forgetting the most important part of this,' Claudius interrupted, 'and that's the dolphins. I mean, we owe it to them to find and stop whatever it is that's causing them to beach themselves.'

'Why don't we start by trying to find out where the divers are operating from?' Ben suggested. 'If we can get them to come to the island, we might be able to follow them.'

'Oh, sure,' Lucy said. 'Let's just phone them up and invite them over!'

Jake snorted. '*Follow* them? In what? The raft we're going to build out of bamboo, I suppose. That's going to be really effective.'

'We'll take their boat,' Ben responded calmly.

'And how do you suppose we're going to do that?'

'Don't tell me,' said Martine, remembering something Ben had once said to her. 'Sometimes the most obvious way is the best way.'

Ben laughed. 'That's right.'

As eager as they were to get started, everyone agreed that, in order for any plan to be effective, sleep was their first priority. Claudius's water-resistant-to-200 metres watch had survived the storm, so he set his alarm for 3 p.m. That would give them four hours of rest, leaving them with three hours to execute phase one before dark.

In the event, they were awoken at 2:10 p.m. by the sound of an aeroplane. Jake heard it first. He scrambled to his feet, brown hair sticking up porcupine-style, stumbled outside, and started leaping up and down and waving his arms. Lucy and Nathan went after him and the three of them did wild dances on top of the dunes.

But the Cessna was circling Dolphin Bay and gave no indication it had seen them.

They ran back into the lighthouse and tried, in a comical way borne of haste, to restart the fire so they could send up a smoke signal. The first flames were just taking when Claudius threw water on them.

Jake snatched the gourd from him. 'Claudius, what the hell are you doing, mate? Has the man-o'-war venom attacked your brain? We've got a chance of getting off this island. Don't you want that?'

'Don't worry about it, Jake,' said Nathan. 'They'll see the SOS on Runway beach.'

Jake glared at Claudius, tossed aside the gourd, and raced outside again. The others joined him. Martine had snatched the tin lid from her survival kit, and she tilted it upwards in the hope the pilot might spot the reflected glare of the sunlight, but the plane flew past without seeming to see them. It dipped low over Runway Beach and circled twice.

'They've seen it,' yelled Jake. 'Whoooee! We're saved. We're out of here. I'm going to play rugby again. I'm going to eat steak and chips again.'

But the plane soared upwards and the drone of its engine soon dissipated in the afternoon blue.

'That's it,' Lucy declared with a loud sniff. 'I'm never going to see my twin again. We're doomed to stay here for eternity.' She slumped to the ground and put her head in her hands.

Jake raked his hands through his hair. 'I don't understand it. How could they miss our sign? It could practically be seen from Mars.' He walked to the edge of the dunes and shaded his eyes. 'Hold on a minute. It's gone. The SOS is gone!'

'Don't be a moron, Jake,' said Lucy, not bothering to raise her head. 'As if anyone would steal your stupid sign.'

'I did,' Claudius said.

Jake gave him a baffled look. 'What are you talking about?'

'I took the SOS away. I moved all the stones late last night when I went to Runway Beach to find my sweater.'

Six appalled faces turned his way. 'But why?' Nathan asked in bewilderment. 'Why would you do that?'

'It's because his rich father hasn't come to save him, and Claudius is afraid it's because his dad doesn't want his fat, bone-idle son any more,' Jake said nastily. 'He's afraid to go home.'

Sherilyn rounded on him. 'Don't be so spiteful, Jake. What's wrong with you?'

'It's true, Sherilyn,' Claudius admitted. 'I have been afraid that my dad doesn't want his fat, bone-idle son back and that that's the real reason he hasn't come looking for me. I *am* afraid of going home. But that isn't why I did it. I did it because I suddenly realized that if we were rescued too soon, we wouldn't be able to save the dolphins. I mean, if that plane had found us and we'd told whoever was on board, "Oh, by the way, we think the dolphins are beaching themselves because of sonar testing, or some weird cables, or divers who plant undersea mines, and we need to stay longer to investigate," they would have said, "In your dreams.

We're taking you back to your families right now."'

He paused and stared hard at his fellow castaways – Jake in particular. 'We've got a chance to make a real difference here. Don't you want that? Isn't that more important than whether or not you get to play centre forward at some rugby match?'

A tense silence greeted this speech. Martine was the first to move. She went over to Claudius and stood beside him. 'What Claudius says makes sense,' she told the rest of the group. 'There's no way we'd be allowed to stay and help the dolphins if any adult found us now.'

'A few more days on the island is nothing compared to that,' agreed Ben.

Lucy gave an exasperated sigh, which Martine took as a yes – albeit a very irritated one; and Sherilyn nodded, although her lower lip wobbled.

'It's not like we have loads of other options,' Nathan reminded Jake. 'People don't seem to be in too much of a hurry to rescue us.'

Jake vented his annoyance on a piece of coconut husk which happened to find itself in front of his foot. 'All right,' he said. 'Two more days. Two more days and then the SOS is going back on the beach and this time it'll be twice the size!'

24

The plan they came up with was three-pronged. First they would attempt to trigger an explosion in order to try to lure the men on the dhow to the island; then Claudius would distract them while Ben and Martine, as the only pair willing to volunteer for the job, would sneak onto the boat, assuming that there was somewhere for them to hide. Once at the divers' headquarters, they would . . . well, they weren't exactly sure what they'd do when they got there, but their main aim was to find the cause of the dolphins' suffering and to try to make contact with the outside world.

That was the idea on paper – or at least on sand.

Claudius sketched it out on Runway Beach with a stick. As they talked, the faces of the seven classmates were grave. There was no fooling around. Everyone knew they could be venturing into the human equivalent of a shark tank.

They made, Martine thought, a motley crew. They'd had a much-needed bath in the lake, but without soap and shampoo there wasn't much improvement. They were all sunburnt or wind-blasted and much thinner, and their clothes were in a dreadful state. Sherilyn looked the most ridiculous in her faded pink pyjamas with missing buttons, but Claudius was almost as bad in tattered jeans, which hung loose on his reduced frame, and a red sweater which was unravelling at one elbow. If he wasn't still delicate following his man-o'-war encounter, Martine would have been sorely tempted to remind him how he'd taunted her for having holes in her jeans back in Cape Town. That said, anyone who saw Ben and Martine's stained T-shirts and threadbare denim shorts would have assumed they'd been castaways for a year, not ten days, and Lucy's white tracksuit was a sight.

Nathan and Jake had fared best in the clothes department. Jake's jeans and forest-green, yellow-collared Springbok rugby jersey were so hard-wearing they had barely been affected by his adventures, and, apart from a few creases, Nathan's checked blue shirt and navy blue chinos were in relatively good shape.

But none of them looked equipped to fight dolphin-killers.

It was phase one of the plan that bothered Martine

most. As the best swimmer and the only person who knew anything at all about undersea explosives – and that was only second-hand from his dad – Ben had been nominated to swim out to the wreck and fix a string to a tripwire. He insisted to Martine that it was not as dangerous as it sounded. 'If they made the trigger too sensitive, then any old fish which bumped into it would cause an explosion,' he said.

She wasn't convinced.

Nevertheless, she helped Lucy collect bark from the trees near the lake. The string in the survival kit was not long enough for their purposes, and Sherilyn worked as quickly as she could to add to it by weaving thin strands of bark together. Length was more important than strength. Regardless of what Ben said, it wouldn't take much to activate the tripwire.

At 4 p.m., they all set off for Dolphin Bay, Ben with a fat coil of stringy bark wrapped around one wrist, Jake carrying a lifejacket. Their strategy was simple. Ben would tie one end of the makeshift rope to the tripwire – assuming, of course, that he could actually find it – and the other end to the wreck. When the sun began to set, Jake would swim out to the wreck, collect the rope, carry it as far as the line would allow and then trigger the explosion. He'd return to the shore as fast as he could and hopefully be concealed by the time the boat men showed up. Then Claudius would go into action with phase two.

Martine wanted more than anyone to help the dolphins, but she was starting to think the plan was insane. These were not a couple of incompetent poachers they were up against. These were men with spear-guns. The best possible outcome was that the dhow men would turn out to be heart-of-gold fishermen, or employees of the cable company, who, once they'd heard Martine and her fellow survivors' story, would assist them in finding what was causing the dolphins to beach themselves, and afterwards return them to their families. The worst case scenario was that they really were pirates or treasure hunters from the mainland, who would not take kindly to having their plans disrupted. Who knew what would happen then?

So lost was she in thought that it wasn't until Ben was calf-deep in water and about to swim out to the wreck that she remembered what he was doing. She went tearing across the white sand, splashed up behind him and grabbed his arm. 'Don't go, Ben,' she said emotionally. 'I couldn't bear it if anything happened to you.'

Ben looked at her in surprise. 'I have to go.'

There was something very still about him, almost as though he'd been meditating.

Martine shook her head. 'No, you don't. It's madness. You could be blown up. We'll figure out some other way to help the dolphins.'

He returned her gaze steadily. 'You know what you said to me the other night . . . ?'

Martine was mortified. The guilt and shame of those excruciating hours came rushing back. She let go of his arm. 'I'm so, so sorry, Ben. I didn't mean it, I promise. I was just being stupid.'

But Ben cut her short. 'You were right about one thing. Sometimes it is important to stand up for what you believe in.'

He dived into the water and was gone.

The first phase of the plan went very smoothly – almost too smoothly. Although Martine covered her eyes and kept reliving the moment when the manta ray blew up and rained down on the sea like lava, Ben accomplished his mission in record time, and Lucy prodded her so she could see him balanced on the edge of the galleon, giving them the thumbs up.

'Easy,' he said as he waded from the turquoise water, but when he went to pick up a gourd to have a drink Martine noticed that his hands trembled so much he almost dropped it.

Next they all sat down to crab soup, which was very watery because they'd only had time to find three undernourished crabs.

'Nothing against your cooking, Sherilyn,' Lucy said, 'but if we ever get off this stupid island, I'm never going to eat another fish, crab or coconut meal in my life. And a herd of stampeding buffaloes couldn't drag me camping. I wouldn't sleep on the freezing, hard ground with bugs again if you paid me a million rand.'

The hardest part was the goodbyes. They'd been through so much together and nobody knew if they'd be separated for a few hours, a few days or for ever. Martine was doubtful that the closeness that now existed between the seven of them would continue if they ever made it back to Caracal Junior, but she did know they would always share a bond. She would always be loyal to them and stand up for them because they had come through for her on the night of the dolphin beaching. Twenty lives would not have been saved without them.

Martine felt in her pocket for the ivory dolphin Jake had given her. He'd carved it that afternoon from the kernel of a palm fruit. 'For good luck,' he'd said. Martine couldn't believe it. She'd been beginning to wonder if he had a rugby ball for a heart. To Ben, Jake had extended his hand and said gruffly, 'You're all right,' which was the closest he ever came to a compliment. Sherilyn had given them each a perfect cowry shell and a kiss on both cheeks, and Nathan had shaken their hands very formally and said, 'See you later,' as if they were tourists going out for a scenic tour of the islands and would be back in time for dinner.

Lucy had just given them a hug and said in a choked-up voice, 'If you find a phone, tell Luke I miss him . . . Don't forget about us, hey.'

Claudius refused to say goodbye, because he said that implied he was never going to see them again. They had to think positively. They would see each other in days, if not hours. Even so, he punched Martine affectionately on the arm and said, 'You'd better take care of yourself. You're not bad for an orphan.'

To which she retorted, 'You're not bad for a boy who

dresses like an orphan!' And he burst out laughing.

At sundown, Jake swam out to the wreck and set off the explosion. He raced back to the beach and joined Nathan, Lucy and Sherilyn up on the ledges above Dolphin Bay. Ben and Martine concealed themselves among the rocks near the shore. They had bits of coconut in their pockets in case they had to go without food for a while, but Martine had left her survival kit with the others. If the plan worked they'd hopefully be reunited soon, but in the meantime the knife, torch and other contents of the kit were essential for island-living. All Martine had taken from it was the root ginger, in case of seasickness.

For twenty minutes nothing happened. The horizon stayed empty. Martine grew anxious. She tried to remind herself that the risk they were taking might save their lives and hurry her home to Jemmy and her friends at Sawubona, but her doubts soon overwhelmed her. Her biggest terror was that there would be room on the dhow for only one of them, and that Ben would disappear into the blue and she'd have no way of knowing what had become of him.

'If we can't go together, I don't think we should do it at all,' she said, standing up and shaking the pins and needles out of her legs. 'It's too dangerous. We should stay here and think of some other way to get rescued and help the dolphins.'

Ben looked up at her. 'What if no one ever comes?'

High on the rocky ledge, Nathan made 'get down' hand signals. Martine dropped to the sand. But it was not the dhow which appeared around the side of the island, it was a motorboat. This time there were only three Africans on board, one in a diving suit. They swooshed to a stop near the wreck.

Phase two of the plan was about to go into operation.

· 25 ·

Claudius had been vague about how exactly he was going to attract the attention of the boatmen, except to say that he'd confuse them with a combination of animal noises and Martine's whistle. 'They'll think they're hearing things,' he explained. 'They'll come to the island to look around but I'll hide really well and be quiet as soon as I see Martine and Ben are safely on board. As long as they don't go to Runway Beach and see our shelter, they won't suspect a thing.'

But that's not what happened at all. Five minutes after the men on the motorboat appeared, Claudius strolled onto the beach and stood in the middle of it in plain

395

view. He had put on his red jumper and rolled up the bottoms of his jeans.

'What is he *doing*?' Martine whispered to Ben. 'He's going to get himself killed.'

Nathan and the others emerged briefly from the shadows of the ledge and called down to him to stop being so crazy and get off the beach immediately, but Claudius pretended he didn't hear them. He took out the whistle Martine had given him and blew three blasts on it. The silhouettes in the boat were thrown into a state of extreme agitation. Pulling the diver back on board, they zoomed to the shore. They gestured for Claudius to come over, but he remained anchored to the spot, waving his arms like a drowning swimmer, until they were forced to leave the boat and go to him.

'Boy, am I glad to see you!' he cried as they approached. 'I thought I was going to be stuck here until I starved to death or grew a long, grey beard.'

He thrust out a hand. 'I'm Claudius. Pleased to meet you.'

'What are you doing here?' barked the boat skipper, a gaunt man with bulging eyes and long, sinewy arms. He made no attempt to take Claudius's outstretched hand. 'How did you get here? Nobody is allowed on this island. *Nobody*. Every boat captain in Mozambique knows that. Every lodge and tour operator knows that.'

'Well, to be honest that was mentioned to us . . . '

'*Us?*' demanded the man. 'Where are the others? How many of you are here?'

'I was just getting to that,' said Claudius, as if he was

oblivious to the threatening advance of the other men. 'They abandoned me. Not on purpose, I'm sure – at least, I hope not, ha, ha – but you know what grown-ups are like when they've had a few beers. I went for a walk up to the lighthouse and returned to find them gone. I'm sure they'll be back, but I'm getting very hungry so I'm really glad you've come. Is there any chance you could give me a lift to the lodge at Benguerra?'

'This is very bad news for you and very bad news for us,' the skipper said, ignoring the question. 'No one comes near Dugong.'

'Dugong?'

'Dugong Island. This is where you are trespassing.'

Down on the shore, Ben and Martine slipped like wraiths onto the motorboat. There was a storage locker under the wheel. They dived in and shut the doors behind them. The space was cramped, wet and stunk of fish and petrol fumes, but they'd done it and they were together.

'Don't worry,' Claudius was saying to the skipper in the same confident, light-hearted tone, 'the people who brought me here will be hearing from my father. Anyway, what's so special about this place? Why is no one allowed to come here? What were you looking for out by the wreck? Are you salvage experts, or from the army or something?'

'There is a saying in English, no? Curiosity killed the pussycat.'

'Fine,' said Claudius. 'I'll just wait here until my friends come back.'

'You must hope that your friends don't come back,' the skipper advised. 'We have put . . . measures . . . around the island to keep people away. You are lucky that you and your tourist friends did not get a big surprise.' He mimicked the sound of a bomb blast and followed it with a gap-toothed grin. His companions laughed.

The diver made a comment in Portuguese. The skipper's retort brought more laughter.

'Carlos thinks he has seen you somewhere before,' he told Claudius. 'Maybe on TV. I told him that, with your long yellow hair, it must have been a story about a princess. One who didn't like to take baths.'

'That's funny,' Claudius said amiably. 'You're funny. Anyway, it's been nice talking to you. I'm sure someone will be along to collect me. Goodbye.'

The skipper shot out a lanky arm and seized Claudius by the sleeve of his jumper. The smile left his face. 'Not so fast, my friend,' he said.

'What are you doing?' demanded Claudius, his voice rising. 'Leave me alone.'

But the man retained his grip on Claudius's sleeve. He said something to his companions, and they moved in a bit closer. The diver seized his other arm.

'It is not the island way to refuse hospitality to a stranger,' the skipper said coldly. 'We must not leave you here. If you please, you will accompany us to Paradise.'

Inside the dark compartment, Martine and Ben heard only snatches of what was said, but enough to gather that Claudius was more or less being kidnapped. He was still protesting, although not particularly convincingly, when the motor roared to life and the boat cruised out towards the open sea. To Martine, it sounded as if he wanted to go with the men. She was quite sure that that had been his intention all along.

As the boat picked up speed and hit rolling ocean swells, she and Ben were thrown around bruisingly. There was nothing beneath them but an anchor and a coil of wet, stiff rope, which made an extremely uncomfortable cushion and which they hoped would not be required when they reached their destination. Dirty water swilled around their space. Petrol fumes floated in. Disoriented, Martine began to feel seasick. Within minutes it was so bad she was convinced that she would vomit and the retching sounds would get them caught. But Ben produced the piece of ginger and insisted she eat it. She sucked on the fiery root and the nausea retreated, although it didn't go away altogether.

It was difficult to hear anything above the roar of the motor and the pounding of the hull against the waves, and the men didn't speak much. Martine kept her spirits up by telling herself that every mile might be taking her nearer to Jemmy and Grace and her grandmother and Tendai, but the journey seemed interminable. Plus there was the knowledge that every mile might really be taking her further away from her loved ones. It was abundantly clear that the men were not friendly fishermen or good-natured islanders. They were up to something. They had as good as admitted that Dugong Island was booby-trapped to keep people away. So what were they hiding? And where did that leave her, Ben and Claudius – or, for that matter, their friends still stuck on the island?

Her thoughts were interrupted by the slowing of the boat. The engine was switched off. They drifted on the tide until the boat bumped into land. It rocked as the men jumped out. Attempts were made to pull it out of the water, but then the movement stopped and the diver could be heard grumbling.

'Carlos is complaining that the boat feels very heavy tonight. It must be you,' the skipper said rudely to Claudius. 'Get off.'

Sand scraped loudly beneath the fibreglass hull as the boat was dragged further up onto the beach. At last, to Martine's immense relief, it was still.

'Welcome to Santa Carolina,' announced the skipper, as though Claudius were a carefree holidaymaker and not a virtual prisoner. 'A lot of people call it Paradise Island, but that will not be you, I think.'

26

Martine and Ben stayed where they were for as long as they could stand it, which was only about another ten minutes because the stench of petrol and the claustrophobia brought on by the damp compartment drove them out. Fortunately, it was early evening and there was no one around. They hopped onto the sand and stood inhaling the clean, salty smell of the ocean, which was pure heaven after the hell of their journey. A long, white beach tailed away, lit by the dim glow of the rising moon. The dhow was moored midway along it. In the distance was the outline of what looked to be a low, sprawling hotel or holiday apartments.

'Maybe it's one of those luxury lodges Lucy was going on about!' Martine said hopefully. Her mind was already racing ahead to the moment when a kindly hotel manager would, after learning of their plight, offer them free accommodation for the night and allow them to phone home. She imagined herself wallowing neck-deep in a bubble-bath before tucking into a dinner of roast chicken, crispy potatoes and loads of fresh vegetables, smothered in gravy, followed by coffee and maybe a trifle. Afterwards, she'd fall into a feather-soft bed and sleep for twenty-four hours.

'Better not get too excited,' cautioned Ben. 'They might not be pirates, but those men didn't exactly behave like hotel employees.'

'They could just be using the island as a base for their operations and have nothing to do with the hotel,' Martine said, determined not to let go of her vision. 'The hotel owner might be very interested to know that there are child kidnappers living on Paradise.'

They set off towards the buildings, the sand squeaking under their bare feet. The island was about half the size of Dugong, with gentle undulations rather than steep dunes, so they decided to follow the glittering black sea all the way round and approach the building from the back. That way they could be sure that the sinister men weren't in sight before showing themselves.

'For a hotel, there don't seem to be too many lights on,' Ben commented, as they peered between the wind-twisted trunks of some pine trees some thirty minutes later.

'It is winter in Mozambique,' Martine pointed out. 'Perhaps there are very few guests at this time of the year, or perhaps they're all at dinner.'

They waited a little while longer before venturing out into the open. It was only then, gazing up at the double-storey block of rooms and the forbidding façade of the hotel itself, its vast, curving terrace suspended over the ocean, they saw that that's all it was: a façade. A ruined shell. Not only was it unoccupied, it looked as if it had been that way for at least thirty years. The civil war or something else – mismanagement perhaps – had driven away the tourists.

Martine didn't know whether to cry or fly into a rage born of total despair. For eleven days she and the others had been trying to escape their island prison, only to end up here: the penal colony Alberto had told her about. She could still hear him saying, 'Over the years, Santa Carolina has been a playground for wealthy tourists. They call it Paradise, but oh, Miss Martine, if only they knew what that paradise had seen: hundreds of hungry, suffering prisoners, tormented beyond what any man could endure, then taken to Death Island to be swallowed by the sea.'

Martine had recounted this story to Ben on the way over. But although he had been braced for the unexpected, and hadn't allowed himself to be carried away with fantasies of feather beds or roast chicken dinners, shock was written all over his face.

'Is this what grown-ups mean when they say "Out of the frying pan and into the fire"?' Martine said.

Ben recovered sufficiently to speak. 'We're still better

off than we were,' he said. 'If there are people here – even if they do turn out to be criminals – there must also be food and some way of contacting the outside world. But no matter what, we need to be off this island by sunrise. I'm pretty sure I could sail the dhow. We'll try to rescue Claudius but if we can't we'll have to leave him and go for help. We'll be no use to him, the dolphins or anyone else if we get caught.'

Martine agreed wholeheartedly – particularly with the part about them leaving Paradise before sunrise, so they resumed their search of the hotel grounds with more urgency. The rooms they saw were all empty, their cracked walls and exposed electricity wires oddly clean, as if they were soon to be put back to use. Most eerie of all was the old ballroom, a sad shadow of its past glory. A weather-beaten, out-of-tune piano still stood in one corner, and Martine could almost hear the tinkle of keys and see the sequin-gowned dancers who must have glided across the floor beneath a brilliant chandelier. Out on the terrace, a gaping chunk of floor was missing and the sea slurped and sucked at the crumbling foundations below.

The next block of rooms was also disused, but close to the beach where they'd come in they could see lights shining among the palms. The two areas were separated by a walkway which ran almost the width of the island. A flagless pole was in the centre of it, and it was lined with weed-filled concrete flower beds in which roses or island flowers must once have bloomed. Martine and Ben were about to dart across the unkempt expanse when a lone guard appeared. He was swinging his truncheon and singing an African song in a low, sad voice. When the light fell on his face, it was young and handsome. He strolled the length of the walkway and disappeared through the palms onto the beach.

'Now!' said Ben, and they sprinted for a flat-roofed building in the centre of the grounds. For the first time in ten days, they were close to human habitation. The windows of the rooms glowed yellow, and there was washing hanging on the line. Smoke and the smell of cooking came from the rear.

They followed the sound of voices to a side window, across which a cloth had been pinned in lieu of curtains. The window was slightly ajar and the cloth hung crookedly, leaving a gap in one corner. Martine and Ben stood on tiptoe so they could see the occupants of what must have once been a dining room or restaurant. Four men were gathered around a wooden table laid with dishes of steaming food. A grainy television flickered in the background. Three of the men were eating and watching the skipper, who was up out of his seat and seemed to be tormenting a fifth person by shoving a plate of prawns and rice at them and then withdrawing it and eating a forkful himself. He stepped back and Martine had to bite her lip to keep from crying out.

Claudius was roped to a chair!

'You're lying,' the skipper was accusing him. 'You are an island spy. Who sent you?'

'Look, I would love to tell you I was a spy if it meant you'd give me some food,' said Claudius, his eyes following the prawns longingly, 'but I'm just an ordinary kid from Cape Town. How many times do I have to tell you that?'

The plate swept under his nose again and Claudius's eyes closed momentarily with the effort of resisting it. He swallowed.

Out in the cold night, Martine swallowed in sympathy.

'Was it Nico from Benguerra?' demanded the skipper. 'He is always trying to keep people from the mainland from coming in and making money from the islands. Those island grandfathers do not understand business. Their heads are in the past. We have a boy working for us, Fernando, from Bazaruto Island. He is just eighteen, but he understands that a person must take opportunities when they come, and stop worrying so much about preserving animals and plants. He is a young man with ambition. He has some things to learn about the world, but he . . . '

Behind him, Carlos let out a strangled squawk. He sprang out of his chair, gave the television two hard thumps and turned up the volume. Distorted sound blared into the room. The picture cleared slightly and the words *Sea Kestrel* Mystery – 11th day, appeared beneath a photo of Claudius. He was younger, plumper and paler, and he was wearing his old jokers' smile, but it was unmistakably him.

'Ah! Ah!' was the skipper's incredulous response, as he looked from the TV to Claudius and back again. The other men reacted the same way.

'Good evening,' intoned the newsreader. 'Eleven nights ago, seven Cape Town schoolchildren fell overboard during a freak storm off the Mozambique coast and have been missing, presumed drowned, ever since. Presumed drowned, that is, by almost everyone except property magnate Ed Rapier, father of Claudius . . . '

Martine watched Claudius turn white.

'The search has been concentrated on the Southern coastline around Inhambane where, marine experts say, currents would have carried the children in the unlikely event they survived the sharks and freezing water temperatures, and Mr Rapier has personally sponsored one of the largest air and sea rescues ever undertaken in these waters. Despite that, not a trace of the seven has been found. Yet Mr Rapier, one of South Africa's most successful businessmen, has refused to accept defeat.'

A broad-shouldered man with a grey-streaked, lion's mane of hair appeared on the screen. He was standing beside a rescue helicopter on a windy beach.

'I don't believe my boy is dead,' he told the camera. 'I will never believe it until I see his body. He is too full of life, too smart and too used to having his own way! He is a survivor. If I have to sift every grain of sand on every beach in Mozambique, I'll find him. I will never give up – and I'm sure my feelings are shared by the families of the other missing children. On their behalf, I am prepared to offer a million rand for information leading to the safe return of my son and any of his classmates.'

A contact number appeared on the bottom of the screen.

'Liar!' roared the skipper, and he struck Claudius across the face. A palm print appeared on the boy's cheek. 'You think you can talk rubbish to us and get away with it? Who else is on Dugong Island? If your friends cause trouble with the test tomorrow, I will feed you to the sharks.'

Claudius lifted his chin a fraction. There was a wobble in his voice and his fingers gripped the arms of the chair very tightly, but there was a light in his eyes that hadn't been there for days and he said determinedly, 'I was alone on the island. Completely alone. I think I must have been the only survivor. I remember getting into an empty lifeboat, but everything after that is a blur. When I woke up I was on Dugong Island. 'Course I didn't know it was called Dugong.'

This latest untruth caused the skipper to lose his temper. He slammed down the plate and lifted his arm as if to strike Claudius. A babble of furious African voices shattered the evening quiet.

The dialect they spoke was not dissimilar to Zulu, so Ben translated in a low voice. 'They are very angry with him,' he reported. 'They say he is not thinking clearly. What is he doing hitting a tourist? Here they have a chance to earn a million rand in reward money for handing over a boy who is very annoying and only going to cause trouble for them, and he is more worried about being loyal to their boss. They say he has been blinded by their boss's power. Can't he see that they are being cheated over the money from the tests? Why else does he think their boss drives a Mercedes when their own cars and bicycles are held together with string?'

The skipper seemed startled by this mutiny. He made a few feeble objections but quickly came to the conclusion they were right. They *were* being cheated. What possible harm could it do if they returned the boy and claimed the reward money for themselves? Was it not their due after all the months they'd spent caretaking Dugong Island, and been bored half to death on Paradise Island? And nobody but the four of them need know anything about it.

He smiled his gap-toothed smile. The other three smiled back. Then he untied Claudius, made a big fuss of dusting him down and straightening his clothes, and shouted to some unseen person to bring him a Coke and a hot plate of prawns and rice. 'My friend, forgive us this small misunderstanding,' he said in English. 'We are paranoid because of some problems with the islanders. Eat now and be happy. Tomorrow we will take you home to your father.'

27

The he men left the room then, locking the door behind them. 'For your own safety,' the skipper told Claudius with a hyena grin. He had given him a blanket and virtually ordered him to use a torn sofa with protruding springs as a bed. After they'd gone, Martine and Ben had to wait an age for the cook to finish in the kitchen. It was only after he, too, had departed, a flick of a switch plunging the building into darkness, that they returned to the window. There were burglar bars across it, so they hissed to Claudius through the opening.

Claudius almost had a heart attack, but soon recovered and rushed over to the window. 'Ben, Martine, thank goodness you guys are here. Whatever happens, don't let anyone catch you. That skipper is nuts. Somehow you've got to try to stop them. I'm not sure what's going on, but they keep talking about a test tomorrow at noon. I haven't been able to find out what's being tested, or who is doing the testing, but it might have something to do with the dolphins.'

'What about you?' Ben whispered. 'Don't you want us to try to get you out first?'

'Are you kidding?' Claudius said. 'What, and run around chasing lunatics when I could just rest on this broken sofa, eat prawn dinners and wait to be returned to my family? No thanks. If somebody brought me a cheeseburger, I'd be in paradise. Oh, I forgot, I am in Paradise! Just go. You don't have much time.'

'Okay,' Ben said uncertainly. 'You were great, by the way.'

'Awesome,' agreed Martine.

Claudius smiled. 'Thanks.'

'Hey, Claudius . . . ' she added.

'Yeah?'

'The kidnapping story beats the yacht story hands down.'

Their first lucky break was finding that the door through which the skipper and his cronies had exited was unlocked. Their second was discovering that it led to a dark kitchen. Judging by the number of cockroaches which scuttled for cover when they walked in, it wasn't a particularly clean one, but they were too hungry to care. Inside the fridge were two big plastic bowls containing cold rice and spicy beans. Aside from a jar of pickled onions, there wasn't much else. The island menu seemed to be a combination of fish caught daily and meat from the freezer humming in the corner.

Martine and Ben fell upon the cold rice and beans and devoured the lot with gusto. It wasn't the roast chicken dinner Martine had been dreaming of, but it was edible and made a pleasant change from the fishy fare on Dugong Island. They finished off the meal with a tin of guavas which had been left out on the bench.

'What do you think we should do now?' Martine asked, wiping guava syrup from her mouth. A grease-smeared clock on the oven showed that it was coming up to ten p.m.

'Look for evidence and a phone,' Ben said. 'If they're working on a project or dealing with tests, they must have some kind of office.'

They tucked the bowls, utensils and guava tin in a cupboard where they couldn't easily be found, and padded silently through the other rooms. Their eyes had adjusted to the darkness and here and there the moonlight offered some illumination. They found a lopsided ping pong table in one room and, in the other, ceiling-high stacks of cardboard boxes with Marlin Communications written crudely on the side in black ink. A stack of copper piping was propped against the doorframe.

Ben levered open one of the boxes. It was filled with nuts and bolts, wire and fuse boxes. He opened three more, each duller than the last.

'Nothing here,' he said. 'It could be that they're ordinary communications or construction workers, and the test they were talking about has something to do with their project. It could be that they're just not very nice people.'

They looked at each other. Then both of them went, 'Nah!'

'Ordinary workers don't have undersea explosives,' Martine reminded him. 'And they don't lock up innocent children.'

'We've got two mysteries to solve,' said Ben. 'Number one, why are these men so determined to keep people away from Dugong Island? Two, who or what is killing the dolphins?'

'And are those things linked in some way?'

'Come on,' said Ben, 'we'd better hurry if we're going to find the answers by morning.'

They already knew that the dining area where Claudius was being held was a phone-free zone, so the office, if indeed there was one, was either in the staff apartments near the beach, where they'd seen the men heading, or in one of the ruined buildings. Since the staff quarters were inaccessible, they decided to start with the blocks of rooms, taking along the torch they'd found in the cutlery drawer in the kitchen. They didn't dare switch it on, but pocketed it anyway in case of emergencies.

'It's like an abandoned film set,' Martine said when they reached the ballroom after a lightning search of the rest of the hotel – a task made easier because many of the rooms were missing doors or windows. 'It's as if a plague or some terrible catastrophe has swept away all the actors and dancers.'

They stood on the terrace, breathing in the salty night air and listening to the rhythmic swish, swish of the sea. It was hard to believe that it was only yesterday that they'd stayed up till dawn trying to save the beached dolphins.

Martine yawned. 'I'm so tired,' she said. 'I feel like we've been awake for days.'

'That's because we have,' was Ben's dry reply.

A sweeping yellow beam sent them diving for cover. They'd temporarily forgotten about the guard. They crawled back into the ballroom and hid behind the piano. After a while they heard his footsteps retreating.

'We'll have to think of a way to get in to the staff apartments,' Ben said. 'There's nothing here.'

Martine put her hand on his arm. 'Wait. We haven't looked upstairs.'

'It's probably just a bar or lounge area. The whole hotel is empty. The bar is not going to be any different.'

Martine's gaze followed the curve of the spiral staircase high into the black darkness of the upper floor. It looked like the last refuge of the ghosts of Paradise

Island's penal colony, the prisoners who'd lived or died in torment centuries before the sunseekers arrived to lounge beside the ocean, or twirl beneath the twinkly lights on the ballroom floor.

'We have to be sure,' she said. 'What if it *is* different?'

The second-storey was, as Ben had suspected, a bar and lounge, but he was wrong about it being empty. Big plastic bundles lined one wall and there was a desk and a filing cabinet in front of the windows. Moonlight spilled in, but it wasn't bright enough for their purposes. They needed the torch if their hunt was to be effective. After several long minutes studying the grounds below for any sign of life, they decided to risk switching it on. The first thing they saw was the contents of the clear plastic bundles.

'The cables!' exclaimed Martine.

'So maybe we are on the right track after all,' Ben said.

But the filing cabinets were as dreary as the boxes had been over in the restaurant area. Whatever else the men were doing, their record keeping could not be faulted. Not if the neatness of their handwriting was anything to go by. File after file revealed nothing more riveting than orders for cement, and letters from the planning department reporting delays to building work.

'I guess if there was anything important here, the door would be locked,' Ben said disappointedly. 'Their computers, phones and radios are probably in their apartments.'

They were just about to leave when Martine spotted a wire basket beneath the desk. Ben handed her the torch and she moved the chair and grabbed it. Inside was a single ball of paper. She smoothed it out. It was a printout of an email. The sender's address had been torn off but the message was still intact.

Dear M, Thank you for your kind permission to conduct a further test near Dugong Island on the date agreed. Please be advised that it will take place at 12:00hrs and will be 235 decibels. Payment is as before. VS

'Sonar testing,' said Ben, crouching down beside her. 'Has to be. What else could they be testing that's measured in decibels? Somehow these guys have got mixed up in it.'

Martine looked at the printout again. 'It doesn't have a date on it, but it could be the test that Claudius was telling us about. That means we have until noon tomorrow to stop it. Or is it today already? Do you think it's past midnight?'

She turned off the torch. 'Oh, Ben, the test that drove the whales to their deaths in the Bahamas was 235 decibels. I remember that because those are the first three digits of our phone number at Sawubona. Under water, 235 decibels sounds like a rocket taking off.'

'If it's true about the test, we're in way over our heads,' Ben said. 'We have to find a phone or a radio and get a message to my father's ship. If we can reach him, he'll contact the coastguard or the navy. We're going to need some outside help.'

Keeping low, they crept over to the arched doorway. Ben put a finger to his lips. 'Shh! Did you hear that?'

'Hear what?' whispered Martine, but by then a hand was descending from the darkness like a club, mashing her face into the floor and wrenching her arm behind her back, and it was already way too late.

· 28 ·

'At least we tried,' Martine said. 'We did everything we possibly could.'

'Yes,' Ben agreed. 'We did our best.'

'We're just kids. It wasn't realistic to think that we could outwit the kind of men who blow up manta rays, 'specially not here, on some island in the middle of nowhere.'

'You're right. We're just kids.'

'It's just that . . . ' Martine's tone was wistful. 'It's just that I keep thinking, what if we'd done things differently? What if we hadn't been caught? What if we still had a chance of saving the dolphins? I can't bear to think of the agony they'll be in if the test goes ahead.'

'I know,' said Ben. 'Unless we can escape and prevent it, I feel as if we'll have failed Cookie and Sun Dancer and the others. I keep thinking that there has to still be a way to keep our promise to Mini.'

It was hard not to feel regretful. They'd had a chance and it had slipped through their fingers like sand.

After capturing them with the help of Fernando, the young guard, the skipper had turned ugly. He'd ranted that Claudius had, as he'd suspected, been lying to him about being alone on the island. He'd said that 'Claudies', as he called Claudius, would be punished – 'but not too much, because we don't want to make the father cross.'

Alarmed, Martine and Ben had insisted that Claudius had in a way been telling the truth because none of them got along. 'When we reached the island, sir, the first thing he did was tell us to get lost,' Ben had informed him.

Unfortunately, that had backfired because the skipper saw an opportunity to get even more extra cash. He would deliver Claudius to his father in the morning but would hold on to Ben and Martine for another few days and try to claim some reward money from their families. Martine noticed that he was careful not to mention the million rand he aimed to extract from Mr Rapier in front of the guard.

That's when she said, 'Why do you need more money? Aren't you getting enough from the tests?'

The skipper reacted as if he had just received several hundred volts in the rear from a cattle prod.

'What do you know about the tests?' he shouted.

'We know everything,' Martine bluffed. 'We even know that there's one tomorrow at noon. The islanders are not going to be happy when they find out what you're up to.'

If looks could kill, the skipper's would have incinerated her. Instead he shouted, 'Lock them up, Fernando. I must think of what to do with them.'

Martine and Ben's big chance came a few minutes after that. It happened when they were fumbling around in the dark for the torch and Ben found a hard, heavy object. Martine found the torch shortly afterwards and she switched it on.

Ben gave an amazed laugh. 'I don't believe it. The guard must have dropped this in the struggle. Martine, he dropped his radio!'

In the distance, Martine caught the ring of boots on concrete. 'Ben, someone's coming!'

But Ben was already adjusting the dial and putting his mouth to the microphone. 'This is Dumisani Khumalo's son, Ben, to the *Aurora*. Do you copy?'

There was no reply.

'This is Ben Khumalo to the *Aurora*. Do you read me?' he repeated.

'Ben!' said Martine. 'We're going to be caught!'

He continued without a pause. 'I can't hear you but I'm just going to hope you can hear me. Over,' he said clearly into the radio. 'At 12:00 hours tomorrow, there's going to be a 235 decibel sonar test near Dugong Island in the Bazaruto Archipelago. Over. There is a possibility that dozens of dolphins might beach themselves because of it. Over. Dad, if you get this message, Martine,

Claudius Rapier and I are on Paradise Island – Santa Carolina – and we're fine, although if you could rescue us after you've helped the dolphins, that would be great. Over and out.'

Nothing happened.

'Do you copy, *Aurora*?' Ben said desperately into the radio. 'Did you read any of that?'

As if to tease him, static crackled and hissed.

A key turned in the lock and the door burst open. A swinging gas lamp showed the panicked face of Fernando, who was carrying blankets and a bottle of water. He looked a little less fraught when he saw them sitting innocently on the windowsill, and gave a visible sigh when he caught sight of the radio, half hidden beneath the desk. Even so, he stared at them suspiciously.

'Lucky for you that you didn't find this,' he said, flinging down his load and snatching up the radio.

'Lucky for you, you mean,' Martine retorted. 'Why are you mixed up in this, anyway? You're Tsonga, aren't you? You're an islander. How can you take money from people who put bombs in the water around your beautiful home? People who murder dolphins? Those dolphins have saved generations of your fishermen.'

'What are you talking about?' he said angrily. 'Nobody is murdering dolphins. They are here to build a hotel, which will bring work to many islanders.'

'Are you sure?' Martine asked him. 'Or maybe they'll just give the work to people from the mainland. As for the tests, what do you think they're for?'

'You are a child and you are not from Bazaruto,' he said. 'You know nothing.'

The door slammed shut and he was gone.

Martine turned to Ben, who'd been quiet throughout this exchange. His knees were scrunched up and he had his face buried in his arms.

'Ben,' she said worriedly. 'Ben, what's wrong?'

But he was too distraught to reply. He kept his head down and spoke so softly that she had to lean close to him to make out what he was saying. 'They couldn't hear me. It didn't get through. The message didn't get through.'

Five-thirty a.m. found them leaning against the sacks of plastic cables, wrapped in blankets, watching the morning star flicker against the fading blue of night. For days they'd yearned for sleep, and now that it was an option – their only option in fact – they were too tired, too hungry and too concerned about what would happen next, to surrender to it.

For the first time since the dolphins had deposited them on Dugong Island, Martine was losing hope that she'd ever return to Sawubona. She thought about the last dawn she'd watched at the game reserve, twenty-four hours before boarding the bus for the school trip. Her grandmother had perched on the side of her bed and watched her with wry affection as Martine propped herself up and looked out at the elephants drinking from the misty waterhole. She could still recall the thrill she'd felt that the game reserve was her home. She'd had no idea then that her home was about to slip away from her, just as the *Sea Kestrel* had slipped away from the continent of Africa. That the sunrise she watched might be the last she ever saw at Sawubona.

'Ben,' she said. 'Do you mind if I ask you a question? Just in case . . . You know, just in case . . . '

He smiled wearily. 'Just in case you're too busy to ask me when we make it back to Cape Town, you mean? Sure. What do you want to know?'

'Why don't you ever speak at school?'

'Promise you won't laugh.'

'Promise.'

'A long time ago I read this Buddhist quote: "Say nothing that doesn't improve on silence." I guess it just . . . '

There was a jingle of keys and the door flew open. Fernando rushed in. 'I can't find the key for the motorboat,' he said. 'Can you sail?'

Ben and Martine tore through the coconut groves to the beach, but their strength was depleted and every stride was an effort. When Martine's feet came into contact with the cold, squeaking sand, she almost collapsed. Her arm was still sore where it had been wrenched by the skipper, she had a stitch in her side and her legs felt like two tree stumps. A large part of her just wanted to give up; lie down on the beach, go to sleep and hope that when she woke up, somebody else would have saved the day. She forced herself on, telling herself that she was running to save the dolphins. Running to get back to Jemmy. Running to be reunited with her grandmother, Grace, Tendai and the sanctuary animals at Sawubona.

'Follow the sun and you'll reach my home island, Bazaruto,' Fernando had promised. 'Somebody there will help you, for sure.'

At first they'd just stood stock still and stared at him, like birds unexpectedly released from a cage.

'You want to know why, don't you?' he said. 'It's because when you spoke to me last night, it reminded me that I went to the mainland to find honest work – to better myself – not to lock up children or work for people who would cause the *mathahi*, the dolphins, to die. So it is time to look for a different job.' He grinned. 'Anyway, I am a terrible guard.'

They'd thanked him profusely and sped off, but as they neared the water, they could see that escaping wasn't going to be quite as easy as it sounded. It wasn't just that there was very little wind. There was no breeze at all. Without it, the dhow was going nowhere.

Ben didn't hesitate. 'We'll take the motorboat.'

'*How?* We don't have a key,' said a frantic Martine, but Ben was already on his way over to the sleek white vessel. He leapt on board. Martine followed more slowly.

'Keep a look out,' Ben told her. 'I'm going to try to start it manually. A lot of boats have a hand crank as a back up.'

This boat did, too, just not a very cooperative one. Time and time again Ben tugged at the cord, but the most he could get out of it was a feeble cough. He paused, panting, for a breather.

Martine was a nervous wreck. 'Let me try,' she said impatiently, leaving her post. She wrenched with all her strength at the cord and the engine roared to life.

'You've done it!' Ben cried in disbelief. 'Martine, you're a star.'

There was a thud and the boat rocked violently. They both swung around.

'Going somewhere?' enquired the skipper.

To Martine, there was a certain symmetry to the whole island adventure. An inevitability. It was almost as if destiny had been in motion since the day Miss Volkner had told them about the Sardine Run, and that no matter how hard Martine had tried to stop it, she was always going to end up speeding across the ocean on a boat steered by a man with only one purpose: to deliver her to Death Island. And she knew without being told that that's where she and Ben were being taken.

'Are you really going to leave us here to die?' she demanded when the boat spluttered to a halt at a shell sandbank and the skipper indicated that they should get off. When she hesitated, he gave her a push.

'What kind of monster are you?' she said furiously.

'Monster? I'm not a monster. If I was, I would have fed you to the sharks. No, I am a kind man – a generous man – as you will see. I am giving you a chance to win your freedom, like the old prison guards used to. You are young and strong. If you can swim to the shore, just eight miles from here, you can go home to your families, and I will forget that you tried to steal my boat and interfere with my business and stop my chance to get some real money. A million rand. Do you know how much that can buy in Mozambique?'

He revved up the engine. 'Enjoy your swim,' he said. 'Perhaps if you are lucky, a fishing boat will come to your aid.' He was gone in a swoosh of flying spray.

Martine looked at the sliver of sandbank and the seething ocean that surrounded it. Her nightmares returned in flashback. She could hear the screams on the night of the storm; feel the slow-motion terror of impending disaster; see the circling, dead-eyed sharks. She knew now how the Paradise Island prisoners must have felt in centuries gone by. At least she could swim a little; most of them had probably been unable to swim at all.

Ben was scared, too, although he was trying hard not to show it. He said, 'I don't suppose one of your powers is holding back the tide? No? Well, hopefully a fishing boat really will come along and rescue us. Until then, why don't we pretend we're on a lovely beach and that

427

we've chosen to be here? I could help you with your sea swimming if you like.'

Martine appreciated the effort, but couldn't bring herself to go along with it. She tried to muster a smile. 'I'd really like you to give me swimming lessons sometime, but it would be nice if it was on a Cape Town beach in the summer, not Death Island in the winter.'

They watched hopefully for passing fishermen or tourist ferries, but nothing but sea birds crossed the horizon. As the sun rose, the sand bank shrunk steadily. Before long, it could barely have accommodated the two of them if they'd sat down and stretched their legs out.

'Ben,' Martine asked, 'do you think that when you're really frightened of things, you sort of attract them? I mean, you know how girls who are afraid of bats are always ending up with bats getting caught in their hair, while people who couldn't care less about them go their whole lives without seeing a single one? Well, I have a phobia about deep water and I seem to keep getting into situations where I have to face it.'

'I suppose it's possible,' Ben said. 'But maybe it's just your destiny.'

'To drown? Great.'

'No, silly. To be put into situations that would lead to you helping the dolphins, and to them helping you.'

Martine thought about it. About Mini, her life needlessly sacrificed; about the suffering in the eyes of the twenty-one dolphins beached at Dolphin Bay; of the whales in the Bahamas with bleeding eardrums. She thought, too, of the joy she'd experienced when the dolphin in Cape Town had swum away; of lying in the turquoise water gazing into the wise-innocent eyes of Little Storm; and of the night of the cyclone when she'd looked up to see a hundred dolphins coming through the wild waves, outlined in silver.

She and the others had helped the dolphins, but not nearly as much as the dolphins had helped her. Yes, they had saved her from the storm, but they'd also given her something far, far greater than that. They'd healed her. For the past two weeks, she had been so preoccupied with surviving that she wasn't even sure when it had happened. She didn't hurt any more. The knot of sadness that had dwelled inside her heart ever since the death of her mum and dad, six and half months earlier, was gone. She still felt very close to them – she felt as if they were watching over her as she stood on Death Island – but it was a good feeling, not a painful feeling.

Some of the fear left her and was replaced by the same sense of acceptance and optimism that had come over her when she first took in the severity of their predicament on the island. 'Ben,' she said, 'you know what's really weird? All of a sudden I'm not afraid any more. The dolphins will save us if they can find us, I know they will.'

'Then why don't we try telling them where we are?'

He took a deep breath and yelled as loudly as he could, 'Sun Dancer, Cookie, Ash, Thunder, Steel, Rain Dancer, Patch, Honey, Little Storm.' Martine did the same and then they took it in turns.

When they were almost hoarse from shouting, Martine took Ben's brown hand in her small white one and squeezed it hard. They were up to their ankles in water. He squeezed back and then they stood together, hand in trembling hand, looking out at the encroaching sea.

'If you could do it all again – I mean, everything that's happened in the last couple of weeks – would you do anything differently?' Ben asked.

'Yes,' said Martine. 'I'd tell my grandmother that I love her.'

· 30 ·

Three days later, as she stared unseeingly from the
window of the South African Airways plane carrying
her and Ben back to Cape Town, those words came back
to Martine. She had meant them with all her heart, but
that didn't make the thought of returning to Sawubona
any easier. She was almost more afraid of going home
than she had been watching the approach of the wintry,
shark-filled sea on Death Island. Who knew what
conclusions her grandmother had come to in her
absence? Maybe she'd decided that it was really rather
pleasant not having a giraffe-mad eleven-year-old around.
Maybe she liked having the house to herself again.

If so, there was not a lot Martine could do about it. She just had to hope that it wasn't too late to say sorry, and that whatever happened she wouldn't be sent away to England or some other place where she'd never again feel the African sun on her skin, ride her beloved giraffe, cuddle a lion cub, or smile at dolphins.

Ben nudged her. 'It doesn't seem real, does it? What happened to us, I mean. We swam with wild dolphins. We actually played with them. They carried us on their backs in a storm. They rescued us, then we rescued them, and then they rescued us right back again.' He laughed. 'It seems like a dream.'

'No,' said Martine, thinking of the shark nightmares that had started everything, 'it's much better than a dream.'

The first person Martine had seen after regaining consciousness in Maputo General Hospital was Alberto. The chef was sitting in a visitor's chair.

'Ah, Miss Martine, you are awake,' he said with a smile, the little ruby sparkling in his front tooth. 'You know, if you had mentioned you might be dropping into the Bazaruto Islands, I would have arranged for you to have a warmer welcome. Although from what I hear, you are quite the expert at building shelters!'

Alberto was wearing a white shirt, and the combination of that, his snowy hair, and the window behind him, framing a sky of pure and perfect blue, was such that Martine, who was still bleary after thirty-six hours of sleep, thought for a second that they were meeting in the afterlife. Then he added: 'You must have used your giraffe magic to talk to the dolphins and sharks, little miss. If it were not for them, you probably wouldn't be alive.' And it all came rushing back to her.

'Are the dolphins okay?' she asked in sudden panic. 'Did they beach themselves?'

'They are very well, thanks to you and your friend,' he assured her. 'I think they would want to know the same about the two of you.'

Martine sat up weakly. She was at the far end of a long hospital ward which smelled of disinfectant and roses. Nurses were gliding about, dispensing pills and trays of food. Ben was asleep in the bed beside her. A dazzling sun was casting stripy patterns on the green-tiled floor. A chubby-cheeked nurse came over, propped her up with pillows and took her temperature.

'Can ay bring you some tea and tosst?'

'Tosst?' queried Martine.

'Toast,' interpreted Alberto, and instructed the nurse, 'Miss Martine and the boy will have some coffee but no food, thank you.'

Martine opened her mouth to protest, but the chef winked at her and nodded in the direction of a large brown bag. No sooner had the nurse departed than he opened it up and produced four bacon and banana rolls, foiled-wrapped to keep them hot, and four pieces of coconut cake. The aroma of these delicacies roused Ben from his sleep, and he was soon sitting up munching on a roll. After he and Martine had been further revived with coffee and cake, Alberto filled them in on the events of the past couple of days.

As far as anyone could tell, they'd both lost consciousness within minutes of being swamped by the sea on Death Island. The doctor who'd examined them said that exhaustion, lack of food and cold water had combined to near-lethal effect.

'I was in the helicopter with the coastguard and Mr Rapier, searching for you,' explained Alberto. 'We had had no success until we saw this beautiful pattern from the air – more than a hundred dolphins in silver circles and, around them, a circle of black, white and speckled-yellow giants – whale sharks. We flew lower to take a closer look and there, in the middle of all these animals, were you and Ben.'

The cave painting, Martine thought. Every prediction on the Memory Room walls had come true.

'Mr Rapier was sure the whale sharks would swallow you whole, like canapés,' Alberto went on, 'but I told him that they are as gentle as porpoises and eat only plankton. But it is the dolphins who really saved you. You were lying across their backs, out of the cold water, and they were cradling you like babies. It was with great difficulty that we persuaded them that we were not there to hurt you.'

Ben and Martine listened in wonder, hardly able to wait to hear what came next.

'Why were you with Mr Rapier?' Martine wanted to

know. 'How did you guess where to look for us? We heard on the news that the rescue teams had been searching in the wrong place.'

'That is correct,' said Alberto. 'The morning after the cyclone, when none of you had been found, I contacted the coastguard's office and told them about my grandfather being helped by the dolphins. I said that maybe that had happened to you and your friends and the dolphins had swum against the current to take you to safety, but they just laughed at me. It was ten days before somebody told Mr Rapier about that possibility, and he contacted me right away to ask if I would help him search the Bazaruto Islands. We were on our way there when we heard from Ben's father that he'd received a message from you.'

'Dad got my message?' cried Ben. 'But he never responded.'

'He did, but he said you couldn't seem to hear him. You may have had the volume turned down on the radio.'

Ben looked sheepish. 'You might be right.'

'It didn't matter because he could hear you speaking so he could tell us that you were on Paradise Island and in great danger. We arrived too late to find you there, but luckily for us the young guard, Fernando, guessed that you might have been taken to Death Island. We did find your friend, Claudius, and he and his father were very overjoyed to see each other. It was quite sweet.'

'Don't let Claudius hear you say that,' Martine advised him.

'Did you manage to rescue our other friends?' asked Ben. 'Did Claudius tell you where to find them?'

'Yes, we took Claudius and flew straight away to Dugong Island, where we found them. There were quite a few tears, I can tell you. We brought them here to Maputo Hospital to be checked out. They were all fine, just very hungry and dehydrated. The two of you had already been carried here by air ambulance and you were sleeping, but they insisted on seeing you. They left something for you.'

Martine saw it then on the bedside locker – her survival kit. A piece of orange notepaper was taped to it. On it was scrawled, 'Cheers, guys. We owe you one. Martine, there'll be a new survival kit waiting for you in Cape Town, but we thought you might like this one as a souvenir. See you at Caracal Junior!!' They had all scribbled their signatures, and Sherilyn's had lots of x's after it.

There was a moment of silence while both Ben and Martine struggled to master their emotions.

Martine cleared her throat. 'Where are they now?'

'They went by plane to Cape Town this morning,' Alberto told her. 'Mr Rapier was going to take them for a fast food feast. Everyone except the big boy – Jake is it? He seemed very keen to get to a rugby match.'

'We still don't know what any of this was about,' Ben said. 'Why did nobody ever visit the island? What were the cables? Who was testing sonar?'

'Well,' said the chef, 'it is a simple story of greed. Ten years ago Dugong Island was bought by a very rich man from overseas. He had seen it once and loved it so much

436

he wanted to preserve it. He rarely came to see it, but he allowed us islanders to picnic, fish or take our children there, so long as we left it the way we found it. Which we always did. We felt it was our heritage, too.

'Last year, this rich man died. His son came into possession of the island and he decided to put a hotel on it. He hired a man from the mainland, Marcos, from Maputo, to manage the project. Unlike his father, he thought of Dugong as private property and he wanted to put a stop to the islanders going there. Marcos's idea was to put underwater mines around the island. The police found out about it and there was a lot of trouble over it, but the son was going to invest millions of dollars and employ many workers, so they let the matter drop with a warning. Marcos recruited some contract workers and they set up a base in the old hotel on Paradise Island. All were from the mainland except for the young boy, Fernando, who had recently arrived in Maputo in search of work.'

Alberto paused to let the nurse take Ben's temperature, and clear away the coffee cups, crumbs and discarded foil. She gave the chef a disapproving glance.

'Perhaps all would have been well,' he continued after she'd gone, 'but planning permission for the lodge was very slow in coming and, two days after the contract workers began laying cables at Dugong Island, Marcos was contacted by the navy of a country whose name I will not mention. Because Dugong is the island furthest out into the Indian Ocean, they asked if he would allow them to test sonar in the waters surrounding it. He saw a

437

chance for some extra cash. He didn't know that dolphins and whales might suffer because of the sonar and the stress caused by naval exercises. It was only when the son started to make enquiries about the lack of progress on Dugong Island that Marcos knew his golden goose would have to go. Still he gave permission for one last test – the one you told Ben's father about in your message.'

'Did anyone manage to stop it?' Ben said worriedly.

Alberto shook his head. 'Unfortunately not. It took time to find Marcos and to get him to admit what he was doing and who was carrying out the tests. The test went ahead before that happened. But we did organize for around thirty islanders to go to Dugong and wait there in case the dolphins tried to get onto the beach. But none came. It seems that every dolphin in the area was at Death Island when the test happened.'

Martine stared at him. 'So by saving us they actually saved themselves?' she said.

Alberto shrugged. 'We will never know. But it looks that way.'

'Do you think it will make a difference?' Martine said. 'Will navies around the world stop using LFA sonar if they know that it's contributing to dolphin deaths?'

'I'm not sure about that,' responded Alberto. 'On the news this morning, they were saying they needed to wait for more scientific evidence, more proof, before they acted. But our own government is talking of banning it in these waters, so at least you will know you have helped to create one sanctuary for dolphins and whales.'

'What happens now to the reward money?' Ben said. 'I take it that the skipper and his friends will not be getting it.'

'Mr Rapier met with the island chiefs yesterday and he has decided that half the money should go to build a new school on Benguerra Island. The other half, he and I are going to use to set up a restaurant on Benguerra. I've already offered Fernando a job as my sous-chef. We need bright young men like him on the islands.'

Alberto stood up to leave then. He was halfway down the ward when he remembered something and came back. 'I'm very sorry, Miss Martine, I should have told you this first, not last. We've had a message from your grandmother to say that she is so looking forward to seeing you.'

Now, as the plane thudded onto the runway and the engines screamed, the nauseous feeling in Martine's stomach intensified. Was her grandmother really looking forward to seeing her or was she dreading it? Was she scared too?

Inside the terminal, she and Ben, wearing colourful sweatshirts and cotton trousers donated by a Bazaruto Archipelago lodge (their own clothes had apparently disintegrated in the hospital washing machine), were escorted through the baggage hall by the flight attendant who had taken care of them since Maputo. Since they had no luggage to collect (their bags had returned to Cape Town on the *Sea Kestrel*), they thanked her and prepared to go into the arrivals hall.

Martine turned to Ben. How did you say goodbye to someone with whom you'd nearly died twice?

He was thinking the same thing, so they shuffled their feet and looked at the ground awkwardly before deciding on a quick hug.

'Everything's going to work out fine, you know,' Ben said. Martine had told him about the row with her grandmother when they were waiting for morning on Paradise Island.

'I s'pose,' mumbled Martine. 'I mean, I hope so.'

He reached out and touched her arm. 'It sounds mad, but I had a great time. Thanks for being my friend. There's no one in the world I'd rather be marooned on a desert island with!'

Martine couldn't help smiling. 'Same here. You're the best friend I've ever had – well, apart from Jemmy.'

Ben grinned. 'That's all right. I don't mind being second to a giraffe.'

31

Tendai was waiting in the arrivals hall, his khaki game ranger clothes and general stillness – the stillness of a man who spent a lot of time in nature – setting him apart from the stressed tourist hordes at the airport. He swept Martine up in his arms and whirled her around, his booming laugh causing people to stop and stare.

'You gave us a few sleepless nights, little one,' he said.

'Us?' queried Martine. She didn't know if she was relieved or devastated that Gwyn Thomas wasn't there to greet her.

Tendai put her down. 'Don't be too disappointed that

your grandmother hasn't come to the airport,' he said. 'This has been hard on her.'

What about me? Martine thought. I'm the one who nearly drowned, came close to being eaten by sharks, narrowly avoided being blown up by an undersea mine, and was left to die on Death Island. Whatever had been going on at Sawubona could hardly have been worse than that.

On the drive back home, Tendai talked to her about the game reserve, updating her on the progress of the sanctuary animals and describing a recent addition: a caracal kitten with a sore paw. 'The giraffe has been pining for you, little one,' he said. 'He hasn't left the waterhole in days. The visitors have been asking why the white giant is so sad.'

Martine couldn't bear the idea of Jemmy being unhappy but it was a nice feeling to know that he'd missed her. Then she remembered that she was banned from riding him.

To keep her mind off what was to come, she told Tendai about some of her adventures on the island. When she thanked him for his advice about keeping the survival kit with her at all times, and told him that that and the pouch he'd given her had helped to save seven lives, he looked proud enough to burst.

An hour and a half later they passed under Sawubona's black arch, and Tendai guided the jeep down the long sandy road to the main house. A white van was parked in the driveway. Martine climbed nervously out of the jeep. She could hear her grandmother's voice in the hallway. 'Quickly,' she was saying to someone. 'We haven't got much time.'

The door was shoved open and two men in overalls appeared. They were carrying Martine's bed. They nodded to Tendai and Martine, loaded the bed onto the back of the van and drove away.

Martine's knees nearly gave way. Was she going to be sent back to England after all?

Gwyn Thomas came out onto the front step. She was pale and seemed to have lost weight. 'Martine!' she cried, rushing over to embrace her. 'I didn't hear you arrive. Look at you! I was expecting a scruffy castaway, but you look so brown and healthy. Grace will definitely want to feed you up though! Come inside. I know you must be exhausted, but I have a surprise for you.'

Martine wriggled out of her grandmother's arms and stood stiffly, but she refused to cry. If she had to go, she would go proudly with her head held high, and she would not leave without saying goodbye to Jemmy. 'I already know what the surprise is,' she said.

Her grandmother looked sharply at Tendai. 'Did you say something?' she accused.

'I said nothing, Mrs Thomas,' the game warden protested. 'Nothing at all.'

When the roar of Tendai's jeep faded, Gwyn Thomas turned and went inside. Martine followed her with dread in her heart. The thought of leaving this lovely, serene house, with its welcoming fireplace and wooden beams and oil paintings of cheetahs and elephants, was agony. Warrior and Shelby, the cats, were snuggled in a worn leather armchair. Her grandmother was halfway up the stairs to Martine's room, her shoes clumping on the wooden stairs.

Martine climbed slowly after her. She walked into her room and stopped short. It had been transformed! The walls had been freshly whitewashed, and there was a new bed by the window, spread with a blue duvet decorated with African batik images of a white giraffe. Above the bookcase were three large silver-framed photographs: one of Martine and her parents laughing on a beach in Cornwall, one of Jemmy by the waterhole, and one of a pod of dolphins playing in the waves.

'I was going to redecorate your room as your Christmas present,' her grandmother said, 'but when you went missing I nearly went out of my mind. I couldn't sleep I was in such a state. Grace persuaded me to do this to pass the time. One of Grace's nieces is a fine arts student at the University of Cape Town and she hand-made the batik giraffe for the duvet cover.'

Despite her resolution, Martine's eyes filled with tears. 'Thank you. It's wonderful. I'm so sorry. I thought that you were sending me away.'

'I know what you thought,' her grandmother said. 'And I don't blame you. I can be a stubborn old woman at times. I cursed myself for letting you go away without resolving our row, and of course once you were on the ship I couldn't contact you. My husband had a very wise saying, "Never go to sleep on an argument." Unfortunately, in the heat of the moment, I forgot that. I was just so afraid that you'd steal out at night once too often and that something would happen to you and I'd lose you like I lost your mum. But I'm sorry for hurting you. Please forgive me.'

She opened her arms and Martine flew into them and they held each other like they'd never let go.

'I'm sorry too,' Martine told her. 'I'm sorry for disobeying you and I'm really, really sorry for saying what I said. I didn't mean it.'

They stepped apart. 'Have I told you how much I love you?' Gwyn Thomas said.

'No.' Martine responded shyly.

'Well, I do. You mean more to me than anything else in the world.'

'Really?'

'Yes, really.'

'Well, I . . . '

'It's okay,' said her grandmother, suddenly embarrassed. 'I know without you having to say it.'

'But I want to,' Martine told her. 'I learned on the island that it's important to say things when you have the chance. I love you, too, and I'm very, very happy to be home with you.'

Her grandmother's reserve got the better of her then, and she ruffled Martine's hair and muttered something about getting dinner started. Martine pretended that she was organizing herself to take a shower. She was desperate to see the white giraffe, but she didn't want to burst the bubble.

Her grandmother lingered at the door. 'Hadn't you better get your boots and jeans on if you're going to go for a ride?' she asked, smiling.

'But you told me I was banned from riding him?'

'You'd better hurry up in case I change my mind. I meant what I said – absolutely no sneaking out at night. But I can't stop you riding the white giraffe. The two of you are inseparable. Jemmy is your soul-mate. You need each other.'

32

For Martine, who had on numerous occasions over the past two weeks thought she'd never see the white giraffe again, the moment when she caught sight of him waiting for her at the waterhole was something that she'd always treasure.

It was hard to tell who was more excited. Jemmy cantered over to her as exuberantly as a pony, lowered his silver head, nuzzled her and made his musical fluttering sound, while Martine spent ages just stroking his silky coat, telling him off for not eating properly, and trying to explain about the storm and the dolphins and how she'd thought about him every minute on the island. Then she climbed onto his sloping, silky back and became a part of him again.

As soon as she was out of sight of the house, she urged him into a flat-out gallop across the golden savannah. Ordinarily, she was careful not to go too fast in daylight in case her grandmother caught sight of her and decided giraffe-riding was a recipe for broken bones, but this afternoon she was on a mission. Not even a snarling lioness, woken from her slumber in the winter sunshine, could detain her.

When she reached the trees near the barren clearing, she halted Jemmy, and spent several minutes scanning the area for prying eyes. Visiting the Secret Valley was another thing she'd resolved never to do in the daytime, but that, too, couldn't be helped. Once through the thorny wall that guarded the crevice, she slid down the white giraffe's neck as if she was shooting down a waterslide, turned on her torch, and positively ran down the tunnel, only slowing to tiptoe through the bats' home in the antechamber.

Grace was in the Memory Room, as Martine had known she would be. She was sitting on the flat rock that served as a sort of bench, wearing Zulu traditional dress and drinking from a flask of *rooibos* tea. When Martine ran in, she gave a cry of delight and enveloped her in a massive hug. 'You're arl bones,' Grace said when they finally parted. 'What ya been eatin' on that island? Bet ya wished you had summa Grace's good food.'

Martine giggled. 'Oh, Grace,' she said, still a little breathless after having the air almost crushed from her lungs, 'I missed more than just your food. When I ended up alone on the island because of some stupid things I said and did, and I felt like everyone in the world was disappointed in me, I wished that you were there to give me a hug and tell me something wise to make everything all right.'

Grace's eyes shone but she didn't say anything. She patted the rock beside her and poured Martine a cup of *rooibos*. They sat there sipping the hot red tea in the light of two torches, surrounded by glowing copper scenes of centuries-old Bushmen life.

After a while Martine said, 'You knew I would be back, didn't you?'

Grace smiled, revealing bright pink gums. 'Sure did, chile. I done tole your grandmamma everythin' would be all right, but she don't ever believe me when I say the bones don't lie. I tole her that the dolphins would see no harm would come to ya.'

'But how did you *know*?' Martine probed. 'How could you know about the dolphins? I mean, if I'd understood what you meant about the boat fence, we would never have ended up in the sea.'

But the *sangoma* just laughed and changed the subject. 'That boy, Claudius, he came to see me yesterday.'

Martine stared at her in disbelief. 'Claudius?! Why? What did he want?'

She couldn't for the life of her imagine how Claudius, of all people, had managed to track Grace down. But it seems he had. Not only that, but he'd impressed her by giving her a magnificent bouquet of flowers to thank her for providing Martine with the plant which saved his life.

'I tole him, that ugly thing! Who knew it would come to any good? It's been followin' me around like a bad smell for years. Every time I dig it out of my garden, it grow back again. Many times I wanted to t'row it in the trash but I's afeared that granny was goin' to come back and haunt me. Then I thought, I'll jest give it to Martine to take on har journey. Maybe she can lose it in the sea.'

'Are you serious?' Martine wasn't sure if this was Grace's idea of a joke. 'Is it something your Caribbean grandmother gave you? You really didn't know that one of the kids on the trip would get stung and need its sap to survive?'

'Chile,' Grace said warmly, 'this is *your* destiny. You have your gift. I weren't the one on the island.'

Martine smothered a sigh. She knew her questions would never really be answered. And as frustrating as that was, she would have to let it go.

'What did you think of Claudius?' she asked, unable to suppress a grin at the thought of Claudius, doubtless scrubbed-up and in his best clothes, sitting among the chickens that pecked around Grace's living room.

'He's a good boy,' Grace told her. 'He done chosen the wrong path before but he learn from that and now maybe if he remember that money can't always buy what matters in this life, he'll grow into a fine young man.'

Martine stood up and went over to examine the two ocean paintings. It felt peculiar to look at them after their predictions had come true. And they were remarkably accurate. Even the sharks were not just painted as random sharks but had the yellow and white markings which identified them as whale sharks.

'You know, Grace,' she said, 'the San people, or the forefathers, or whoever it was who created these pictures, they saw nearly everything that was to come. They even knew the number of beached dolphins, twenty-one, and the species of shark and that there were at least a hundred dolphins in rings surrounding us. They just got one thing wrong. There were two of us on Death Island – my friend Ben and me. There should be two swimmers in this picture and there's only one.'

'Are ya, sure, chile?' Grace said. 'Look closely.'

Martine did and she still saw only one swimmer. Then she noticed that there was a flake of shimmering rock, almost like mica, clinging to the centre of the painting. She peeled it away. Beneath it was the second swimmer.

Martine's blood ran cold. As much as she loved the cave, the knowledge that someone, centuries ago, could have predicted her future in such detail, gave her chills. Before Martine had got to know Ben, when she was still isolated at school, Grace had told her that she would find the friend she sought in the last place she looked. And so it had proven. So maybe Ben himself was part of everything. Maybe everything was linked, even their friendship.

'That's spooky,' Martine said. 'Do you think that the second swimmer was there all the time or do you think . . . I know it sounds weird, but do you think it could have just appeared recently, by some kind of Bushmen magic?'

Grace gave her a strange smile. 'I tole you before, chile, everythin' is already written, but only time and experience will give you the eyes to see it.'

33

To celebrate their safe return, Gwyn Thomas suggested to Ben's mum and dad that the five of them have lunch the following Sunday at the beach kitchen in Uiserfontein, the place where Martine had healed the dolphin. It was usually shut all winter, but there had been a run of unseasonably mild weather and Gwyn Thomas had seen an advert announcing it would be open for the next two weekends.

Martine had been introduced to Ben's parents at the airport, and she'd found his Zulu father almost as quiet as his son was, although he exuded an unmistakable authority. In appearance, though, they were nothing alike. Where Ben was small and wiry, Dumisani was well over six feet, with a dignified bearing, his muscles so broad and defined they might have been sculpted. Ben's Indian mother, Sinita, by contrast, was tiny, talkative, and delicately beautiful, with long glossy black hair which smelled of coconut. It was she who Ben resembled most closely. But his inner strength, thought Martine, his inner strength came from Dumisani.

The Khumalos picked Martine and Gwyn Thomas up from Sawubona in an old station wagon, stopping briefly to meet Tendai, Jemmy and Grace. Jemmy still refused to allow anyone but Martine to touch him, but he hovered near enough for them to appreciate his lustrous white coat and great height.

'He *looks* like a creature of legend,' Dumisani remarked. 'A wonder horse.'

For once Grace said little, although she was very interested to meet Ben. When she came to the car to say goodbye, she hugged him as if she'd always known him and Martine was pleased to see that he didn't act embarrassed, like most boys his age would have done. Instead he looked Grace in the eye and there was a respectful familiarity in the way he spoke, as if he, too, felt a kinship with her.

Two hours later, they pulled into the carpark at Uiserfontein. It was a fine, fresh afternoon. Heathery plants in rich purples and maroons, their colours startling against the creamy sand, crowded up to the dunes, and sea birds wheeled above the waves. They walked along a path of crushed shells to the restaurant and Martine found, to her delight, that it really was a beach kitchen. Rustic tables were set on a wooden deck on the sand's edge, just beyond the reach of the waves, and even the ovens were open to the elements. The aroma of baking bread greeted them. The sunshine took the edge off the winter chill, and the sky was so blue it seemed infinite.

Soon they were tucking into one of the best meals Martine had ever eaten. There was a delicious seafood bisque to start, accompanied by hot, doughy bread baked in clay ovens. After an interval, big bowls of Greek salad, coleslaw and watermelon appeared, followed by the main attraction – snoek, a smoked game fish. Martine had so many plates of it she was sure that she'd have to be transported back to the car in a wheelbarrow!

While they ate, Sinita reminisced about her early life as a dancer in Rajasthan and told them about Pushkar, a festival held once a year, where people came from all over India to trade silks, crafts and jewellery, and to race camels and magnificent Arab horses from the Punjab. It was a world away from the experiences Martine had had so far and it made her realize how much more of the planet there was to see. 'You will travel to the ends of the earth and have a whole lotta adventures before you're done,' Grace had once told her. Martine liked the sound of that, but she wasn't so sure about the 'many, many challenges' which Grace had mentioned would also be coming her way. She'd had enough challenges in the past six months to last a lifetime.

After the main course, Gwyn Thomas suggested that

they go for a walk in an effort to make room for dessert – *koeksisters,* twists of deep-fried batter, drenched in syrup. Martine was too full and too sleepily contented to talk, so she dawdled along the fringes of the surf while the others went ahead. When she reached the spot where she'd healed the dolphin, she stopped and stared out to sea. She was thrilled to be home at Sawubona with Jemmy, but that didn't mean that she missed the dolphins any less. Everything about them was graceful and smart and a celebration of each precious moment of life. Dolphins made it easy to feel happy.

'Funny thing about dolphins,' the kite surfer had said, 'ever noticed that you can't help smiling when you're around them?' And she had.

At that exact moment a dolphin jumped in the bay. Martine wondered if it was the dolphin she'd helped. It was incredibly unlikely, but then so many fantastical things had happened to her recently nothing would have surprised her. But although she fixed her eyes on the patch of ocean where she fancied she'd seen him, he didn't reappear, and after a while Martine came to the conclusion that it was probably wishful thinking on her part.

She was about to walk on when she noticed something drawn on the sand. It was a leopard. Every detail of it was lovingly recreated, right down to its claws and whiskers, and it was full-size, drawn to scale. At least, she thought it was. It seemed an extra large leopard. Its teeth were bared in a snarl and there was something coiled about it, as if it was poised to attack.

It was so realistic that Martine took a step back. She

checked behind her, wondering where the artist was. She hadn't seen anyone on the shoreline. The tide was coming in and the image was too crisp and sharp to have been there more than a few minutes. But, apart from Ben, his parents and Gwyn Thomas, and a couple of fishermen unloading their catch in the distance, the beach was empty.

'Grandmother! Ben! Come and have a look at this,' she called.

Ben sprinted over, and his parents and Gwyn Thomas followed more slowly. 'What is it?' he asked when he reached her. 'What have you seen?'

Martine went to show him and halted in disbelief. In the few seconds that her back had been turned, a wave had rushed in and washed the pale sand smooth. Flecks of glistening foam marked its path. Not a trace of the leopard remained.

A shiver went through Martine and, at the back of her mind, a warning bell tolled.

'What is it?' Ben asked again.

'It's nothing,' Martine said. 'I made a mistake. It must have been a trick of the light.'

'Come,' urged her grandmother, walking up to her and putting an arm around her shoulders, 'it's getting cold now. Look at you! You're covered in goosebumps. Let's go in for some coffee and *koeksisters*.'

Out in the bay, a dolphin breached the waves, gave a flick of its tail and dived deep again.

AUTHOR'S NOTE

A few years ago, I went to Monkey Mia in Shark's Bay, Western Australia, where I'd heard it was possible to swim with wild dolphins. On arrival, I found that it wasn't quite so simple. There was no actual swimming involved. We just stood knee-deep in the sea stroking the dolphins, or took turns, with other tourists, to feed them.

Of course, that was amazing enough. The thing that really struck me was the dolphins' eyes. They'd lie on their sides gazing up, and when I stared back it was like looking into eyes as innocent as those of a new-born baby and, simultaneously, those of the wisest creature on earth. Their gaze was all-knowing. It seemed to me that the dolphins understood more than we ever could. Their skin was remarkable too! I had expected it to be cold and slightly slimy. Instead, it was silky-smooth and beautiful to touch and I could feel their powerful muscles rippling underneath.

This made me want to swim with them more desperately than ever. I pleaded with the owners of the resort and even the research scientists to make my dream come true, but they insisted it wasn't possible. One evening I was sitting alone on the beach watching the sunset turn the water to molten gold when a fishing boat came in, followed by a mother dolphin, known at Monkey Mia as Nicky, and her calf. Well, I didn't hesitate. I dived into the sea in my shorts and T-shirt and swum out a little distance from them. Nicky had a reputation for being greedy and was preoccupied with waiting for stray fish from the fishing boat, but I noticed her calf watching me inquisitively.

After a couple of minutes, he started to swim in my direction. The water is very buoyant in that part of Australia, so I lay on my stomach and stretched my arms out and, slowly and very shyly, he moved closer. Eventually we were only a couple of inches apart. That moment, lying in the red-gold sea, gazing into the wise-innocent eyes of a baby dolphin, was unforgettable. I borrowed from it for the scene in *Dolphin Song* where Martine first swims with Little Storm.

My fascination with dolphins didn't end with my visit to Monkey Mia. I was always trying to find an opportunity to get close to them again, and whenever I read about dolphin and whale strandings, most of which seem to end in tragedy, it broke my heart. As the number of animals involved in these strandings increased, I started to wonder what caused it, what the common denominator might be.

Then I heard that the testing of low-frequency active sonar had been directly linked to the deaths of whales in the Bahamas. Since that day, the weight of evidence gathered by marine scientists and conservationists proving – beyond doubt in many cases – that active sonar is linked to the strandings of whales (particularly species such as beaked whales), has continued to mount.

Forced to surface too quickly, the whales die of a condition similar to the bends in humans and are frequently found with bleeding brains and ears. Dolphin experts are divided over whether the increased use of sonar is directly responsible for the rise in beachings of dolphins, or whether activity such as naval exercises in the area causes them so much stress and fear that they literally try to flee the ocean. Either way the outcome is the same.

Reading about the impact of sonar testing on marine mammals gave me the idea for *Dolphin Song*. I knew I wanted it to be about a school trip that goes disastrously wrong, and when my mum, who lives in South Africa's Western Cape, close to Martine's fictional home, Sawubona, started sending me regular reports on the miracle of nature that is the Sardine Run, that provided a perfect reason for a school adventure. All I needed was a location. I wanted to find a remote African island which was still home to wild dolphins. I'd heard that Mozambique's Bazaruto Archipelago was such a place, and I decided to go to see it for myself.

There are five main islands in the Bazaruto Archipelago, so I hope the Mozambicans won't mind that I've taken the liberty of adding a sixth, Dugong, for the purposes of my story. However, the Death Island sandbar and other islands mentioned – Benguerra, Bazaruto, and Santa Carolina, with its eerie, abandoned hotel, which I explored – all exist. They are a true African paradise. The sand is so clean that it squeaks when you walk, the water is aquamarine, and the islanders are extremely proud that their islands are friendly and free of crime.

The islands also happen to be home to several hundred-strong pods of dolphins. Late one afternoon a boatman took me out in a rubber dinghy to look for them. We found them close to the reef hunting shoals of little fish. The sight of their lithe, graceful bodies glinting in the clear water as they darted like quicksilver all around us, surfacing periodically to take a puff of oxygen, was beyond beautiful. This time I felt no urge to swim with them. I was content to watch dolphins at play in their natural environment; dolphins left alone to be free. I prayed that sonar testing would never find its way to the Bazaruto Islands as it does in *Dolphin Song*.

Writing this book and being able to spend months immersed in a world of dolphins was one of the best experiences of my life. In *Dolphin Song,* Martine's gift allows her and her friends to help twenty-one beached dolphins and return all but one to the sea. In real life, dolphins and whales rely on marine welfare organizations and ordinary people like you and me to take an interest in them and try to protect them.

We only have one planet. Let's do our best to care for it.

Lauren St John
London 2007

Also by Lauren St John

THE LAST LEOPARD

With one bound, the leopard smashed Martine to the earth. His great paws thudded against her chest, his claws pierced her skin, and then she was on the ground winded and in pain . . . 'Please don't hurt me,' she whispered. 'All I want to do is help you.'

Martine is looking forward to the holidays and riding Jemmy, her white giraffe, until an accident sends her and Ben on a journey to the Matobo Hills in Zimbabwe. There they uncover a plot in which the fate of a magnificent leopard and the lost treasure of an African King are mysteriously linked, their friendship faces its greatest test.

In this third African adventure, Martine and Ben must use every survival skill they possess as they race against time to save the world's rarest leopard – and each other.

THE ELEPHANT'S TALE

The elephant's whole body trembled; a tear rolled down her face . . . Some sixth sense told Martine that the elephant's heart was failing because it had been broken. Her freedom and family had been stolen from her. She had nothing left to live for.

When a sinister stranger threatens Martine's home at Sawubona Game Reserve and her beloved white giraffe, Jemmy, she is determined to try everything in her power to save them. To do that she and her best friend, Ben, must risk their lives by travelling to the Namibian desert. There they uncover a plot so terrible it threatens the existence of every person and animal in the land.